DEATH OF A PAINTER

Mark Poynter – No. 1

MATTHEW ROSS

RED DOG

Published by RED DOG PRESS 2020

Cover Design by Oliver Smyth

ISBN 978-1-913331-36-8

www.reddogpress.co.uk

For IGR

-1-

SOME SAY BEING in the building trade isn't a job, they say it's a way of life. What they never tell you about is the problems – every day of every week of every year – nothing but problems.

Everyone you work with wants money off you, everyone you work for wants to keep money from you, and everyone – and I mean everyone – wants it done by yesterday. It's problem after problem after bloody problem.

And right now, I seem to have more than anyone. I've got a hysterical woman screaming down the house, a dead man on her kitchen floor, and I've got absolutely no idea what's going on. All I do know... there's no way now this job's going to be finished by Friday.

MRS WILKES SQUEEZED my hand and sobbed. I looked at the mess that was once Tommy and couldn't help wondering – had he been having a bit of a dabble with Mrs Wilkes? It wouldn't be the first time he'd entertained the client, and it would explain the overly dramatic wailing that quite frankly was starting to give me the hump.

I figured he probably had been. He definitely had a magic touch with married stay-at-home mums harbouring secret fantasies for no-strings with a rascal – and he was that alright, all smiles and laughs and a little bit of teasing to make them blush – it was as though he'd walked straight out of a crappy 70s sex comedy, only now it wasn't so funny – *Carry On Dying*.

There is a Mr Wilkes. We'd greet him every morning as he headed off in his smart suit and sense of self-importance. It was no wonder the wife treated herself to a bit of fun with a cheeky painter when she was married to such a miserable belligerent arse. He does something in the City and thinks he's very busy and important; maybe he is, I don't care. Mrs Wilkes was alright, but he'd been a nuisance since the job began, in fact since before the job began – he'd insisted on having a proper contract between us.

So far, he'd tried and failed to knock our money for genuine variations, and tried (and failed) to refuse us an extension of time after his wife's changes of mind added a fortnight to the job. His contract wasn't really working in his favour and it only seemed to add to his general state of ill-temper. However, we'd run out of smart excuses. We had to finish by Friday, and Mr Wilkes was exactly the sort who'd want his penalty payments out of principle. I could picture him willing us to fail just so he can feel like he's won something. But I don't know where the contract stands on when the work's delayed by the site becoming a crime scene – is that force majeure? It was certainly a force of something, looking at the damage done to poor Tommy.

This wasn't a fall or an accident on site, this was violence, this was brutal. Just below his ear, his head yawned open wide, smashed white bones and grey jelly. His face had been rinsed red by the steady flow of blood, now pooled and tacky like spilled paint on the granite tiles beneath him.

He was the best decorator I've ever worked with; morally questionable, but he'd do a lovely job, which is why, as soon as I saw his brushes on the side, I knew something was up. They hadn't been washed out, he'd still been working, must have been interrupted and put them down for a moment. If he'd intended leaving them for a while, he'd have wrapped them in clingfilm to keep the bristles soft. That's what he always did. I knew his brushes would stiffen and become brittle, like the bloody wound in the side of his head that was turning black around the edges. Thankfully I was pulled out of these dark thoughts by a voice beside me.

'I said, what are we going to do?' asked Mrs Wilkes.

'Police... I suppose,' was my rather feeble response.

No doubt Mr Wilkes and his swaggering pomposity would have thrived in such a moment, issuing commandments left right and centre, but my immediate reaction – and it probably doesn't show me in any great light to admit it – was *Thank God she found him first*, as I could just imagine how the police's questions would go if she hadn't, although it didn't seem to matter because, twenty minutes later:

'He worked for you for how long, roughly, would you say?' the uniformed copper asked me. He looked so familiar, I'm sure I'd seen him before, maybe from one of the Sunday league teams that drink at the Golden Lamb post-match; he looked the football sort – tall, slim, bit of a swagger. 'And were there any disagreements? Disputes about money?'

There it is, that's the one I'd been waiting for – the sub-contractor's dead, must've been an argument over payment, must've been me; brilliant, well done Medway's finest for jumping to the bleeding obvious!

A man entered the room, a small man with a face like a fox – all dark eyes, pointy nose and teeth, with white hair. He was very smartly dressed and obviously took a great deal of pride in his appearance judging by his shiny shoes and even shinier cufflinks. The uniform stopped his somewhat insulting questions, looked at the dapper little fellow, gave a respectful nod and moved away.

Mr Cufflinks approached me, reaching into the inside pocket of his tailored suit jacket. 'I have been appointed investigating officer here,' he informed me in a monotone voice, pulling out a warrant card and holding it six inches from my face. I tried to read his name, unusual, never seen it before but I decided to give it my best shot.

'Inspector Senior, I'm—'

'Sen Ya' he interrupted 'Senia, it's pronounced Senia, Detective Chief Inspector Senia. It's Italian.' His patronising tone was already beginning to annoy me.

'So, you're Italian?' I still don't know why I asked that, ease the tension I suppose.

'Do I fucking look Italian?'

Well, that threw me, no-one's ever asked me that before; what does an Italian look like? I could only think of Pavarotti and he didn't look anything like him. I must have pondered for too long as he barked his next question at me.

'You're the one that called it in? Mark Poynter?'

I confirmed I was both of those, and then started explaining that Tommy worked for me and the job we were doing. He didn't seem to understand.

'But you're an electrician?'

'Yes.'

'And the deceased was a painter?'

'Yes.'

'So why does an electrician need a painter?'

'Err, to paint.'

'I know a painter does the bloody painting, don't get smart with me. Why is an electrician employing a painter?'

'Because I've been fitting the new kitchen here, and I had him decorating.'

'Fitting a kitchen? Isn't that a carpenter's job?'

'Yes, but the carpenter's finished, the plumber's finished, the plasterer's finished so now it's just the decorator to finish.'

'But you're an electrician!'

4

I thought carefully about my next words, he was starting to wind me up, but the last thing I wanted was to annoy the Law when they were looking for someone to blame a murder on.

'Yes, I'm an electrician. Most of my work is electrical. But on occasion people have asked me to take on bigger projects because they know I know all the right trades and it's easier having me manage the thing start to finish.'

'Like a main contractor?'

'Yes, like a main contractor.'

'Well, why didn't you say that to begin with instead of farting about saying you're an electrician?'

I didn't know how to respond to that, so I didn't.

'So, you two were friends, good friends?'

I felt a bit guilty – to Tommy not to this foxy-faced fuckwit – to find myself denying we'd been friends for, must be, fifteen years now. Instead I gabbled around the edges staying nondescript, I told him we'd done a lot of work together – he'd get jobs and recommend me, I'd get jobs and recommend him – and that's how things tend to go in this industry.

'Can you think of anyone that'd want to harm him, or bore a grudge?' asked Senia.

I immediately thought of Tommy's tendency to dabble, and wondered whether Mr Wilkes had found out he'd been dipping more than his brushes whilst he was at work. But I didn't say anything, firstly because Mr Wilkes may have been a petulant nobhead but I knew he was nothing more than bluster and bullshit, also it didn't make sense to accuse him of murder when he still owed me a month's money. I've got the bill for his granite worktops due this week, they're the price of a new car alone, the last thing I wanted was to risk him knocking my payment, so I told Senia no.

Senia stared patiently at me, for ages, unblinking, like a crocodile. 'Did he work for you as a direct employee?'

I explained, again, he was a sub-contractor; this was beginning to feel like hard work.

'Well why in that case,' the frustration in his voice matching mine, 'are you both wearing the same shirt?'

He was right. We were both wearing a purple sweatshirt with my silver 'MP Electrical' logo. I tried explaining the concept of corporate branding: 'my job, my firm, my rules', meaning Tommy would wear my shirt when on my project.

'So, if you can't think of anyone that may have wanted to harm him,' said Senia, 'what about you? Your job, your firm – your shirt. Could it be mistaken identity and it was, in fact, you they were after? Has anyone threatened you, anyone bear a grudge against you?'

'No,' I lied, but by the way those dark eyes stared back I don't think he believed me.

-2-

BLUNT HAD SAID he'd back off, promised to give me until the weekend. Now I was scared.

Senia's team had taken my fingerprints and statement, but all the while I was inside my own head, looking out, on auto-pilot. The rest of the world passed by but I was one pace out of step. My body participated, yet any thought or understanding had been switched off. I don't know how I managed to keep myself going. Senia's words had frightened me, not to mention the sight of Tommy like that. Up until today Dad's was the only dead body I'd seen, but that was different, Dad looked almost glad of it. The only way I can describe it is to imagine bleeding a radiator: as if someone had unscrewed a little cap behind his ear and all the pain had whistled away on the air, pushed out by peace.

Tommy however: his dry eyes fixed open, his skull smashed apart, damaged beyond repair, his face twisted in terror and confusion. Realising those were the last emotions he'd experienced: the prospect that this job wouldn't be finished on Friday had suddenly taken on a deadly meaning for me.

I JABBED AT Chapman's number again, it rang out until the voicemail prompt took over. 'Anthony, where's my money? Things are serious. Where is it? You promised I'd get it this week.' I finished by telling him to call me back straight away. He wouldn't, he hadn't done to any of the dozens I'd already left him.

I'll be honest with you, I was in a bit of a bind. A little while ago I finished a big wrap-around extension for this man, Chapman, who'd knocked me my last payment. I've a third of my money unpaid and hanging out – seriously overdue, almost twelve weeks. He'd given me promise after promise, lie after lie, same old same old, more broken records than a boot fair. In the end, the threat of going legal got him to swear he'd pay up. Needless to say, he's now avoiding my calls.

Twelve weeks is too long. Any money in the business had been spent, any personal savings long gone. No money makes life very awkward. Even people I've dealt with for years treat me like the enemy. For instance, Thorpe Timber And Building Supplies: I'd gone in there today with Mrs Wilkes so she could choose her door handles. Before you ask why I was in there instead of giving it a wide berth and heading to a place they don't know me, first ask anyone that's ever run a business, they'll tell you: it's always easier to get credit from someone you know, especially if you already owe them money. And besides, I like Thorpe's. There's all the big national chains nearby but there's something nice about a local family firm, and that something nice is the Magnificent Maria who spent the whole time giving me pained faces and gestures towards the cash register.

'What are you doing Mark?' she said. 'Uncle Trevor'll go nuts if he catches you here. You know he's suspended your account until you pay what you owe? You're not expecting to buy anything for her over there?'

I love the way women can manage to put so much contempt into a simple little word like 'her'. It amused me she was more annoyed about me being there with another woman than the state of my account. We'd had history, a little dabble a long time ago. I've often wondered whether there could have been a rematch, but the timing's never been right and now I hear she's engaged to a panel beater from Strood. If there's one thing I've learnt, you don't mess with the woman of a man who wields a big hammer.

Anyway, money's tight. I'm forced to do what I'd promised I'd never do (again), I'm passing the problem down the chain. I've not been paid, so I can't pay, won't pay. I'm getting by on fumes, telling everyone to be patient, bear with me, I'll have the money in a few days. Even I don't believe me when I say it anymore.

It's not fair, I don't like it one little bit, but what can I do? Go to the bank? Since some head office nitwit decided to do away with actual people in banks, I can't get a meeting with anyone for at least two weeks and even if I could wait that long, there'd be another fortnight on top of that before anyone can make a decision. So, no, going to the bank is not an option. Payday lender? I suppose it would get me the money quicker, but at fifteen hundred percent interest rate, would you do it? No, nor will I.

My very last hope had been to get this job finished on Friday, get paid and use that money to buy a bit of breathing space. Rob Peter to pay Paul. Literally. Paul Blunt, my biggest creditor whose volatile temper is matched only by his lack of patience.

Blunt is a roofer from a long line of roofers, like he's been genetically modified to be a roofer. He's short and he's squat. His low centre of gravity makes him ideal for scuttling over rooftops. And he has got immense upper body strength from clambering up and down ladders all day fully laden. Coupled with a neck as thick as your waist, a heavy brow and a covering of short black hair, you can't help thinking he resembles a chimp – that, and the feeling he'd tear your arm off without provocation.

But I thought we had an understanding. He agreed to give me a clear run until the end of the week to finish this job then as soon as they pay me, I pay him, that was the deal.

I know, it was only one part of a bigger problem, but I wanted the monkey off my back.

-3-

THERE'S PEOPLE BEEN in this area since, well, since people. They were here long before the Romans jabbed Watling Street straight through the middle of it. The three towns of Rochester, Chatham and Gillingham are so ancient that the entry in the Domesday Book probably read 'old and shitty and falling to pieces' even back then.

As centuries passed, they bled in to a dense sprawling conurbation known as the Medway Towns, after the river around which they all were built, each town flowing seamlessly into the other. Unless you've lived here all your life you wouldn't know where one stops and the other starts. Three hundred thousand people crammed into a space a mere eight miles across, no wonder tempers fray from time to time around here.

The Wilkes's large modern home was in the affluent and leafy Walderslade Woods area of the Towns. When the police were finished with me, I left there and headed for the Golden Lamb. I couldn't think of anywhere else to go. The police had closed the house off as a crime scene, so I couldn't get back to work, and no doubt Mr Wilkes was already poring over the contract to see whether becoming someone's last resting place represented a breach. So, pub it was.

As I drew to a halt in the Golden Lamb's car park, I recognised at least five of the vans, a couple sign-written, the others left plain. You can always spot a tradesman's van, it's backed up tight against the wall, if you can't slip a credit card between the bumper and the brickwork then no-one can break in and steal your tools.

Sure enough, eight or nine thirsty grafters congregated about the bar, and right in the middle holding court was Disco. The building trade thrives on gossip and rumours, so I figured Disco was the best person to go to if I wanted to get the true story about Tommy out there before it's exaggerated out of all proportion. Around here, nothing gets past Disco, he knows exactly where everyone is and exactly what they're up to, he's just like Google – if Google wore saggy-arsed track pants and smelt of sawdust and roll-ups.

'Mr Poynter,' he said, raising his pint glass in greeting towards me.

'Mr Dancer,' I replied. 'Disco, listen, can I have a quick word?'

David Dancer could have been the greatest carpenter in the Towns, he had a natural eye and instinct, he was more like a cabinet maker of old in the quality and craftsmanship he'd bring to his work, but the drink had got hold of him young and held him tight ever since. Somehow, he made it work for him. Instead of taking his time to deliver an outstanding piece of workmanship he became fast at delivering a standard one. He could crash out in a morning what most people would take a day and a half to do. He had to because around lunch time he'd start getting the shakes, it's lucky he's not sawn off a couple of fingers by now.

As we made our way outside to the smoker's shelter, I told Disco about Tommy. Disco rolled himself a fag, lit it and took a long deep drag on it. A peculiar moment of silence had fallen between us, neither knowing what to say next. Disco picked sticky white dots of mastic from his sleeve. He caught me watching him.

'Boris the Plastic,' he offered by way of explanation, meaning he'd been fitting upvc replacement fascias and soffits for Boris Gruber. Pretty boring, and straightforward but it was quick and easy price work, which suited Disco down to the ground.

'Shit,' he muttered after taking in my story. 'What about Jen? Have you spoken to her?'

I hadn't. Senia had told me: 'The police shall be informing the next of kin, and providing the appropriate victim support' – the pompous twat. But I needed to talk to Jen sooner rather than later because I felt responsible for what had happened. It wasn't an accident, it wasn't a shaky scaffold or a dropped hammer: this was violence, this was murder. I knew I couldn't have predicted anything like that. But, somehow, it still felt like I should have, especially if it should have been me lying there.

Jen and Tommy had been together since school, but only got married a few years ago when Chloe came along – oh God, that poor little love, what's she going to do now? This situation's getting worse and worse.

And yes, Tommy the compulsive shagger was married. I don't know what compelled him, maybe he saw it as a perk of the job like the way other blokes help themselves to a bag of nails from site. But yes, he was married, very happily too. And now I must face his widow, offer sympathies and then apologise for my failure to not foresee someone coming into my job and doing this.

Disco ground out his cigarette with a twist of his toes, the uncomfortable silence resumed and hung for a few seconds until a tap on the window released us. Disco was being beckoned back inside for the next round.

'You coming in?' he asked. I shook my head, I wasn't in the mood. 'Okay, I'll, err, I'll see you around I guess.'

'Got much on?' I asked.

'Boris's got enough to keep me going for the rest of the week, weather permitting.'

'Oh, right, ok, I've maybe got a couple of bits coming up I can do with a hand on, so I'll give you a call next week, maybe.'

'Righto,' he replied, and with that, headed back inside the bar. As I unlocked my van, I looked back at the pub. It was a funny place. Like so many others in the area it had been refurbished and redecorated, made fancy and gastro to appeal to a 'better clientele'.

Instead, its secure car park at the back and a misjudged happy-hour promotion saw it become the epicentre for the local building industry: meetings were held there, deals were done there, jobs were awarded there, accounts were settled there, and I could see that today Tommy's demise was being announced there. As I moved away, I saw a toast being led by Disco.

'Good luck Tommy,' I whispered, and pulled out into the traffic heading towards home.

As I waited for the lights to change at the corner my phone rang. In bold capitals a name that I'd hoped had forgotten mine leapt from the screen. Hamlet. Shit, that's all I need. I pressed the Accept button – no one, I repeat no one, ever sends Hamlet to voicemail.

'Hello,' I called out, in my most jovial of tones, 'long time no speak, how are you?'

'I want to see you,' came the reply.

'Well, I'm... in the middle of something, tricky job, need to get it finished before the—'

He cut me short with an angry 'Bollocks! You've just been in the Golden Lamb!'

Great – he knows where I am. There's no point trying to second-guess who told him – to say he's got people in his pocket would be an understatement, they reckon there's so many you could make a pretty decent five-a-side league. And he knew I'd lied to him. I didn't have a good feeling about this.

'However,' he said, with the benevolence of a shark scenting blood, granting me a favour I neither asked for nor wanted, 'as you are no doubt extremely busy this afternoon, I will see you tomorrow. My office. Ten a.m. Don't be late.'

-4-

THE LOCAL EVENING news had just started when I swung the van into my little cul-de-sac. Tommy was the top headline, I didn't want to listen and switched the radio off, coasting the final few hundred metres in silence. It had just turned six, but it was already cold and dark and, given the day I'd had, felt claustrophobic in the way it smothered me. I couldn't be bothered decanting my tools from the van to the safekeeping of the adjacent lock-up garage. I wanted to be indoors. I backed up tight to the wall, if anyone was determined enough to rob the van, they were welcome to whatever they found, most of my stuff was still sealed off at the crime scene. I headed towards the house, and then finally, at last ...

Home! Just like the sudden escape of warm air from inside, relief washed over me as I opened the door. Other than my parents', this is the only home I've ever had, the first person in my family to buy their own house. Starter homes they called them when they were built in the 80s. I say built, more like mass-produced; huge estates of them popped up all over the place – remember Mickey Mouse with all the brooms? Imagine it had been the Town Planner that'd taken him on as an apprentice instead - pop pop pop, street after street, all the same.

They were built with young couples in mind, just starting out on the property ladder or maybe retired people downsizing, and when I moved in, it was a nice community of folk all swimming in the same direction. But in recent years the Buy-To-Let mob outbid the newlyweds and up went the rental boards. Now no-one stays more than a year, no-one knows their neighbours and no-one cares. A new tenant had moved in next door to me this week. I'd been kicking cardboard boxes back onto their side of the path for days but still not seen them yet, probably never would. I don't remember ever seeing the last lot either. Sad really.

Mine's the left-hand end of terrace, built in a yellow sand faced brick bought when I was nineteen with my then girlfriend who, I'm happy to say, three years later gave me the enormous pleasure of becoming my ex-wife.

Small and plain – the house I mean, obviously – two bedrooms upstairs, small kitchen and living room downstairs, plenty big enough for just me. Plus, more importantly, almost paid off. I'd had a few good years, some nice contracts, and many more not so nice ones involving a lot of unsocial hours far from home, grafting through the night and sleeping in the van. Back-breaking, ball-aching work scurrying like vermin through dark confined ceiling voids, working in the tightest spaces to even tighter deadlines, ploughing on whilst the skin on your knuckles gets flayed off at every turn by hidden sharp edges, being unable to stand straight without it hurting for a week. Lots and lots of head-down, arse-up, nose flat against the grindstone hard work. But in three years I'm clear, a decade early on the repayment period. To be able to pick and choose my work would be a nice position to be in, and that's my big ambition – at least, it was. The house was all I had left, everything else had gone to keep me afloat. The prospect of losing it now just didn't bear thinking about.

The comfort in taking my boots off was immediate and welcome, it meant I could relax – if 'relax' is the right word. 'Process', I think that's perhaps the better word – I could at last process the events of the day without a sense of responsibility for everybody else. I could take my time to understand what had happened and how it had affected me.

Fifteen minutes in the shower cleared my head as it cleaned my skin, washing away all the crap and bad news that had piled up on top of me in the hours prior. Being alone with space to think, it suddenly struck me, and struck me hard, that I would miss Tommy greatly. I turned to face the showerhead above me and let the spray wash away my tears.

An hour or so later, cleaned, fed and watered, with no appetite for watching television and the chance of sleep feeling more and more remote, I found myself reflecting on the day I'd had. I needed to find a solution, I needed it fast. But the more I thought the more I went round and round in circles.

I returned from the kitchen clutching an '*I love Belgrade*' mug, bugger only knows whose it was and how it had found its way into my house, but it was clean, unchipped and didn't leak so the whys and wherefores weren't important. I didn't particularly want a drink, I simply hoped ten minutes of something mindless and mechanical like putting the kettle on would give me enough distance and space to make the grief-induced insomnia go away. No such luck.

On my coffee table, in my lounge, in my best handwriting, was a list of everything I could sell, and believe me, I mean everything. But even if I managed to get top dollar for all of it, it still wouldn't be enough to pay off Blunt alone, never mind the rest of them.

One thing was certain, I needed cash, and needed it fast. In the past I'd been around huge piles of it, table tops carpeted in the stuff: 'You haven't seen anything, you don't look, you don't touch, do what you're here for, do as you're told and then get out, you have never been here.' But that was another lifetime ago, that door was closed and I'd promised myself I would never step back through it. But I began to wonder whether I had any other choice. No, I knew what I had to do, where I had to go... and I already regretted it.

-5-

HEY... IT'S ME... *you there? Can you hear me? Yes? No? Whatever, I'm just going to carry on, so listen.*

I don't know what I'm doing any more. I thought I'd got my head straight, but quick as a flash it flips again. I don't know my own mind anymore. That scares me.

But I can't be scared, that's not me, I'm Marky Mark... everyone's friend, always bouncing, always moving, give them a smile, crack a joke, another pint mate, keep the change darling, that's me, Marky Mark. I don't let anything get me down, because I know as soon you give in to the piss-takers they've won. I'm Marky Mark, cause no offence, take none either, just keep bobbing along, everybody's happy, and if you keep on bouncing, they can't hit a moving target.

But they did. And that wasn't meant to happen. That was never meant to happen.

You've heard about Tommy? You must've. Poor, dopey, silly bollocks Tommy, Casanova in vinyl matt. It's my fault, I mean, whichever way I look at it, it's down to me. Again, someone I care about. Again I'm powerless. Now he's dead.

Chapman, he caused this. If he hadn't disappeared with the money he owed, I could have paid everyone out, happy days all round. But no, he thinks he's clever, he thinks he's smart, he thinks he can tuck me up and knock me my money. Now I've got Blunt and all the rest after me, getting restless, getting angry... and rightly so. I'm angry, I'm furious. Worth killing for? This morning I'd have said no, but after seeing Tommy, now I'm not so sure. And why Tommy? Supposed to be me? It was my job, he was wearing my colours, from behind, heat of the moment, it's possible they thought it was me. Or was it always meant to be him, as a message to me? It's got my attention that's for sure. I need my money and I need it fast, no-one else is going to suffer because Chapman robbed me.

And now Hamlet's summoned me in, as if things weren't bad enough. I know, I promised – walk away, never go back, especially with what happened to... well, you know... but what can I do? The only good I can see coming from this is if anyone can get me retribution for Chapman – because I swear he's the root cause of all of this – it's Hamlet. If getting pulled back in to Hamlet's orbit gets me my money, and gets Chapman his comeuppance, then it's worth it, right?

No, it's not, I knew that's what you'd say, I knew it. Why aren't you here? Why aren't you here to talk me out of this, Dad? Can't you tell me it'll all be alright?

-6-

SIX AM, WOKEN by my own snore, I snapped awake. Through the open window I could see the street outside was quiet and still, not even the tail lights of a station-bound early starter. At some point, I must have fallen asleep in the chair. Belgrade was at high tide, the tea untouched and spoiled beside my scribbled list of everything I owned, valuing my worth – adding up to not good enough.

By the time I'd dressed, the day was awake and the street had come to life. The schoolchildren were making noisy nuisances of themselves. '*I love Belgrade*' had been refilled, and as I sipped, I spotted Mr Skinner watching the kids from the opposite side of the road with suspicion. I raised him my mug in greeting, but he blanked me and walked away.

My phone began to ring. 'Number withheld'. No, I don't think so. I ignored it and waited for the ringing to stop while watching Mr Skinner shoo a couple of fat magpies off the lawn. A chime told me a voicemail message was waiting, I listened, it was Senia: 'It would be greatly appreciated if you could come into the station to assist us with a few questions please.' He was polite, I'll give him that, but he'd have to wait. I had a meeting with Hamlet at ten, and I must not be late.

WHEN THE RUMOUR went round that Ian Hamlet was opening a new club someone joked he should call it Elsinore, but no-one got it. In the end, he chose the rather mundane 'Town And Country Club.' Just before ten I'd pulled up outside it.

Located midway between Chatham and Rochester, it was a basement bar beneath a once-grand Georgian townhouse that had long since been carved up into units and then carved up once again into even smaller units, and then carved up yet again. He's not getting any younger so I suspect he bought the property for its opportunities above ground: far easier money as a slumlord packing it full to bursting with vulnerable migrants than dealing with drunk punters every night. But then on the other hand, does his vanity still thrive on the local celebrity of being a club owner, who knows?

There'd been a club here for as long as I can remember, in every incarnation you can think of – live music, live comedy, strippers, gay, goth, gay goth, you name it, they've tried it but nothing had ever stayed very long. Hamlet had relaunched it as an upmarket cocktail club and, for now at least, it was proving popular with young orange women and bushy-bearded tattooed hipsters.

Two boneheads were unloading a lorry parked in front of me. They stacked crates at the top of the stone steps leading down into the club. The square-headed ginger one in the gold Brazil football shirt had the shape of someone who had spent too much time in the gym out of conceit rather than fitness: big chest, big arms, skinny chicken legs. His mate wore a t-shirt with a Dunlop logo, he didn't look like a gym-goer, but instead had that sinewy, long-limbed, lean physique of a greyhound. Both looked as though they didn't trouble themselves with too much thinking.

Seeing me approach the entrance they together blocked my way. I knew exactly what they were, by day they hump crates, and by night they're club security: nothing more than Hamlet's dumb muscle. They're there for the heavy lifting, the fetching and carrying, they'll guard closed doors but won't know what's behind them: a disposable human shield to protect the girls, the drugs and the cash, and they don't even have the brains to realise it.

'Club's closed,' said Brazil, to which I replied, 'I'm expected. Tell him Mark Poynter's here.' Brazil gave a nod to Dunlop who scurried down through the doors and then re-emerged thirty seconds later with a thumbs-up. Brazil stepped aside to let me pass. I entered the club leaving them to their crates.

Inside I found Hamlet sitting at a tall circular cocktail table, a newspaper laid out in front of him, coffee mug in hand. What a piece of work is this man? He looked ridiculous. Every strand of hair was jet black and styled like a teen popstar. His T-shirt and jeans were young, trendy kids' brands with Japanese symbols all over them. His forehead had that fresh Botox sheen. Perhaps in the artificial twilight of a busy nightclub he can get away with it, but under the harsh glare of daytime he looked every day of his fifty-five years and nothing could mask that.

'Marky Mark,' he said, beckoning me towards him. I knew what he was going to say next and I really didn't want to hear it. 'Marky the Sparky.' There it was, the rhyming couplet, the bastard.

'Marky Mark,' said Hamlet, roaring with laughter. 'It's good to see you again, man. How are you? Haven't seen you since, what, my Christmas party?'

Of course, it suddenly came back to me, Hamlet's Christmas party. I say party, more like conscription – you get an invite, you *will* attend. This place had been packed with two hundred of his most intimate friends and acquaintances – including that uniformed policeman with his insulting questions and footballer swagger from the Wilkes's kitchen – that's where I'd seen him before, that's who must have tipped him off, he was one of Hamlet's men.

'No, I guess it must have been Christmas,' I said. 'How've you been?'

'As merry as the day is long. That's me. Tip-top, as if you care. How come we don't see you around anymore Marky Mark? I thought we were friends, but then you just disappeared. Anyone would think you were trying to avoid me. I mean, you come to my party, first time we've clapped eyes on you since God knows when, but even then, it was blink and you're gone, don't think we didn't notice.'

'Sorry, things have been busy, no offence meant,' I said, but he was right, I'd wanted distance. The problem is you never get away in the end, as today was proving.

'I was sorry to hear about Tommy,' he said. 'Such a shame, he was a good lad. And a very good worker, he did this place for me, did you know?' I replied that I did. 'And so very clean – you could always rely on him to clean up.'

Behind us, Brazil and Dunlop were fetching in the supplies and making a noisy job of it in the process. To be heard over the clinking of glass and rattling of crates, Hamlet leaned in towards me.

'What he did, and indeed what you do, Marky Mark, is very skilled. I can always find opportunities for people with skills, people like Tommy and like you, even like your numbskull of a brother.'

I said nothing.

'Ah, still a sore point I see.'

I said nothing.

Hamlet readjusted his posture, slightly more upright, more formal.

'Take these two dickheads,' he said gesturing towards Brazil and Dunlop. 'Thick as pigshit the pair of them. Both bloody useless. I can replace them in a second, I've got them queueing up round the block to work for me.'

He was right about that, there's a strange glamour attached to him, you think if you're in his shadow some of his notoriety will rub off on you like stardust. I did, at least I used to once upon a time.

'But the likes of you and Tommy and… others, let's say – you're special, you're valuable to people like me because you understand how things are, how the world turns.'

His attempts at flattery made me uncomfortable, but he either didn't notice or didn't care. He continued talking: 'I hear Senia is investigating Tommy's…' He tailed off on the last word, either not wanting to say murder or not wanting to be seen to know too much.

I didn't respond, assuming he'd already had a full account from his inside man, quite literally the Police Informer.

'What do you think of acting Detective Chief Inspector Senia then?' he asked. 'You know his pedigree?'

I shook my head. Hamlet continued: 'Our Mr Senia is something of a rising star, the man of the future no less. You know old Ted Gaffney? No, I don't suppose you do. Well, Ted heads up the Medway Serious Crimes Squad here, but last month the poor old git had a heart attack. Shame, only fifty-six. Anyway, they needed an interim head. Young Mr Senia's been the golden boy of the Met, so he's come down here to the 'burbs on secondment and if all goes well for him, he could be staying, as I've heard Ted's trying to pension out early on medical grounds. So, what do you reckon of Senia?'

'He doesn't look Italian.'

Hamlet looked confused at my observation. I didn't elaborate. He leaned in close to me.

'Now, this is important, think carefully,' his voice had taken a serious tone, but his forehead looked unconcerned. 'Has Senia mentioned me?'

'You? Why would he mention you? What, regarding Tommy's...' I too tailed off on the final word.

'Yes. Has he? I am relying on you Marky Mark to keep my name out of this. I repeat, I do not want my name coming up regarding anything to do with this.'

'But why would it? I don't understand.'

'Oh, come off it, you two were as close as stink on shit, don't pretend you weren't. Just keep me out of it, okay?'

I mumbled my agreement, but didn't have a clue what he was talking about. What had Tommy got himself involved in? I looked around to make sure the dumb muscles were far enough away – I didn't want to be overheard. They looked busy, I felt it safe enough to talk freely.

'Listen,' I said, 'I really need your help, please.' He didn't say anything, just a quizzical look. I continued, 'I've been let down and need to borrow some money, quickly.'

He asked how much, and I gave him the full story about Chapman running away and hiding, and about Blunt getting impatient.

'You know your problem? You're stuck between a Cock and a Hard Case!'

I knew it wasn't the first time he'd used that joke, yet he clearly still found it very funny judging by the time it took him to calm down.

'Look, we're friends, and because of that, and because you've agreed to keep my name away from Senia – haven't you?' Again I muttered my agreement, only this time with a bit more vigour. 'I'm prepared to do you a big, big favour.'

I waited, wondering what I was letting myself in for.

'I can lend you the money at mates' rates, you pay me back plus fifteen percent or I can buy the debt off you wholesale for eighty-five percent. Up to you.'

So, there were my choices. Either way it'd cost me any residual hope of ever breaking even, but at least the only one left short would be me. I could live with that. The Devil had tabled his deals, now all that was left was bending over to take the least painful one. If I went for the first option, I was just another mug punter, and mates' rates or not, the interest would go on and on and the repaying would never stop. If I went for the second, I get the cash, Chapman becomes the mug punter, and it becomes Hamlet's job to recover it from him. He'd probably unleash the goons to find Chapman and get what he owed, probably hurt him. But it was Chapman's fault, he started the whole chain of events, I held him one hundred percent responsible for Tommy.

'The debt's all yours, thanks,' I said.

'You'll get the money by Friday, someone'll call you when it's ready, okay?' Hamlet phrased it as a question but I took it as the instruction it was. I confirmed Friday would be fine and that I appreciated what he was doing for me – you deal with the Devil, but you still need to bow and scrape.

'Now, whilst you're here, there's some jobs for you, go and see Sally in the back office.' He paused, then, 'It's good to see you again Mark, really good, we should hang out again soon.'

And with that I knew I had been dismissed.

-7-

SALLY LOOKED UP at me over the top of her thin monitor, the light of the display reflecting off her fashionable black-framed glasses. She leaned back in her seat, removed her glasses, and broke into a smile.

'Well, well, well. Marky Mark, the prodigal returns,' she said. 'I was told you were popping in, but I didn't believe it.'

She rose from her seat and hugged me, which I found both surprising and comforting at the same time. She was a good kid – that's all she was, only in her early twenties and already the most sensible member of my family, so composed and self-possessed. I certainly never had that kind of confidence at her age, not that I'm suggesting any family resemblance between us, in fact I'm not even sure if I can say we were family. Sally's my uncle's wife's niece: what does that makes us, second cousins, anything, nothing? I only even knew of any link a few years ago when my uncle introduced us. Funny isn't it? It's a small town but you could walk past someone in the street and not even realise you're related. But like I say, she's a good kid, making her way on her own, dealing with gurning idiots like Brazil and Dunlop all day and Hamlet, a smiling damned villain, by night.

I'd grown to hate the way he treated women. Maybe its territorial, *my club, my property*, maybe it's a throwback to all the ecstasy he'd gorged on over the years, maybe he was just an arsehole. Whatever the reason, if the Prince behaved like that, then his court would follow, giving socially inept boneheads like Brazil and Dunlop entitlement to paw women and treat them like livestock. It sickened me and was one of the reasons, not the main one I admit, but nonetheless a reason, I had wanted to get some distance from this whole thing.

I never said anything to her, but for a while I felt compelled to keep a watchful eye over Sally, making sure she was alright and being treated respectfully, even though I'm sure Sally could more than take care of herself. But in any event, she was protected, Hamlet made sure of that. The reasons why were on her desk. Several photos in varied frames were assembled around the stem of her computer screen, pictures of Sally and a little girl, her daughter Sophia. Hamlet's granddaughter. Possibly.

Sally, as efficient as always, had produced a short list of repairs she wanted done. As we walked around the club, she pointed out each item, and we caught up in the gaps in between talking about family, and I nodded along politely as she spoke of people I didn't know and would never meet but I was somehow linked to. She seemed happy when I told her I'd get the materials on order and come back in a few days, but she persuaded me to stay on to look at a blown security lamp over the external entrance stairs. I couldn't think of any justifiable reason to turn her down, and told her so. We both smiled. Breaking the mood of the moment, my phone buzzed in my pocket. Without hesitating, I killed the call, and it chimed a notification at me a minute later. Apologising to Sally I listened to the voicemail message, Senia again. I put the phone away and said, 'Okay, let's have a look at this lamp.'

It only took twenty minutes or so to change the lamp over. As I was packing away my ladder, Sally emerged with two mugs, handing one to me, and gestured towards the low boundary wall as somewhere to sit. Following her lead, I sat and thanked her for the coffee. The warm bright Spring day was all around us and the low sun felt welcome on my face.

'I was ever so sad to hear about Tommy,' she said. 'He was such a lovely guy.' I muttered my agreement.

'He'd been down here quite a bit recently, I think he'd been doing stuff for Ian, working in his properties.' Perhaps she picked up on my lack of understanding as she explained, 'He was dealing with him direct, anything to do with the club or the pubs come through me, so I assumed it was to do with his other properties. Who did it, Mark? Do you know?'

I shook my head and told her no matter which way I looked at it, I couldn't understand why anyone would want to hurt him; he was the best. I didn't mention my guilt and my shame that it might have been because of me, unable to pay the debts I'd stacked up on the promise of a fat bastard travel agent in absentia.

And then she asked me, the first person to do so, how I felt, how I was coping, how I was bearing up. Sometimes all you want is someone to listen, isn't it? You don't want opinions, or solutions, you just want someone who can hear you. I was so grateful to her for understanding this.

She didn't speak, she sat and she listened, knowing that was the correct way to deal with me, that's how we do things round here. Every now and then just lift the lid, let out some of the steam, and then straight away seal it up again as though nothing had happened.

A shrill comedy wolf whistle broke the sombre mood. Blushing, Sally reached into her pocket and pulled out a smartphone, 'Oops, text message.' She became coy as she read it.

'Go on then,' I gently teased her, 'who's that? Got much going on?'

Sally contemplated her answer looking upwards. She unrolled her hunched shoulders and arched towards the clear blue sky above us, she gnawed her lip and nodded with faint embarrassment. The sunlight reflected a warm glow off her coffee-coloured complexion. This was someone happy, someone with good news, exactly what I needed.

'Come on, share.'

'Things are good. I've met someone. Sophia's met him, she likes him, always a good sign, and she adores his little boy. He's the same age, says she wants him to be her brother. So, yeah, things are good.'

I congratulated her, and encouraged her to continue.

'We want to move in together, like a ready-made family. Problems with his ex though, bit of a nightmare. We want to get away, start somewhere new. Plus, there's all this here, I could do with getting away from here. Don't tell Himself downstairs though, I don't want him to know yet.'

I promised to be the soul of discretion and wished her success whilst she fumbled about with her smartphone. On her cue, I grinned a cheesy smile to the small lens in the sparkly red cover. She giggled as I heard the shutter sound-effect.

'New toy. Got it at the weekend, took them ages to transfer everything across to it from the old phone but it was worth it because it's brilliant, only thing is I have to keep charging it, the battery doesn't seem to last anywhere nearly as long as my old Samsung.'

She looked at me as though expecting me to have the answer to her battery woes, I just shrugged my shoulders and drank my coffee.

'There you are, don't you look pretty?'

Some sort of photo app had turned my face into a fluffy white kitten. I smiled, but she found it hysterical and began to sing *'Pussy cat, pussy cat I love you, yes I do...'*

'Small things...' I muttered in mock indignation, 'How's Sophia? Still gorgeous?'

Sally swiped her finger across the screen then tilted it towards me to show me a charming little girl with the same coffee complexion as her mother and tight black curls dropping in ringlets across her beaming face. 'A proper little mini-me, isn't she?'

Her next swipe brought up an image of Sophia dressed as a Disney princess and a little boy of similar age dressed as a superhero flapping his cape behind him, 'That's my Sophia, and that's Joseph – I told you, we're a ready-made family'

I murmured pleasantries, but our conversation was interrupted by the sullen arrival of Brazil. 'Oh no, what's he want now?' I heard her softly mutter.

'No rest for the wicked, eh?' I said.

'Something like that.' Sally's whole demeanour had changed. Gone was the happy care-free young woman with dreams for the future, tired eyes took their place and the hunched shoulders had rolled back.

'Boss wants to know if you're finished. He wants you inside. Now.'

I handed Sally my empty mug and thanked her – more for the chat than the drink – then watched her follow Brazil back downstairs.

LATER, BACK IN traffic, heading for home, waiting for the lights to change, I looked around. It's all poor and low rent round here now. The nice stores have all long gone, replaced by coffee shops, takeaways, charities and empty units, sad when you stop to think about it, all those businesses that had been part of the local landscape, wiped away forever – like the furniture store that had been there ever since its founder came back a war hero. It had closed exactly seventy years later and stood empty for a while, decaying day by day as the traffic trundled past. Its new occupant had painted the exterior a gaudy red and gold, 'Cash X Changer', where hard-up individuals can peddle valuables for cash enticed by the big banners screaming '*We pay you for electronics! We pay you for games! We pay you for phones!*' A modern-day pawn shop or a legalised fence? I guess that's a matter of opinion, but it shows an area's on its knees when something like this is welcomed on to the high street like a conquering hero.

A single chime took my focus away from concerns about the local decline, but my heart sank to read the incoming message from Sally, *'Forgot to mention, Uncle B is coming back this week'*. But then she made up for the bad news by attaching an image file which when opened brought up my fluffy white kitten face – it was quite funny after all. I was still smiling when an angry blast of horn from behind told me the lights had changed and the traffic had begun to move.

-8-

THERE WERE THREE people I needed to contact. The first was Chapman. I dialled his number, no surprise, voicemail:

'Anthony, this is important, I want my money, you've got until Thursday night, then it's out of my hands and I can't take responsibility for whatever happens. You have to phone me back.'

The second was Blunt, but I really didn't want to talk to him, I didn't think I could stay polite and plead that he doesn't pulverise me whilst wanting to rant and rave about Tommy at the same time, so I took the coward's way out and sent him a text message *'Paul, good news, one way or the other I'm getting your money on Friday. Call me, let me know where to find you Friday. I'll bring it over.'*

The third and final person I needed to speak to was Jen, Tommy's widow. I hadn't had any contact with her since finding Tommy like that. I figured Senia's warning to stay away should've lapsed by now. I needed to see her, the guilt and shame was coursing through me with such ferocity I realised I was shivering; it was that long-forgotten dread sensation of being sent to the headmaster to face your punishment. Her man was working on my job, he should have come home safe. He shouldn't have been injured and killed, particularly not if it was meant to be me. If I was to clear my conscience, if I was to atone for Tommy, I needed to look Jen in the eye and apologise.

It was almost dark by the time I got to Jen's, yet it wasn't much past five. Spring was just starting. I like Spring, the season of new life and expectation, not that that's much comfort for Jen though I realised.

This was the hardest thing I've ever had to do, I just wanted to stay in the van and go home.

I couldn't see any police presence outside the house or on the street, but I recognised her mother's smart new Toyota on the driveway thanks to all the golfing tat. '*Keep Calm and Play Golf*' read one sticker in the back window, '*Queen Of The Green*' and '*Chicks With Sticks*' said others. I knew right then that something difficult had become even harder. Now I really didn't want to be here, I wanted to drive on.

After a few very long minutes prevaricating, I was on the doorstep. I looked up and down the road for nothing in particular and checked my pockets a second time, glad to feel the soft latex between my fingertips, and after a couple of deep breaths to steady my nerves found myself ringing the doorbell.

'I'll get it,' said a loud voice which I knew belonged to Jen's mother, and made me want to run away as fast as I could.

Through the glass in the door I saw a wibbly-wobbly underwater depiction of the interior and watched as she appeared through an adjacent doorway. As she opened the door, she recognised me and didn't hide her displeasure.

'What do you want?'

She leaned against the jamb to block the entrance, a physical barrier in golfing casuals: the bastard lovechild of Theresa May and Rory McIlroy. Jen's mother had always been sharp-tongued and cantankerous, not that it ever bothered me before as our paths crossed so seldom, but now given the opportunity to vent all her spite and fury on me she wasn't going to waste a second of it.

'You aren't welcome here, piss off before I call the police.'

'Hey,' a weak voice called from a room out of sight. 'It's okay Mum. Let him in please.'

I made to step forward, but she refused to budge, she had no intention of letting me past. She may be a lady in her sixties, but she is still very active, she probably figured she could hold me back if it came to it – she was probably right.

'Mum, that's enough. Let him in.'

She rolled back and walked off with all the grace of a sulking pit bull, leaving the door swinging open.

I ventured into the lounge – it looked great – one of the benefits of living with a decorator I suppose. Jen sat alone in the middle of a huge leather sofa, looking like she'd been cast adrift in a lifeboat. She really looked a mess, understandable given the circumstances, but nonetheless it was a shock to find her this way. She looked up at me with hollow red eyes, held my gaze for a couple of seconds and then, with effort, rose from the sofa with her arms outstretched.

'Mark, I'm so glad to see you.' She hugged me. 'So glad.'

'Jen, I'm so sorry, so sorry, are you okay?'

'Of course she's not okay, you dick,' came Old Mother Faldo's pleasant tones from behind me. 'I've given her some of my Temazepam to calm her down.'

Strange, I never imagined her mother – that spitting, hissing demon of the sand traps – to be one for the tranquilizers.

'What do you want?' It's funny isn't it how, even when you can't see them, you somehow know if someone's sneering at you.

'I just wanted to make sure Jen's ok. Can I do anything for you Jen? Or Chloe?'

'They're fine! We don't need anything from you. Go!'

'Okay, okay, I'll be off.' I knew there was nothing to be gained from having a row.

'Uncle Mark!' squealed a cheerful voice from the other end of the room.

Chloe sat at the dining table; paper and crayons spread out in front of her. The world outside the large patio doors had been lost in the evening's early darkness, but as I turned to face her, the garden became awash with bright light. It backlit her, adding an almost angelic glow through her straggly blonde hair. In the garden, a woman paced up and down. Karen – Jen's sister: by going out for a vape, Karen had triggered the external lamp. She didn't move her eyes off the ground before her, lost in her own thoughts as she puffed and paced with equal fury.

'Hello, my darling,' I said to the charming little girl who, judging from her enthusiastic scamper towards me and tight hug around the thighs appeared oblivious to what had happened to her family, 'I've got something for you.'

I reached in my pocket. I pulled out a long thin orange balloon and gave it a couple of stretches, letting it snap back against my knuckles, 'Ouch!' and a quick shake of the hand to show the pain – always gets a laugh from the kids and did again this time – then a big long puff and the balloon inflated. As I knotted the end, I asked her what she wanted, and a few twists later handed over a balloon dog to squeals of delight. My adoring audience of one demanded an encore, and using two balloons, one green one yellow, I handed her a daffodil.

'Mummy, look, I've got a flower, and a doggy.' Jen smiled and we heard the garden door click shut. 'Auntie Karen, look,' said Chloe running out to the kitchen to show off her new gifts.

'Right, I'll be off then,' I said to Jen. Her mother stood beside her glowering. 'But Jen, remember, anything I can do, anything, just let me know.' And with that I turned to leave. As I reached the threshold Jen called me back.

'Please, Mark…' with genuine concern in her voice. 'There is something.'

'Sure,' I replied. 'What?'

Jen rose with even greater effort this time, and, dazed, shuffled across the lounge to a sideboard against the opposite wall. She moved with such uncertainty I wondered how much Granny Ballesteros had doped her up.

'Tommy's jobs,' she slurred on the 's' sounds, the meds having taken hold.

Jen was trying to pull something out of the cabinet, something her muddled fingers couldn't grasp. I knelt beside her and saw she was reaching for two small metal filing chests. I reached in, pulled them out and sat them on the sideboard. They were nothing special, just ordinary home filing chests that I knew would have a few hanging files inside for paperwork.

'Tommy's jobs,' Jen repeated. 'Please help, Mark.'

I could see what was coming. I knew Tommy had a few current jobs on the go, a lot recently finished, and according to him several ready to start. But something like that could be a treasure trove to anyone a bit sharp. Picture the scene: they get invited to finish off the job, and lo and behold they begin finding problem after problem with the work already done, the client starts panicking because their job has already been held up what with losing the first guy and then having to find the new one, they want it finished and will throw money at the new guy then they simply deduct it off the first guy – we call this holding the job to ransom, because they know they will get paid whatever they want to get the job done. A convincing ransom contractor would clean the client out and ensure that the original contractor won't be left with a penny.

I knew what Jen was asking. She wanted me to complete Tommy's jobs and collect his debts on her behalf as she knew I wouldn't rob them.

'Of course,' I whispered, I put my arm around her and guided her back to the safety of her sofa, and then picked up the filing chests, 'I'll take a look and we'll talk again in a few days, is that ok darling?' I don't think she understood what I was saying by that point, so I kissed her lightly on the forehead and left.

I placed the two filing chests beside me in the van – like I say, they didn't look anything special. If only I'd known, I'd never have gone near them. Her mother glowered at me from the window as I drove off, but I was beyond caring by that point. However, looking back I should have taken it as an omen.

-9-

THE EVENING CLEAR and crisp, the fresh dusting of frost crunched underfoot as I parked the van and headed home. Two paces and then – d'oh! – my Dad was the same, always forgetting what he'd come into a room for – I spun on the balls of my feet, back to the van to retrieve the filing chests, and then finally, I was unlocking my front door.

The new incoming neighbour still hadn't cleared their pile of cardboard from the front path, if anything they'd added to it. I kicked some of the spillage back to their side.

ANOTHER EVENING UNABLE to sleep and nothing on television to distract my thoughts. To waste some time I decided to look through Tommy's files. I'd promised to protect Jen and mitigate any risks on Tommy's business from sharks and chancers, and I fully intended keeping my promise. I reached for the nearest chest and snapped open the chrome buckles.

Inside, as expected, were a series of hangers. I flicked through them seeing loose papers and correspondence, quotations on his headed paper and his build-up calculations stapled behind them. There were invoices from merchants and suppliers, bank statements and a half-used cheque book, there were letters from accountants and returns to the Tax Man. The chest didn't yield any surprises, it was nothing more than a snapshot of an ordinary small business, no more no less.

In the final hanger, I found what I wanted: Tommy's invoices for works complete. I took them out, then flicked through again looking for the bank statements – a quick reconciliation of the two would soon reveal how much money he had outstanding waiting to be paid. The hardest part, I feared, would be getting people to pay up once they'd heard he was dead, so it was something I needed to chase quickly. Leaning into the chest for the statements I noticed an envelope I hadn't spotted on my first rummage. It was an ordinary large white envelope, used, with a window for the address and blue inked postage marks with the sender's logo, which I recognised as a local builder's merchant. I get these in the post almost every day stuffed full of unwanted promotional rubbish – vouchers for this and discounts on that. Mine go straight to recycling unopened, so it seemed a little strange to me Tommy would want to keep anything like that. I assumed he'd reused the envelope to keep certain paperwork together. That made me curious. I didn't want to miss anything.

I removed it. It contained a wodge of loose papers held together by a clip. I slid them out and saw a stylish grey and green letterhead for Quentin Property Holdings. Reading on I realised it was a purchase order, nothing complicated, nothing onerous, just a bog-standard set of terms and conditions employing Tommy for a small maintenance job at an address I knew at once: Queen Mary's Retirement Home, a private sheltered housing complex for senior citizens.

I don't remember him saying he'd worked there, but right away I could picture Tommy in his element, the centre of attention for the frisky old land girls and bobbysoxers, using his charm and innuendo to transport them back to giddy young things when they spent hot sunny days in Kentish hop fields and warm summer nights in American nylons.

I knew the place because it was no more than two minutes from Tommy's house: to the bottom of the road and around the corner. I leafed through the contents of the envelope, there must have been thirty or forty purchase orders all from Quentin Property Holdings. It made sense for them I suppose, why not have a pet contractor on call nearby to handle all your repairs. I put them back in the envelope and then back in the chest.

'Let's see what's in the other chest,' I thought, reaching for it, but unlike the first one this was locked. I rattled the buckles, they wouldn't open.

'I hope this isn't an old family heirloom, Tommy,' I said to the empty room, attacking it with a thin-bladed screwdriver. A few minutes later, and with a bit of brute force the buckles popped open. I raised the lid and peered inside.

Well... it's fair to say I wasn't expecting that!

-10-

I FISHED '*I love Belgrade*' out of the sink, rinsed it clean and brewed myself a tea. I don't know what I was doing, perhaps hoping it would have disappeared like a passing mirage, but no, as I walked back into the room it was still there.

One hundred and fifty-two thousand and seventy pounds in cash, the complete contents of the second chest. I'd counted it twice and laid it out like tombstones in neat regular little rows. All used notes, mainly twenties, a few fifties, even fewer tens. One hundred and fifty-two thousand and seventy pounds. Cash.

This didn't make any sense at all. What was Tommy doing with a box full of money? Did Jen know about it? No, of course not, she wouldn't have given it to me otherwise.

We've all been paid cash in hand once in a while, it would be silly to deny it, but this much? This isn't right. I didn't understand this at all, and it concerned me. Believe me, cash is not king, cash is trouble. Anyone who thinks a bundle of cash is a gift from God has clearly never had any. It's incredibly hard to get rid of large amounts of cash nowadays – new cars every year, lots of exotic holidays, solid gold watches? That'll be when people begin to notice, and you have to explain to the Taxman how you can afford a champagne lifestyle on tap water earnings. And you most definitely can't put it in the bank! No, too much cash is a problematic pain in the arse.

What was Tommy intending to do with it? I'd promised to look after Jen and little Chloe, and all of this must now be theirs so I need to be certain this won't get them in trouble. But really, what can I do? It was this confusion that made me dizzy enough to get up and leave the room in the first place.

The *Belgrade* break had untangled my thinking. I knew what needed to be done. I had to return it. This was Tommy's money and, knowing him as I did, he would want it to look after his family, so there was no question, Jen would get it. But then, there was also the question of the formalities. The bank and the Taxman would soon be creaming off what they could, leaving Jen to fend for herself. Never mind the newspaper talk about Death Duties being only for rich men, they'll pick over the bones like carrion whether you're a billionaire or a bus driver.

I remembered my Dad's estate, the resentment flooded back, that conniving bastard of a lawyer: '*You see, your father died intestate, that complicates things considerably*'. My Dad had absolutely nothing when he died and by the time that lawyer had finished there was even less. No, I'd made a promise, they'd be looked after, or else I could never clear my conscience for what had happened.

But then a new thought crept into my head, and expanded to fill it to bursting point. This was serious, I couldn't get rid of it and it terrified me: *What if this is what got Tommy killed?*

This added a brand-new level of craziness, now I was really worried about creating trouble for Jen. I had to trust my judgement, the best thing all round would be to hold on to it, somewhere safe, and give it to Jen later. Once the dust had settled and the vultures had gone. Once I was sure no-one would come looking for it.

The money went back into the chest and I at once regretted breaking off the buckles as it wouldn't fasten shut any more. It would need a secure hiding place, but where? I was struggling to think, my head was starting to ache and a pain screamed behind my eyes in a skull-splitting mix of tiredness, sadness, fear and regret.

It was two in the morning; any prospect of sleep had long flown. I'd tried, but it was a struggle to get off and when sleep at last came I was awoken by dreams of Tommy, lying glassy-eyed on the floor, looking up at me with his usual dopey grin, his yawning head wound meting out banknote after banknote, each fluttering down like autumn leaves landing in the bloody pools beneath him, their edges curling through contact with the moisture, a crimson red bloom being drawn up through the fibres of the paper.

As a way to distract myself, I set about working out Tommy's accounts. It didn't take too long as, luckily, I found his handwritten ledger slipped within his invoices It was about a month old and only took a quick exercise to bring it up to date. I identified three distinct elements – invoices raised with money due, invoices to be raised for works complete, and works in progress.

The first category seemed the greatest by number, with around twenty invoices, although the bulk of it was owed by only a few contractors and I knew them, so I made a note to deal with that in the morning. The second category would be the most time-consuming. I'd need to go through a lot of paperwork to sort that out, but the fatigue and the headache made reading too hard so I parked that one for the night. I was most interested by the final category. I made a list of live jobs, and it was complete as far as I knew, although the only way I'd know if I'd missed anyone would be getting their irate complaints later in the week when no-one's turned up for three days running. I could add them on the list then, if and when it happened. I estimated there would be six, maybe eight weeks work for one man, I'd contact a few decorators in the morning, see if anyone was interested.

Then I turned back to the Quentin purchase orders, and separated them out. There were forty-four in total and from what I could make out eleven of them were completed, billed and paid; twenty had invoices raised against them but I couldn't find any payment, and thirteen were all dated only a few days ago. Seeing as he'd been with me all week, I assumed they hadn't been done yet.

I flicked through the orders to get an idea of what was required. *You've done well there, Tommy!* Sheet after sheet, the money offered was incredible. Silly little repair jobs that would take anyone sensible all of fifteen minutes were being awarded for half a day's money. I made a quick estimate – these thirteen jobs would take at most ten days, but the money on offer was well over a month's-worth. I'd head over to Queen Mary's tomorrow to see the manager, chase up payment on the outstanding invoices and see what's needed for the work to be done, so that I can get started with it.

-11-

THE MORNING SUN in my eyes woke me just before seven a.m., and after pulling on yesterday's clothes I hauled myself downstairs, cursing that I should have woken earlier. Sure enough, alongside the sofa sat the broken filing chest. I flipped open the lid and the notes grinned back at me regally. I had a plan, perhaps it was my mind and body shutting down and rebooting in the wee small hours, but I knew how to keep the money safe. I gathered up the chest and headed outside.

I'd spotted something on the path when I came home last night, and the only advantage of being awake before the binmen was that it was still there: a discarded cardboard box from a new kettle. I looked around, the street was deserted. I took the box and, with the broken filing chest, carried them to my lock-up garage.

Gentle, ever so gentle. Up went the steel door with great care, no noise to wake up nosy neighbours. Shelving lined the walls, floor to ceiling, and freestanding racking filled the centre. It was stacked with everything I could ever need to run my business, apart from one shelf at the back where three transparent plastic storage boxes sat in a row. They were grimy with dust and cobwebs, their lids snapped shut and unopened since they'd been put there, the contents of Dad's flat – stuff I don't have a use for but at the same time can't bear to part with. Without time to waste getting maudlin, I transferred the cash into the kettle box and pushed Dad's boxes along to make enough space to squeeze it on the same shelf. A small palm-shaped window emerged in the grime where grey filth transferred from Dad's boxes to my hands, and as I wiped it off on my jeans I could see Mum's china Staffordshire Dogs through it. I think Granny Parsons won them at bingo, certainly not an antique, but they meant something to her, and meant something to Mum, so by rights they should mean something to me. Isn't that how it works?

Wedged in the dark corner, deep amongst the cobwebs, I was satisfied the kettle box was inconspicuous enough not to catch the eye. Besides, there were lots of lovely power tools at the front of the garage to appeal to your average friendly neighbourhood junkie, should he decide to break in on the off-chance. All my power tools were leading brands, they had to be. If you turn up on site with expensive, branded kit you look like a professional from the off. But also, when you're working on a price you want reliability, you want to bash the job out as fast as you can, the very last thing you need is being forced to stop because the motor in your cheap, crappy, no-mark drill has burnt itself out, especially if you're working through the night and everywhere's closed. De Walt, Hilti, Bosch and the like. Big, chunky cases in their corporate yellow, red and green stood shoulder to shoulder like proud soldiers on the shelf. Any opportunistic thief would see them as an easy win long before they ventured to the back for a kettle. I closed and locked the door, satisfied Tommy's cash would be safe.

I WENT BACK indoors to shower and dress for the day ahead. Through the kitchen window I saw a sparrow hop across the lawn with hungry expectation He'd have to wait, I had a couple of calls I needed to make first.

Suspecting he'd still be at home, I phoned Disco. After a lot of swearing and complaining about being woken up at *'the filthy bleeding arse crack of dawn'*, I told him to get something to write on, and threw out a few biscuit crumbs to the sparrow while listening to

Disco's further volley of very imaginative profanities in between bangs and thumps as he hunted for a notepad.

After muttering something particularly inventive and disgusting, he was at last ready. I recited a list of names and what they owed, telling him, 'They're all drinkers at the Lamb. I need your obvious charm and diplomacy to get them to pay up. Woo them, shame them, harangue them, bully them, I don't care, just get them to pay what they owe. Tommy was our friend, he's got a family, we all know it's the right thing to do, so if you can get them to play fair it'd be much appreciated, okay?'

Disco assured me he would do his best.

'And what are you up to later? Can I borrow you for an hour?'

Cue more complaining, but I persisted and explained about the Quentin purchase orders. 'Fair bit of work, and good rates too if you're up for it?' That caught his attention. 'I need you to come with me, we can walk around the job, see what's needed and then I can order it all up for when we start.'

'Okay, fine with me. Where is it?' See, told you he was interested, it's amazing how eager to please people become at the promise of good money.

'Queen Mary's? Really?' he sounded surprised. 'I thought Old John had that buttoned up nice and tight? You remember Old John?'

'Hadrian's hod-carrier? I've not heard his name mentioned for ages, I'd assumed he'd retired years ago. Maybe he has, maybe that's how Tommy got a foot in the door? Anyway, I'll come and pick you up later.'

THE PHONE JIGGLED about in my pocket like a burrowing hamster. I looked at the name on the screen and wanted to go back to bed and hide – just when I thought things couldn't get any worse.

'Mark, it's me.'

The voice was unmistakeable, to be fair Sally had warned me, but her text had gone straight out of my mind. I adopted my politest telephone manner.

'Hello Uncle Bern, how are you?' *And how much is it going to cost me*, I wondered.

'Good, good as gold. Look, I'm coming back day after tomorrow—'

Here it comes. *What's he after this time?*

'Got any work for me? Anything I can do?'

'Funnily enough, I've had some painting jobs come up – interested?' I said, filling him in on what had happened to Tommy and my role in closing out his jobs.

'I don't know, Mark, sounds dangerous. What if they come after me?'

'Oh, don't talk wet, why would anyone want to kill you?' I said realising what a silly question that was as soon as I said it, you'd only need to spend a few minutes with Uncle Bern before you noticed your fingers limbering up for a spot of light strangulation, 'Look, if you don't want it, fine, I'll get someone else. Good rates though.'

A moment of silence passed, just enough to weigh up the money against his perceived murder threat, 'Okay, I'll do it. I'll need some T-shirts.'

'Bloody will you now? Don't you have any T-shirts of your own?'

'No.'

'But, you live in Spain, you spend all day every day in T-shirts and flip flops, haven't you packed any?' I asked, knowing full well he'd bought another bargain flight for two quid: the sort with no food or water, six-hour delays, double booked seats and hand baggage only.

'Espadrilles, not flip flops, it's the Costa not bloody Margate,' said Uncle Bern rising to the bait. Sometimes it's too easy. 'And I don't mean the kind of T-shirt you wear on the beach. If I'm working for you, I'll need T-shirts, you know, uniform.'

'What happened to the ones I gave you last time you were here?'

'Them? I took them back with me.'

'To Fuengirola? To wear on the beach?'

'You bloody well know it's Marbella! They were knackered, you need to buy better quality fabric – after a couple of washes they're only any good for taking to the beach.'

'Okay, I'll set aside a couple of T-shirts for you.'

'And a sweatshirt, actually, you got a fleece? I bet it's bloody freezing over there, I don't know why I bother coming back this time of year, it's always bloody miserable.'

Well don't bloody come then, no-one asked you to, I thought, but instead took a deep breath and said, 'I'll see what I've got left.'

'Thanks Mark, you're a good lad,' said Uncle Bern. Then, after letting his compliment hang just long enough, 'If you could find me some tracky pants too?'

We chatted for a moment about mutual friends and what had been happening here since he was last home. Bern's worse than Disco when it comes to gossip, and after I'd had enough, I started saying my goodbyes.

'Actually, Mark, I've an idea, you still got the key to my flat?'

I confirmed indeed I did.

'Then why don't you let yourself in, drop off the T-shirts and stuff there before I get back, that way you won't need to make a special visit will you?'

That didn't sound like a bad idea, it'd still be a special visit, but at least if I let myself in when he's not there I wouldn't have to see him, so I agreed.

'Good. Makes sense, doesn't it?' A pause. The pause became a long pause, a longer pause, then: 'So, seeing as you're going to the flat, can you get me some milk and bread, and bacon, and teabags and—'

Schoolboy error, I should have seen that one coming, now I have to do a grocery shop for the sneaky old git. I really needed to get off this call before he gets me declared bankrupt.

'Before you go, you didn't say what time you'll be picking me up for work.'

'I won't be picking you up, I've got my own work to be getting on with,' I lied, but I wasn't in the mood for enduring dark early mornings trapped in the small cabin of the van with the smell of Bern's farts and his constant moaning.

'Well can I have a float then? I'll need to get taxis in that case.'

How did this happen? I thought I was doing him a favour, chance to earn a bit of cash in hand, now it looks like it's going to cost me simply for the privilege of offering him work. A quiet few seconds passed, I could hear him breathing, and could picture him in his hacienda puffing and panting like an asthmatic mole.

'You still there? This call's costing me money. Still there?'

'Look, I can't imagine Jen's got any use for Tommy's van. I'll see if I can borrow it for a few days, maybe sell it for her.'

'I'm not driving a dead man's van, it's unlucky, it might be haunted.'

'Oh, shut up. Look, tell you what, if she lets me have it, I'll use it and you can use mine. How's that sound?'

'Thanks Mark, you're a good lad. Listen, my flight lands at eighteen twen—' but I cut the call before he could rope me into a three-hour round trip to Gatwick.

JEN WAS HAPPY to let me use Tommy's van – well, I say happy, she sounded so spaced out I doubt she really knew what she was agreeing to. Her mum stood over her like a bodyguard in pastel waterproofs. She made me write a receipt on the back of a golf lub scorecard she found in her handbag to say that I'd taken the keys to Tommy's van. I told Jen that I'd try to sell it, raise a bit of cash, but her mum had already run her eye over Tommy's estate it seemed.

'That van's worth at least five grand, I've checked, so don't you go robbing her, Mark Poynter.'

The vultures are circling close to home it seems.

A MINI-CAB dropped me off outside the Wilkes house. Blue-and-white tape fluttered across the front lawn. A bored female police officer stood on the doorstep, her thick, padded fluorescent jacket unable to keep out the cold it seemed from the way she shuffled from foot to foot, clapping her gloved hands in front of her.

The officer, grateful for someone to talk to, told me that the house was still closed off as a crime scene, waiting for the men in the white paper suits to turn up and find that crucial flake of dandruff to trace the killer. I told her I was a friend of the family here to take the van, and then lost all feeling in my toes and fingers while she had a conversation on the radio attached at her shoulder. Just when I'd lost all sensation in my lips, she told me that the van could be released, and not wasting any time I opened it, hopped in and fired up the heaters.

TOMMY'S VAN WAS nice to drive. The dry warm air circulated with the smell of paints and solvents trapped inside, and I became pleasantly light-headed as the heat seeped into my bones. The Citroën was based on a proper car, so it was small and low to the ground. It felt nippy and easy to throw around, unlike my high-sided panel van. It was useful to have had a go driving it as I'd know what I'm talking about when I come to sell it for Jen. But Old Mother Faldo was wrong, you wouldn't get five grand for it. In ordinary circumstances, you might – it was in good condition with quite a low mileage and as a rule a decorator's van will have a far softer life than, say, a brickie's van, as the lumpiest thing they ever need to ferry about is a stepladder and they only turn up at the end of the job when the site's been cleared and the roads are in. However, Tommy had painted it. Don't get me wrong, it looked fantastic, but for resale value it's a big no-no. On the side panels and rear doors, he'd hand-painted livery in a style that always made me think of 1930s New York: upright gold and black letters and horizontal lines of differing thicknesses.

Signwriting was one of his many talents, learned when he started off as an apprentice from an old-timer out the Dockyard that had applied the finishing touches to battleships and submarines for the Arctic Convoys. I think it was one of Tommy's hobbies, he always kept his hand in. I recall him doing all the boards and signs for Chloe's school fetes: 'Tombola', 'Coconut Shy' and the like, all in that beautiful, nostalgic fairground style, and all done properly, they'll be using them for years, long after she's moved on to big school. But nobody wants their vans painted any more they want laser-cut vinyl stickers that don't fade and don't damage the paintwork and when no longer wanted can be peeled off with a hairdryer.

Made me a little sad to think an old traditional skill like that had died with Tommy and I felt my eyes start to prickle, although that could have been the warmed-up solvent fumes getting to me. No, a painted van is a nuisance and Granny Ballesteros won't get her five grand because I'll need to discount it to cover the buyer's respray cost. It wouldn't have been a problem for Tommy though: with his last van, he sold it to some woman starting a florist-cum-coffee shop so he over-painted the panels with her designs and she was delighted, he'd always pop in there whenever passing for a steaming extra-hot flat white – and a cup of coffee too, probably.

At the traffic lights, and warm enough that I could at last move my fingers without hurting, I punched in the numbers. The phone rang a few times, then a few more. By now I was hoping for voicemail and panicked when I heard a human voice speak after so many rings.

'Hello?'

'Mrs Wilkes?' I said struggling to remember what to say next. 'Hello, it's Mark Poynter. How are you?'

Mrs Wilkes and I muttered the standard pleasantries back and forth but in the background I could hear, '*Is that him? Is it? Let me speak to him.*'

'Mrs Wilkes, I was just checking in, see what's happening, whether you know when we can come back and finish off?'

She told me the police still had her home sealed off as a crime scene, confirming what I'd just encountered, and they were staying in the Holiday Inn for the meantime.

'*Give me the phone, Alison,*' said the distant voice.

'Any idea when they'll be finished?' I was keen to get back to work but, bollocks, the police had said expect the house to be out of bounds until at least next week. 'Mrs Wilkes, I know it might be a bit cheeky given the circumstances, but I was wondering if there was any chance of an interim payment, you know, just to keep everything ticking over?'

'Just a moment,' she said and I heard her repeat everything.

'*What!*' said the very angry distant voice, '*Give me the phone right now Alison.*'

'I'll just pass you over to my husband,' said Mrs Wilkes.

Now, I don't know, call me clairvoyant, maybe it was the mystical magic of the soft warm fumes, but something told me I wouldn't be getting paid, so I hung up before he could get to the phone.

-12-

A LITTLE AFTER one, I collected Disco from Boris The Plastic's job at a bland boxy detached house built in an era when frontage was more important than character. Fed up with the barrage of abuse I was getting for cutting into his drinking time and bored of having to explain for the third time why I was driving Tommy's van, I raised finishing Tommy's jobs.

'Uncle Bern's coming back tomorrow, I thought I'd offer him some of the painting,' I said and heard him mutter 'Useless' under his breath. It was clear Disco wasn't impressed by Uncle Bern's work ethic, but to call him useless wasn't fair – he was absolutely, totally, double dog-shit useless. But he was family, and I don't have much of that anymore, honour told me I should fight my corner. 'He is quick and cheap though,' I said.

'So's sticking your arm in a woodchipper for a manicure – and, both of them, you'll end up scraping lumps out the carpet for months after.'

'I'm only talking about odds and sods, just a touch-up, he should be alright for that,' I said, and took the low grumble beside me as Disco reserving judgement.

Putting Uncle Bern's malingering aside, we drew up outside a substantial piece of Victoriana in one of Rochester's grand historic avenues. Solid handsome bays extended from the basement to three storeys above with tall elegant double-hung sashes in each window. The ornate stone lintels and burnt orange brickwork radiated warmth and character in stark contrast to the monstrosity I'd found Disco at. They call these old imperial bricks 'rubbers' on account of how soft they are, the bricklayers of times past would rub them by hand to straighten out any defects which is why Victorian brickwork is still the best for being straight and plumb.

Once upon a time, back when Charles Dickens walked these wide leafy streets looking for inspiration, this property would have been home to one of Rochester's wealthy and respected gentlemen: wife, children, domestics, staunch pillar of the community, faithful servant of the Empire. Now it was owned by a charity and had been sub-divided into flats, only four of them, one per floor, and sympathetically done to provide decent accommodation for people in need, not like Hamlet's rat-traps.

'What are we doing here?' said Disco, pulling a manky looking roll-up cigarette from behind his ear, 'I thought we were going to the old folks' home.'

'Later,' I replied as he picked loose shreds of tobacco from his tongue 'This is one of Tommy's, a full external redec front back and sides, so we've got a meeting about it.'

'Who? Oh jeez, don't say Bern,' Disco said between splutters. I don't know what he'd rolled in that cigarette but it wasn't agreeing with him.

'Behave. Can you imagine Uncle Bern on this, it'd give him double incontinence? No, I want the Two Ronnies to do it.'

'The Two Ronnies? Yeah, that sounds more like it,' said Disco. The spluttering had stopped, but a dense black smoke and the smell of burnt hair hung around him.

Chris and Gavin Roncskevitz set up 'CGR Decorations' several years ago. Partly because of their ridiculously unpronounceable surname, and partly because of them being identical twins, but mostly because everyone loves a silly nickname, it was almost inevitable they'd become better known as the Two Ronnies – unusually for a nickname, they loved it too and had even started using the famous spectacles logo on their letterhead.

Disco and I looked round to the sound of doors slamming. The Two Ronnies' van – new, Mercedes, business must be good – was parked up slightly ahead of us on the other side of the road behind a stationary silver Mondeo whose driver appeared to be having a furious row on his phone as the Two Ronnies waddled past.

'Remind me, how do you tell them apart again?'

'It's easy,' said Disco. 'Chris is the hairy one with the beard, and Gav wears glasses.'

Well that makes it nice and easy, no problem I thought when two smooth-faced, shiny-headed identical clones in matching sweatshirts faced me, not a spectacle in sight.

'Hair … beard … glasses?' was all I could muster.

'Oh, yeah right,' said One Ronnie rubbing his face. Could this be Chris? 'We did a sponsored shave for charity at my boy's school.'

'I got lasered,' said the Other Ronnie, I'm guessing Gavin. 'It's brilliant, it's like seeing everything now in HD.'

'Nice to see you again boys,' said Disco, stepping forwards to shake their hands. The Ronnies moved in towards Disco, one stepped aside, then one walked towards the building and the other followed, one went one way, the other went the other, one stepped forwards, one stepped backwards. My mouth puckered up in frustration, all their moving about, it was giving me the hump – now they were all jumbled up and I had no idea who was who.

'We priced this job a little while ago,' said One Ronnie. 'Obviously didn't get it though, surveyor said we were too expensive.'

'I don't know anything about that,' I said. 'All I do know is Tommy won it and for obvious reasons he can't do it. So, do you want it?'

'Why don't you go back to the surveyor, tell him about Tommy and tell him to re-tender it?' the Other Ronnie asked.

'Two reasons: one, if all the other prices were already too high, he'd probably just shelve it and then nobody gets any work. And two, I want to do it for his wife and kiddie.'

The breakdown to Tommy's quote had built in a tidy little profit and as it was only a straightforward redecoration, it wouldn't take much to manage it, especially with an experienced crew like the Two Ronnies on board, and then the profit could go to Jen to help her out.

I explained all this to the Two Ronnies. No benefit in trying to deceive them, and thinking I'd be best off trying to appeal to their consciences, I laid on the bit about trying to help the poor widow and child as thick as I could before it began to sound like a Catherine Cookson. They didn't walk away, so I guess it worked.

'Look, I'm being honest with you, here's Tommy's breakdown, so let's take off the profit and set that aside for his family, and here,' I said jabbing a finger at a figure on the page in front of us, 'here's what he's got in for the job. I'm earning nothing from it, you take all of it and make what you can.'

'I don't know,' said One Ronnie to another. 'What do you reckon?'

'We've already priced this and were too dear. We couldn't match his price then, but now you want us to come down to his price and then down by another twenty per cent on top of that. I don't think we can.'

'Maybe you could think about using cheaper materials?'

'Look at his rates, how'd he expect to do it for that? What was he painting it with, a fucking magic wand?'

Disco chipped in, pointing to their shiny new van, telling them they could afford to do the right thing occasionally. I noticed one of them bristle, but Disco ploughed on regardless, getting right under their skin.

'We're all the same, all we want is to work safely,' he reminded them. 'It could just as easily be one of you that didn't make it home one day and God forbid if that happened, you'd hope your mates would rally round to help your loved ones left behind.' God, he was good, I could almost feel myself welling up.

'I suppose we could try to make a bit of extra margin on the subbies,' said a Ronnie.

'I guess so,' said the second Ronnie. 'We could get Cookie to do the scaffold, he's been complaining he needs more work.'

I felt a sudden lurch roll in my stomach at the mention of the name, making me slightly lightheaded, slightly sick. 'No. No Cookie. Promise me. No Cookie on this job.'

The Two Ronnies looked at me like I'd soiled myself, but nonetheless murmured their agreement.

'Look, we'll talk about it, and we'll call you later, is that okay?' suggested a Ronnie. I gave my agreement, we all shook hands and headed back to our respective vehicles.

As we rolled away from the kerb Disco turned to me, 'What was all that about Cookie? Why are you so against him?'

'Hmm... let me see.' I tapped a mock thoughtful finger against my cheek. 'How about the fact that he's uncontrollable? He'll never turn up when you need him, he comes and goes when he feels like it.' Disco nodded as though he was mentally weighing up my words. 'And how about that all his gear's stolen off everybody else's sites?'

'Careful. You can't prove that.'

'Apart from the fact that it's all painted different colours, branded and labelled with everyone else's name on it.'

'Fair point, I stand corrected.'

'And how about the fact he's a violent, racist, Nazi arsehole?'

'Not any more, he's not. He's changed.'

'Just because he's covered over the tattoos doesn't mean anything.'

'Maybe, still seems a bit of an overreaction though.' Disco gazed out the window. I could almost see the gears turning over, until... 'You owe him money!'

'I don't want to talk about it,' I said, snapping more anger into my reply than I intended and at once felt guilty when the embarrassment burned on Disco's face. But he was right, I did, I owed a small fortune to the very cheap and extremely nasty Cookie, so the longer I stayed out of Cookie's way the longer I stayed out of hospital.

WE TRAVELLED IN silence to our next destination. A large modern, low-level, red-bricked complex with charcoal concrete roof tiles creating wide overhanging eaves across the paved walkways around it. Lots of windows and doors gave the place an open and airy appearance, and it looked nice sat amongst mature gardens laid mostly to lawn. At crawling pace, I rolled Tommy's van along the service road, coming to a halt in the far corner of the car park, stopping beside a steel ship's container. A fresh coat of deep forest green paint and a chunky padlock gave it the look of a semi-permanent fixture.

The stern heavyset woman behind the reception counter looked at us with utter contempt as we entered. I suppose we looked a sight, me red-eyed from grief and two hours sleep and Disco, well, Disco was Disco.

I asked for the manager and was told – in quite an unnecessarily haughty manner I might add – 'Ms Fuller has just gone out for lunch,' and that we'd have to come back later. I asked if we could have a walk around the home, but that was rejected without the merest hesitation, it was clear she didn't want a couple of scruffs spoiling her well-ordered fiefdom. Despite my protestations and waving the Quentin purchase orders at her, she stood her ground and like an Alsatian in a polyester blouse, refused to let us in.

Realising we were on to a loser, Disco and I headed back out to the van. I apologised to him which prompted a further torrent of fruity swearing. Just then I saw a face, vaguely familiar, aged and weathered in the maybe fifteen years since I'd last seen it and, even then, I wasn't convinced until…

'Hello Mark, you alright?', Rob Beach, now there's someone from a very long time ago. He was a little heavier, a little grey at the temples but, on the whole, he looked much the same. Beside him stood a young boy in a Spiderman T-shirt, four maybe five, and the resemblance was very strong. It seemed Beach had settled down and become domesticated in recent years, the gold band on his finger adding to that assumption. We tried to exchange pleasantries, the smallest of small talk, but I found it difficult to establish common ground with someone that I barely knew years ago. I think he was in the same position until he surprised me with, 'I heard about your brother.'

'Heard what?'

'Well… you know…?' An awkward lull fell across our stilted conversation, and to escape from it he did that thing parents do when they start talking through their children: 'Got to go, we're meeting Mummy, aren't we Joe? She works here.'

'I didn't think she was one of the inmates,' piped up Disco. Using that as our opportunity to leave, I bid Beach all the best, and pushed Disco, who was giggling at his own grab-a-granny jokes, in the general direction of the van.

'Who was that?' he asked.

I looked back to make sure we were out of earshot, watching as the little boy in his Spiderman shirt ran up to a gaggle of ladies in their corporate navy-blue uniforms, the subject of much fuss and affection from all of them.

'Nobody. Forget about him,' I said, but Disco didn't want to let it lie.

'He's a dick,' I said. 'No friend of mine, he just used to be around, on the fringes, in the same places as me. Way back when, end of the Nineties, back when everyone went clubbing. Rumour was he was a dealer, Es and Whizz, not my thing at all, so I can't say whether he was or not for sure, but he'd always be hanging about at all the clubs and parties. So, I sort of got to know him as a mutual friend of mutual acquaintance sort of thing.'

'Seems like he knows about your brother,' said Disco.

'Everybody says they know about my brother,' I replied. 'Trouble is nobody knows anything about my brother.'

'Well, on the bright side, he looks like he's all settled down and loved up now,' said Disco.

'Yes, that struck me as odd as well,' I said.

'I guess age calmed him down. Maybe he's grown up and matured,' said Disco. 'And speaking of getting old…'

From across the car park we could see that the container doors had been opened wide, and propped up for all the world to see was a sign-written board with the words '*JP Overy, Building Contractor*'. Old John. So he was still about. And then as we got closer, there was the man himself, sitting in front of it on a plastic folding chair, munching away on a sandwich and he'd seen us: 'Hello chaps, what brings you here?'

They call him Old John because he's very very old – that, and his name's John – not all nicknames need to be clever. I don't know how old he actually is, but they do say he started out as Brunel's apprentice.

Old John looked up at us from his seated position. His face is perfectly round like an apple, his cheeks are round and rosy, his glasses are round and his mouth is small and upturned. He looks like a cartoon caterpillar, so you'd expect him to be kind and avuncular, wouldn't you? Wrong! You have never met a more prissy and pissy man than Old John. There's being precise, and then there's being a pain in the arse. And then there's Old John.

He was everything I hate about the building trade, never a good word to say about anyone, always picking faults in other people's work. I'd only ever worked for him once but vowed never again.

And he's so slow, it takes him so long to finish anything. And that's not just because of his age either, there's a lot of chin stroking on Old John's jobs – twists a screw half a turn, steps back and strokes his chin, fixes a handle, steps back and stroke his chin. Blokes like this drive me mad. If you're working on a price you want a nice clear run at the job to get it all hit in one go, you can't make any money if you're always stopping and starting waiting for someone else to finish ahead of you, or even worse, being forced to do things out of sequence to try to work around them.

Old John rose to his feet, brushing the crumbs from his lap, and adjusted his spotless white polo shirt, buttoned at the collar and neat ironing creases on the sleeves – like I say, prissy. 'Welcome to my office, lads,' he said, waving a grand sweep towards the container. 'So, what are you after?'

'Disco's looking for a girlfriend, he likes the older woman,' I said and, getting no reaction from anyone I continued, 'Actually we were hoping to see the manager but she's not about.'

'Kate Fuller? I've just seen her go,' he said pointing vaguely towards the main gates. 'What do you want with her?'

'Not a lot, we've got some work to do for her, that's all,' I said, and as I spoke Old John's demeanour changed, he stood up straight, fists clenched, feet firmly planted shoulder width apart.

'Work? What do you mean work? What sort of work?' I raised the Quentin purchase orders to show him the list of general maintenance items to get on with but, startling me, he slapped the papers out of my hand.

'I do all the work here. This is my patch, my client. I've worked for it, bloody hard too.' Disco was scrabbling about on the ground trying to gather up the papers before they were taken on the breeze. Old John continued his tirade.

I asked him to calm down but it was pointless, he was livid. I tried telling him we were finishing off Tommy's jobs, but I don't think he understood what I was saying.

'Him? That randy little git. No way. He's not coming here. I don't want him here. I'm not having him on my job, he's not coming here!'

The more I tried to explain, the angrier he got. I felt a gentle tug on my elbow and I let Disco guide me to the van.

At walking pace, the van rolled us back up through the grounds towards the main road. By now the car park had cleared out a bit and cars stood isolated amongst the empty bays and as we trundled past a silver Mondeo parked under the shady canopy of a large ash tree I noticed the driver appeared to be in the middle of a heated debate on his phone; the faint chimes of recognition jingled somewhere in my head, but any attempt to flesh out the familiarity was soon forgotten when Disco blew out his cheeks in expressions of amazement at Old John's outburst, 'Help the aged, my arse!'

I was laughing when the phone rang: Senia requesting to see me again, I couldn't put it off any longer so agreed that I would be there shortly.

-13-

I'D PROMISED DISCO I'd buy him lunch, so we pulled into the McDonalds drive-thru on the way to the Police Station. Parked up and plucking through the paper bags on our laps I broached the question I'd been putting off all day,

'I've been looking through Tommy's stuff, but something doesn't quite add up, there's a few queries.' About a hundred and fifty thousand queries I thought. 'Do you know who he'd been working for recently? What he'd been doing?'

'He did the disabled riding school with Pervy Ken.'

'Yes, that one I know, but anything else? Off the books?' I said. 'You know what I mean?'

'No, not really,' replied Disco.

I thought hard; to be honest, this way of trying to talk around the issue was beginning to annoy me. I wasn't very good at it and it was giving me a headache.

'Was there anything... low profile, high value?' I said, wishing I hadn't bothered starting this, my nuggets were getting cold.

'Oh, you mean dodgy?' At last that penny had dropped. 'Why didn't you just say that instead of tiptoeing all round the houses?'

'Don't know,' I said, mid-mouthful of tepid chicken. 'Well, was he?'

'Yeah, course he was,' said Disco, although he seemed more interested in prising the sliced gherkin from his burger. 'I thought everyone knew that.'

EVER HAD THAT sensation when the world moves in slow motion? Everything around me had ground to a halt – the lady with the pushchair crossing the road, the gaggle of schoolboy footballers heading towards their training pitches, the smoker sheltering from the wind – outside my body it all moved at a glacial speed, the tendril of cigarette smoke hung frozen in the sky, but inside my head I was reeling, struggling to understand.

After what seemed like a lifetime and a half, my internal and external balance was restored, the schoolboys sauntered past, their boot studs rattling on the footpath like hailstones on glass, and I begged Disco to tell me more.

According to Disco, 'everyone' meant his network of gossips at the Golden Lamb, and 'knew' amounted to not much more than suspicion and rumour. Apparently Little Nicky, who has been Tommy's number one man for as long as anyone can remember, had been complaining whilst partaking in his Friday inebriation. Disco said he'd been moaning that Tommy had picked up a lot of night work at fantastic money, but Nicky wasn't getting a sniff anywhere close to it, despite being with him for years, scratching by on crappy low prices. When Disco and his chattering circle told him to take it up with Tommy, he said that he already had and was told he wasn't right for the job. Nicky said that was bullshit, he'd got all the current certificates and clearances for railways, schools and even prisons but was told no, he doesn't want to get him involved with this work.

That immediately led Disco and pals to define that as dodgy, a three wise monkeys job: see nothing, hear nothing, say nothing. Sounds plausible, I suppose, and I admit I'd not seen Nicky around for a while, not that I'd go out of my way to look him up as he was a whingey little bitch. He might do a nice job but he'd do my head in if I had to listen to him all day. I don't know how Tommy put up with it to be honest.

'Do you reckon you could find out what he was up to? Discreetly, mind.'

'Of course I can, why?' he said, between chews of his burger.

'I'm wondering whether it might be what got him killed?'

I'd never given anyone the Heimlich manoeuvre before.

THAT'S NOT TRUE, sorry. It just makes a better story than what really happened.

Disco did say, 'Yeah, course he was. I thought everyone knew that,' and my world did go into a temporary freefall – that bit's true. And Disco told me about Tommy and the cash, that bit's also true. But Disco didn't choke and I didn't do anything heroic.

Instead Disco started singing along to an old Blondie song that had come on the radio, while I shrunk inwards with embarrassment and questioned how I could have been so stupid. I felt ashamed, and I think also a bit cheated. Everyone knew that, everyone, except me. Why? Did I even know him, properly?

I suppose it was natural we became friends; we often worked together on the same sort of projects and knew many of the same people. We made each other laugh, we both liked a drink and we'd hang out after work, some weekends, sometimes when there was a significant other to invite we'd do things as couples like fancy meals out. But what does that amount to though?

Should I have known what he was up to every minute of every day? Known how he earned and spent every penny?

I began to realise our friendship was based in the present – going to work, going for a drink – we're there, we're together, we're enjoying the time as it's occurring. But with Tommy, like with all my other friends, it never went too far below the surface, only discovering things about each other if it had an impact on the present.

For instance, I know Tommy supported Tottenham, took two sugars in tea but none in coffee and liked 90s Britpop, because these are things that arise in the present – a song on the radio, a headline on a newspaper back page, an order in the cafe. But beyond the superficial, how well are you meant to know anyone?

So many conversations, little more than *What did you get up to at the weekend?* *Not much, you?* *Not a lot*, and straight into the present, the here and now. It's as if we understand the polite thing to do is show an interest, but we'd rather not actually know.

Should Tommy and I have tried more to scratch below the surface, perhaps trusted each other a little more? 'How was your weekend?' *Well I've just amassed a secret fortune, but shh it's all highly illegal.*

The truth about that moment in the van? I discovered two things: one, I was embarrassed at being shocked, but more embarrassed for being so complacent and lazy, and two, Disco's a terrible singer.

-14-

SO, THIS IS what an interview room looks like is it? This police station is quite new, I remember it being built about ten years ago after they decided to make it regional for the whole of Medway rather than modernise the old local stations. The new police station has been sited on what always used to be an indistinct boundary, an odd no-man's land between Gillingham and Chatham.

Unless you knew the building's true purpose you could be forgiven for thinking it was a new college on the edge of the nearby university campus due to the way its red brick and glass elevations dominated its corner location.

I'd lost track of how long I'd been sitting in there alone trying to mask out the stench of cabbagey farts that seemed ingrained in the place. I was just about to walk out when the only door in the room opened and in strode Senia, who took the seat opposite me and shot out his arms to adjust his shiny cufflinks. Another man followed behind him laden with files, notebooks and other paraphernalia.

'Mr Poynter,' said Senia, 'Thank you for gracing us with your presence, you're a very difficult man to get hold of.'

'Not really. Just trying to earn a living, been a bit busy.'

'Well, we're all truly grateful you could make time in your very full diary to come and help us, it's very much appreciated,' he said, with all the sincerity of someone that didn't have a single ounce of it in his body.

'As you know I am the senior investigating officer and my name is Detective Chief Inspector Senia, and my colleague here is...'

'Hello Nick, you alright?' I said.

'…Detective Constable Witham.' Senia trailed his sentence to a slow halt.

'Yeah, I'm fine Mark, you?' was the cheerful reply from the aforesaid Detective Constable Witham.

'Not bad, considering. I'm okay. I saw Tim the other day.'

'Tim,' his response had a fond, nostalgic tone.

'I see that you and DC Witham are already acquainted,' snapped Senia. He was unsettled by this. I liked it.

'Not a problem is it, Mr Senia? After all, as you say, I'm only here to help, aren't I? I'm not under arrest, am I? Do I need a lawyer present?'

'No. You are free to leave at any time, Mr Poynter.'

The tone of his voice was resentful. Behind him I could see Nick Witham tense a little, he'd probably get bawled out after this by Senia, and it was my fault. I'd have to catch up with him later to apologise, as Nick was a decent guy, plus I could see the benefit of having an ear inside the investigation now I'm back in Hamlet's debt.

Senia paused and looked straight at me. He'd done this to me before, which made me wonder if it was something he'd learnt on a course. The way he stared was quite unsettling. He took a deep breath through his nose, and then in a fluid motion heralded by the scrape of chair legs he sprung to his feet and left the room. Nick Witham looked at me, looked at the open door, looked at me again, gathered up everything from the table, then disappeared out of the door too.

After ten minutes of looking at the wall again, the door reopened and Senia reappeared, this time flanked by a young man who looked all of about seventeen; it was his turn to be laden with all of the files, notebooks and paraphernalia.

'Detective Constable Witham has been called away on urgent matters. So, allow me to do the introductions.' He was enjoying his little moment. 'We are joined this morning by DC Nwakobu.'

Young Mr Nwakobu looked like he'd found his role model and mentor in Senia, judging by his matching navy-blue suit, white shirt and shiny cufflinks.

'So,' Senia took a deep breath and then exhaled. 'We think we've identified the murder weapon.'

That took me by surprise. To be honest I hadn't given it any thought. I remember seeing Tommy and his blood channelled in the square gridlines of the tile joints, bits of bone and gristle on his collar – but it never occurred to me look for a weapon, why would it? I'm a spark not Sherlock Holmes.

'DC Nwakobu, the weapon if you please.'

With a loud thump that resonated off the room's hard flat surfaces he dropped on to the table a transparent plastic bag through which I could see a 4lb hammer. The varnish to the wooden handle was worn and flat, one face of the hammer's head was pocked and chipped from repeated use, the other face was matted with clumps of hair and blood. The hairs on my arms began to rise, a chill cold fell across my skin; suddenly, I felt vulnerable.

'Do you know what this is?' said Senia.

'It's a hammer,' I replied.

'Do you recognise it?'

'No, it's just a hammer, you can buy them anywhere.'

'Anywhere?'

'Anywhere. Any builders merchant sells them. Millions of them.'

'So, it's the sort of thing a carpenter would carry in his kit, then is it?'

'Maybe.'

'Or, maybe not. After all, this is a club hammer, is it not, the proverbial blunt instrument. It's not a joinery tool, is it? People use these if they want to break something. Or someone. Is this your hammer Mr Poynter?'

'No!'

'Are you sure?'

'Yes! No! Well, like I say, they're ten a penny, everyone's got one!' I protested.

'True, but do they all have this?' And with the great flourish and delight of a conjuror doing a magic trick, The Great Bastardo, he turned it over.

Exactly as I feared, the initials 'MP' were scratched deep into the wooden handle. I had to fight down the rising feeling in my stomach. The carved letters had been stained dark red by Tommy's blood rinsing across them, and I could see more clearly the greasy, fatty smears on the hammer head. I hadn't expected to see anything like this, not today, not ever. My tool had been used to end my friend's life. I felt violated.

'We shall be taking fingerprints from the hammer. And seeing as you and the lady of the house co-operatively gave us yours at the scene, we will be able to rule you out,' he informed me, and then, as a cruel aside, added: 'Assuming we find anyone else's on it.'

I used that hammer every day, my fingerprints would be all over it. I wanted to faint. I wanted to vomit. I knew I mustn't do either, I needed to regain control, I needed to say something, I needed to make sure he knew was mistaken.

'So, back to my first question, is this your hammer?' Senia's arrogance was overwhelming. Nwakobu sat by scribbling down every word, the master's eager student. 'Your initials are MP are they not?'

'Yes, but not just me,' I protested. Nwakobu looked up from his notebook. 'What about Monty Panesar?'

Nwakobu started scribbling again. 'Panesar, how's that spelt?'

Senia's head snapped round to the young man beside him. He vented his substantial outrage, 'Idiot! Do not write that name down. He's a spin bowler.'

So Senia knows his cricket, he can't be all bad then.

Seeing Senia's fury directed at poor Nwakobu rather than me eased my state of panic and my confidence began to rise.

'And Manny Pacquiao,' I suggested, looking straight at Nwakobu, for it was for his benefit I added, 'He's a boxer.'

Senia stifled a grunt, I could see that he knew he was losing control of the situation.

'And Michael Portillo, he's a—'

'Yes, thank you, we all bloody well know who Michael Portillo is, thank you very much. But seeing as the Right Honourable Mr Michael Portillo MP was not working at the crime scene on the date of the murder, I think it's safe to rule him out of the investigation for now, don't you? Likewise, Monty Panesar, Manny Pacquiao, Mary Poppins and Marco bloody Polo! You however, Mark Poynter, were there. So, tell me, please, is this your hammer.'

Of course it was my hammer, I knew it and he knew it. 'No comment. You know it wasn't me, I was out with my client at the merchants when he was killed, it's in my statement, you haven't got anything on me and you know it.'

'I'll grant you your statement matches Mrs Wilkes's, and that is the only reason I'm not arresting you right here and now. But be warned, we're looking at you.'

His words hit me, his meaning was clear, I'm his one and only suspect, and by the sound of it he's not going to put too much effort into finding anyone else. I need to pay attention, sharpen up, as he's going to use any opportunity he can to put this on me.

'We know you're skint. You have been for months.'

To be fair, months was a bit of an exaggeration, but I didn't think it the best time to correct him so I kept quiet and shrugged.

'He'd almost finished his works, you said yourself the client's added a lot of extras to the job – did he want more money, money you haven't got, is that why you killed him?'

'I wasn't there, you know that already.'

'Convenient that, but then that's what you do isn't it, sub-contract? Get a man in?'

'Yeah, great, very funny. Look, we all know, I'm potless, I can't even afford to pay the window cleaner so how do you think I can afford an assassin?'

'You could have come to sort some of arrangement.'

'What, so you can get a hitman on instalments now can you?'

'You tell me, you seem to know a lot about it.'

It's started, he's twisting my words, trying to catch me out. But I'm not being fitted up for anything, this is a fight or flight situation. I choose flight.

'I think I'd like to leave now.'

Senia slammed his hand down on the table, he stared at me without speaking for a few seconds, then, 'Nwakobu, please show Mr Poynter out. Just remember this, you are a person of interest.' And with that he stormed out of the room.

Keen to obey instructions, complemented by a matching hostile attitude, young Nwakobu escorted me through the building to the street. I followed a pace or two behind him and spotted Nick Witham through a glazed panel. As far as I could tell he'd been called away no further than the vending machine. He'd seen me too, we gave each other a small nod of recognition and that little gesture lifted me.

I left the building and got into the van. As soon as I was out of sight round the first corner I pulled over, threw the door open and vomited in the gutter.

-15-

I FOUND DISCO in the same pub I'd left him in, chatting with great authority to the landlord. He saw me beckon him from the doorway, downed the final third of his pint in one gulp, and hurried towards me giving the landlord a cursory wave as he went.

'You look rough,' he said falling into the van with the ease of a collapsing chimney. He fumbled for the buckle of the seat belt and I thanked him for his welcomed opinion. After a moment or two he remembered where I'd been and asked, 'How did it go with your mate, has he got someone in the frame for it yet?'

'You could say that,' was my non-committal response but, being a semi-professional rumourmonger, Disco couldn't let it lie and kept asking who. I ignored him, but the questioning was relentless. In the end I broke.

'I don't want to talk about it, alright?'

Perhaps my tone of voice was a touch too aggressive, as he shut up and sat back, looked straight ahead for a second or two, then, 'You? Seriously? You? Oh my god, that's hilarious.'

Well, that wasn't the reaction I was expecting. Disco roared a raspy, throaty laugh seasoned by twenty years of sawdust and roll-ups.

'That is the funniest thing I've heard all day.'

His laughter rolled around the van and I must admit, despite my concerns, it was infectious and I began to smile, realising it was the first time in what seemed like ages I'd felt cheerful about anything.

The phone rang, I answered it, 'Marky Mark, Hamlet here.' His voice rang out loud and clear through the speakers as I slowed the van to a stop beside the kerb. Disco looked terrified by the disembodied voice, I held a finger to my lips to keep him quiet. 'A little bird tells me you've just been to see our friend Mr Senia.'

Yet more eyes and inside men, I thought.

'What did he want? What's he know?'

So how close to things are your insiders? Why can't they tell you? Or do you already know and this is a test?

'Not a lot,' I replied. 'He asked a few questions, to learn a bit more about Tommy, you know? Habits, friends, lifestyle and the like.'

'Anything else? Was I mentioned?'

Disco silently mouthed shock and awe profanities; I hoped my eyes looked angry enough to make him keep quiet and still.

'No, you weren't.'

I think I had reassured him as he said 'Good' and cut the call.

'Hamlet? No. Don't say you're back in with him again Mark, not after… you know,' said Disco, his tone implying panic more than fascination. I said nothing. 'What was "was I mentioned" all about? Hey, did he kill Tommy?'

I tried to ignore him, but the bouncing of his leg and the clenching and unclenching of his fists was driving me mad, I needed him to calm down. I wanted to reassure him he had nothing to worry about, assuming he could break the habit of a lifetime and keep his mouth shut about everything he'd just heard. I pulled up outside the first pub I could find.

The Eagle. A small tatty-looking pub built as the end corner unit of a row of Victorian terraced houses that stepped out straight on to the pavement. Its white painted render had blown in places, the black gloss to the joinery had faded and lost its bloom, its two windows had heavy opaque frosting masking the interior. Despite having never set foot in this pub before I knew exactly what it would be like.

Sure enough – it was dark and dingy. The windows blocked any sunlight penetration, and the walls – lined with heavy deep brown wood panelling – added to the general gloom. The wooden chairs and tables were stained a deep brown too, the slightly sticky carpet was a dense pattern of dark colours and shades, and the smell of frying hung so thickly in the air you could feel it on your skin. It was exactly as I imagined, right down to the aged collection of wilting beermats pinned up behind the bar and a huge jar of copper coins, three quarters full, beside the till. It's a talent I have, although I can't see TV paying me for it just yet: *'And your specialist subject is, shitty pubs of the Medway Towns.'*

A bored, middle-aged barmaid leafed through a magazine, occasionally looking up to glance at the racing on a television behind her every time the old man perched on a stool murmured any reaction. They were the only people in the place, but privacy was prudent so I motioned for Disco to go and sit in the furthest corner whilst I got us drinks. The woman's displeasure at being inconvenienced was all too evident from her clumsy serving and couldn't-be-arsed attitude.

Disco's hands shook as he reached for his medicinal pint.

'Hamlet? I'm serious, Mark, I don't want to get involved in anything if he's part of it, no way.'

'Relax. Take it easy for a second. He's not part of anything. Just slow down and think things through: Tommy has died, Tommy had some work to do, I've been asked to finish the work, I'm asking you to help me, that's it. That's all it is. It's all okay.' *'I hope'*, I thought but didn't add.

'What you were asking, earlier, about… what did you call it, low profile high value, do you think Tommy was involved with Hamlet, is that why he was asking if he'd been mentioned?'

'No, of course not,' I said, but I'd already given up trying to convince myself he wasn't.

AS THE LAGER began to replenish his alcohol stream, Disco seemed to relax and by the time he started his second pint he was back to his normal gossipy self.

'So, you know Hamlet, you know how he got his money don't you? You know how he got where he is today?'

My answer to all three questions was yes, but one thing I have learnt is that there are some things you never, ever, talk about and this was one. There was no way Disco could draw me out on anything. I'm allergic to getting my head kicked in, it doesn't agree with me.

I reached for my phone and made a great show of studying the screen, not answering or reacting to any of Disco's fairytales, letting it wash over me, although the fantasies I was hearing were remarkable.

'They say that he was the brains behind the Securitas depot robbery in 2006.'

He wasn't.

'...they got away with fifty-three million but the police only found ten, they say he's got two million buried under his swimming pool...'

Apart from the fact he doesn't have a pool.

'They say he was involved with the Millennium Dome diamond raid in 2000, that he was going to ship the diamonds overseas...'

He wasn't, now this is getting silly.

'They say he's the missing man from the Hatton Garden safety deposit break-in, you know the one they never caught...'

Oh, for god's sake.

'...they say he made a lot of his money out of Raves...'

That was true.

'And that he's been stabbed three times by a Triad with a sword...'

But that's not.

I wonder how much of this nonsense has Hamlet put out himself? Talk about fake news. Does every bloke in every pub swap stories adding their own little nugget each time? This mythology of a local thug was ludicrous because that's all he is. A thug with a bit of charm and patter, a local celebrity: one may smile, and smile, and be a villain. I'd known Hamlet quite well, as well as anyone could probably know him, and he's certainly no criminal mastermind. Tony Soprano? Tony Hadley more like, especially with that silly pop-star haircut. I was beginning to get annoyed by Disco's fan worship of him.

Now, listen closely, I know exactly how he got started, how he made his money and who keeps him in a position of power. Do you want to know? Really? Can you keep a secret? Well – so can I.

-16-

'LOOK, I'VE APOLOGISED, what else can I do?'

'You can stop the van and let me out, that's what! You've kidnapped me under false pretences.'

Disco was probably right, but I needed him, so I picked my words carefully to try and placate him: 'Oh shut up and quit your moaning, it won't take long.'

Unfortunately for Disco, he was outside having a smoke when Hamlet called with a bit of work. The implication was clear, if I wanted a favour, first I had to earn it. I knew this would happen. I regretted from the outset ever asking him, but if you're going to be in a jam, be prepared to have your pips squeezed. Hamlet had been very clear; time was of the essence.

Without hanging about, I left the dismal and slightly sticky confines of the Eagle, pulling Disco along with me, and waited until we were well on the way before telling him where we were going, and for who. I braced myself for a very colourful onslaught of some of his finest swearing, but not a peep. Poor old Disco must have been so disorientated he couldn't even string an obscenity laden sentence together anymore, and I have to admit the lack of fruity language made me feel a little bad about misleading him like this, so we sat quietly for the remainder of the journey, awkwardly pretending to listen to some unfunny sketch show on the radio.

We pulled up outside a row of empty shop units in a dilapidated housing estate of ugly, dark square blocks and a flat-roof pub that looked so unappealing even Disco didn't want to go there. Looking around, it was a run-down and cheerless environment. All I could think was *Thank God I don't have to live here*. My Dad used to say, '*Pay cheap, pay twice*', but judging by the general squalor all around, 'twice' won't be coming any time soon.

Even the road was cheap and nasty: poured concrete finished roughly. Large cracks split the surface, breaking off corners and lifting edges, moving apart like melting ice floes. Cars never glide gracefully over concrete roads and I could hear our tyres *thup, thup, thup*, arguing with the uneven surface.

Wire mesh caged the only unit still trading, suggesting the shopkeeper considered himself at risk, more the endangered species than the last man standing. Pebble-dashed walls gave it the look of weathered sea defences, only adding to the sense of desolation.

Newspaper and whitewash obscured the other four units. Above one, the lettering for a butcher was visible in reflection where the nameboard had been taken out and refitted back to front. Where a community once flourished, it was now reduced to empty dark voids. It made me think of graves and, by association, my head filled with thoughts of Tommy. I felt a prickling sensation around my eyes again. I shook it off with a forced cough and rub of my face before Disco noticed.

We parked up and waited. The daylight was fading and the one working streetlamp cast a dull nicotine-stained glow across everything.

A black Mercedes pulled up, about twelve years old, not worth a lot, but it looked flawless – straight out of the box. Brazil emerged from the driver's side, and Dunlop the passenger's. I motioned to Disco to get out and we went across to them. It was clear that the Merc was Brazil's pride and joy. He'd invested a lot of love and time in it and I knew the proper thing to do would be to compliment him on it, so I didn't. Instead, I remained silent waiting for one of them to speak first.

'This way ladies,' said Dunlop, nodding his head towards a unit that according to its nameboard was once a carpet remnant seller. Disco and I stood obediently outside the shopfront while Dunlop faffed about with a massive ring of keys, trying one after another without success. At the sound of a gentle *thup thup thup* Disco and I looked up to see a slow-moving Mondeo trundle past us. As the reflected light caught it, we could see the driver was looking straight at us, nosy git. A bit of activity in an empty property and all the neighbourhood curtain-twitchers are out in force desperate to find out what's happening.

With a twist of a key, Dunlop finally opened the door and ushered us in through an ankle-deep drift of junk mail. Disco looked around the bare empty shell of a place, then at me, perplexed, and I tried to reassure him with a small nod. From the road came the heavy breathing of an overworked diesel engine reverberating off the hard concrete beneath.

'Truck's here,' said Dunlop. 'Come on then, let's get you started.'

DISCO AND I ferried everything in from the lorry. Brazil and Dunlop of course didn't lift a finger, instead they loitered outside and got in the way smoking and swapping porn by Bluetooth, eventually giving us our instructions after everything was inside.

Disco was assigned to erecting a screen right inside the doorway, floor to ceiling – for most passers-by the whitewashed glass obscured any view of the interior, but for the more prying of eye Disco's screen blocked everything.

Me, I ran cables and connected lamps – lots and lots of bright halogen lamps across the entire area, as well as servicing the air-conditioning units and checking the existing wiring could carry the increased electrical loading. As we worked through the night, Brazil and Dunlop made several inspections from outside to be sure my bright light didn't bleed through Disco's screen.

We finished just before two in the morning and were told to follow Brazil to his black Mercedes where he reached into the glove box to remove a carrier bag.

'Mr Hamlet says to be sure you know the rules.'

'I didn't see anything, I don't know anything, I wasn't here, I have never been here,' I recited, proving I still knew them.

'Then this is for you.' Brazil tossed the bag at me which I caught and brought into my chest like a rugby ball. 'You can count it if you like but you aren't getting any more. It was good enough for your mate, what he always used to get paid, so as far as Mr Hamlet's concerned that's a fair rate. You can go now. Ta ta.'

We loaded our tools back into the van, and flopped our tired bodies into the seats. I opened the bag and shared the money equally with Disco. It was worth more than three days work for both of us, but then we weren't being paid for our labour, were we.

A beam of headlights came straight at us, just for a moment but long enough to make us blink away white blurs from our eyes after it passed. The driver of the vehicle, a large box van, stopped directly outside the shop unit and high-fived Dunlop. Brazil emerged in the doorway and took a high five too. Neither Disco or I spoke, watching the driver drop the tail lift and open the back of his vehicle. He hopped up inside and re-emerged pushing a large, black, square container, lowered it to the pavement, and with the assistance of Brazil took it into the shop unit. Judging by their faces and grunts it was heavy.

'What do you think they're going to do in there, Mark?' said Disco, but I slowly shook my head.

'Best not to know. We don't ask questions, we don't know anything, and that's the best way to leave it. Forget about tonight, it never happened.'

In the quiet of the van, as the adrenaline rush of panic from being purloined to work for Hamlet faded, Disco's body clock finally caught up with him.

'I need a drink' he said.

-17-

'HELLO, WHO IS THIS?'

I'd been yanked from sleep by an insistent ringing phone. Bleary eyed and wanting it to stop, I picked it up and answered without looking – a fiery temper for a cold caller.

'Mark?' I was awake, I was alert, I was afraid. 'You know who this is, don't insult my intelligence.'

The very sound of the voice frightened me. Alone in my bed, wearing only yesterday's underpants, I'd never felt so vulnerable. I was aware that I'd pulled the duvet up over me, perhaps my subconscious hoped it would bring me protection.

'You still there?' I hadn't spoken since answering, I needed to form the words in my head to make them come out.

'I'm here. What do you want?'

'What do you think I want?' said Blunt. 'I do hope you've not forgotten you owe us a considerable lot of money.'

'I know. I messaged you to confirm you'll get it on Friday.'

'I saw that, but I've heard you've downed tools on your job and haven't been on site for the past couple of days. Seems a funny way of topping out and getting paid to me.'

I didn't respond and instead remained quiet.

'You promised me my dough by Friday. How're you going to do that if you're not working?'

'You should have thought about that before getting me shut down shouldn't you.' I said without thinking, and at once regretted it.

'What does that mean? I've been very fair with you Mark, but this is starting to worry me. I don't want us falling out.'

'I've told you you're getting it on Friday, I'll be in the Lamb at lunchtime. Find me there,' and I killed the call.

Blunt's always been a punch-first-think-later primitive, his ideal night out ends in a fight or a fuck, or if he's lucky both, and if he's really really lucky both at the same time. He's been barred from every pub in the area at least twice. He's trouble and he's troubled, but I never expected him to be quite so blasé: *'I don't want us falling out.'* Murder's nothing more than a couple of names off the Christmas card list?

I sat there dazed and amazed to discover it was ten o'clock. I realised two things that morning: one, I had to clear myself of Blunt and get out from under his debt as quickly as I could – I'd be a fool not to recognise that call had been my final warning, and two, I'm too old to be working through the night anymore.

I opened the drawer beside the bed, relieved to find my money still there. My half of last night's proceeds. Hamlet had been generous in his payment, it'd keep me going for the rest of this week, but it wasn't enough to dig me out of trouble. As if on cue, the uncaring postman pushed more bills and demands through the letterbox. Great, that's a few more people to avoid for the foreseeable future.

Among them, an envelope with the Macmillan Nurses logo. I opened it: *Dear Mr Poynter thank you for supporting us in making the lives of those suffering with cancer more bearable, unfortunately our direct debit request this month was declined by your bank...* Bastard bank! Couldn't they have let that one through? It's only a few pounds a month, it'll cost them more than that to write telling me they've refused it. Bastards. I owed the charity so much for all they did. At this moment I'd never felt so embarrassed about my finances, and the more I thought about it the tighter my breathing became.

Having a self-induced panic attack was a pointless exercise, so I tried to clear my head and take stock of the situation. My notes valuing everything I owned were still on the side. I gathered them, along with all the other loose papers strewn about, and stacked them in a neat pile. Problem solved. If I can't fix it, I can pretend to ignore it.

The dismal valuation of my entire worldly possessions sat on top of Tommy's stuff which sat on top of all the bills and my freshly awoken brain cells made the connection. Maybe Tommy could help me out? Maybe Tommy could lend me the money? There's over a hundred and fifty thousand sitting out in my garage gathering dust. Would he mind if I borrowed a little, only until I sorted myself out? I'd pay it back as soon as everyone had paid me, plus I'd add a little bit of interest, surely, he wouldn't object to that? Would he? By the time I'd showered and dressed and was leaving the house, I'd convinced myself that he'd be happy to lend me the money, and not only that, being such good mates, he'd waive the interest too.

I'd heard the expression *'like a weight off your shoulders'* all my life but I'd never appreciated what it meant until today. It feels exactly what it sounds like, I found I was standing straighter, I felt lighter, bouncy and free in my walk, I was as happy as a frog at a wedding, my problems had gone.

'Oi!' My daydream was popped. A woman's voice came from behind, 'Hey, can you hear me?'

I turned to see who had spoiled my happy high, and was faced with a woman of about thirty who, although dressed in shapeless blue medical scrubs, looked stunning. Her eyes were breathtaking, her cheekbones sharp and her hair razored short into a trendy style – pixie crop, is that what they call it? She wore minimal, but expertly applied, make-up. She was astonishing. The morning seemed to be getting better and better.

'I called you a couple of times but you looked a little distracted,' she said. 'I'm your new neighbour. Hello, I'm Perry.'

'Hi, I'm Mark.'

I approached to shake her outstretched hand and noticed the name badge on her uniform. Perry was short for Parminder.

'Look, I know it's a bit cheeky to ask, seeing as it was in the rubbish and all, and the binmen have been and everything...' She had that upward inflection at the end of her sentences that I find annoying in others but she was getting away with it. 'Can I have my box back?'

I must have stood there a second or two too long like a stunned fish as she gave up waiting for a response.

'For the kettle? I saw you take it yesterday.'

Oh, *that* box. This could be awkward.

'I'm not a nosy neighbour, honest. You see, I only moved in two days ago and look,' she gestured up to the top window, 'no curtains yet. I noticed you when I was getting ready yesterday.'

'Sorry, I don't have it any more. I needed a box to put some materials in, made it easier to deliver to the client's house. Sorry.'

Her smile dropped and I felt as though I'd destroyed some spectacular work of art. She began explaining that due to the perils of on-line shopping she needed the original packaging to return her expensive but faulty new kettle. Of all the problems I've had this week, this was the only one that mattered, this was the one I wanted to fix right here, right now. Telling her I was an electrician got me ushered indoors straight away.

When I first moved in, a wonderful old lady called Vi lived in this house next door. I'd be happy to pop round and help with whatever odd job she wanted. I always had time for Vi. I loved her stories about when, as a little girl, her brothers took her to the river's edge. Scrambled from nearby airfields, the Spitfires flew low above the water, the roar of the engines blew warm across her face, and the rolling waves in their wake splashed her shoes. The vapour trails braided with the rising plumes of smoke in a tapestry, and the sirens wailed all around her. The Luftwaffe, in formation high above, carried their bombs towards Chatham's naval dockyard – the same dockyard that would kill my Dad sixty years later. The big anti-aircraft cruiser moored out on the Medway opposed them with its huge guns, and every time it fired, the vibration shook the ground where she sat. Her tired, jowly face shone with excitement as she recounted her story, and from it I could see her at seven, watching it all play out around her. After she died, after the funeral, I went to the spot at Sharps Green she'd described and threw a flower into the water for her memories. I realised that I hadn't been back to that spot, nor indeed inside this house since that day nearly eight years ago.

There had been four or five new tenants since then. The living room was now redecorated with the rental standard of bland cream walls and pale laminate flooring, but as I was led through, I discovered the kitchen was still the same, even the cooker and tumble dryer that I'd installed for Vi were still there. That's the trouble with Buy-to-Let landlords, they never spend any money. The units looked a lot more tired than I remembered. The vinyl flooring was sun-bleached in parts, and the counter top chipped and scuffed. The gleaming Ferrari red kettle looked very modern and out of place in the kitchen that time forgot.

As it turned out, there wasn't anything wrong with it, nothing an expert fiddle couldn't fix and Perry offered to make the inaugural brew with it as a way of saying thanks. I gratefully accepted.

We chatted and it was easy, it flowed freely. She told me she'd moved up from Brighton for a nursing position at Medway Hospital. I found, for once, I was enjoying myself. She was bright, she was funny and she was one of those people that touch you when they talk – the sensation of her hand on my forearm as she laughed stayed with me long after she'd removed it.

And then, '…so I figured I've just qualified, I've got no ties, I'm single so why not take the opportunity, make a fresh start in a new place, so here I am…' Bingo!

From its awful start, this morning has got better and better, what could possibly go wrong?

-18-

WHAT COULD GO wrong? How about a visit from Uncle Bern? Normally as much fun as pissing on the live rail, but he seemed in good form today, probably because Auntie Val hadn't come with him this time.

Uncle Bern's my mum's younger brother. He lives an itinerant, low-cost lifestyle that seems to work for him. He'll spend the winter in his apartment in Spain, which he'll then rent out during the Summer and come back here to pick up whatever work he can, usually from me and any other contacts he's got. The rest of the year he flits back and forth whenever the money or Val's patience runs out, whichever comes sooner. When he's here he might spend a few days helping me out pulling cables and holding ladders, or he might be washing cars at his mate's second-hand lot. In this day and age of all things digital he's the master of finding cash-in-hand casual jobs.

As promised, I'd dropped off the t-shirts and groceries at his flat: he likes to think that because it's over an estate agent it adds a bit of grandeur, but it is what it is, a grotty flat in lower Gillingham. He still managed to whinge though that I'd got the wrong brand of teabags and no biscuits on his march towards my kitchen to raid my larder.

If there's one thing Uncle Bern knows, it's the value of a pound. Uncle Bern hoards every penny he gets to fund his semi-retirement in the sun. His only luxuries when here are a few pints a couple of times a week at the Palm Cottage, and maybe a few home games at Gillingham depending on how well they're doing at the time.

Sometimes Auntie Val comes too, but that's always struck me as a marriage of convenience because usually when he's in Spain she's here and vice versa. She's an odd one Auntie Val, one of those women that find a look that suits them and they then keep it for the rest of their lives. Val found her look a long time ago, she modelled herself entirely on the blonde one from ABBA – well, up until he grew his beard. But no, she really did look like the blonde woman from ABBA. The only problem is she still looks like the blonde one from ABBA forty years on with the blue eyeshadow, long boots, floaty skirts and berets. I've no idea what the blonde one from ABBA looks like now, but I'll bet it's not like Auntie Val.

None of Tommy's unfinished works seemed particularly difficult and I'd made a shortlist of jobs that would be comfortably within Uncle Bern's abilities. It was a very short shortlist.

Tommy, Disco and myself, we'd all been apprentice trained, we were professional trades. Uncle Bern was what you'd call a handyman, he'd had no formal training in anything, but when pushed he was able to turn his hand with varying success to a number of different tasks.

Even he should manage fine with what I was giving him to do, but true to form, faced with the prospect of doing some proper work Uncle Bern did what he does best – he panicked – and I was starting to lose patience. All I'd done was tell him I wanted him to check in on the Two Ronnies every other day to make sure they were getting on okay, you'd think I'd just told him he'd been put in charge of Brexit negotiations.

'I can't do that. You can't expect me to climb up and down scaffolds, not with my knees, and then there's my vertigo, I can't go up there, I'll get all giddy, it's not safe.'

'Oh, calm down. It's only a basic painting job, there's nothing to it, just relax.'

'But I don't know anything about painting, they're the pros, why would they listen to me?'

'Because we're in charge of the money, that's why.' I'd hoped that would reassure him but he stood there blinking behind his thick glasses like a bemused weasel. 'Look, if you don't want to go up the ladder here's an old trick I saw a clerk of works pull years ago.' He nodded in eager anticipation, any trick to make life easier was always popular with Uncle Bern.

'The scope says rub down all the joinery then prime, undercoat and two coats of gloss, understand?' Nod nod, eager nod. 'So, tell them to mix a drop of red paint into the primer. That way when you turn up it's easy, you can stay on the ground and look up, if the timber's pink they've primed it. Then next time you visit, if it's all gone back to white they've undercoated it, and then next time you go after that, if it's all shiny then they've glossed it – understand?'

Uncle Bern pushed his glasses back up to the bridge of his nose and nodded, causing them to slide back down again, and a confused expression settled on his face. 'So, that's how to spot if they've done the timber, but what about the stone work? How can you tell if they've done that?'

'Oh, I don't know! I suppose it'll be clean of pigeon shit. So, are you happy, know what you're doing?'

'Yep, got it, make it pink and no pigeon shit,' said Uncle Bern, looking for praise and a pat on the head. He didn't get either. It's not fair, what did I do to deserve being saddled with an idiot for an uncle?

'Okay, fine, got it,' said Uncle Bern, nodding his head then pushing his glasses back up his nose.

Every time he comes back from Viva España he looks a little bit older, the hair a little wispier, the face a little heavier. I suppose with my own parents gone he's my only yardstick to chart the progress of generations passing. I always remember my mum to have been quite glamorous, she must have got the good genes because there's something of the mole about Bern. I guess, thinking about it now, him and Val must have made quite a strange pairing back in the day – her a tall, attractive, Eurovision blonde, him the short, dark mole man. Mind you it was the early 70s, Dustin Hoffman was quite the heartthrob back then, I blame Hoffman, I'm sure Val does now.

I handed the keys of my van over to him and watched him fiddle with all the knobs and buttons, twiddle with the mirror and disturb and disrupt everything else to get comfortable. With a downturned mouth and a shrug of the shoulders, I was given the grateful praise, 'It'll do.' *You're welcome Bern.*

I bid him adieu and he rolled away, only to slam on the anchors about a hundred metres away, then came flying backwards at about forty miles an hour in a manner that'd give the 'Fast and The Furious' second thoughts. I asked him what he thought he was doing with some particularly fruity swears that I'd learnt from Disco added in for flavour.

'Forgot to say, Harpo wants to meet up with you, got a bit of work for you, I'll call you later with the details, toodle-oo.' And with a crunching of gears that made my wallet wince he sped off like Lewis Hamilton with his arse on fire.

UNCLE BERN ARRANGED for us to meet Harpo at lunchtime in a pub in Wigmore, a well-heeled corner of the Medway Towns largely populated by bungalows that are being picked off for loft conversions and rebuilds at an alarming rate. The pub had recently been refurbished. Disco wasn't impressed.

'What have they done here?' he said, wandering around getting a full look at the place. They'd removed every internal wall, knocking the bars and dining areas into one long narrow space with hard surfaces, hard floors and low ceilings. 'It feels like one of those pubs you get in Heathrow Airport. You know, where everyone's knocking back gin at six in the morning. They've given this place the same soulless charm.'

Disco was right. I honestly think in twenty or thirty years people will look back on the present and think it was a terrible time for pubs. They're closing down every day and those that survive get this sort of treatment. Why is virtually every pub nowadays decked out with pale hardwood floors and hard plaster wall finishes so that the noise ricochets off every surface making it too loud for comfortable talking? And why is every available space filled with a huge tv screen that never gets turned off despite nobody ever watching it? But it wasn't my fault so I didn't feel the need to defend the pub's refurb, I just shrugged.

'They're all much of a muchness round here now.'

Disco ordered us a round – soft drinks only, I've had it drummed into me for so long now that alcohol and building sites don't mix that I've got out of the habit of drinking at lunchtime. Disco whinged and moaned a bit, but I'd already lost someone working for me this week so I think he understood why I was being a bit touchy about health and safety. He ordered for himself some brightly coloured energy drink that smelt foul and began rolling a fag.

'I got a taste for it in Thailand, although it tastes better with rum.'

He poked his fag behind his ear for later, and then loudly, probably more loudly than was necessary, informed me and the rest of the bar he was going for a piss.

I was standing there trying to overlay this miserable barn of a place against the pub I remember it used to be when I spotted the disgusting but familiar face in the corner.

'Hello Mark,' said Duncan Harper, for it was he. He put his phone face down on the table, and pushed his glasses back to the bridge of his nose with a pudgy finger.

'Beard looks good, Harpo' I said. It didn't. 'Really suits you.' It didn't. It was a nasty patchy yellow-and-brown mess but Harpo seemed to like the compliment.

When Harpo smiled his face looked as if it was being devoured by wasps, jeez it was horrible. Clean shaven he was no lady killer but bearded he looked like a child killer. It was vile. He looked like he should be living rough out of a skip, less hipster, more dumpster. What is this fascination everyone has with beards? There's a reason why they went out of fashion before, they should be consigned to history, things done in the 70s, and should never be seen again, like brynylon sweaters and home-done abortions.

Harpo was the man you went to if you needed the unusual, obsolete or odd. He had a large sprawling yard full of what he called architectural salvage but everyone else called old shit – however, if you needed a Bakelite door knob or a single Victorian encaustic tile, he was always the man who could help you out.

'I understand you've been looking for me, Harpo,' I said, pulling out a stool and settling opposite him.

'And here I am looking at you.' The thing about Harpo is that he can be a pedantic sod when he wants to, which is most of the time. 'I'm glad you're here Mark, I require your help.'

Great, someone else's problems, as if I haven't got enough of my own, I'm now importing them.

Harpo looked straight at me and smiled. 'There's a fox living in my yard. The problem is he's not paying any rent but he keeps on turning on all the lights.' He grinned, thinking himself a great wit, his revolting beard rolled and rippled like a doormat with worms. 'As you will no doubt recall, you installed the lights so I need you to put them right.'

'Lights? But? That was what four, five years ago Harpo?'

'Five in May.' Pedantic, see, told you so. 'What about my warranty?'

'Warranty? For a couple of halogen lamps? You're joking?'

Harpo looked affronted, his grin fell away, like pissed off roadkill, 'I thought you were an honest trader Mark, your Uncle Bern says –'

Uncle Bern! Back in the country five minutes and he's already costing me money. For the sake of a quiet life I agreed to go over to Harpo's yard in the next day or two, causing Harpo to sit back in his chair grinning like a smug merkin thinking he'd chalked up a win. I bid him farewell and returned to Disco who was now back from his ablutions.

'Jesus, is that Harpo?' said Disco looking over my shoulder. 'Hey Harpo,' he shouted, the entire bar stopped and turned. 'Did you know there's a squirrel trying to shag your chin?'

The bar seemed to hold its breath for a second, Harpo fixed Disco with a stare and then raised the middle fingers on both hands simultaneously, giving it to his friendly tormentor with both barrels.

-19-

DISCO AND I rolled into Queen Mary's and parked on the opposite side of the car park, deciding it best not to face the wrath of Old John again.

As we walked towards the entrance, I gestured to Disco the blue VW Golf we'd seen yesterday.

'Looks like she's back.'

'Why does everyone have these?' said Disco, pointing at a Baby on Board sticker in the car's back window. I shrugged and walked past into the lobby beckoning him to keep up with me.

The same haughty attitude was waiting for us in Reception, and our return was met with as much contempt as our previous visit although the Receptionist did this time at least call the Manager. She had that special knack of letting us know it was the greatest inconvenience imaginable for her without saying a word.

We were made to wait in the lobby, more people than I'd expected, until several minutes later we were met by a woman who clearly regarded herself far too busy and important to waste her time with the likes of us. She seemed to expect us to be grateful and doff our caps to her for merely granting an audience. Another one that thinks simply because they wear a suit they're better than us in dirty boots.

'Hello, I'm Kate Fuller. I understand you wanted to see me,' she said in a tone that made perfectly clear that she didn't want to see me.

'Hello Kate, how do you do?' She bristled at the casual use of her first name, that amused me. 'You owe us quite a bit of money. Can we talk about your unpaid bills?'

She seemed uncomfortable when people began looking at the poor workmen who hadn't been paid.

'This way,' she said, ushering us towards an adjacent corridor, I find you can never beat the threat of airing dirty secrets in public to get a reaction. Disco left to roll a fag outside, so I followed her alone.

Overall, she gave me the impression of someone trying too hard to keep it all together, and failing. Her grey woollen suit pulled tightly in places where it shouldn't and the way she stomped along the corridor on heels that were too high and too thick put me in mind of the Wicked Witch of the West. Her lank, greasy hair was tied back with an elastic band.

She led me to a large untidy open-plan office area, and off that to a private room formed by glazed partitions. We entered, and she closed the door behind her. It rattled noisily in its frame. From the certificates on the wall I knew this was her office. As well as the certificates, the walls were decorated with motivational slogans.

'Now then, you claim we owe you money. I've never heard of you,' she said.

I laid out the Quentin purchase orders on her desk and explained I was there on behalf of Tommy. She glanced at Tommy's name and address at the top of the orders.

'I've never heard of him either.'

'You must have, you've paid him enough times. Check and you'll see,' I said, trying very hard to keep my voice level because whilst I didn't believe her, I could see the benefit of diplomacy.

She took one of the purchase orders, and began pecking away at her keyboard.

'Right,' she said, 'here's his account, although...' she paused and squinted at her screen. 'He's been paid by handwritten cheque.'

'Yes, and?' I didn't understand the dithering.

'He's been paid by cheque nine, ten, no eleven times. That's very odd. Regular contractors and suppliers go on our system and are paid electronically. We normally only bother with cheques for one-offs.'

She tapped on the glass wall beside her and a young man's face popped up; she beckoned him into her office. The phone on her desk rang loudly and she jabbed at a button to answer it on speaker.

'Yes, what, I'm in a meeting.'

'Sorry to interrupt, but it's the dealership returning your call, shall I tell them to call back?'

'No, put them through,' Fuller demanded.

I noticed there was no acknowledgement towards me, clearly my time didn't matter. The young man from the other office entered and gently squeezed the door closed behind him to minimise any noise just as the voice on the phone began apologising for being late returning her car. The young man was dressed a lot more casually than his manager, a wooden beaded necklace dangled in the gap of the open collar of his white linen shirt. As the voice on the phone promised to have the car ready in a few days he waved a loose and languid friendly greeting towards me.

'It's not good enough, you didn't have this attitude when you sold me the bloody car so don't think you can get away with it now. I haven't paid you all that money for you to dick around doing nothing, I want that car back and I want it tomorrow –'

The young man gave an exaggerated grimace and rolled his eyes that I took to mean *'Awkward'*. The poor sap on the phone got a pasting, and the young man kept fiddling with the leather bracelets around his wrist as we waited. After a few minutes of hurling demands at the phone she was finished. The person at the dealership deserved a round of applause for remaining civil at the end of it, most people would have lost their tempers by now, I know I would have.

'Idiots!' she said upon cutting the call. 'Bloody useless the lot of them. I'll never buy another Merc from those people, I'm going to go back to Audi when this lease is up, nothing but problems with that firm.'

She rubbed her temples, gave a sigh and then turned to face me, at last acknowledging I was still in the room.

'This is our director.'

She gestured to the young man who had flopped into a visitor chair. Director? I've always been a great believer in first impressions, but director, really? From the body language, from the communication, I'd have said he was deferential to her, she was the boss, I didn't get it.

'Charles Quentin,' he said holding out a floppy hand for a limp handshake.

'Quentin, as in…?'

He bobbed his head and shrugged his shoulders in a gesture I think was meant to signal embarrassment but came across as gormless.

'Yeah, one of the family I'm afraid, but I'm just Charlie, call me Charlie,' he said.

Now I got it.

'This man says we owe him money, and has come in with these,' she said, pointing at the orders and sneering on the 'these'. 'The system says there's an account history, all paid by cheque. Do you know anything about them?' And then addressing me directly, 'Only a company director has authority to sign cheques.'

'Oh, yeah, think so, but, where's Tommy?'

I explained to him that Tommy was dead. He gripped the chair to steady himself, pulled his fingers through his hair, rubbed his face, rocked back and forth muttering, 'Oh my god, that's awful, awful.'

His histrionics were, to be honest, a bit embarrassing so I thought it better for all concerned to get us back on track. 'Mrs Fuller…' I began but was cut off.

'Ms, it's Ms,' she said. 'I haven't worked all my life, I didn't get a first at Cambridge, just to be judged by my marital status.'

I'd seen the gold band on her finger, but clearly, I'd assumed wrong. It was then I actually read the motivational signs decorating the walls: '*Behind every successful woman is herself*' said the one nearest to me, a small print showed a 40s factory girl in spotted headscarf and overalls rolling her sleeves up with a speech bubble saying '*What exactly can you do for me that I can't do for myself?*' Clearly, I'd assumed very wrongly indeed, she was more than a woman succeeding, this was a woman in competition with the rest of the world.

As if to prove my point, unprompted, she seemed compelled to add, 'I'm the breadwinner in my family. I earn the money, and he stays home like Daddy Daycare.'

I didn't like her to begin with, and now I liked her even less. Don't get me wrong, I have no problem with career women, far from it. My problem lies with people that think that to get on they need to treat everyone around them with contempt: much like her, much like Mr Wilkes. All I'm saying is just a little respect goes a long way, we've all got a job to do and a role to play. It makes things so much easier if we all show each other a little appreciation, otherwise all you end up doing is pissing everyone else off, like she has now. Anyway, I was keen to get her back on topic.

'Ms Fuller, according to this paperwork from you, you owe quite a significant sum, can you please tell me when it'll be paid?'

She fanned out the invoices in front of her, read them all, before looking back up at me. She shocked me with her answer: 'Never.'

Now she was really giving me the hump, and Charlie sat beside her looking as confused as me.

'This one here, redecorate garden room following leak. We haven't had a leak. This one, room 1/7, full redecoration for incoming resident. She's been in that room for over two years and has no plans to go anywhere. All of them, they're all bogus,' and before I could say anything, she picked them all up and ripped them in half. I was speechless at her arrogance. Charlie looked stunned.

'Now I'd like you to leave, otherwise I will call the police and ask them to make you leave,' she said.

OUTSIDE I FOUND Disco having a fag with the Receptionist of all people, gossiping away like the best of friends. I told him we were leaving.

'What's happening?'

'I've got absolutely no idea, but come on we're off,' I said and started marching. Disco bid farewell with the promise to call her later.

'Wait,' a voice called out from behind us. I stopped and looked back to see Charlie scuttling after us. Disco shrugged and carried on without me.

'Don't go, look, I can sort this out,' he said, 'Did Tommy say anything to you? About me? No, no, never mind... Did he have anything, you know, for me?'

'What're you talking about?' I asked, but by now he was crossing and uncrossing his arms in embarrassment.

'No, no forget I said anything. But... if you find anything from him for me, I can give you purchase orders, as many as you like, next time come straight to me, I'll sort them out, not her.'

'So, what about these ones?' I said, showing him the clutch of jobs that hadn't been done yet.

'Yes, I'll pay you for them. In return, for, you know...' He kept looking around him as he spoke, pausing any time anyone was remotely within earshot, 'You, you know, you give it to me and I'll get them paid, right away, there and then, not her, forget about her.'

I didn't understand what he was talking about, and I honestly didn't have the stamina to find out. There was a heat inside me, my face was burning, my hands were beginning to tremble, I knew this feeling, nothing good comes from it – the milk pan bubbling before it boils over. To my relief, the impatient Disco was banging on the roof of the van telling me to get a move-on, and without another word to Charlie, I walked away before he could say anything else and before my rage erupted.

'WHAT'S BEEN GOING ON?' said Disco, as we pulled away 'You looked like you were about to start a fight.'

I explained about Kate Fuller's obnoxious attitude, about her ripping up Tommy's invoices.

'So, we're not going to be working there then?'

Based on the balance of probability and all things considered, I told him it was highly unlikely we'd be working in there any time soon.

'Shame,' he said. 'According to Helen it'll all be buttoned up with framework contractors once they're sold next month.'

'Helen? Who the bloody hell's Helen?'

'Helen! On reception, back there. Helen.'

'How'd you get talking to her then? When I left you, she looked like she wanted to stab you, when I come back it's all "Helen says".'

'I don't know, just did. Here, you'll never guess who her next door neighbour but one is?' I shook my head. 'Tim!'

'Tim?' I said with fond, nostalgic tones, 'Good old Tim. Golden Lamb?' And so we spent the afternoon toasting absent friends.

ALL IN ALL, it had been a pretty dismal day, and by the time the mini-cab turned into my cul-de-sac shortly after seven I couldn't wait to get inside and hide myself away until tomorrow.

The cold dark night was suddenly illuminated with supernova brightness thanks to the lamp on the front of my house triggering as soon as my foot hit the path. It filled my boozy head with thoughts of Harpo's fox. The brilliant white light dazzled me and made my hand difficult to steer. I was finding it a challenge to get the key in the lock. The brass tongue wouldn't line up with the latch. I'd made a couple of near misses and now with it held firmly in both hands I gently made my third attempt.

If ... only ... I ... could ... get ... this ... bloody ... door ... open.

This had become a matter of principle. I would not be defeated. I directed all my concentration on it. I became focussed, so much so I didn't hear the approaching footsteps behind me. I don't think I fully noticed the first blow to the back of my head – there was no mistaking the second though.

It caught me squarely just behind my ear and knocked me off my feet. Even as I clattered on to the path, face scraping against the concrete, my hair falling into the dirt, I still don't think I realised what was happening.

By the time I felt the kick between my shoulders forcing the air out of my lungs I knew I was under attack. Another kick, same place. I coughed and retched, unable to draw a breath quick enough. Reactions took over, pleading with me to get away, I rolled on to my hands and knees steadying myself, but another kick, this one to the ribs, knocked me flat again. The kicks flew in, all down my side, stamps pounded on my back. It was coming so fast, so ferociously that I couldn't tell whether it was one attacker or many, but I could only hear one muffled voice over the top of my groaning.

Stamp, 'You can't have what *kick* belongs *kick* to *stamp* me,' *kick* 'Bastard *kick* thinking *stamp* you can *kick* take what's *stamp* mine, I want what's *stamp* mine.'

The paving, cold and damp against my face, burned as my ear dragged across it. My hands were under me still trying to push up to a standing position and the pain ripped through me when my elbow was crushed under foot. I thought I heard a far-off second voice calling out, and force of reflex caused me to turn towards it just as the heavy foot connected with my cheek.

-20-

I CAME TO propped up in a hospital bed, squinting into the bright glare overhead. My face felt tender and every breath hurt. My clothes had been removed and replaced by a thin hospital gown, and becoming aware of this made my skin shiver. I rubbed the goose bumps on my forearm until the pain across my shoulders forced me to stop.

I sat still, silently, whilst the rest of the ward swarmed with noise and activity. I tried to understand my surroundings, but looking around made my head swim. I held myself upright and motionless until the nausea wore off. I drew in a few long deep breaths, that old cure-all, and tasted dried blood in my mouth, metallic and earthy.

'Hello again,' said a voice beside me. I carefully twisted around and was surprised by just how happy I was to see Perry. 'We must stop meeting like this!'

Looking back, I know the first rule of trying to pull your hot new next-door neighbour is laugh at her corny jokes, but at the time I figured, in the grand scheme of things, it wasn't worth the pain my ribs would have had to endure – jeez, I must have been more hurt than I realised. Instead I asked her what happened.

'Initial thoughts were you were in a fight, but your hands and knuckles are undamaged which suggests you were attacked instead.' I murmured that this much I knew, 'You were brought in by a man who didn't stay, he dropped you off and left. It happens from time to time, they're concerned, but not enough to get involved with the paperwork.'

I didn't remember anything beyond being on the ground, I had no recollection of how I got there, and certainly not of a guardian angel, did she get a name or a number?

'No. All he said was he's a driver. One of the porters helped him carry you in and then he disappeared off into the night.'

Perry offered me a flimsy white plastic cup, and I gratefully took a sip from it. The water tasted warmish.

'Do you want this?' she offered a moulded cardboard bowl. I took it and gratefully spat, it looked pale pink under the harsh lighting. There had been blood in my mouth. My tongue checked my teeth, they were all present and standing firm, but the coarse texture my tongue detected suggested I must have bitten my cheek at some point.

'As I say, your Good Samaritan dropped you and ran. We don't know anything.'

She paused, picking her next words with great tact, 'Because you came in through... let's call it an unusual route – no ambulance, no 999 calls – the police haven't been involved. It's up to you if you want to them to be.' Another cautious pause. 'Would you like us to report this for you?'

I told her no, I hadn't seen anything, it would be pointless. I didn't tell her our kind don't go to the police, and that we sort our own problems out. Instead I told her I wanted to go home.

'You can soon, the doctor wants you observed for a couple of hours to make sure there's no concussion. Look, I finish at one a.m., so if you can wait until then I'll give you a lift home.'

She gave me a couple of painkillers and left me to sit quietly. Robbie Williams sang 'Angels' on a constant loop inside my mind as I drifted in and out of sleep.

HALF PAST ONE and Perry was helping me out of her small Fiat, leading us towards our adjoining houses. As we got closer, I noticed something.

'Look,' I said, pointing at my keys dangling from the door like a lonely Christmas decoration, 'I managed to get it in the lock after all.'

-21-

I'D HAD A broken night's sleep, and then, finally, when I'd got off, I was roused by the doorbell. I ignored it and rolled over. It rang again. And again. When it was clear they weren't going away I began to haul myself out of bed in the usual manner, but the sleepy ache around my ribs suddenly woke up and filled my head with white pain. Slowly I lifted myself into a seated position and then with great care twisted around until my feet touched the floor. The doorbell rang again.

Now standing, I shuffled like a hundred-year-old man until I could find a rhythm and pace that didn't hurt. Still the doorbell rang. Eventually I made it to the front door. The doorbell was ringing again as I opened it. Perry.

'Ah look at your poor face,' she said, and reached up to hold my cheek in the palm of her hand. I wasn't used to such kindness but welcomed it gratefully. 'I'm just leaving for work now, thought I'd check in to see how you are, make sure you're ok.'

She did that rising inflection at the end of her sentences again, I wasn't certain if she was asking me or telling me, so I muttered, 'I'll be fine, a few painkillers and I'll be right as rain,' before remembering my manners. 'Thank you.'

She smiled, and that alone made me feel a lot, lot better. She said she'd look in again later, and waved goodbye as she walked towards her car. I closed the door. It hurt to smile, but this time I didn't care.

I STOOD IN front of the bathroom mirror, naked, and looked at myself properly for the first time. My left eye was swollen, flowering grey and yellow on my cheek beneath it. An angry scab had formed across the bridge of my nose. My nostrils were lined with dried blood, but I found the tension and the cracking of it each time I flared them oddly pleasurable. All down my left side, from my shoulder to my hip, was a patchwork of bruises in varying shades of grey, green and maroon. The bruising to my upper arm bore a half boot print where it stamped across my elbow, a crude rainbow of red, purple and black.

Twisting caused the pain to bite and clamp across my ribs, conjuring up visions of Gnasher from *The Beano*, my own black dog to suffer, with every movement he would grip me in his jaws. By taking it slowly, I managed to look over my shoulder to see my back reflected in the mirror. Boot prints, full and partial, glared back at me, fierce in their red, raw form. Decorating my shoulder blades were round bruises, perfectly circular – toe punts. That meant one thing for certain – my attacker wore steel toecaps, protective boots, a tradesman straight off site. I examined myself and remembered his words as he booted me up and down the garden path: '*You can't have what belongs to me. I want what's mine.*'

I STOOD AT the front window stepping from foot to foot, checking my watch, checking my phone, checking my watch. Where was he? Ten minutes, they promised he'd be here in ten minutes twenty minutes ago. At last, a shabby silver Nissan saloon pulled up, I grabbed the box at my feet and left the house.

I pulled the car door shut and instructed the driver to take me to the Golden Lamb, wincing through the unexpected gnash that bit me, son of a bitch: I'd crouched too quickly when boarding the back of the Nissan, and vowed not to make that mistake again.

'You remember me?' I said to the eyes in the mirror once we were in motion.

'Don't know boss,' came the reply from the front seat. 'So many passengers, can't remember everyone.'

'I asked for you specifically.' I noticed the eyes hadn't left me since I'd sat down. 'I asked them who was on last night, in a silver car that picked up at the Golden Lamb.'

The eyes in the mirror narrowed and stayed fixed on me, but the body in the front seat didn't move.

'All I wanted to do was say thank you. If you hadn't stepped in things could have been a lot worse, thanks.'

'Look man, I don't want any trouble, I don't want to get involved.'

'You aren't involved in anything, you won't be, relax. But can you tell me what you saw, who did it? Please?'

The eyes in the mirror looked left, then right. I knew he was debating whether to say anything. I had thought something like this might happen so I opened the box beside me, the one with a Ferrari red kettle on the side, and removed some notes, roughly the equivalent of two day's money for him. I offered it up to the eyes in the mirror. I heard a long sigh and then he began to speak.

BY THE TIME we'd reached the Golden Lamb, I'd learned that Devinder – for that was his name – had indeed been my mini-cab driver home last night. As he was turning around at the toe of the cul-de-sac he saw me, floodlit, on the ground getting a beating. He shouted, hoping it would scare the attacker away, which it did, but then he saw I was in a proper mess. He dragged me to the car, and as Perry had already told me, he took me to hospital. At this point I felt compelled to give him a few more notes to cover the fare to the hospital last night, and a few more to get the upholstery cleaned even though I was pretty sure I wasn't responsible for most of the unpleasant stains crusting his seats. He couldn't give any description of my attacker though as he'd taken off in the opposite direction, but I was beginning to form a fair idea who did it.

THE VAN WAS parked where I'd left it last night, and after thanking Devinder, I was soon on my way again. Twenty minutes later I was outside the white and red hoarding of a large housing development. In about a year's time there will be a dozen new five-bed luxurious executive homes but right now, behind the gates they're still shells, some further along in the programme than others.

To my left the houses had been topped out and the windows were going in, they'd soon be waterproof and the finishing trades would be racing through to make them habitable. To my right the bricklayers were finishing off doing the awkward cuts around the gables and the carpenters were still manhandling the triangular trusses into position: the timber preservative treatment gave them a ghostly greenish tinge against the sterile grey sky. And directly in front were the halfway houses: their states midway between those left and right. The roofs had been covered in tacky bitumen-coated felt pinned down by thin timber battens. Piled precariously across the roof were stacks of roof tiles, they'd started fitting them at one end and were now beginning to sweep their way across, changing the colour of the roofs from tar black to a warm russet.

I could see Blunt, standing astride the ridge of a roof, one foot on each slope, watching and commanding all around him, the ape-man king of the jungle.

A bored, minimum-wage guard paid from the neck down had seen the van with writing down the side of it and assumed I had business there. He opened the site gates and waved me through without saying a word – and they wonder why theft on building sites is so high.

At the designated parking area, I got out of the van, taking my box with me and looked around to get my bearings. Last thing I wanted was to get too near the works – every site has its own unique combination for protective wear, so I really didn't want to lose the element of surprise by being bawled out by an overzealous site manager for being in the wrong kit. Instead I waited around the little encampment of cabins and containers, realising it would soon be lunchtime.

Without a sound or signal, the operatives dotted around the site began to drift in towards the cabins at the stroke of noon. Blunt and his crew came down off their roof, dropping their tools at the foot of the ladder, and came towards the mess hut.

I stepped out to block his path; he approached, getting a bit too close for my liking, virtually touching me, squaring up to me toe-to-toe like a boxer.

'That's a nasty eye,' he said. 'Rough night, was it? What's her name?' His crew laughed sycophantically at his jibe. 'You know your trouble? You and your mate, you need to toughen up.'

My mate? Did he mean Tommy? I heard the pack laughing, I saw him sneering, I felt the burning on my face and the trembling through my fingers.

'You need a bit more fight in you.'

I swung and my fist connected with his jaw, his head jerked back on impact, I'd put a lot of power and anger behind the punch, but his low squat centre of gravity kept him firmly upright, I may as well have punched a tree.

The box dropped from my grip as I lunged at him with both hands and this time he went over, flat on his back in the mud. I reached out, grasping for a weapon, and pulled a shovel out of someone's hands who cursed at me in a language I didn't recognise. I stood over Blunt and raised the shovel skyward ready to smash in his thick, primate skull but paused on the down swing, not long, only a second but it was long enough to feel strong arms dragging me backwards. I was disarmed by the shovel owner, who snatched it back, shouting foreign swears as he walked away.

I was held tight unable to move, the rage numbing any pain my injuries might have been screaming at me from being gripped so tightly. Blunt got up, wiped the mud from his hands against his shirt. He looked at me and then launched, his teeth bared and eyes wide, ready to inflict maximum damage. Thankfully, his brother Gary stepped in the way, grabbed him and with the help of another member of their crew pulled Blunt away from me. The way Gary spoke to him and calmed him down was definitely for Blunt's benefit rather than mine. Luckily, Blunt was out on licence, if Gary hadn't stopped him, he could quite easily have been back inside by the end of the day. But I had no doubt that if it hadn't been for that, Gary would have stood aside and let him rip me limb from limb.

We both stood facing each other, squirming within our restraints. He was desperate to break free and batter me. I now regretted starting this and was quite glad of the restraints, but kept up the pretence.

'What's all this about?' said Gary to me, over the sound of his brother's animalistic grunts of anger. 'You better have a good explanation because we can't hold him much longer.'

'I told him you'd get your money. Told him Friday.'

'We already know that. But what are you doing here? Today?' Blunt twisted and writhed in his brother's arms, his face red and contorted with fury.

'Look at me! Just look at me. And my friend, clubbed to death. Over a bad debt? I told you Friday. We had a deal.'

'Whoa! Wait right there' said Gary, 'You think… you actually think that's something to do with him, us?'

Gary was staring directly at Blunt as he spoke, maybe it was a sibling thing, maybe he was seeking reassurance from his younger brother. As if understanding, and to give the reassurance sought, Blunt stopped resisting and his body lost its tension, the veins in his neck faded from view and his complexion returned to normal.

'So, you came here... what... for revenge? To kill him? An eye for eye?'

As he spoke Gary realised that the heat had evaporated from the situation and gestured for me to be released.

'No' I said, the adrenaline was still streaming through me, my hands were pulsing and I could hear that I was shouting, 'I'm here to give you this.'

I picked up the box that had been kicked over in the melee and threw it at Blunt. As it dropped to the ground in front of him the lid opened and banknotes fell into the mud at his feet.

'Take it! Take it and leave me alone. This ends now.' The guy previously restraining Blunt was now on his knees scooping the loose notes back into the box. He passed the box up to Gary who looked inside and then passed it to Blunt who peered in at the contents.

'We need to talk,' said Gary. 'You lot, eat, I'll be along in a minute,' and he ushered his crew inside the mess hut, then beckoned me to walk with him back to the van.

'Thanks for that, we appreciate it,' he said to me. 'I can calm him down, convince him it was a misunderstanding, anyway you know what he's like, there's nothing he likes more than a good tear-up so you probably made his day. But you've made a big mistake coming here. You can't go shooting your mouth off, Mark, accusing us of things in public.'

We'd reached the van. I knew this would be the part where he warns me off and tells me he'll let the psycho chimp off the leash to kill me next time, but no, he surprised me. He checked with me the day Tommy was murdered. He was correct. It had been all over the news, it was a big event in the Towns so of course he'd be aware of when it happened, but I think he wanted me to verify, to take ownership of the date. He then pulled out his phone and began scrolling through his photos. Dozens and dozens of pictures of him, Blunt and their crew in green boiler suits and crash helmets in amongst lots of other similarly dressed men.

'Look, see, we were all go-karting at Buckmore Park for—' he searched and then pointed at a face in a picture. 'His stag do'. The time and date was embedded in the phone's memory and he was right, they had been taken at roughly the same time Tommy was bludgeoned.

I SAT IN the van watching Gary walk away, back to his brother, relieved that he'd been there with his cool head, otherwise things could have got very nasty for Blunt, very nasty indeed – he might have got my brain matter all over his shirt.

So, Blunt hadn't killed Tommy and hadn't gone back on our deal, he was waiting patiently until Friday as promised. I'd made a big mistake. It suddenly struck me just how big a mistake I'd made and I quickly pulled out my phone and dialled in panic, hurry up and answer, hurry up and answer. Voicemail.

'Anthony, Mark Poynter, listen, Anthony it's about my money. You need to call me back. Trust me, this is urgent. Call me back. Bad things will happen if you don't.'

I'd got it all wrong. I had no idea who killed Tommy or why, but I'd set Hamlet on to Chapman believing he lay at the root cause of all of this. Yes, he was a slimy weasel who hadn't paid what he owed, but he wasn't the first and he certainly won't be the last. I'd made a mistake. Tommy wasn't killed because of Chapman's debt, but unless I could call off Hamlet quickly, Chapman was going to pay for my mistake.

-22-

WHEN THEY CAME mob-handed into the café, the girls behind the counter disappeared out the back double quick, thinking it was a raid on illegal foreign workers, but then suddenly it was me surrounded and being led out.

I'd never been in an interview room before and now I'm back again, second time in the same week, the same cabbagey fart smell hung in the air. Nobody so far said a word to me, all I could assume was Senia was still intent on fitting me up for Tommy's murder.

If they were keeping me isolated to frighten me – it was working. The only way to counter the giddiness I felt was to sit very still, very upright. And breathe slowly, in through my nose, out through my mouth, to keep the rising nausea down. I felt a desperate need for the toilet so tried my hardest not to think about it. No matter how much I rubbed my hands together they wouldn't warm up.

After the longest thirty minutes I'd ever endured, Senia burst into the room slapping a folder on the tabletop between us. A po-faced woman in a black suit followed behind. Her gentle action of closing the door contrasted Senia's powerful entry.

'I want a lawyer,' I said, hoping my voice didn't break.

'What for?' asked Senia, sitting back in his seat, crossing one leg over the other, unbuttoning his suit jacket, draping his elbow over the empty seat beside him.

I struggled for an answer, grasping for words but none came. Eventually the best I could manage was, 'I don't know.'

'You don't know? He doesn't know,' said Senia to the woman. She'd chosen to stand by the door, a bully's smile began to curl under the sullen cast of her eyes. Senia's mocking wasn't over yet. 'Mr Poynter, this is what is known as a Voluntary Attendance, and you have not been arrested. When you were cautioned you were given the opportunity for legal representation, but we only have a few questions for you. Do you need a lawyer to answer a few questions for you? Or would you rather we cut to the chase and arrest you?'

I was out of my depth and didn't know what to do. The age-old instinct took over, tell them nothing. I looked straight at Senia, breathing slowly, hoping my trembling wasn't too noticeable. He stared straight back. Eventually, thankfully, he broke the silence.

'That's quite a bruise. You look terrible, what happened?'

'Fell off my bike.'

'Nasty. You want to be more careful.'

'I won't be doing it again.'

'Now, you're no doubt wondering why you're here.' If he was expecting a reply, he didn't get one. 'No? Well, we're going to look at some photographs, and then we're going to talk about them.' Again, no response. 'Are you sitting comfortably? Then we'll begin.'

He opened his folder, pulled out three photographs and laid them on the table face-down, giving each a little twiddle at the corners and a tweak at the edges until they sat perfectly straight and level with each other, a trio of white, blank rectangles neatly in a row. He tapped on the first one, 'Let's look under here shall we?' He was playing with me, his take on the Find-The-Lady three-card trick. With an exaggerated gesture he flipped it over.

'Now, we've all seen this before haven't we? Oh, I don't think I mentioned, we didn't find any fingerprints on your hammer, none at all.' I didn't like the emphasis he placed on the word 'your'.

I glanced down to a head and shoulders close-up of Tommy. I looked past the vicious head wound exposing bone and jelly by concentrating on the elasticated white cover over someone's shoe caught in the background of the picture. The photographer caught Tommy in sharp focus in the foreground, the shoe behind him was a softly blurred white cloud floating him off to Paradise. Despite best efforts to resist, my eyes naturally kept drifting from the vague to the clearly defined. There was a very thin diagonal stripe of stubble on his cheek about half an inch long where Tommy had missed when shaving, funny, I don't recall noticing it when we sat and talked that morning but then, I guess, his face had been animated, full of movement and laughs and tall tales.

'So, without any fingerprints, we don't have any further leads. But here's something new you might be interested in.'

He turned the second photograph. Chapman's sallow, flabby face. Lifeless, the skin white, the lips red, his Mr Punch nose curling down towards his chin – well the first chin at least. His head had been propped on a small pillow, the flash of the camera off the stainless steel tabletop beneath him resembled a white sun against a cold grey sky. I couldn't breathe, I couldn't focus, I couldn't speak. The darkness around the edges of my vision suggested that my head was trying to black out but I fought against it, trying to regain control over my own body.

'I'm assuming you recognise this man? Mr Anthony Chapman, you do know him? Now, this is a strange one, Mrs Chapman comes home from a business trip to find him dead in his favourite armchair, assumes her dearly beloved had a heart attack and calls an ambulance. It's only when she's on the phone and notices that the kitchen door has been forced open that it becomes a suspicious death and it crosses my desk. So, what do you know about this chap?' Again, his questions were met with absolute silence.

'Nothing to say? Well, we checked his phone, and weren't we surprised to hear your voice, only three days ago you left the following message: *"Anthony, this is important, I want my money, you've got until Thursday night…".'*

His delivery was robotic and emotionless, twisting the words totally out of context.

"'…I can't take responsibility for whatever happens." Now that sounds very ominous to me, does it you Leigh?'

The woman nodded her agreement. Leigh, I wondered, first name or surname?

'In fact,' continued Senia, 'I'd go so far as to say it sounds downright threatening. So, Mr Poynter, where were you the night before last?'

My head was throbbing. The blood pulsed hard and rapid across my temples, fast track on the Aneurysm Express. My heart bounced inside my chest like a caged animal desperate to burst out. Still I remained silent, I turned away from the photographs on the table and looked straight ahead. Directly in my eyeline was the thin silver chain around the woman, Leigh's, neck, above her white blouse. I held on to the vain hope that concentrating on a neutral point in the distance like that would calm me down. Fine silver links held a pendant at the base of her throat, in the shape of a feather, or was it a fern, its slender central spine curved naturally and diamond-adorned fronds sprouted either side in a herring-bone layout. A copper couldn't afford diamonds, they had to be zirconas. The flashes and sparkles in the light were quite hypnotic, quite pacifying; relaxing thoughts of swimming pools on sunny holidays filled my head. The beast in my chest began to fade, the drumming at my temples slowed to a comfortable halt, all change all change this train terminates here.

'Still with us Mr Poynter?' said Senia, rousing me from my meditation. 'Because we have one last piccy for you.'

He flipped my mind when he flipped the photograph. I glanced down. Something didn't look right, I couldn't at first work out what was wrong, like an optical illusion it needed a second look and a squint and a moment or two to process what I was seeing.

Sally! It was Sally. Sally. Sally, from the club. My Auntie Val's niece, my cousin, sort of, but family nonetheless. Sally who looked so content arched up to face the bright blue winter sky. Sally, excited for the future. Sally.

Only it wasn't Sally, not *that* Sally, this Sally was inert, this Sally was unresponsive, this Sally was empty of any energy, any vitality, anything that made Sally my Sally.

I began to dry-retch. Senia immediately recoiled, and drew back his shiny shoes from the potential splatter zone. I composed myself. The woman passed me a thin plastic beaker of water, and a tissue which I used to wipe my mouth.

It was a struggle, but I found my voice and I asked Senia how and why. As I spoke, the photograph became clearer. Sally was slumped forwards on the floor, her leg jutted out at an unnatural angle. Surrounding her, an almost black outline where her blood had soaked into the pale carpet. Her visible arm was cut several times and her hand slashed twice with tramlines carved either side of her knuckles. Her back and shoulders were cut and hacked, an ugly crude gouge ran from nose to ear. But despite these awful, horrendous wounds it was clear what had killed her. A thick open tear sliced her neck apart, so deep it was almost as though her head was hinged from her body. It gaped wide apart, edged by raw stems of flesh.

I turned the photograph over, grateful to meet its plain white back once again. My eyes prickled, I could sense tears welling, but I wasn't going to give Senia the pleasure of seeing me weep. I diverted my gaze to the ceiling until the sensation went away.

Senia produced another photograph from his folder and laid it on the table. It was a natural, unposed photograph taken of the subjects, unaware. I looked closer, it was me, me and Sally, the other day, outside the club sitting on the wall, she's holding her new red phone, I'm smiling, she's laughing. It must have been when she was making that daft kitten-face picture of me. I didn't know what to say and looked up at Senia hoping for an explanation.

'We've had you under surveillance. I did tell you last time we spoke that you were a person of interest Mr Poynter.'

I was emotionally exhausted, but at the same time anger coursed through me. My hands began to tremble. The flashpoint bubbled up towards the surface. I felt abused and manipulated. Then it suddenly occurred to me, of course, the silver Mondeo I'd been seeing around. I tried to compose my words but was struggling to express myself in a way that wouldn't get me into more trouble. I was biting down on my rage when Senia leaned closely in towards me. It took everything I had to stop me smacking him in the mouth. He knew it and he laughed, right in my face.

'So, Marky Mark, as you can see, I have got three suspicious deaths all occurring within the same week and the only common denominator is you! Now, where were you the night before last?'

-23-

THE SLAM OF the door behind me made me jump. I was disoriented and groggy. The night was damp and cold and I didn't have a jacket. My shoulders hunched by reflex to keep out the chill. I decanted my possessions from the plastic bag – wallet, phone, keys, loose change – and as I snapped the buckle shut on my watch, I saw that it was almost ten o'clock.

I'd been held for over nine hours; did it really take them that long to check my story? I'd told Senia exactly what he wanted to know and he wasn't happy about it. He'd shown me the surveillance photo his snoops had taken of me and bragged they'd had me under observation, but he looked ready to explode when I told him I had a cast iron alibi, where were his snoops then? Someone somewhere will get a roasting tomorrow I'm sure.

However, as alibis go, five hours in an Accident & Emergency bed is pretty solid. I guess it checked out, as I was woken up fifteen minutes ago, my valuables returned and then shoved out the back door to rejoin the rest of the world.

My phone's dead, brilliant! I've absolutely no idea how I'm going to get home. The van's parked up miles away on a pay and display, I'm bound to have got a ticket, brilliant! And now it's started to rain, brilliant! Everything is so fucking brilliant!

I started walking in the direction of the nearby university campus, my hands bunched up inside my sleeves to keep them warm, a habit I've always had. My dad used to say it made me look like Dennis Law. He loved Dennis Law ever since he sent Man United down. I figured there must be a pub or a coffee shop or something open for students that will have a payphone then I can call for a cab. Maybe I could ask for Devinder? Then I can apologise. I'd promised him he wasn't going to be drawn into anything, but I had no choice other than to give his name to Senia. I felt a bit guilty about that now.

I was thinking about Perry when the car pulled up. God knows what she must think, first I turn up battered and bruised, then she's roped in as the alibi for the prime suspect to a triple murder. That'll put the kybosh on anything happening there. Shame. I trudged on, lost in my thoughts of what might have been, idle daydreams of Perry, me and happily ever after. I didn't notice the car crawling beside me, not until it flashed its blue lights and gave a short sharp scream of its siren to grab my attention.

The patrol car window slid down.

'Mark Poynter, get in.'

I hesitated, and decided I'm not going back. If they wanted me again, then this time I'd want a lawyer and I'd want everything done official and on record. I kept walking.

'I'm your ride home, get in,' the voice said. I hesitated again, my feet were cold and damp, and my clothes weren't any protection against the chill seeping deep into my bones. I opened the rear door and sat in the back of the patrol car. As I did so the car's interior lit up for a second. I immediately recognised the driver – the policeman from the Wilkes's house with the footballer swagger. The door slammed closed and the car went dark again.

'Thanks,' I said.

The heating burned fiercely inside the car. I sat on my hands to try to warm them up and felt my face tingle as the dry heat began to thaw it out. The silver details of the driver's uniform flashed in the shadows, but otherwise he was masked by the dark. The driver proceeded in the direction of the university channelled by the one-way flow of the dual carriageway, but against my expectations he didn't do a full loop of the roundabout at the university approach to head back on the opposite side towards my house, instead he continued straight ahead into the gaping mouth of the tunnel taking us down and under the River Medway only to emerge on the other side a couple of minutes later in the heart of a sprawling industrial estate full of huge crinkly tin warehouses locked up and deserted for the night. The driver slowly cruised the network of estate roads, flashing his full beam to read the street signs, picking his way through the maze until he finally came to a stop behind a dilapidated old unit, its perimeter guarded by spiky bare metal palisade fencing.

'What's all this about?' I said. I hoped my voice carried enough annoyance and belligerence to mask the worry and fear trembling inside me. Why was I here? Part of me tried to urge calm, knowing cops couldn't just pick people off the street and take them to dark deserted areas to beat confessions out of them, but another part of me was anything but calm as I knew this cop was dirty, and he knew I knew.

'Just wait. You'll see,' he said.

The opposite door opened, again the car's interior lit up for a second, then the door slammed closed and the car went dark once more. Hamlet shuffled to get comfortable in the back seat, he leaned up close to me, and then, to be sure, flicked the interior light on then off. 'Shit mate, what happened to your face? Did Senia do that?'

'No,' I self-consciously rubbed my forehead. 'I fell off my bike.'

'Yeah? Well if you need a couple of guys to help you sort out your *bike* let me know, okay? Danny, give us a minute?'

Obediently the driver got out of the car. I looked to Hamlet for an explanation. 'Senia's after you, Mark, he's trying to get authority to tap your phone calls and have you watched full time. The only safe way to talk privately is by using the hospitality of friendlies, such as PC Brennan here.'

PC Brennan sheltered in the doorway of the building to keep out the drizzle. He looked cold and pissed off.

'Listen, Marky, I need your help.' His voice had changed, it was weak, helpless, and he carried the smell of whiskey on his breath. I didn't need to see him in the dim light to know he was in a bad way.

'Danny says they told you about Sally, what happened to her,' he sniffed. 'I want you to help me find out who did this; she liked you, she'd want you to. Whoever it was, I'll make them pay for it.'

I didn't know what to say, so gazed out of the window. PC Brennan was using this opportunity to relieve himself and stood with his back to us unloading his bladder; a small cloud of steam emerged between his knees as the hot flow hit the cold brickwork.

'He could get nicked for that, lucky there's not a copper around,' I said.

I couldn't help myself, always one for gallows humour: lighten the mood, change the subject, if they're laughing it means they're not hitting you. As soon as I said it, I regretted it, knowing it wasn't the right time or place, but Hamlet wasn't listening anyway.

'You've got the…' Hamlet struggled to find the right word, and I sat quietly letting him find it. 'You've got the way with people Mark, they like you, they open up to you.'

'I don't know about that,' I said, thinking how little I actually knew Tommy despite all our history.

'The other day when you were at the club, what'd you talk about?'

'Tommy mostly.'

'And?'

'Her kid.' I thought it prudent to leave out the bits about her hoping to get away to set up a new life with a new family, I didn't want to be the messenger Hamlet was planning to shoot.

'Did she say anything about a new boyfriend? About getting serious?'

'Yes.' I replied, he obviously knew so there was no point in denying it.

'And?'

'That's all. She had a boyfriend, sounded keen, hoped it would go somewhere.'

'Who is he?'

'I've no idea. Honestly. No idea.'

'Then that's what I want you to find out. Who is he? You will come to me with his name.'

'But...'

'No buts. Look, here's the deal. You get me his name, I let you off what you owe me.'

'What I owe you? What are you talking about, we agreed, you bought the debt off me.'

'He's dead Mark.'

'And whose fault is that?'

'Don't go blaming me! The boys went to collect, no answer at the door they thought your man was avoiding them, they get inside and find the silly fat bastard dead in his chair. They never laid a finger on him.'

'That'd explain why he didn't answer any of my calls.'

'Well he wouldn't, carked out in front of the telly, all over and out, Elvis has left the building.'

'Hold on, you haven't even given me any money yet, you said Friday, so I don't actually owe you anything.'

'Oh yeah, I forgot, this is for you.' He passed across a small Peppa Pig tote bag that had been between his feet. 'Happy Christmas.'

'Piss off, I don't want it now, you can keep it.'

'Too late, you asked for it, you've got it. You've got no idea what I had to go through to get that, so you're bloody well having it. As for the fat man, he's no good to me in that state, so the debt comes back to you, sorry but that's how it works.'

'Seriously, you're telling me you have a refund policy?'

'Look, relax, I've told you I'll let it go, just get me that name.'

'Me? Why? You don't need me. You've clearly got PC Pissy over there who's better equipped than I'll ever be to find out, ask him.'

'I have. You seem to forget just how large your debt is Mark. This right now is the most important thing to me. I'm asking everyone who owes me a favour, I want this sorted in days not weeks or months. I'm perfectly aware your debt is way in excess of the task in hand, that's the same as everyone. I want people hungry for this so I'm stirring up a bit of competition, winner takes all, scoops the jackpot, if one of you finds the bastard, it's money well spent as far as I'm concerned. Senia knows exactly who Sally was to me, so he'll keep a tight lid on it – as soon as he has him, he'll be whisked off in to the wide blue yonder of protective custody. I want him before Senia's even out of bed. I will take care of this, not Senia.'

He opened the car door and stepped out, but before closing it he leaned in and added, 'First instalment's due a week today. Get that name.'

Hamlet walked off into the shadows, a slam, then headlights pierced the darkness and a big car, it was too dark to be specific, whisked him away.

'Come on then, I'll give you that lift home,' said PC Brennan, climbing back into the car.

I sat quietly watching the scenery slip by. I wondered how I'd managed to get myself into this mess, and tried working out the sums. Chapman owed me a load of money, that meant I couldn't pay anyone, the money from the Wilkes job would have enabled me to pay off some of the debt, but went wrong when the police shut the job down. I've given most of Tommy's money to Blunt to avoid bloodshed and I need to find a way to repay that, and to cap it all, I've now been handed another bag of cash which even if I give it straight back to Hamlet tomorrow will cost me fifteen percent on top for the privilege of just looking at it. Basically by my rough calculation that adds up to, more or less, a heap load of trouble I can't afford, squared.

'I'VE NEVER SEEN him like that before,' said Brennan after a couple of miles in silence. 'Who was she, girlfriend?'

'No, most definitely not.' Sally was more important than that, but I knew better than to gossip about Hamlet's private life, especially to the police – he might be Hamlet's man but it doesn't mean he's mine.

'Shit, she's not his daughter, is she?'

'No.'

We were back through the tunnel by now, back to the back-to-back houses, walls caked in grey traffic grime, the occasional all-night shop or petrol station lit up brightly against the gloom. I held my gaze out the window to let him know I wasn't in a chatty mood. He wouldn't hear it from me. If Hamlet wanted him to know he'd tell him, like he told me.

Way back, when we were close, at a long boozy lunch, holding court, he got a little maudlin and took the conversation in a peculiar turn. He talked about his son. During the 1989 Summer of Love, after seventy-two hours dancing in a field, he first came down and then came home to find his wife had gone, and the baby with her. *'She used my boy as a weapon, turned him against me.'* The boy Jonathan had grown up with the wife's family and a top-grade education paid for by a father they tried to forget. But aged 18 and with the promise of a car, a reconciliation between Jonathan and Hamlet was attempted

Jonathan took a shine to one of Hamlet's new barmaids, a pretty young thing called Sally, but a fortnight later after one paternal bust-up too many, Jonathan returned home in his new motor, the same one he would spread across a bridge support on the M3 a few years later. Sally, on the other hand, left her job and her college course suddenly, only to show up again eighteen months later looking for part-time work to fit around her childcare arrangements. Hamlet, adding two and two together and coming up with eleventy-seven, gave her a nice responsible job and protected her like his own blood. As far as he was concerned, Sophia was his granddaughter and Sally his family. Was she Jonathan's kiddie? I don't know, but Hamlet had decided she was and if that was good enough for him, it was good enough for everyone else. And now he's out for blood. Someone has attacked his family, and he wants retribution. How did I get stuck in the middle of all of this?

I asked PC Brennan to drive me to where I'd left the van, no point wasting money on a taxi tomorrow. It looked sad and abandoned in the corner of the otherwise empty car park, thankfully it didn't have a parking penalty stuck to the windscreen, so at least I can be grateful for one little win today. As I got out of the car Brennan called me back.

'Don't forget this,' he said, handing me the Peppa Pig tote bag, and then a brown envelope. 'And take this, you might find it useful.'

I took them both from him without speaking, opened the van door and tossed them on the passenger seat before buckling up and driving away.

-24-

I LAY BACK in bed watching the morning sunlight track across the ceiling, wondering what might have been. Everything had seemed so simple. Get the Wilkes job finished, get the money, pay Blunt, breathe out and relax. It had all been planned so nicely, but that plan was now more tits up than a nudist beach in July.

My phone, sat on the window sill, began to ring, forcing me to haul my tired carcass out of bed. I didn't recognise the number and let it ring off to voicemail. I looked out the window hoping to see Mr Skinner, and spotted him on a shed roof a few gardens over. He stretched out to his full length and rolled over to expose his tummy to the warmth from above. He looked content, lucky chap. The phone chimed the voicemail prompt. Mr Skinner wriggled against the rough surface of the shed's roof felt to ease an itch that simply couldn't be reached. 'I know just how you feel, mate,' I thought as the message began to play.

'*Hi, hello, Mark? It's Charlie. Just phoning to say hi. And wondering whether you've had the chance to look, did Tommy leave anything with you for me? Anything at all? Let me know. Oh, and purchase orders, all of them, don't forget, I'll pay you for them, all of them. Call me back, cheers.*'

He's becoming a nuisance I thought. I cut the call midway through him reciting his phone number, and I mentally filed it as one to ignore in future. I plugged the phone back on to the charging lead and then put it on the bedroom window sill beside my keys, loose change and the other pocket junk that had been dumped there when I got home late last night, including I noticed, Brennan's envelope. I'd forgotten all about that. '*You might find it useful.*' Those were his words. Feeling curious, I ripped it open and found a plain brown unmarked folder, nothing else.

I flicked through the folder's contents. The front sheet had handwritten at the head of it '*DeFreitas, Sally*' and then a list of documents. It looked as though Brennan had given me a copy of Sally's case notes. I wasn't comfortable about this, convinced I could get into a brand-new level of trouble if anyone caught me with it. I debated whether to rip it into shreds and then burn the pieces and then bury the ashes. The doorbell rang. I flipped the folder shut and slid it out of sight under the bed, next to the Peppa Pig tote bag already hidden there, and went to the door.

I OPENED THE door, and was taken aback. Perry. And adding to my genuine surprise she didn't look angry.

'Hello,' she said. 'Can I come in?'

I ushered her in, and followed her through to the kitchen.

'How have you been? I've not seen you for a couple of days, I looked out for you but you weren't home. Although, I later found out you were a little, err, busy yesterday afternoon,' her rising inflection on the end gave it a teasing tone from which I took I wasn't in trouble with her.

'That's one way of putting it I suppose. I'm guessing the police spoke with you.' She nodded. 'Thanks, I'd probably still be in there if you hadn't vouched for me.'

'That's right. You owe me. Big time!' she said, prodding me in the side; this was getting playful. 'So, I was thinking you could take me out for dinner to say thank you. All I've had to eat since getting here is hospital food, so how's about you show the new girl somewhere nice.'

This morning had suddenly changed for the better. 'Okay, sure, I'd love to,' I said. 'Tonight?'

'Tonight suits me fine, pick me up at seven?'

I agreed, we looked at each other and smiled, holding the moment long enough to mean something. She took a sip of the tea I'd passed her and noticed the mug. 'When did you go to Belgrade?' but before I could answer something outside caught her eye. 'You see that cat?' she said.

'Mr Skinner?'

'Yes. Wait. What? Never mind. That cat, who does it belong to?'

'Me, I suppose' I said.

'You, you suppose?'

'He just appeared in the garden one day.'

'Doesn't make him yours.'

'Agreed. But nobody stays long around here anymore, I didn't know if he got forgotten or maybe abandoned because they got told no cats by the landlord, or whether he just ran away one day and got lost.'

We both watched Mr Skinner as he hoisted his back leg perfectly straight up across his shoulder and behind his head making Perry chuckle. 'He looks like he's about to play the cello,' she said.

'You can tell he's been loved and cared for, but something's happened that's made him wary of people, something he can't recover from. Not yet anyway.'

'But how does that make him your cat then?'

'I don't know, maybe we recognised each other as kindred spirits. It wasn't long after my dad died. I was under a dark cloud feeling down and lonely. Then he appeared, this skinny sad little thing hiding from the rain near my bins.'

'Ah, two lost souls.'

'But anytime I tried to go near him, he'd run away. Poor little fella's terrified of hands, won't go anywhere near them. He's always kept his distance. I feed him every day, and he's beginning to trust me, he'll approach now, and he'll sit near me but it's always more than an arm's-length away.'

'Close enough for company, far enough for safety?'

'Exactly. But he will never ever come indoors, he simply doesn't trust people.'

'That's what I was going to tell you. I found him asleep on my sofa this morning. I came down and there he was, curled up fast asleep like he owned the place.'

'Mr Skinner? Never. Mr Skinner doesn't go indoors. It couldn't have been him.'

'It was, I promise. Look, let's see.' She opened up my back door and stepped outside on to the patio deck. 'Come on,' she gestured to me. I obeyed and followed her.

'Pusspusspuss,' said Perry, leaning forwards with her arm straight out before her, her thumb rubbing between her fingers.

Mr Skinner looked up from his ablutions to see what all the noise was about, saw the pretty lady billing and cooing and came bounding over to rub himself against her legs.

'No way. Surely not, Mr Skinner? Have you been messing with me?' I said, and reached forwards to stroke him. He recoiled behind Perry making himself small behind her legs.

'You don't like men do you darling?' said Perry to Mr Skinner. 'Were they bad to you? You don't need to be afraid of this one Mr Skinner, he's ok.'

'Looks like you've adopted a cat then. Enjoy your new owner Mr Skinner.'

'Why's he called Mr Skinner?'

'He had to be called something, every cat needs a name. No-one's ever come looking for him, or stuck a sign on a lamp post with his photo under a big red LOST, so I chose it.'

'But why Mr Skinner?'

'Because he looks like an old client I used to have.'

'Yeah? What was his name?'

'Mr ... oh, funny!' she was mocking me but I was enjoying the teasing.

'Right, things to do, I need to go. See you at seven. Are you coming with me Mr Skinner?'

-25-

I RETRIEVED THE folder from under the bed after Perry left. I had no alternative other than help Hamlet and I needed to get ahead of the pack, I couldn't afford not to. I looked at the contents again. A lot of it sounded pretty straightforward, titles such as Photos, Statements, SoCo Reports and the like, all pretty familiar from countless TV shows.

However, I was intrigued by a tab marked 'Third Party Legal Correspondence' and flicked to find a single document, the letterhead for Anderson Capel & Shale solicitors. The letter identified them as Hamlet's lawyers. I made a mental note to remember that name if Senia tried pulling me in again, if they're good enough for Hamlet then they must be good. From what I could gather it objected to Senia's plans to search Hamlet's club, using heavy legalese, *the police must not discriminate nor victimise*, but basically said any search would be opportunistic because Hamlet had been a person of long-time interest to the police. It set out that the only area appropriate to search was Sally's office and that nothing could be taken away that might have an adverse affect on Hamlet's business, including her computer. Credit where it's due; these lawyers were impressive.

I honestly didn't know what I was looking at, or what I was looking for. I'd deliberately avoided the section called 'Photos' as I didn't want to see Sally like that again, but all the documents, all the words, all the jargon, gave me a headache.

The phone began to ring. Saved by the bell, I put away the folder and hoped the distraction would clear my head.

I glanced at the caller display and inwardly sighed, it was Tommy's widow Jen. No doubt she wanted some sort of update. Guilt sent a shudder through me. On top of everything she had been forced to deal with she shouldn't need to chase me, I should have been in touch sooner. I'd been too focussed on my own problems. I resolved to do better, and I pressed to accept the call.

'Hello. Mark?' she sounded vague, wrapped up in a warm and fuzzy anti-depressant blanket.

'Hello Jen. How are you darling? Are you ok?'

'I'm getting through it, Mark, my mum's here and Karen's been great too.'

'That's good. So, what can I do for you Jen?'

'I'm just calling to see how things are going with Tommy's stuff.'

'Fine.'

'I knew I could rely on you.'

I thought it best not to mention that I'd given away all of her inheritance to save my own skin, unnecessarily as it turned out. Or that I'd been thrown out by Kate Fuller when trying to get paid his money, or that he still had three weeks money owed from me on the Wilkes job that I can't pay, or that I'd been accused of his murder, or that he'd been on the payroll of Medway's leading villain and I'd been dragged down into it in his wake, none of that seemed worth mentioning so I stuck with, 'It's all in hand, don't worry.'

'You are coming to the funeral on Tuesday aren't you Mark?'

'Of course I am.'

Silence. A bit more silence. I assumed she'd finished and I was about to gently end the call when she added, 'A man's been to the house Mark, I don't know him, I've never seen him before, Tommy never mentioned him, but he's been twice now and he was getting quite aggressive by the end of it. Luckily Karen was here.'

'Who is he? Did you get his name?'

'Charlie… something.'

'Quentin?'

'Yes, that's him, kept saying he was a friend of Tommy's. Tommy promised him something; he wouldn't believe me when I said I didn't know what he was talking about and when I said he should speak to you, that's when he kicked off saying all sorts of things about you, you can't be trusted, you want it – whatever *it* is – for yourself. It was horrible, Mark.'

'I know him,' I said. 'Leave him to me, he won't bother you again. I promise.'

'THINK,' I SAID to myself. 'Come on think.' I had no idea what Charlie Quentin wanted from Tommy. I hadn't found his name on any of Tommy's paperwork. What were you going to give him, Tommy.?

I listened to Charlie's voicemail message again '... *did Tommy leave anything with you for me? Anything at all? Let me know. Oh, and purchase orders, all of them, don't forget, I'll pay you for them, all of them.*'

No, I couldn't see it. My phone began buzzing like an angry wasp. I left it and it rang through to voicemail.

'*Mark, it's Michael Morlake,*' said the voice belonging to the surveyor from the Rochester job, '*I'm at the job, what's going on? Everything's hot pink, looks like a tart's knickers, you'd better get down here fast.*'

Hot pink? Uncle Bern!

-26-

I TRACKED DOWN Uncle Bern loafing at his mate's car lot. *'Genuine low mileage used vehicles'* fluttered the fluorescent green letters. *'Death traps are us'*, more likely I thought, carefully sidestepping a fragile-looking Vauxhall that was ready to split along the join.

I dragged Bern into the van, ignoring his complaints that he was watching the cricket on the telly and told him three times to stop fiddling with the radio as we sped across to Rochester. He ignored me, and by the time we got there, he'd found himself coverage of the Test Match.

There was no mistaking the property we were looking for. Every surface made me squint. It glowed like the neon sign in a kebab shop window. It looked as though someone couldn't decide whether to open a sweet shop or a sex shop so decided on both. This once proud, elegant building stood there big and robust, glossy and pink: like an enormous butt plug. I couldn't speak, I literally couldn't speak, I was struck dumb.

'Yeah, it looks shit doesn't it,' said Uncle Bern, chirpily throwing it out as conversation before turning his full attention to the radio commentary. I could only nod, I still hadn't found my voice. 'I thought it looked crap when they were doing it, but they seemed to know what they were doing.'

'You... you saw them doing this and you didn't stop it?' I said finally when the power of speech returned.

'Why would I stop them? It's what was wanted, you were very clear, paint it pink.'

'That's not what I said.'

'You did. Paint it pink, and no pigeon shit, that's what you said. Why? Someone got a problem with it?'

'You could say that, yes, someone's most definitely got a problem with it,' I replied, slowly opening the door.

Morlake was instantly recognisable, his hair shaved down to the bone – much like his prices. I'd met his kind many times before: never want to talk to you when things are going okay, go out of their way to avoid you when you need to talk to them about the extras, but when things go wrong they're harder to get off the phone than a lovestruck teenager. Whatever had happened here, one thing was certain, it was going to cost me. And now he'd seen me, it was time to face him. I knew I should have listened to Disco, he'd been right all along about Bern, bloody useless. Hindsight, eh?

I wished the pavement's thick yorkstone slabs could swallow me whole. Morlake approached. He probably had a dozen paces before he reached me, I needed to think fast if I was to talk my way out of this. I prayed for divine intervention.

'Poynter! I can see you!' a voice screamed, dripping with menace and anger. I looked around, saw no-one. 'Poynter, I want you.' It seemed to be coming from the sky, was this my moment, was I being summoned to meet my maker? If so, it must have been the angriest ever product recall.

'Wait right there, I'm coming down now,' the voice commanded.

I turned my eyes heavenward and saw him – Cookie – hanging off the top lift of the scaffold, his face red with rage – 'I want you Poynter. Don't move.'

Cookie started his descent. Guessing it would take him about sixty seconds to reach the ground, I ran like Billy Whizz with the shits, as quick as I could, shouting: 'I'll call you later, Michael!' to the bewildered surveyor from the window of the speeding van. I was out of there and gone before Cookie touched down.

My heart was pounding like a fucked train, I could feel it banging out its rhythm in my head, my breathing was rapid and shallow.

'New Zealand's just dropped another wicket,' said the oblivious Bern as I drove for safe cover.

HIDING UPSTAIRS IN my bedroom, thoughts of Cookie and extreme violence swirled through my head. To try to divert my restless imagination I picked up Brennan's file again. There was a briefing note giving a summary of events leading up to Sally's death. I noticed the author was my pal Nick Witham and it seemed pretty straightforward.

Sally was working at the club as normal; around two in the afternoon she told her employer she had been contacted by her childminder telling her that her daughter had been in a fall and she needed to come home immediately. Seeing as Hamlet was her 'employer' it was clear he had co-operated with the investigators, obviously the rules of strict silence are flexible when it comes to family. He told her to drop everything and go immediately, which she did, and CCTV images from the club's entry show her leaving at 14:12 clutching a small handbag.

Her body was found at approximately 17:30 by the childminder arriving at her house to drop off her daughter. When she couldn't get a response, she looked through the living room window, discovered Sally, and called 999. The conclusion was that the killer pretended to be the childminder to lure her home. It was a grim read to be honest.

The file confirmed her handbag had been found close beside her, and it listed the contents: a purse containing £22:61 in cash, four debit and credit cards, postage stamps, driving licence, receipts and a couple of photographs; the modestly described 'sanitary products'; chewing gum; mobile phone; house keys; car keys; keys to the club; hair brush; and, spectacles.

On the pages that followed were photographs of the individual items. I quickly flicked through them with little interest: two ten-pound notes and loose change, tampons, hair brush, Samsung phone with cracked screen and packets of Juicy Fruit. I couldn't see the point of taking photographs, and assumed it was a back-covering exercise in case the nearest and dearest ever accused the police of grave robbing.

I stopped on the last page of the document when I reached more text. It was a postscript note confirming that Sally's bank account had been checked and all associated cards were present, and that Hamlet had confirmed that all keys to the club were present and correct, so I guess they were considering whether the attack had been either opportunistic or related to Hamlet, and were satisfied it wasn't.

There wasn't a great deal else in the folder. Even to my untrained eyes it was clear the search had been very narrow, which I guess was good for Hamlet – his lawyers had earned their high fees, but it didn't help me at all.

-27-

I'D GOT US a table in a bistro I used to be fond of. I'd not been there for a couple of years after falling out of the dating habit.

'Do you know much of the area?'

'No, not really, I haven't gone much further than work and back,' said Perry. 'But I've heard Rochester's meant to be nice.'

'Yes, it's lovely, very historic, with the castle and the cathedral. It's always good to visit. I'll take you if you like,' I offered, reminding myself to give Uncle Bern's giant pink sex toy a wide berth.

'Sure, that'd be great,' she smiled. I was determined to relax and have a good time, put everything to one side for one night, enjoy myself for once. If those cheekbones and those eyes couldn't distract me from all the crap I'd been dealing with lately then I didn't deserve to be let out of the house any more.

'So, where's your family?' Perry raised a glass of red wine to her lips, peering over the top at me with a kitten's playfulness.

'I don't have any, just me now.'

'Really? That's sad.'

I've discovered people normally respond like that when I tell them. There's nowhere for me to go from there. If I say it's okay it feels flippant and disrespectful and I hate myself for it. If I tell the truth I pull everyone into my own personal black hole and I hate myself for it. So, I've found a shrug works best. I shrugged my response.

'Were you young?'

'We lost Mum when I was twelve. That was tough. And I lost Dad almost two years ago, that was tougher.'

'No brothers or sisters?'

'Pass. Move on.'

'O...kay.' She looked a little unsure, and I hoped to my core that he hadn't mucked things up for me again.

She dabbed at the corner of her mouth with the napkin, the smile had slipped from her eyes, 'Righty ho. So, your dad, was he an electrician too? What did he do?'

'He was a clown' I said, she laughed, her eyes restored their smile. 'Honestly.'

'No way.'

'True. Well, I say clown, probably children's entertainer would be better. He said it was what he always wanted to do.'

'Good for him.'

'Mum was furious, she couldn't believe it, blowing all his severance on it. I can still remember the day he told her. Uncle Chuckie, Uncle Chuckie, Uncle Fucking Chuckie, and my Mum never swore so I knew it was serious.'

Perry did that laugh that some women do when they hold a crooked finger below their nose as though they're trying to mask it. That was wrong, that smile was too good to be hidden.

'He was actually very good, he did magic tricks, played his banjo, sang silly songs, earned a pretty good living out of it.'

Which was true. He told me, this was before he got ill, he could do three parties on a Saturday, three on a Sunday and take home more than he'd ever earned slogging it out forty hours a week in the dockyard.

'Did you ever get involved? The glamorous magician's assistant?'

'I'd help out now and again, you know, load the car, help him set up, that kind of thing. He taught me a few tricks.'

'I bet you could show me a few tricks,' she said, laughing as she did. 'Hey, stop it, card tricks I meant,' she'd turned the teasing up to eleven.

'I'm sure Fuzzy Duck's somewhere at home, you want to meet Fuzzy Duck?'

She snorted, but it was charming, her finger shot to her nose again, she seemed surprised by her own snort and that set her off into a further fit of laughter.

'Yeah, Fuzzy Duck. He's a duck, obviously, and you choose a card then put it back in the deck, the deck goes in the contraption, and the boys and girls shout 'Best of luck Fuzzy Duck...' I gestured with raised eyebrows that audience participation was required at this point.

'Best of luck Fuzzy Duck,' my companion said through fits of laughter.

'And snap!' I shot out my hand towards her, pecking like a beak, causing her to jump back in her seat with a hoot of laughter. 'Is this your card Miss?'

'Six of hearts, amazing. How did you do that?' she said in mock wonder, playing along with the pantomime. She took a deep breath and fluttered her hands under her eyes to calm herself down.

'He was great. He absolutely loved being Uncle Chuckie. He did it right up until the end.'

She'd gotten her breathing back under control, and she leaned in close towards me. Without realising it I'd taken on a more reflective tone, as she was nodding the nod of sympathy.

'He died on the job, so to speak. He was running a bit late, had trouble finding the house, got there in the end, fully prepared, all in costume ready to go, rang the doorbell and then fell to the ground clutching his chest.' Perry sat up with a look of concern. 'The birthday girl's mother thought it was a gag. But another mother, who happened to be an off-duty nurse, realised he was having a massive heart attack and began giving him CPR. Eventually the ambulance arrived. They used the big pads to try and jump start him, but it was no use – and they electrocuted the two white doves in his jacket. My Dad died under a flurry of white feathers and the smell of barbecued poultry.'

It took a moment or two for her to understand what I'd done; to my relief she laughed and muttered that I was awful.

'Sorry, that was a joke, that didn't happen,' I said. Perhaps I'd got too comfortable, because without thinking I added, 'But I wish it did, it'd be better than the truth.'

I'd said too much, I muttered something to leave the table and disappeared to the Gents before she could see my eyes were moistening.

I RETURNED A few minutes later, hoping the previous happy high could be salvaged. She'd seen me weaving between the tables and her smile guided me back.

'Are you okay?' Again, I shrugged and nodded. 'Why do you feel you always have to make a joke about everything?' Oh man, how do I even begin to answer a question like that? 'I'm guessing Uncle Chuckie wasn't his real name, was it?'

'Eric'

'Okay, Eric, how did Eric really pass? Can you tell me, do you think?'

'Mesothelioma,' and immediately my eyes moistened again.

'Asbestos? He died from lung cancer?' Her voice had changed, gone was the giddy playful teasing, now she was using her professional voice, the care-giver's voice. 'Was it bad?'

'Ever seen a nice version?' I was wrong to snap, it wasn't her fault. 'Sorry.'

'No. No. Don't be silly,' she reached across to take my hand. 'And if you ever want it, I've got a waterproof shoulder you can borrow. Any time.'

WELL DONE ME, nothing gets the ladies into bed quicker than the slow painful death of a close relative. Way to go Numb Nuts! That had successfully dampened any heat that had been simmering during the evening. As we waited on the pavement for our cab, I tried to make small talk, but my attempts were clunky and awkward, and before I'd even realised it I'd resorted to pointing to the shops up and down the road.

'That one there, that used to be a piano shop when I was growing up. My Uncle Bern used to help out in there now and again giving demonstrations. I've no idea nowadays where you'd buy a piano round here, can't think of anywhere.' I was just gabbling by now. 'Pianos dot com maybe.'

Perry slipped her hand in mine. 'You're a strange one, Mark Poynter,' she said. 'But you're alright.'

'And that big red one,' my confidence was returning, I cast out the invitation to be teased. 'That was the furniture store. The old fella that ran it was a war hero, came back from Monte Cassino with a wooden leg, now it's the Cash X Changer...' I tailed off because I saw it; about a hundred metres away, on the other side of the zebra crossing, the silver Mondeo, the same one I'm sure.

'Oh, interesting.' the teasing had resumed, snapping my attention back to Perry. 'And Mr Electrician, do you have any electronics? We could make you some money, look.' She pointed across the road. 'We pay you for electronics, we pay you for phones, it says. So, got any we can sell?'

'No,' I said, but there was something about that, something odd but something familiar too. I cursed as I knew it would annoy me now until I could work it out.

Twenty minutes later I paid the cab driver and when I turned round, Perry was waiting, standing outside our side-by-side front doors.

'Thank you for a lovely night,' she said. 'Now, seeing as this is only a first date and I'm a nice girl – don't go believing what's written on toilet walls – I'm going to give you a kiss on the cheek. Goodnight. Maybe we can do something over the weekend?'

'Sure, I'd like that,' I said, watching the door close behind her.

-28-

I TWISTED THE lock open to my front door and stepped inside as giddy as a schoolboy with his first crush. It had been so long since I'd felt this way it was almost alien, but it excited me. I was coming home as King of the World.

'You took your bloody time.'

Instantly, the King had been deposed.

'Thought you were going to spend all night out there.'

Sitting in my armchair, one leg crossed over the other, empty bottle of beer beside him, never looking more comfortable, was Hamlet. Brazil was sitting on the sofa, eyes fixed to the television.

'I was worried you'd be bringing the tart home.' That word, that description, made me bristle. 'Ah, he's sweet on her, sorry mate, just banter. Anyway, the lads said you had no chance, so I lose.'

Lads? I looked around, as if on cue the toilet flushed, and out walked Dunlop who simply sauntered past as though he owned the place.

'Nah, no chance,' said Brazil, looking at me before turning his attention back to the screen.

'What's that, where did you get that from?' I said, realising he was watching porn on my tv.

'It's on telly,' he said without looking back.

'What? Pay per view? So, you mean that's going on my account then?'

'Yeah. Cheers, nice one mate.'

'No, not cheers, not nice one. How? What?' I was confused, I had so many questions it was difficult to get them all out at once.

'Marky,' said Hamlet as though trying to pacify a terrible-two tantrum. 'Marky, you've written your PIN number on the back of the remote, so you can't get all lemony if people then use it, can you? He's not doing any harm, and it keeps him quiet. He likes it, he watches it all the time.'

That might have been true but it didn't bring me any closer to understanding what was going on. I was just about to ask again when the doorbell rang.

'Bit late isn't it, Marky?' said Hamlet. 'Tell them to sling their hook, we're not buying anything.' And as the dumb muscle chuckled sycophantically at his quip, I answered the door.

Perry stood on the doorstep, beaming smile, 'I was thinking, look, well, I may have been a bit rude,' she said. 'No, not rude, but too quick. Well, you know what I mean. Anyway, I had a really nice time and wondered if you'd want a coffee, you can come over, or I'll come in, I don't mind.'

'I'd love to,' I said, and it crippled me to say it but, 'But I'm sorry, I've got company.'

'Company? We only got back a few minutes ago.'

'I know, I'm sorry, it's kind of complicated,' I said, and a chorus of laughter bellowed from the doorway behind me, no doubt caused by some joke at my expense again.

'Oh. I see. Okay. Forget it, it was a silly idea, I need to be up early in the morning anyway. Thanks once again for a nice night.'

I watched her disappear again, only when my door closed this time, I felt crushed.

BACK INSIDE, I saw Dunlop, and an icy chill ran through me.

'Put it down, give it back.'

I moved towards him, my arms outstretched. Dunlop sat down on the arm of the sofa, gripping Dad's banjo by the neck.

'Please,' I said, 'Just give it to me, don't break it, please,' this was beginning to feel like a hostage situation.

'I only want a quick strum,' said Dunlop

'No, please. Give it back.'

'Let him,' said Hamlet. 'Go on, give us a tune,' and Dunlop duly obliged.

To my relief he genuinely only wanted to play it. To my astonishment he was actually very good. His fingers moved nimbly over the strings and he, Hamlet and Brazil sang along together pretty well in unison, in the same way drunk rugby teams can surprise you with their harmonies, '*Your smile is like a breath of spring, your voice is soft like summer rain, And I cannot compete with you, Jolene.*' This was becoming one of the most surreal nights I'd ever had, particularly when they all gave themselves a round of applause at the end.

Dunlop then decided he'd done his warm-up and wanted to show off his skills. He launched into a song full of fancy finger picks and twiddly bits. The others couldn't have recognised it as they didn't sing but I knew it right away, '*...I watch the birds fly south across the autumn sky, and one by one they disappear...*' it was Dad's favourite. I never thought I'd hear it again from those strings. He didn't do a bad version, he even knew the words, '*...through autumn's golden gown we used to kick our way, you always loved this time of year...*'

Hamlet and Brazil seemed to be loving it and sat there enthralled, but it didn't feel right to me, it felt disrespectful, I felt guilty, unfaithful, '*...'Cause you're not here...*'

Dunlop finished to applause and cheers from Hamlet and Brazil. Before he could launch in to another I snatched the banjo from him in a fit of jealousy. It didn't seem enough merely to prop it back on its stand, I wanted it away from him. I snapped open the buckles of Dad's battered and scuffed case and with love and reverence laid it to rest.

'Did you see them too?' said Dunlop. I hadn't realised he was standing behind me, he leant over and picked up a flyer from inside the case. 'Eric 'n' Bernie. Ever see them?'

'That was my Dad, Eric, on banjo, and my Uncle Bern played the piano.'

'No way. Really. Are you winding me up? I saw them a few times at the Tap 'n' Tin, they were amazing. That's where I first heard an acoustic version of that song, that's what made me want to learn it.'

No, no, no. I didn't want this to happen, I didn't want to find myself liking him or having anything in common, so I ignored him and tried to get back to the point.

'What's going on, why are you here?'

'I wanted to see you,' said Hamlet.

'It's Friday night, don't you have a club to run?'

'Club's closed all weekend,' he said.

'We haven't got a manager any more,' added Dunlop.

'Closed out of respect,' said Hamlet, louder than before, annoyed by Dunlop's interruption.

'Yeah, show some respect,' said Brazil, smacking Dunlop sharply round the back of the head. Dunlop winced, so did I, it looked more forceful than a simple telling off. Hamlet didn't seem to notice, and continued, 'So, I thought I'd come and see you, see what you know, what you've found out for me.'

'Seriously? It's only been a day.' Hamlet didn't look happy, Brazil and Dunlop reared up like attack dogs. 'But I've had a few thoughts, a couple of possible avenues to explore.' This seemed to relax them a little.

'Look,' I said, trying to find a way to buy some time, 'The stuff your man gave me, there wasn't much there. I get the impression they didn't get a lot of help at the club.'

Hamlet smirked. 'No,' he said. 'My boys here, if there's one thing they're good at its getting in the way. They made sure Senia kept his nose stuck exactly where my lawyer had told him he could stick it.'

'I think maybe they missed something. Can I get back inside? You know, now I'm under observation?'

'Sure, I'll get someone to call you tomorrow, make it all official.'

'Come to think of it, if I'm being watched, how did you even get in?'

'Oh, didn't anyone tell you, you aren't being watched anymore. Senia couldn't get the budget for it,' Hamlet yawned as he spoke. 'This is Austerity Britain Marky, don't you read the papers? Budget cuts galore. They can't afford the overtime to play gooseberry on your nights out with lady-friends. It's shocking these cuts in public services it really is.'

I thought about the silver Mondeo and maybe I looked unconvinced as he then added, 'Marky Mark, relax, the police aren't watching you, trust me, I get their shift rotas before most of them do. So, if you've nothing else to tell me, just make us a nice cup of tea and then we'll bid you so long, farewell, auf wiedersehen, goodbye. Put the kettle on.'

Dunlop sprung to his feet and headed out to the kitchen, from where I heard the slamming of drawers and doors. Before he woke up the entire street, I went and got out the mugs, teabags and spoons for him.

'Look,' I said as I sat down again, 'I need you to be honest with me.'

Hamlet pulled a funny face to make Brazil laugh, but realising I was serious he dismissed Brazil with a flick of the head in the direction of the kitchen.

'Just for my own peace of mind, Tommy was working for you, yes? Is it done, over, there's nothing going to come back? I'm thinking of his wife, so she can move on smoothly.'

'You know he'd been doing bits and pieces for me,' said Hamlet. I didn't respond but I could feel my face burning. 'You didn't know? Marky Mark, I thought you two were close.'

I didn't reply and tried to fight back the embarrassment.

'What was he doing?' I asked eventually.

'You really want to know? You realise this puts you back in the circle of trust? I know you've been trying to get away from all of it, put it behind you, and I respect that Mark I really do. So, are you sure, do you really want to know?' I nodded. 'Okay then, Tommy worked for me as a cleaner. You know what that means? Well, some of my business gets a little messy. He was paid to come in afterwards and clean up, and I have to say he'd do a lovely job, full redecorations, he'd make the place look like a show home, you'd never know.'

'Are you talking murders?'

'Murders?' He found this amusing. After his hollow false laughter faded: 'What do you think this is, Chicago 1920? Who am I, Bugsy Malone?'

'Well what then?' Apprehension: now I wasn't so sure I wanted to know.

'Do you know how hard it is to make an honest living these days? There's no money in porn any more since the internet started giving it away for free. The Russians now run the whoring racket and everyone knows you don't want to get into a fight with them. As for drugs, that's a young man's game these days. So, I've had to branch out: dog fighting. Not very nice, in fact it's bloody disgusting truth be told. I can't watch it myself. But it's cheap to stage and earns a huge amount of money. I've got a speccy twat from the college who sets up the video coverage, it's as clear as being there, different camera angles, the works. It's like watching *Match Of The Day*, it's that professional. And I've got them paying fortunes to log in and watch it live from all over the world, it's exceptionally popular in China, who'd have thought it, eh? And

I've got me a kid out in India putting together a portal, they call it, so that very soon they'll be able to bet on-line on live fights. It's becoming colossal. And that's because I give them the full HD 4K crystal-clear experience. In the past it was all done on grotty building sites, or in shitty car parks, but my fights are indoors, multimedia. Trouble is it's very messy, all that blood and piss, and that's only the punters. So that's where Tommy came in. He'd clean up, tosh new paint on the walls and no-one would ever know. In fact, he was doing such an impressive job, it'd got to the stage where I was getting the venues for free on the promise of a full redec afterwards. And he was very well paid for his efforts.'

Things certainly made a lot more sense now, and probably also explained why he never spoke about it. I felt reassured for Jen now; Hamlet was a satisfied customer who'd paid his bills, it didn't sound as though there'd be any comeback on her and she could keep the money. If I could get it back that is.

'Any idea what he planned to do with the cash you were paying him?'

'Don't know, don't care.'

'I think he fancied becoming a property developer,' said Dunlop. We both turned to see him in the doorway holding a tray laden with mugs, slowly shuffling his way towards us.

'Go on.'

'Last time I saw him, I asked him what he was going to do with all the cash he was earning – maybe a new car, just trying to make conversation, you know.'

'And?'

'He said he'd got in with someone in property who was helping him out.'

'Who? How?'

'I don't know. He said the property guy was helping him to get his accounts in order, I figured he wanted a good set of books so as to expand. He never told me the guy's name though.'

Dunlop handed out the mugs, Hamlet told Brazil to switch off his porn, and then we all sat quietly in front of the tv watching the highlights of the night's earlier Chelsea match. I imagine should anyone have peered through the window they'd have found it a cosy sight. If only they'd known. It's hard to relax sitting next to Hamlet, it's like being beside a mildly annoyed grizzly bear in a suicide vest, you're terrified the slightest thing might set it off. Luckily, Chelsea won and Hamlet left happy.

-29-

PARANOIA. HAMLET SWORE there was no surveillance on me, but I was convinced the same silver Mondeo was following me again. Was he wrong? I'd spent so much time checking my mirror, I'd nearly gone in to the back of two cars this morning. I think I'd lost it. I couldn't see him, but to err on the cautious side, I deliberately parked some distance away and approached the rest of the way on foot unnoticed. Almost there, not much further. I moved behind and around the parked cars, keeping low, just in case.

I reached my target without being seen, a couple of deep breaths, straighten up, shoulders back, chest out, ready.

As I rounded the front of the container Old John recognised me and turned in the opposite direction but found Disco blocking his way.

'Morning lads, what brings you here then?' said Old John, trying to bluff his way out of it.

'See this,' I pointed to my face. 'Five hours in A&E. Two days off work. You owe me John.'

'What? I don't know what you're.... your face... ooh, nasty... what happened there?'

'Don't lie to me John, I know it was you.'

Old John seemed about to speak, his mouth flapped but nothing came out. Then he surprised us by dropping into his white garden chair and burying his head in his hands. As we looked at each other across the top of Old John's bald patch, I swear I heard a low chuckle coming from him.

'What do we do now?' asked Disco.

DURING A SLEEPLESS night I'd mulled over every possible permutation, looking for a way out of the mess I was in. I'd even considered buying back Dad's act and doing some children's parties. I'd heard the guy that bought it off me was desperate to offload it due to a 'personal setback' — he'd been caught by the birthday boy's dad scuttling the birthday boy's mum over the chest freezer in full Uncle Chuckie clown costume complete with spinning bow tie and squeaky red nose. Honky honky.

Needless to say, the birthday boy was traumatised at the sight of his irate father kicking the shit out of Uncle Chuckie up and down the front garden. And so I gave that idea up as a non-starter seeing as Uncle Chuckie's name is now verboten amongst parents. In the dark, I silently prayed that I'd hear from Mrs Wilkes soon to say that her job's been released and I can get back in and collect my money for it. But I kept coming back to the point that most of Tommy's money had paid off Blunt and Hamlet's money was the only way to replace it. Whatever way I looked at it, I owed someone somewhere a lot of money, and with Chapman's death changing 'unlikely to be paid' to 'definitely won't be paid' there was no quick fix, no windfall. And all the time Senia was circling, desperate to set me up for Tommy's murder. I couldn't see any alternative, I had to help Hamlet and hope he stayed true to his word to waive the debt, while at the same time find a way to keep myself out prison.

Having reached that conclusion, I finally found sleep. Inspiration had come to me overnight because when I woke up it was fully formed in my head, and I knew it needed two of us to make it work. I called Disco right away. He discharged a volley of incredibly complicated profanity at being woken up so early, and put the phone down before I could even say a word, so I called his house-phone and asked his Mum to have him up and dressed within the hour, and here we are.

OLD JOHN LOOKED up at Disco and me, gone was the cute cartoon caterpillar face, replaced by a snarling lip curling to meet red-veined eyes.

'You fucking bastard twats!' he said, slowly rising from his chair. No more the sloping shoulders and old man stoop. He'd unrolled himself from his docile, senior cocoon and had emerged a vicious predator. Disco and I hadn't expected this, and I realised that by instinct we'd taken a couple of steps back.

'This is mine,' Old John swung out a long gangly arm making Disco flinch as the knobbly knuckles swept past, 'and I'm not having little pricks like you or your pisstaking mate come here thinking they can take it off me.'

Flecks of white foam flew from the corner of his mouth on the popping P sounds, pisstaking, that could only mean Tommy, so John had seen him here after all.

John dropped his arm to his side. His spine no longer shot up straight like a piston and began to sag slightly from the vertical. Getting angry, it seems, is still a young man's game. Feeling the heat had subsided I stepped forwards. Disco followed my lead and edged closer. John saw this as a threat and reared up again, arms outstretched both sides marking out his exclusion zone, prepared to repel anyone that breached it.

'Look at my face John. You did this.' I leaned in to him, never breaking eye contact as I shouted my words.

'Says who?'

'"I've got witnesses,' I lied. 'Remember the mini cab driver?' Judging by how his stance suddenly dropped, I had him doubting himself.

'You were very territorial when we saw you here before John,' I said, trying to speak calmly. 'You kept saying you didn't want Tommy here, that this is your job.' He gave a weak nod. 'And then I get a kicking to the tune of *'you can't have what belongs to me'*, it doesn't take a genius to work out who gave me it does it?'

Old John stared, his nostril flaring, his lip flickering with the start of a snarl, and then with a speed no-one would have expected he lunged at me. By some freak of nature he may have retained the reflexes of a young man, but he still had at least thirty years on me and it didn't take much effort to push him off. He stumbled backwards, tripped, and was caught by Disco as he started to fall. Old John wriggled and twisted, a caught fish trying to break free, but Disco gripped him tight until he'd worn himself out.

'Have you quite finished, John?' I got up close, almost nose to nose. He writhed in Disco's bearhug, but after only a few seconds gave up. Disco directed him towards his chair, and he flopped defeated into it.

'Okay John, you're going to explain exactly what is going on?' I said.

Old John took a deep breath, looked around, and then began, 'This is a sweet little number, nice easy work, I'm nothing but a glorified caretaker really keeping things clean and tidy, I figured there's enough here to keep me busy until retirement and no need to go out chasing every lead, just keep my head down and get on with it. The last thing I want is someone else coming in, pushing me out. I thought that was what his meetings were about. Not that it matters now I suppose.'

'Meaning?'

'They're selling this place to a national chain, one of the big boys.'

'Yeah, that's what I heard too,' said Disco, hoiking up his saggy-arsed track pants. He had rolled two cigarettes and handed one to

Old John, who gratefully lit it from Disco's shared match, inhaled a lungful and then spoke.

'What they're saying's everyone's going to do nicely out of it. The Quentins offload it for a truckload of cash straight into their trust funds. The manager's been offered a seat on the board by the new firm. And the staff have been offered better pension rights. Everyone's doing well out of it, except me. I'm out.'

'Explain?'

'These national firms have frameworks in place for their maintenance, they don't use little one-man-bands like me. So as soon as the takeover happens at the end of the month I'm finished.'

He muttered some self-pitying nonsense that was barely audible, and then stared appreciatively at the roll-up between his fingers.

'What I want from you John, as a way to make amends, is for you to tell me what Tommy was doing here?'

'Nothing. He's never worked here in all the while I've been here.'

'You're starting to annoy me now, John, so if you don't want to feel my boot up your arse as payback, don't give me any more lies. He's got a bundle of paperwork from this place – orders, instructions, payment slips, the full works. You saw it, I showed it to you.'

'I'm telling you, he did absolutely nothing.'

'He's never been here?'

'He'd been here two or three times, yes. But he's never done any work here.' He could tell that I was confused and starting to get frustrated so he quickly continued without prompting, 'After the second time, I spoke to him and asked if he was visiting family here, he said no he had a meeting but didn't say anything else, he couldn't have been here longer than ten minutes. I don't know what he was doing, honest.'

He lifted off his glasses, instantly making his big round cartoon caterpillar eyes shrink back to normal size, and he wiped his lenses on a loose fold of his shirt. Disco meanwhile had got bored and wandered off, he'd found someone to have a smoke with, a skinny old man in a way-too-big dressing gown. They were sat on a garden bench merrily chatting away like old friends.

'So, tell me about Charlie Quentin.' My patience with Old John was running out. 'Why *was* Tommy meeting him?'

'I never said anything about Charlie Quentin,' said Old John, but he hadn't needed to. I'd managed to square off that piece of the puzzle myself. I'd been told Tommy had a friend in property helping him out: Charlie Quentin came from a property investment family, he was desperate for something Tommy had promised him, and Old John had confirmed Tommy had been coming here. It had to be Charlie Quentin who was helping Tommy with his plan.

'I don't know anything about Charlie,' said Old John.

'Don't give me that, you're giving me the hump now, John. You know something about everyone, that's what you do, you're a gossipy old woman, now I can either call Disco back to give you a slap or you can talk to me.'

I stepped towards him and he cowered. 'Okay, okay. Charlie, yes, they met. I saw them twice together, they came out and sat in his van, ten minutes later Charlie would get out and go back inside. I've no idea what they were up to.'

'And what do you know about him?'

'Charlie?'

'What was the big property deal he was advising Tommy on?'

'Property deal? Charlie? I don't think so.' He gave an involuntary laugh, 'Charlie doesn't know the first thing about property, or business. He's nothing but a spoilt, bored, rich kid.'

Old John directed his eyes towards the building, I followed and could see Charlie yawning in the office suite. He was here, good, I wanted to talk to him once I'd finished with Old John.

'His dad got fed up with him loafing about all day, mooching off the family money, said he wanted him to learn the business, so sent him here. Gave him "executive" powers to make him feel important, but as far as I can tell it's no more than being in charge of the company cheque book, making the tea and filling the photocopier.'

What he was saying was striking a chord with me. When I met him in his office that day, he seemed surplus to requirements, a nice guy but pointless.

'So, Kate Fuller?'

'Kate's the brains, she runs the place, makes all the decisions, works around Charlie rather than with Charlie, if you know what I mean,' he said. 'From what I hear from the staff here she's the one that's put this whole takeover deal together. You know me, speak as I find, she's not an easy person to like, she's rubbed a lot of people up the wrong way with her attitude, but hats off to her, she's done well to put this all together.'

'But Charlie?'

'Tell you the truth, I think she prefers it when Charlie's out the way, so she ignores him and leaves him to it.'

'To what?'

'Champagne Charlie. I heard all he'd do, on the days he actually turns up, is organise parties. Big lavish parties for other rich kids. He'd have the copiers churning out hundreds of invitations, probably what he's doing now, no other reason he'd be in on a Saturday morning. And then he'll spend the rest of the day on the phone taking orders and arranging supplies, special supplies, you know?'

I had a vague idea what Old John was hinting at but kept my silence, let him come to me, I thought, rather than ask too many questions. His character study married up entirely with my first impression of Charlie but I still couldn't understand where Tommy fitted into all of this though, it's not as though he hung out with the rich and famous.

'Supplies, you know, cocaine, ecstasy all of that. Apparently, he used to be a proper out of control cokehead. One of the nurses here, she used to work at a private clinic, says she recognised him from when he was there doing rehab. That's another reason his dad stuck him here in God's waiting room, you couldn't find anywhere less debauched.'

Disco, I noticed, had now been joined on his bench by the receptionist that had been so snooty to me last time, what was her name again, Helen, was that it? And Old John seemed comfortable. He'd gone from fighting for his life to quite relaxed enjoying a good gossip and gripe. He was getting quite loose-lipped so I thought it best to keep relaxed, he seemed to respond better to it than threats.

'His dad,' said Old John, 'and speak as I find, I rather admire him, I mean what father doesn't want their boy safe, healthy and earning an honest living. The Quentins are worth more than you can ever imagine, but he's made him clean himself up, get a job and he's paying him a proper salary that he has to work for. You've got to admire him for that.'

Old John wittered on but I'd stopped listening. The final pieces had clicked into place, I think I knew what was going on between Tommy and Charlie, but only one way to find out. 'Bye John.'

Disco and Helen were still deep in conversation, looked like it was going well between them: a derelict, semi-alcoholic chippie and a frosty, uptight receptionist, but then they do say opposites attract. Disco's flirtation was the perfect distraction for what I wanted. I picked a route around the perimeter of the grounds, entering the building through a side door and with the reception unguarded I quickly followed the corridors I'd walked before, back to the office suite. To say Charlie was surprised to see me is an understatement.

As he got off the floor and back into his seat, I closed the door behind me so we could talk in private.

TWENTY MINUTES LATER, walking at a brisk pace, quicker than normal, but not so quick it'd draw attention, I left the building. Disco was still on the bench with his companion. I tapped him on the shoulder and without breaking stride said, 'Come on we're leaving.'

He took too long saying his fond farewells – I was in the van, engine on and ready to go by the time he got in, and I pulled away whilst he was still getting comfortable and buckling his seat belt.

'What's the rush?' he said, then suddenly guessing I'd been inside the building. 'Oh no, don't say you've done something stupid?'

'No. I've found out what Tommy was up to with Charlie, it makes sense now.'

-30-

FOR DAYS THAT slogan in the Cash X Changers window bugged me, *We pay you for electronics*. I couldn't think why, but then... of course, Charlie's voicemail, *I'll pay you for them*. It was the same phrasing. But he'd been talking about Tommy's invoices against the purchase orders, and that's why the phrasing sounded so awkward and clunky – you pay an invoice, but you don't pay *for* an invoice. Adding the word *'for'* makes it sound as though you are buying the invoice. And from my chat with Charlie, that's exactly what he'd meant.

Coming at him unexpected put Charlie on the back foot. I started the conversation with the fact that I knew he'd been badmouthing me to Jen, and that had frightened him into thinking that he was about to be beaten black and blue. I asked him questions. He held nothing back.

Charlie resented being made to work by his father, it got in the way of his social life, but more significantly to Charlie, it came nowhere close to being able to fund his social life, and Charlie I've found has no intention of scaling back. Charlie's solution was to do a little dealing of what he euphemistically called 'party favours' amongst his friends and associates. The trouble was, his boring nine-to-five doesn't pay enough to bulk buy his wares. You'd think that wouldn't be a problem, the Quentin family is exceptionally wealthy and Charlie has a trust fund. However, the reason why the family has remained so wealthy is because it's not stupid: there's processes in place to stop its younger members spending it all on, say, enough cocaine to stun a dozen donkeys. In short, Charlie is worth a lot of money but it's very difficult for him to get his hands on any of it – and that's where Tommy came in.

Charlie had quickly mastered his job, which wasn't hard seeing as Kate Fuller had removed any responsibility from it as successfully as she'd eviscerated the poor sap on the other end of the phone that time. The only role he had was the keeper and sole signatory of the cheque book, a largely ceremonial role seeing as practically every transaction is done electronically, controlled by Kate Fuller.

Now, by chance, Charlie and Tommy had a mutual friend, a certain Rob Beach. He was the matchmaker, introducing them to a partnership made in heaven. Tommy had a bundle of dirty cash he wanted to launder. Charlie had the means to legitimise it.

Charlie basically bought Tommy's cash from him. Say Tommy had two grand of Hamlet's dirty cash. Charlie would raise a purchase order to Tommy for a non-existent piece of work at Queen Mary's to the value of two thousand pounds. Tommy then submitted an invoice to correspond with the purchase order, hand over the cash, and receive a clean corporate cheque in return, et voilà, Charlie has his pocket money to spend, the fiddle is lost within Quentin Property Holdings records behind a full paper audit trail and Tommy has a clean transaction in his books.

All in all, a tidy, clever little scam, not bad for a bone idle rich-kid slacker. The only trouble is, like all good things, it'll come to an end when the business is sold. I guess that's why he was so persistent with me and Jen. He wanted to try and get as much cash as he could before the sale goes through.

Disco listened to all of this in rapt silence. I think he understood most of it. After letting it sink in, he asked, 'So how does this Rob Beach fit into it again?'

'Mutual friend, that's what Charlie said. We know he's married to someone working there, so he must have got to know Charlie, and he would have known Tommy from years back because they were both into the clubbing scene.'

'Fair enough,' said Disco, then after a thoughtful scratch added, 'But how would he know about Charlie needing cash and Tommy having too much? Also, does this get us any closer to finding out who killed him?'

Those questions hadn't even occurred to me and I certainly didn't have any answers, so I turned up the radio and ignored him and all his conspiracy theories until we got back to the Golden Lamb.

-31-

THE GOLDEN LAMB was busy for a Saturday lunchtime, and Disco was welcomed home to a chorus of cheers. I was getting progressively bored chatting to a data cabler I knew loosely and was relieved to feel a tap on my shoulder from the very last person I was expecting to see.

'I was hoping to find you in here,' said Nick Witham. Despite him joining the Rozzers, he was alright. Nick was, at heart, still the same shit-for-brains, good-natured idiot he was at school and I was pleased to see him.

I ordered him a drink and a fresh one for myself because I knew Mr Data Cables wasn't going to offer. They're all the same, they all think they're a grade above your humble electrician, they all want to tell you how big their job is and how much they're earning, but do they ever buy you a drink when they're telling you all this? Of course not. He was a tedious prick anyway, so with beers in hand I motioned Nick towards a nearby table, and left him where he stood without even a goodbye.

'Cheers! Nice to see you Nick, don't often see you in here.'

'No, I know. And I'm not stopping, I'm meeting Spencer, he says hello by the way.'

'Hello back, how is he, alright? Got any more tattoos?'

'Has he? I should say so, he's just had this oriental looking thing all down his leg, it's huge. Looks good though. Mum hates it.'

'So, what, is Spencer totally covered in tattoos now?'

'Yeah, more or less' Nick laughed, 'But none on his hands, neck or face. He's paranoid about work and being in uniform. Worried about it affecting his career prospects.'

'But I've seen plenty of them in uniform covered in tattoos and piercings.'

'I know, I know. But you never know with these supermarkets, always changing policies. He's deputy manager now, so I guess he doesn't want to take the risk.'

'Fair enough,' I replied, 'Cheers Nick.'

He took a noisy slurp, 'I wasn't even going to have a pint, I only wanted a quick word. Still, be rude not to wouldn't it.'

He was a big daft bastard, he really was. When we were at school Nick was string-bean thin with a mop of shaggy black curls and sticky-out teeth. Now he's a heavy lump with a baldy head and sticky-out ears, but somehow still looks exactly the same with that big daft bastard face.

'I only wanted to let you know about Chapman,' he said. The surprise mention of the name felt like ice water dripping down my spine.

'Chapman? What about him?' I hoped my reply sounded disinterested enough.

'The Coroner came back. Said he died of natural causes two or possibly three days before he was found. He was grossly overweight, suffered a massive heart attack. We think a burglar broke in on the off-chance, saw him and fled in panic.'

A couple of familiar faces entered from the street, I looked up to give a wave and a hello as they passed to keep up appearances. No need for the world to know my business. I may have lost a day in the cells, convinced that if the key hadn't yet been thrown away it had certainly been mislaid at the bottom of a distant, forgotten drawer, but as far as they're concerned it's all an adventure, a jape, a funny anecdote. You don't mention your guts still ache from heaving up sour yellow bile in fear, or your eyes still sting after seeing your past, present and future all crash together like a derailed train, you just wave and smile and pretend all's right with the world.

'So, in short, your alibi checked out fine, there's nothing to link you with the scene. It's being written up that Mr Chapman died from natural causes. Senia doesn't want to tell you yet, but you know me Mark, I don't think it's fair letting you dangle, not when you're off the hook. But, let's be crystal clear, you didn't hear it from me.'

'Sure, thanks Nick. So, how is Mr Senia settling in to Medway life?'

'I don't think he can make it out. He says it's too far out to be London, and too far in to be Country.'

He was right, Medway's a peculiar little hybrid all of its own, adopting customs and expressions from near and far, has been for centuries, ever since the dockyard opened its gates and ships started arriving from all over the four corners of the globe. Bit of a mongrel race, that's us. I realised it was good to see Nick again and we spent the remainder of our pints talking about old times like normal people do.

'NICK...' HE WAS putting his jacket on, ready on to leave. 'Do you remember Rob Beach? Do you know what ever happened to him?'

'Rob Beach, now there's a blast from the past. Funnily enough I'd not heard his name mentioned for years and years, and now that's the second time I've heard it this week.'

The friendly conversation and lunchtime drinking had loosened him up, he was now on the verge of telling me things he probably shouldn't. By the look on his face he realised this seconds after me, as he quickly fumbled with his jacket, suddenly in a hurry to leave. I placed a gentle hand on his forearm to encourage him to calm down and assure him I wouldn't deliberately put him in a predicament. He looked around to see who was nearby, then sat back down and leaned inwards. I copied him, two conspirators together.

'Rob Beach was a dirty little peddler back in the day selling all kinds of shit, and I mean proper nasty shit, cut with all sorts of stuff, to just about anyone. Even schoolkids. He was filth. Rumour had it he had a falling out with Hamlet.'

'That's right, I remember.'

'Then he vanished off the scene for several years.'

'Banged up?'

'No, other than a couple of motoring offences he's got a clean record. He moved away, that's all. Anyway, he came back here about two years ago.'

'Don't tell me, he's a reformed character, a family man.'

Nick gave a sideways smile. 'Not quite.' He looked over his hunched shoulders at the room again then back to me. 'I shouldn't be telling you this, but we think he's still dealing, but it's such small-fry stuff it's not been worth wasting the manpower to chase it down.'

Across the room I could see Disco giving Boris The Plastic a big wet kiss on the top of his wrinkly bald walnut of a head. I'm guessing he'd just been paid, so that meant Disco would be in here for the rest of the day drinking through his wages. Disco saw me looking at him and did the internationally recognised 'Pint?' gesture to Nick and me. I nodded gratefully on behalf of both of us.

After a half-hearted resistance Nick began his next pint and continued talking about Beach.

'He's not important. From what I gather he fancies himself as a bit of a boutique.'

Now that was a new term on me and I told him so.

'What I mean,' said Nick, 'is that he now only has a few choice clients. He's going for quality over quantity, he's given up on that crap mixed with curry powder and brick dust and now supplies premium grade stuff to spoilt rich kids who like the personal service.'

Against much insistence and despite hesitation on his part, Nick left after his third pint. It had been good to see him and thanks to him I was even more confident now that I was right about who Charlie's mutual friend supplying the 'party favours' was. I decided to leave at the same time but it took me a while to get out as there were so many familiar faces to say hello to. Disco caught up with me at the back door and bundled me through before I could realise what he was doing.

'Cookie's after you,' he said, using being outside as an opportunity to light up a smoke, a proper one, not a roll-up, so clearly he had been paid if he's splashing out on branded cigarettes. I told him: 'Calm down, I've no problem with Cookie.'

'That's what I said to Boris.' Disco looked very agitated. 'But he said Cookie was in here today looking very angry, we missed him by about half an hour.'

'It's probably nothing,' I said knowing exactly what it was and it was so far from nothing you could barely see nothing without a telescope, nothing was a dot way, way back on the horizon. I wished him a happy weekend overflowing with hops and barley.

Heading home, I didn't give Tommy, Champagne Charlie and Rob Beach a second thought, I was more concerned about Cookie.

-32-

I WAS MOTHER.

'Thanks,' said Perry. I'd poured her enough tea. She mixed in a dash of milk and then whilst leaving it to stand, broke off the corner of a biscuit.

I sat back in my seat, but found everything a little uncomfortable and cold – the chair, the coffee shop, the atmosphere. It had been decorated art deco style: glossy tiled walls, marble table-tops and straight high-backed chairs in black tubular steel. The only way I could sit comfortably was leaning forwards, elbows on the table. Mum would have been appalled. We'd beaten the lunchtime crowd, although it was now beginning to fill up.

Perry was polite, pleasant company but that was all. The spark from Friday night was missing. It had taken a lot of charm and persuasion to get her to come out, and I genuinely thought the historic beauties of Rochester High Street would be a sure-fire winner. We'd spent a couple of hours wandering around the Castle garden, around the Cathedral, and up and down the red bricked High Street and when I suggested stopping for a drink and bite to eat before heading home Perry chose this place because it was an independent. Being too eager to please I agreed, but my aching back was beginning to regret it.

Small talk felt like hard work. Before too long we had stopped speaking and sat there smiling fake smiles. I couldn't think of anything new to say and my mind started drifting. I didn't like this place – white glazed brick tiles with a black band course screamed public toilet to me rather than roaring twenties. Black-and-white prints of Rochester landmarks in identical black frames were fixed to the walls symmetrically, although the fourth one along was pissed and stood misaligned, not by much, but enough to notice if you were trying to pass the time waiting for the other person to speak.

The low midday sun coming through the front windows cast shadows across the ceiling making the skips in the plaster stand out. They hadn't trowelled it firmly enough, the trowel's meant to glide smoothly in long strokes but if it's held too flat to the ceiling it can drag, leading to marks like those. Mind you the decorator's equally at fault for not fine filling and smoothing it out when he painted it. Putting it all together – the misaligned picture frame, the shaky plaster and the poor decoration – it said DIY to me, the guy buttering the baguettes is probably the same guy who grouted the tiles. Thinking Tommy would have got that ceiling as smooth as glass, it took me a few seconds to notice Perry speaking to me.

'I like you Mark, you're a nice guy, but what's going on with you? It's all a bit too…'

'Complicated?' I said, pre-empting what she was struggling to say.

'I was going to say weird, but complicated will do.'

'It's work stuff, but yeah, it's all a bit weird.'

'Really? All this with the police? How can that be work?'

'It just is,' I said, and it was true, all I wanted to do was earn a living yet somehow, I'm up to my neck in everyone else's problems.

From the way she reached for her teacup and sat sideways on from me I could tell Perry wasn't convinced.

'Look, the other night, I'd had a drink and I got jumped. I can't be the first mugging victim you've ever seen surely?' She slowly shook her head as if carefully considering this thought. 'And the murders, that's the police clutching at straws. Tommy was my friend and Sally, as well as being someone I'd done some work for recently is – was – family, of sorts, distantly. The police have pounced upon the fact that I knew them both and tried to fit me up for an easy result, but as soon as they actually looked into it seriously that all fell apart. Hopefully they'll now start doing their job properly.'

She relaxed a little, and turned herself back towards me. I took this as a good sign.

'Forget about all of that stuff, it's noise, don't worry about it, I'm not,' I lied. 'It'll all work itself out in the end.'

Perry reached across the table and placed her hand over mine. 'Okay,' she said. 'Okay. Let's go home.'

PERRY HAD MADE a point of telling me on the drive home she had some studying she needed to do when she got back. I took that to be a diplomatic way of kicking me into touch, so when I say I was pleasantly surprised I actually mean I was astounded when she suggested getting together later in the evening. Naturally I agreed. She offered to bring the pizza and the wine if I sorted out a movie – sounded a good deal to me.

Mr Skinner had been asleep under a nearby tree, but bounded up the path to greet his new lady as we approached. Perry tiptoed up and planted a kiss on my cheek then said goodbye. I watched them both disappear inside the house, feeling the warm sensation on my cheek linger long after they'd gone. I was happy.

THINKING THINGS HAD gone far better than expected I sat in front of the television and started to drowse, only to be prodded back to life by my ringing phone.

'Mark, it's Cookie, are you home?'

I confirmed I most definitely was not.

'I know you are, I'll be there in five minutes.'

THREE AND A half minutes later my window exploded inwards and a tsunami of glass splinters rained down on me. A steel scaffold clip embedded itself in my sofa. Cookie's angry face rose up through the window frame.

'Outside. Now.'

Stunned, I rose, shaking the glass from my hair, hearing it crunch beneath me. The sudden jolt of adrenaline meant I didn't register it slicing into my bare feet. Outside waited the Cookie crew: Neil Cook and three of his scaffolding gang. None of them looked happy, but neither was I. The confusion had worn off, replaced by other emotions. My hands were shaking and the rage was erupting through me.

'Cookie. What…You could have killed me!'

'You're lucky they're here,' he said. 'I was going throw it straight at you.'

'But… why? What?'

'I want paying. You've paid the Blunts, I want mine.'

This was what I was afraid of. Chapman really dropped me in it by dropping dead, because everyone from his job was entitled to their final payment. Everyone's equally entitled, but being the most vicious of all animals gave Blunt more entitlement. The rest stood back to let him eat first, but once he was satisfied, I knew a feeding frenzy would ensue, they'd have all smelt blood and come in their packs for what's left.

Cookie was physically the complete opposite to Blunt. Roofers tend to be short, squat and agile with a lot of upper body strength. Scaffolders tend to be tall and lanky, with incredibly strong forearms and massive hands from juggling and tossing around twenty-foot steel tubes as easily as a cheerleader's baton. Cookie looked like Steptoe on steroids.

I felt the fury coursing through my veins, hot and spiky, I knew this was my last warning signal before my rage erupted, and looking at Cookie's expression, I could tell he was in the same state. Instinctively, I felt myself all over, searching for anything that could be used as a weapon, as I could see he was preparing to charge.

'Don't insult me! I want my money.' Cookie flexed the fingers of his massive hands, doubling them into even more massive fists. Sleeves of dense black 'Maori' tattoos ran from wrist to shoulder and the veins in his forearms bulged in tension beneath the ink. Those of us unfortunate enough to know Cookie from old knew those big solid black patterns masked copious Nazi filth beneath, but nobody could misread the hate burning in his eyes.

'I don't have it yet,' I said. 'I need a bit more time, I'm working on it. You know this.'

'Blunty says you're back in the money now,' said Cookie. The dull sheen of his steel toecap poked through the boot's worn leather; the last thing I want is that connecting with my head like a Ronaldo penalty. His hands twitched and his eyes were wide, any second now and he'd be on me. I'd found a splinter of glass, about four inches long, in the folds of my T-shirt and I gripped it down by my side, its edges cut the pads of my fingers but the discomfort would be worth it if I could use it like a shiv once he's on me.

'Blunt's wrong.'

'You've had long enough to pay me Mark, this has been going on for months. You either pay now, or—' He didn't finish the sentence, he didn't need to. I had nowhere to go from here, I knew at that point I was as good as dead, they were going to kill me for sure and I couldn't think of any reason that'd persuade them not to. I felt the splinter of glass bite into my hand as I squeezed it firmly. If I'm going down, I'm going down fighting. The blood pooling in my fist felt warm, I was ready, bring it on.

'*GET OUT OF HERE, go on, fuck off!*' Everyone froze, taken aback by the interruption and turned to see where it was coming from. Perry was standing in her doorway.

'I've called the police, now fuck off!'

The crew looked at Cookie for instruction, Cookie seemed to be weighing up his options, before giving a nod in the opposite direction. 'This isn't finished. We will get this sorted,' said Cookie. He wouldn't break his eye contact with me so I didn't notice one of his men had moved until he was delivering a powerful right hook that landed against the side of my neck and knocked me straight over. I struggled on to all fours and spat blood watching the Cookie crew make their exit.

Cookie looked back. 'Paki bitch!' and spat a glob of milky mucus at Perry's feet. The ink might be hidden on the skin but the ignorance had leached deep into the bones.

Perry helped me to my feet and led me into her house. She sat me down gently. Neither of us spoke as she cleaned and bandaged my wounds, expertly extracting tiny diamonds of glass and dabbing antiseptic to my cuts.

'Work stuff, eh? Complicated, eh?' she said, and her upward inflection sounding like she was teasing. I looked at her and realised she wasn't. 'Do you think they'll come back?'

Probably, I thought. 'No,' I said.

-33-

WE SURVEYED THE damage. The front window had gone, glass sprayed in all directions over every surface. The scaffold clip stuck out between my sofa cushions like a solitary jagged old tooth. It hadn't ripped it, but looking at the size of the loose hanging bolt I imagine I'd be missing an eye if it had indeed come straight at me.

'Cookie,' I said to his voicemail, 'listen, just give me a couple more days and I'll sort this, just a couple of days. Please.'

We took it in turns with the vacuum cleaner. It was well into the night before we could go over the same area of carpet without hearing that distinctive crunching sound as it sucked up miniscule splinters.

In the shower, I held my head under the jet to feel the abrasive edges of countless tiny slivers scrape across my scalp, and over my face. I watched the blood sparkle as the light caught the fragments, blood diamonds swirling down the drain.

Downstairs, Perry had wiped clean all the shelves and surfaces. 'I think that's the best we're going to get it,' she said, seeing me return. 'Although I suspect there'll be fine splinters everywhere for a long time to come; you'd better buy yourself some slippers.'

'Whatever happened to the police? Too busy for a domestic dispute, I suppose.'

'I've a confession to make.' Suddenly she looked very girlish. 'I never actually called them. Well, knowing you as I do, I thought you probably wouldn't want them involved. Was that okay?'

'Probably for the best. You were pretty impressive back then, standing up to that lunatic.'

'A few weekend shifts in A&E hardens you up quick enough, you soon get used to drunks, thugs and racist arseholes.'

I fixed a sheet of ply across the window as a temporary overnight measure and phoned Disco asking him to repair it properly in the morning for me. Whilst Perry set about heating up a pizza in my kitchen I let myself in to her house – there were things I simply didn't want to risk having in mine whilst it was unsecure. I clutched my spare toolbox – Hamlet's Peppa Pig tote bag full of money and Brennan's file locked inside it – and I pushed it deep into the dark corner of Perry's understairs cupboard, obscuring it with a few bags and shoes, figuring it'd be safe there.

By the time I'd got back, the pizza was cooked and the wine poured. We sat on the floor eating like normal people – normal people if they lived in a war zone that is. As I shifted my weight from side to side I twinged, the painkillers Perry had given me were wearing off. My neck had swollen and it hurt to turn my head too far. I let out an involuntary groan, she moved closer, put an arm around me and laid her head on my shoulder. She smelt delicious.

'Listen Mark, I like you, I really do, but all this, it's too much. If we can take this anywhere, and believe me I really hope we can, I want you to be honest with me. Totally honest.'

And so, I was. Within reason.

PAST EXPERIENCE HAS taught me women want you to be honest with them, right up until the moment you are. But there's something about her that's different, I wanted to be totally honest yet an ingrained caution made me hold back. I told her I'd borrowed cash to pay off Blunt, but I didn't tell her I'd borrowed it from a chemically coshed widow who didn't even know she had it to lend me. And I told her there was a friend offering to lend me more money as a stopgap to clear my debts, but prudence told me not to mention that the friend was the area's villain who now has me well and truly bent bare-arsed over a barrel playing Poirot.

What she'd heard seemed enough to keep her happy and she snuggled up to me. We watched a celebrity-based elimination show. I didn't recognise any of the celebrities and didn't understand the point of the challenges, but it didn't require much concentration and I found it quite relaxing to be able to switch my thoughts off.

-34-

THE SOUND OF thumping on the door woke me up, followed by Disco's charming alarm call: 'Get up, you lazy bastard!' shouted at the top of his voice through the letter box.

'Uncle Bern dropped me off, you'll have to take me home.' Disco never bothered reapplying for his driving licence after losing it about fifteen years ago and when faced with the choice of drive or imbibe, the licensed victuallers of the Medway Towns rejoiced.

Disco had got everything needed on the way over and was quickly well underway. Even though it pisses me right off when people do it to me, I stood beside him and chatted while he worked. Disco didn't seem to mind though, as he had all the weekend gossip he was burning to get out.

'So…Pervy Ken's working down the organic farm shop, the owner comes back unexpected and finds all the butternut squashes—' he stopped mid-sentence. Disco had been struck dumb by the sight of Perry descending my stairs in just an MP Electrical t-shirt.

'Morning lads. Tea, coffee?' she offered with a cheeky grin before disappearing to the kitchen. Disco looked at me with new eyes.

'Marky Marky, who's that then?'

'Perry, she lives next door.' I was startled by the defensiveness in my tone, but then I knew where exactly this was headed.

'Go on then, give us the details, share,' said Disco downing tools, ready to take notes for his daily address to the industry at large.

'No. There's nothing to say.' I hoped that would shut down the interrogation. And honestly, there wasn't anything to say. A gentleman never divulges about his overnight visitors. Believe me, I was as surprised as anyone when I woke up and found her asleep on my pillow, but in this case, it was totally innocent. After the excitement of yesterday, and a bellyful of pizza, wine and painkillers, I fell asleep in front of the telly. Perry helped me upstairs to bed, but the dutiful nurse was concerned about leaving me alone with a head injury and decided to stay the night once I was safely all tucked up and far away in the Land of Nod.

Disco, knowing I wasn't going to discuss this any further with him, saw Perry's re-emergence as an alternative route to this golden nugget of gossip, and switched on the chat. I've always been amazed by people like Disco that can strike up a conversation with absolutely anyone. It's a skill I've often wished I had, but I'm old enough now to realise that I lack that sort of openness and approachability. It instantly made me think of Tommy, and an enormous wave of regret and guilt hit me in the back like a juggernaut; too many missed opportunities wasted by the superficial.

Disco on the other hand is the kind of bloke who can walk in to a pub without a penny in his pocket and walk out of it six pints refreshed and his taxi fare home. I'd seen him thaw the surliest of pub landlords, delivery drivers and even that frosty receptionist at Queen Mary's... Of course, Queen Mary's. I left the two of them nattering away and headed to the privacy of upstairs where I made the call.

When I came back down again, I saw Disco and Perry on my front lawn. My window was still a gaping hole, clearly not much work had taken place, but slaloming between their legs was Mr Skinner, purring with contentment as he rubbed himself against their shins. Perry picked him up, holding him close to her chest and nuzzled her face against his fur.

'He's a friendly one alright,' said Disco reaching in to tickle the top of his head. Mr Skinner reacted with delight by closing his eyes and flattening his ears; he looked happy and I too was happy that Mr Skinner at last had found peace. I reached out to stroke him. Mr Skinner hissed and raked a spiky claw across the back of my hand, and then settled back down to his Zen-like state between the other two. *Et tu Mr Skinner* I thought, but I knew it wasn't his fault, like I say, some people have that easy approachability. Not me.

-35-

'GOOD MORNING MR POYNTER,' said the voicemail message. *This is the Town and Country Club. We have a broken hand dryer in the ladies' toilet. Could you drop by today to take a look and give us an estimate please?'*

So, there it was, my official summons from Hamlet in case anyone was listening in. Disco had finally finished the window, and Perry had got him putting together some flat pack furniture in her house. Looking out the window, trying to work out what to do next, I saw them arrive.

Senia, young Nwakobu and a couple of uniforms were heading in the direction of my house. Nwakobu had a new haircut, it made him look like that French midfielder Arsenal had wasted millions on a few years back.

The bell rang – once, twice - I knew I needed to welcome my guests.

'Good afternoon Mr Senia, how lovely to see you again. What can I do you for?' I said, throwing the door open to him.

'Mark Poynter, I have a warrant to search these premises,' said Senia, dispensing with any kind of pleasantry. I stepped aside and let Senia and his team in. They snapped on thin latex gloves whilst he assigned them different areas to search.

'I would offer you a cup of tea Mr Senia but then I doubt you'll be here that long; after all it's not a big place, is it? What is it you're looking for by the way?'

He didn't answer, but instead gave me a look of utter disdain, obviously not one for small talk. I decided not to ask him if he was following the cricket. He looked across to the first uniform who was busy looking in my cupboards but only finding old DVDs and CDs.

'We're still looking very closely at you Mr Poynter. You owed Tommy Davies money you don't have, that's motive. And we know that it's definitely your hammer that killed him, that's opportunity.'

'But you told me yourself there was no fingerprints at all on the hammer. Are you seriously suggesting I would batter my friend with my own hammer, and have the presence of mind to wipe it clean afterwards but be daft enough to leave it lying around?'

'I've seen people make stupider mistakes in the heat of the moment.' But Senia didn't sound very convinced by his response.

'Sounds more like someone's trying to set me up.'

Senia smiled the smug sort of smile of someone enjoying the smell of his own farts a bit too much. 'And who would want to do that then?'

'How about the person that killed him? It doesn't have to be aimed at me directly. All I mean is, say, the killer creeps up on him, sees our tools lying around, picks up something handy and heavy and "bosh", stoves his head in. Then all they need to do is wipe their prints off the handle and leave it lying around covered in Tommy's, well, covered in Tommy and hope that, hypothetically speaking, a lazy dim copper would see it and immediately assume I did it. Just hypothetically, no offence.'

Senia wasn't impressed, but I knew he had no evidence, otherwise he would have arrested me a long time ago. I was confident there was nothing here to incriminate me.

'Sir, I think I've found something.'

Oh bugger!

IN MY MIND, I walked through my house room by room, cupboard by cupboard; I couldn't think of anything. The only stuff that would have been difficult to explain was hiding next door under Perry's stairs.

Nwakobu emerged looking very pleased with his find, so desperate to be Senia's pet. He brandished Tommy's file chest.

'What's this?' said Senia, peering inside, flicking through the hangers.

'Nothing, just paperwork.'

'Not your paperwork though is it,' said Nwakobu, eager for a pat on the head. 'It belonged to the deceased Sir, all his bank records, cheque book, paying in book, that sort of thing.'

'Interesting. So, what were you doing with this? Trying to get your hands on his bank account perhaps?' said Senia. 'I see you've already purloined his vehicle.'

'His wife gave it to me,' I said, 'after he was killed. And the van.'

'And she will corroborate that will she?'

I replied that she would, and if he wanted further witnesses he could also ask her sister and mother who were both there at the time, and: 'While you're at it you can ask her mum for the receipt for the van.'

Senia gave a look to Nwakobu that told me they'd be checking immediately as soon as they left.

'When did she give this to you exactly?' asked Senia, to which I truthfully told him the day after Tommy died. A darkness went across Senia's eyes, he looked straight and direct at me. 'You took something from the victim's home without our knowledge or prior consent. I could charge you for withholding vital evidence.'

'If it's that vital you should have taken it yourself then shouldn't you. Your people had been there all day the day it happened, why didn't they take it?'

From the bulge around his jaw and the widening of his eyes I could tell he didn't have an answer. Instead he gave a flick of a finger and the nearest uniform took the chest and carried it out of the house.

'By the way, Mr Senia, whilst you're here…' I felt brave enough to push my advantage. 'What about Anthony Chapman? Have you found out who killed him yet? I'd like to know I'm not still in the frame for his tragic death please.'

'Mr Chapman? The Coroner found that he died from natural causes. Didn't we tell you, I do apologise,' he said in a tone that told me he knew that I knew he didn't mean it.

'So, what you are saying is that you're satisfied I have no connection to his death?' Senia grunted a non-committal response. I pressed on, 'And Sally DeFreitas, can you please confirm I'm not your man there either.'

'Don't get too smug Poynter, you're still very much "my man" for Tommy Davies and will be until I decide differently.'

The second uniform came from upstairs empty-handed shaking his head, he hadn't found anything. Hopefully this farcical show of strength was over and they'd be going.

'Sir,' called a voice from outside. The first uniform had returned and was standing beside the front door. 'Would you like to look at this?'

Senia strode over, swiftly followed by me as I was as keen to see what he'd found as Senia. The uniform had the lid off my recycling bin, and was pointing at the broken glass within.

'That's an awful lot in there, you've done more than drop your postprandial glass of port,' said Senia. *Postprandial*, now there's a word I hadn't heard before, I liked the popping sound it made as he said it. I looked it up, it means after a formal dinner. I suspect Senia goes to a lot of formal dinners, passing port to the left and swapping postprandial funny handshakes with the Grand Poobah.

'The window got broken, look you can see the putty and beads are new, I've not had the chance to repaint it yet.' I directed their attention to the window, holding both hands out like a glamour girl on a gameshow. The uniform peered at it and nodded confirmation back to Senia. 'A bird flew into it,' I added.

'Must've been a big bird.'

'A pigeon. It was lying around here somewhere; a cat must've taken it. Anyway, what's my window got to do with anything?'

'Nothing. Nothing at all. But it all seems to be happening to you this week doesn't it: friends killed, clients dying, windows breaking and of course there was that nasty fall from your bike. You seem to be on a run of incredibly bad luck of late, don't you?'

'They say it comes in threes don't they? If so, I'm probably in credit by now.' As I said it, I wished it was true. 'I'll buy myself a lottery ticket next time I'm out because if anyone is due a spot of good luck it's me.'

Senia was getting restless. He'd found Tommy's chest, there was nothing in it except boring paperwork, but at least he could mark it up as a small victory. Other than that, I could see the frustration mount each time he wiped his hand across his mouth. He'd be leaving soon and hopefully it would be one step, even a tiny baby step, closer to getting me off his most wanted list.

'Sir, may I have a quick word?' interrupted Nwakobu, and he and Senia stepped a few paces away from earshot whilst Nwakobu appeared to brief Senia on points from his notebook. Senia turned back at me with a wide shit-eating grin.

'Mr Poynter, I've been informed that we had report of an incident this afternoon, one of your neighbours phoned about fighting in the street and the sound of breaking glass. Know anything about that?'

'Nope.' Perry had said she definitely didn't call, I wondered who did. I bet the net curtains were twitching like mad, the nosy bastards. 'Nothing at all, sounds rather unpleasant if you ask me, this area's really gone downhill recently.'

Senia fixed his stare on me, and I swear I heard him growl; it was low, but a growl nonetheless.

'What about the garage Sir, would you like that searched?' said one of the uniforms, snapping Senia back to focus. 'I believe it's in that block over there.'

'Yes. Get on with it right away,' Senia said.

'Hold on, hold on.' I waved the warrant document he'd given me. 'This says you can only search the premises which is defined as the house. The garage isn't part of the house, it's en bloc over there, it's a completely different premises. You don't have the authority.'

I had no idea whether that was true and as I was saying it aloud, I thought back to when I bought the house. I'm sure according to the Land Registry the house and garage were one item but does that go the same for a police warrant? I had absolutely no idea, but from the glances between Senia and Nwakobu it was clear neither did they.

'I can get a warrant for your garage and come back, or we can save time and look now. Please may we have your permission to inspect your garage?' The diplomatic tone Senia was managing to hold on to was admirable given the frustration evident in his balled fists.

'I have nothing to hide, but I want it all done properly and on the record. You need a warrant.'

'Fine, we'll be back, come on.' Senia marshalled his troops out of my house. I watched from the window as they stood around their cars discussing what to do next, then Senia and Nwakobu left with the first uniform, leaving the second uniform to sentry duty outside the garage.

They didn't find anything, I didn't expect them to, but wasting a few hours of their time made me feel as though I'd got my own back.

-36-

HAVING GOT RID of Senia and his mob, I found Disco and dropped him back home. I briefly stopped to say hello to his mum and give her the money I owed him for the window. He didn't object, knowing it would cover his board and housekeeping before it could drink a hole in his pocket.

I pulled up outside the club to find it locked up. Nobody was about to challenge me when I approached the door. I was wearing my logo branded workwear and I carried my big chunky black and yellow tool box. There was nothing to draw any suspicion about me, I was simply a tradesman going about his business.

Keeping up the charade for any snoops out there, convinced I'd seen a silver Mondeo pull up on the petrol forecourt about one hundred metres down the road, I told the voice box on the door I was the electrician and at the sound of the buzz I let myself in. If you've never seen one naked in the daytime, believe me, a nightclub isn't a particularly glamorous place when the lights are on and the stains in the carpet grin back at you. As I entered, I was met by a cleaning crew of three women talking to each other in a language I didn't recognise whilst they mopped and polished. I gave them a polite smile and headed straight to the office.

Hamlet was sitting behind Sally's desk, head in hands, looking like he was struggling with paperwork.

'I've got to find me a manager, and quick. Want a job?' he gestured for me to sit down. I pulled out a visitor chair and complied. I looked around the small office, not sure what I was looking for but hoping something jumped out at me that the police may have missed. As I turned my head to survey the small room my bruised and swollen neck bit with pain, Hamlet noticed me wince.

'Jeez, look at your face. What happened this time? Another fight with your bike? Looks like you lost,' he said, pointing at the bandage around my cut hand. Hamlet pushed all the paperwork to one side, and directed his full attention at me. 'So, got a name for me yet?'

'Not yet. But there's something I want to be sure about, the deal, still as agreed? I find you the name, you waive the debt? Yes?'

'Sure,' said Hamlet, but his tone was as non-committal as his posture. Leaning back against the chair with his hands behind his head, the sleeves of his T-shirt rode up exposing tribal tails and oriental finials of black ink. I wasn't convinced.

'Is that the agreement?'

Hamlet was about to speak then paused, raised his eyes to the ceiling, and then a lazy, disinterested tone of voice followed an exhale of breath, 'Yeah, sure.'

'Not good enough. I know how you operate. I want it confirmed, clear and beyond any doubt, otherwise forget about it, I won't help you.' I realised too late that I'd raised my voice to a shout and I was jabbing my finger at him as I spoke.

'Fine,' he said, with a derisive laugh in his voice. He rose to his feet and leaned across the desk towards me. 'I do solemnly swear that if you can deliver me the scumbag who killed our Sally, I will waive your debt in full and final settlement. Happy?'

We both sat down, the heat had gone out of the situation. Behind me the door slammed open and I saw Brazil framed in the doorway; he'd heard the raised voices.

'It's okay, stand down soldier, it's all under control,' said Hamlet to Brazil, who obediently sloped off.

'Right, where were we?" asked Hamlet, he clearly remembered because in a heartbeat his body stiffened and his voice changed, becoming harder, 'Be clear, if you can't or won't deliver your end then you will owe me the full value plus interest, understand?'

I couldn't think of anything to say in response and sat looking at him. Eventually I nodded my agreement.

'Somebody put the kettle on,' shouted Hamlet through the open door. The noises of taps running and the whoosh of steam rising quickly followed. Hamlet relaxed back in his seat, folding his hands across his stomach, the inked patterns disappeared as his sleeves dropped back into place. Before either of us said anything more, Dunlop poked his head around the door frame.

'Visitor, Boss,' he said. Hamlet gestured to bring them in then turned to me, commanding, 'You, stay there.'

Heavy footsteps tapped along the corridor, a sniff and the clearing of the throat, and then the visitor was there, framed in the doorway, six foot of aggression: Cookie, flanked front and back by Dunlop and Brazil.

I'd seen him before he'd seen me, his eyes were fixed on Hamlet, but as he glanced around he recognised me and his shoulders stiffened, his lip snarled upwards, his hands curled into fists, he lunged at me, 'Poynter —'

I flinched, eyes closed, head down, clutching my big toolbox hoping it would shield me, and braced myself for the onslaught. Nothing happened. I looked up, Cookie was restrained by both Dunlop and Brazil, they had him locked up good and tight, flecks of white sputum sputtered from the corner of his mouth.

Hamlet leaned back in his chair, and rolled his head, the sound of stiff bones crackled in the silence, eventually he spoke, 'Hello Cookie, thanks for coming in today. Now, if the lads release you, will you sit down quietly like a good boy?'

All eyes on Cookie, after what seemed an impossible age he nodded and the tension dropped out of his body. Hamlet nodded and Cookie, as promised, was released. Hamlet gestured at the chair opposite him. Cookie sat down.

'Cookie, Cookie, Cookie. You need to calm down mate, you'll give yourself a heart attack carrying on like this.' Hamlet's voice was patronising, deliberately so.

'That little bollocks—' said Cookie pointing at me, but Hamlet shushed him into silence, mocking him with his finger to his lips as though telling a toddler to quieten down.

'Cookie. Listen very carefully, I shall say ziz only once – remember that, who used to say that? Anyway, pay attention. You are making a nuisance of yourself.'

'Look, I—' but Hamlet waved away his protests.

'Your dispute with Mark, it's over.'

'But—'

'It's over. Understand?'

'No. That little shit owes me—'

'Listen to me Cookie. You had your chance to settle it civilly. You had your chance and you blew it. You have been far too loud, far too...' Hamlet took a moment to select the right word. 'Far too obvious.'

Cookie looked around the room, looked at me, but I was as much confused as he was.

'Your carrying ons, smashing windows. Really?' continued Hamlet, 'It's attracting attention. It draws a lot of attention to him, and I don't want any attention being drawn to him in case it gets drawn to me, now do you understand?'

Cookie nodded his head, he looked drained, exhausted, as his chin struck his chest with a slight bounce.

'Yes,' he eventually whispered.

'So, you will leave Marky alone, understand. Any gripe is over, any debt is written off.' Cookie made to protest but Hamlet pointed his finger straight into Cookie's face. 'You owe me remember Cookie, you owe me.'

I had no idea what that was about, but I guessed it was one of those things you don't want to know about. What you don't know can't hurt you.

Cookie slowly nodded and held up his hands, acknowledgement of his surrender and rose from his chair. He shuffled to the doorway with the jaunty stride of the gallows-bound condemned man. As he reached it, he turned back, and then pounced. He was quick, like a rattlesnake, his massive fist launched straight at my face. But Brazil was quicker, and got in between us taking Cookie's haymaker right on the jaw. With a lightning quick reaction, he drove an elbow straight into Cookie's cheek, flooring him. Hamlet leaped around from his side of the desk, and with a knee bearing down on Cookie's chest he grabbed him by the hair yanking his head up – one, two, three – rapid fire jabs, powerful and delivered straight to the centre of Cookie's face blood sprayed from his busted nose; even sat on the other side of the room I noticed a fine scarlet mist settling on the toes of my boots.

Hamlet rose, a delirious grin on his face, eyes wide and the lightest sheen of sweat glossing his forehead. 'Still got it! Fucking love it!' he laughed to his underlings. He raised his fist to his face, and I've only ever seen a child on the playground do this, he dabbed his tongue on his bloody and damaged knuckles before caution caught up and took over. 'Better not, don't know where he's been. Chuck him out.'

Brazil and Dunlop hoiked Cookie to his feet and hauled him off the premises, 'Remember, it's over Cookie. Over, so behave!' shouted Hamlet to his back as it disappeared through the entrance doors towards the street, 'And you, you can fuck off too.' I didn't need telling twice, only I did because as I was standing to leave he spoke again, 'You sorted those jobs out that Sally gave you yet? Get them done, tomorrow!'

I flinched as the flash of silver came at my head, 'And you'll be needing these too,' said Hamlet. I picked up the ring of keys from where they landed and left.

At the entrance doors, I came across the returning Brazil and Dunlop, 'It's okay. You can go out there, he's gone,' said Dunlop.

Brazil rubbed his jaw, it was already beginning to bloom its purple bruising, 'Thanks. I appreciate it,' I said to him, genuinely grateful for his intervention. He sent a hard, fast punch into my guts.

'You're lucky you're his little pet.'

They left me on my knees gasping for breath and walked back inside, slamming the door behind them.

-37-

I'D BEEN TO Sally's flat before, several years ago to do some repair or other. It was one of Hamlet's vast portfolio and if he wants me investigating Sally's death, I figured I'd be better off starting off by investigating her life. Her flat was the obvious place to begin.

Darland, a large imposing Victorian terrace house, sliced into two flats, one on the first floor and the other, Sally's, on the ground floor. The painted brick frontage was a pleasant magnolia colour and the stonework painted white, with the ornate carved details expertly picked out in grey. It looked clean and warm, as though it had been recently done, Tommy's handiwork no doubt.

Curiosity led me around the back, using the narrow alleyway that ran the length of the terrace. The back gate was locked, but with somebody's recycling bin to stand on I got a clear view of the house's rear. It had been a long time since it last saw a paintbrush, but the windows looked new. UPVC double glazed units, fairly robust and no obvious sign of damage. Likewise, the uPVC French doors looked secure and undamaged. Nobody had come this way to get to Sally.

I returned to the front, paying attention to the entrance. There was only one door from the street and it gave access to both flats. That door too was robust uPVC. A silver box was fixed to the wall: controlled entry, no-one comes in without buzzing first and having the electronic lock released by the resident. The windows and door to the front all looked undamaged too, Sally's killer must have been buzzed in. Did she know them?

INSIDE THE STREET door was a small lobby with two internal doors, one leading to the upstairs flat, the other with police tape stretched diagonally corner to corner. I slipped the key in the lock, shimmied around the tape and let myself in, black and yellow toolbox in hand.

The flat felt musty and damp, I doubt it had had much of an airing in recent days, trapping the residual moisture from the clean-up operation. Retrieving Brennan's file from the toolbox I held the crime scene photograph, and tried overlaying it against what was in front of me. The first thing I noticed was the carpet had gone. In the photo Sally's blood had drained into it, spreading all around her like an aura. But there was no mistaking where she'd died, as the exposed floorboards were washed in pink, the volume of blood must have been that extreme it saturated the carpet and underlay to the point it stained the very structure beneath.

As my eyes got used to the compare and contrast game I was playing, photo/room/photo/room, I began spotting gaps where things were missing: a silver laptop from the table, a red iPad from the mantelpiece, the second shelf in the bookcase looked sparser than the photo. I supposed the police took anything that might have been remotely useful to them, and I began to wonder what I was hoping to find. Without any kind of plan, I meandered around, looking and poking and rummaging, but nothing sprang out at me.

I sat on the sofa and looked out at the street, Sally would have seen anyone approaching her front door sitting there, it gave a clear view. As I pondered what it meant, if anything, I saw movement around my van, parked on the opposite side of the street. I walked to the window for a better view, and I was right, someone was taking a keen interest in it: a tall-ish skinny guy, black jeans and grey hoodie pulled up over his face. I watched him circle the van, and peer through the windows, a junkie looking for tools he can steal to trade for drugs, and when he began pulling the door handles, I'd seen enough: 'Hey, you, fuck off!' I shouted, thumping on the window pane. He looked up, startled, darting his head left and right to find the source of the noise. 'Go on, get out of here,' I continued, until he looked straight at me, his eyes channelled by the tunnel of his tightly drawn hood. I paused my noise. *No, it couldn't be* I thought as he took off, sprinting away. I watched him run, following the footpath around the corner until he disappeared from view.

I realised my hand was still pressed against the window pane leaving a perfect greasy print on the glass. I began opening and closing kitchen drawers looking for something to wipe it off with, eventually finding some spray cleaner and a soft cloth. Slowly I sprayed and wiped, removing the print, waiting for the man to return, I wanted to see him again, I needed to be sure. But he was long gone, I'd spooked him and finally, leaving the glass polished to sparkling sheen, I returned the cleaning materials back where I found them.

I spotted the landline phone standing upright in its cradle on the kitchen countertop, and remembering why I was there, I pressed the playback button, *'You have six old messages'* said the lady robot voice and it began to play the first one, some cold call about insurance, I continued ferreting about whilst I listened to the messages tick over.

On my hands and knees peering under the sofa, *'Sally, hi, it's Steve,'* I sprang up bolt upright, I recognised that voice from somewhere, *'I had a really great time last night at the party, I hope you did, and I was wondering, like, if... err... perhaps you'd fancy going out for a drink. With me.'*

Where have I heard that voice? The lady robot told me that call was received a week before Sally died, then moved on to the next message: *'Hi Sally, Steve again, you haven't replied to my call. So, err, drink? Or food? My shout.'*

Lady robot gave the date as a day later than the other one. *'Hi Sally, Steve here. Why are you blanking me? I thought we were friends?'* from the next day. *'Sally. I don't like this, I'm not impressed, who do you think you are, coming on to me and then blanking me, stuck up bitch!'* the day after. Whose voice is that? I know it, it'll come to me, give it time. *'Sally, I'm sorry, I didn't mean to call you names, I hope I didn't upset you, I hope we can still be friends. I'll see you at work tomorrow.'* Bingo, I knew whose voice it was.

Realising that if the voice did indeed belong to who I thought it belonged to, things had become a lot more complicated. I knelt back on my heels to consider my options and a shape passed by the window just catching the edges of my field of vision, snapping me back into focus. Could it be him?

I froze and listened for the letter flap to rattle, hoping it was just a junk mail delivery. Instead I heard the metallic rasp and tock of a key being sunk up to the hilt in the latch. It must be the upstairs neighbour coming home, I thought, but to be safe I gathered up my belongings and hid in the bathroom. I pushed the door almost, but not quite, shut giving myself a narrow slit between the hinges to look through.

Hearing the slam, I knew the street door had been closed. I held my breath waiting to hear the soft thud thud thud of feet climbing stairs but it never came. Instead I heard the rip of the police tape pulling away from the door frame, and another metallic rasp and tock as the key sunk into the latch. I heard the flat door open, sweeping across the coir matting.

I looked around the bathroom, a tiny square window was set high in the wall, there was no emergency way out of here. I looked around for somewhere to hide, but nowhere was suitable. I was a sitting duck. The only way out of here would be by overpowering whoever was out there and hoping they didn't wake up until I was gone. I gripped my toolbox, a good wallop across the back of the head should do the trick, I lifted it up close to my chest preparing to swing. I peered through the slit. I couldn't see anyone yet but they couldn't be far away as their cough sounded as though it was right beside me. I kept peering, then a shadow fell across the slit, he was directly outside the door, my white knuckles gripped the toolbox and goose bumps appeared across my arms. *I have to do this if I want to live*, my mind tried to rationalise what I was about to do. Daylight shone through the slit once again, he'd moved away, I peered through and I saw him, this was it.

I peered again, and then once more to be sure, my knuckles released their grip on the toolbox. Nick Witham?

Nick was slowly making his way around the room, lost in deep concentration, I shivered with relief that it was a friendly, but then new problems kept popping up: how do I explain being here? How do I get out of here without giving him a heart attack?

Inspiration struck, I flushed the toilet, I saw Nick whirl round in reaction to the noise, confused. I swung the door open and sauntered out keeping my face pointing down whilst I pretended to fiddle with my fly, 'What the bloody hell? Mark? What are you doing here?' he said

'What?' I hoped he'd buy my fake astonishment. 'Nick? What are you doing here? You scared the life out of me jumping out like that.'

'Me? What about you?' he said. 'Anyway, this is a crime scene, why are you here?'

'It's not a crime scene any more, is it? Surely you've got everything you need?'

'It's a crime scene for as long as we say it is, and stop trying to change the subject, for the third time, why are you here?'

'Landlord test and inspection.' I raised my set of keys and jingled them at him. 'See, I've got permission from the landlord. He's going to have to get it ready to re-let, asked me to take a look.'

'We all know who the landlord is.' Nick sounded disappointed, as though I'd let him down getting back involved with Hamlet. 'You can't be in here, you need to go.'

I raised my hands and gave a single nod to show I conceded, and I picked up my toolbox. 'Before I go Nick, what can you tell me, come on, you know me, we're mates.'

Nick puffed out his cheeks, and rubbed his palm across his shaved head; he continued for several seconds before saying, 'You've probably seen it all for yourself already anyway: no forced entry, so either the killer had a key or was let in by the victim.'

'Have you spoken to the upstairs neighbour?'

'Believe it or not we have done this before, thank you. We spoke to them, a young lady, works in insurance up in London. Not aware of any false buzzes on the door entry, hasn't heard any raised voices or fighting coming up from downstairs, and was out of the property at work all day the day it happened. We've checked the CCTV at the train station that shows her leaving, and the CCTV showing her coming back and she's got at least a dozen people who say she was in her place of work in the City of London all day, so she's clear.'

'She's not seen anyone or anything, no cars hanging about?'

'Funny you should ask that, she said she saw a car parked up across the road a couple of times last week that she hadn't seen before, a Mercedes. But nobody saw it the day of the murder, just ordinary cars: a few Fords, Vauxhalls, a Volkswagen, a Kia and so forth. But we're interested in tracing the Merc though as she said it stood out, she said it was a nice one.' Of course she did, and I know someone with a nice Mercedes, someone who sounds very similar to Steve, speaking of which ...

'Who's Steve?'

'Oh, you've been listening to her messages, have you?' Nick was beginning to sound annoyed. 'We don't know. Yet. We've got people looking into her phone records, hopefully we can trace the number Steve, whoever Steve may be, called from and then we can trace him.'

'Unless it's a pay as you go burner.'

'Thanks. Then we'll cross that bridge when we come to it.'

'So, who do you reckon he is? Boyfriend?'

Nick looked as though he was about to laugh, 'Stalker, more like, he sounds delusional.'

'So, the mysterious Steve's your favourite for it, is he?'

'I think it's time you for you to go Mark,' said Nick. I didn't think he had any more to share with me and I didn't want to fall out, so I agreed and left him to lock up, giving a friendly wave as I drove away.

I waited fifteen minutes before heading back to Sally's flat. No sign of Nick anywhere. I left myself in, walked over to the answerphone, and pressed 'delete all'. It flashed a red digital zero as I locked up and left.

I knew who Steve was, the police didn't, and neither did the competition. I was ahead of the pack.

-38-

NEXT MORNING, WANTING to get the jobs at Hamlet's club out the way, I headed across to Thorpe Timber and Building Supplies. In my pocket was a thick envelope decanted from the Peppa Pig tote bag. There was something satisfying about knowing I carried enough cash in my pocket to clear my account's overdue balance, and something amusingly smutty about offering the Magnificent Maria the chance to take my wad.

'Well get you Mr Big Stuff, how's life among the rich and famous?' she said after twice counting through all the notes and testing them with her special pen.

'Great, but I'm keeping true to my roots, I'm still Marky from the Block, that's why I'm slumming it here with you.'

'Funny. What else do you want?' she said, I'd known her long enough to know she was only pretending to be annoyed and I managed to cadge a cup of coffee – proper coffee, not the automated pish from the machine on the counter. Eventually I walked back to the van laden with brochures, sundry bits and pieces, and the slight feeling of arousal from the innuendo-laden chatter between us. I was trying to get better discounts but I think she was having more fun embarrassing me. I was honestly unsure whether she was mocking me or coming on to me.

Lost in my daydream of playtimes with Magnificent Maria I didn't notice him until I was fishing around for the van keys. The silver Mondeo. In the opposite corner of the car park. It was so close I got a good look at the driver: closely shaved hair, round forehead, no chin, a head shaped like a light bulb.

This was my chance. I dropped everything and dashed towards him but he'd seen me and was off, bollocks, he was gone before I'd made it halfway across the car park.

As I gathered my brochures off the ground, tossing them into the passenger footwell, I wondered whether to mention it to Hamlet, find out whether he knew more than he'd previously let on. I decided not until I've made some enquiries of my own.

I pulled a credit card out of my wallet and went back into Thorpe's. Holding it in front of me I marched up to the counter. Maria by now was serving a big beast in an orange hi-viz jacket, logos of a motorway contractor across the back. I didn't care and leant across him.

'Maria, quick one, some guy outside, head like the reflection in a spoon, drives a silver Mondeo, dropped his card. Know who he is so I can get it back to him?'

'Hmmm' said Maria looking thoughtful, Motorway Hi-Viz turned and stared as though he was considering where to hit me first. 'No, we've not had anyone like that in here today, can't help, sorry, don't know him.'

'Doesn't it say?' said Motorway Hi-Viz 'On the credit card? It'll tell you what his name is.'

He was right. I hadn't thought of that. Maria looked at me with pity and despair. I needed to think of a smart and witty response to get out of this. 'Mind your own fucking business,' was the best I could manage.

I left pretty sharpish and was back in the van before he could get hold of me.

NO SIGN OF Hamlet when I got to the club, I was told he was away all day on business, and I knew better than to ask any more. No sign of Brazil and Dunlop either, no doubt they'd gone too as his entourage. Without any distraction, the jobs I had didn't take too long, only a couple of switch-outs, and by mid-afternoon I was packing up when I realised where I had parked – right in front of Brazil's Mercedes, the nice one, the loved and cherished one. I peered through the windows but couldn't see much due to the black privacy tint he'd added.

I went back inside for my last remaining items and then a final visual sweep through to make sure nothing'd been left behind when I spotted it: Brazil's denim jacket. He'd folded it in half and laid on the counter behind the bar. Knowing there was nobody around, I approached it, slowly, and I patted it down, feeling a lump through the fabric. I reached into the pocket, success, he'd left his keys.

I took them, but caution told me not to take them outside the club, just in case. I half opened the main door, pointed the fob at the Mercedes, blipped the locks open then quickly returned the keys to the jacket back on the counter. I figured if he came back, Brazil could be persuaded he'd forgotten to lock it when he parked, it'd certainly be easier to explain than finding the keys on me.

Inside, the Mercedes smelt of polish and cleaning products, it was spotless, not a crumb anywhere. The wood veneered console shone, a magnet for fingerprints and smudges, so I knew I needed to be careful where I touched.

With just my little finger I flipped open the glovebox, but found nothing of interest. The boot only contained a stinky gym bag and lightweight boxing gloves. I began to think this was a waste of time and was ready to lock it back up again when as a last resort I flipped down the driver's sun visor. Something was slipped into the pocket, a photograph, I pulled it out and held it up. It showed Sally and Brazil. They were in the club looking relaxed, even though it was a photo, I could see they were both a bit drunk. Sally had her arm draped over his shoulder but was looking away from him, he was looking in the same direction as her. Something wasn't right about the photo, the proportions were wrong, the way it was composed, something was off. Maybe it was the way the two of them filled the picture so completely that her left side wasn't even in the picture, from her left shoulder down, cut off by the edge of the photo. It simply didn't look right.

The aspects of good photography aside, it only reinforced my suspicion – Brazil was Steve, and Steve had a severe crush on Sally. It wouldn't be the first time a stalker has killed the one they desire.

I slipped the photo back where I found it and gently closed the Mercedes, making sure it was as spotless as when I opened it, then I was gone.

-39-

TWO FUNERALS, two days apart. I didn't expect to have a week like that until a cold snap in my dotage. First Tommy's, then Sally's, same place, different styles… both bloody miserable.

Tommy's was a bleak damp day, heavy top coats and breath misting in the air: a young, over-enthusiastic vicar who knew nothing about him and tried too hard to pretend otherwise. Sally's had a bright, low spring sun, shirt sleeves and sunglasses: and a compassionate vicar who was a friend of the family.

The crematorium was full for Tommy, people having to stand at the back. Jen didn't speak, leaving it to Tommy's family to deliver the eulogies. Sally's barely filled three rows but her dad trembled with emotion as he recalled summer holidays past when Sally enchanted his family back home in Trinidad, and school friends gave lively and energetic speeches about her. When the Vicar spoke, she spoke fondly with the warmth that only comes from familiarity, Sally and her family were valued members of her parish. I don't think Tommy ever set foot inside a church unless it needed two coats of emulsion. Tommy wasn't a religious man, and so his Vicar resorted to generic, standard issue material, 'In my Father's house are many rooms …' I've heard that before, maybe it's the go-to text for building trade burials: 'How about this – houses, rooms – that'll do.'

I knew most of the people at Tommy's, I didn't at Sally's. To tell you the truth I wondered why I was there, it felt like I was intruding on something profoundly personal, yes we were somehow, distantly, related and yes, she was a nice kid who had shown me a kindness recently, but really, would I have been there if it wasn't to keep Uncle Bern company? Or more significantly, if I hadn't been under Hamlet's thumb?

Brazil and Dunlop arrived late and unexpectedly causing heads to turn as the big ornate doors slammed shut. The Vicar beckoned them to come and join the family and friends at the front but they ignored her and sat scowling in the back row, their expressions letting everyone know they were there under sufferance, on instructions from the absent Hamlet I assumed.

At the end of Sally's, we filed out of the crematorium to the Garden of Remembrance. Brazil and Dunlop were already there, smoking and smirking against the doorway. The family manoeuvred past their uninvited guests with suspicion and distaste, and Bern scurried ahead to catch up with Sally's mum and give Auntie Val's apologies for not being there. As he began explaining something about the problems with Spanish air traffic control, I took it as my opportunity to peel off to a quiet corner away from the core group, feeling something of an impostor amongst them. I could see Brazil and Dunlop already heading towards the exit, clearly having decided they'd done enough, made an appearance and could go back and report to Hamlet.

I meandered around the small terraced holding area, looked at the flowers and read the small square cards attached and I'm sure it was the low sun in my eyes that caused me to blink a few times to shake away the prickling sensation as I read the tribute 'to my mummy, the angel'. I looked around to find Sally's dad ahead of me, in conversation with none other than Senia. Hoping not to look too obvious, I leaned forward paying greater attention to the flowers and eavesdropped, but could only hear the load of old granny Senia was spouting, about how he's working tirelessly to bring her killer to justice. I wondered if Nick Witham eating biscuits and young Nwaboku arresting top class cricketers are what he had in mind as he reassured her dad that his *'top men are on the case'.*

Bern beckoned me over with a jerk of the head. Obligingly I approached him.

'Here he is, this is him,' he said to Sally's mum.

'What? This is little Mark?' she said with a happy squawk to her voice, pointing a crooked finger approximately in my direction. 'You was only this big last time I saw you', she squawked, waving her hand down below her knees. 'Do you remember?'

I didn't, I could have only been 18 months but what's the point in contradicting a woman on the day of her only child's funeral. 'Of course I do,' I said.

She laughed, 'No you don't, you was only a toddler, but you're a charmer, I can see that, like your dad. I was ever so sorry to hear he'd, you know, gone. You don't half look like him, you know?'

I thanked her, as that's what you're supposed to do, and noticed a few ladies had gathered behind her, presumably waiting to give their condolences.

'So, now you're end of the line, the head of the family...' she began, no doubt thinking she was about to impart some great wisdom, the usual crap people come up with at funerals. 'Oh no, wait, silly me, I was forgetting, there's—' Before she could finish, Bern gripped her arm and turned her towards the waiting ladies. Her thoughts were sufficiently distracted as she greeted them with another happy squawk.

I gestured to Bern I was leaving, and turned to go. Head down, brushing dust from the sleeve of my best and only suit I walked straight into someone. I immediately apologised, looked up apologising again and, was staring straight into the face of someone I hadn't expected to see.

'Karen,' I said in my surprise, 'Sorry.'

'Arsehole.'

'Fine. You're probably right. Look, Karen, I'm sorry, it was an accident, I've had a difficult day. I'm not in the mood for this. It's ok, I'm leaving, forget I was here, I'll get out of your way'.

'That's the problem with you Mark, you're always in the way, always in the bloody way. What are you even doing here?'

'What's that mean? In the way?'

'You. You're always there, messing things up. And then when she needs you, you're nowhere to be seen. You told her you'd sort it!'

People by now were turning towards us, wondering what the raised voices were all about, I was rapidly being pointed out as the strange distant relation with the bruised face.

'Karen, I'm going.' I had no intention of hanging around any longer, by now I was as welcome as a dog poo sandwich in your packed lunch, and so I walked away. Karen, like her mother, was never one to back down and kept it going, following me out to the car park. 'Go on, run away, think you're the big man but can't take the truth'.

'Karen, I honestly have no idea what you're talking about, I really don't, but I'm off.' I was almost at the van, reaching for my keys, but still she kept following me, shouting at me, hounding me, but then a yelp.

I looked back, she was hobbling, she'd turned her ankle stepping off the kerb and was rubbing it.

'Are you okay?' I took her elbow and guided her towards the van, 'Here, come and sit down,' and eased her into the passenger seat. Reaching behind it I pulled out the first aid kit, and set about strapping her ankle. From the door pocket, I pulled a bottle of water that I handed to her, and as she twisted the cap open I passed her a couple of paracetamol also from the first aid kit which she gulped down.

Her anger and her fury had faded away, she sat looking out of the window and in a quiet voice said, 'Thank you'. She returned to observe the comings and goings of the crematorium, 'Why did you help me?'

'What kind of bloke do you think I am? You really think I'm that callous?'

She paused. 'No. No, I guess not.' Another pause, then, 'Thanks.'

In silence, we watched Sally's family board the waiting funeral cars and slowly trundle out towards the main road before joining the traffic and disappearing. It felt to me like a truce had been declared, making the van the Somme football pitch I guess, so I decided to broach the subject again. 'Karen, why are you so angry with me, what have I done?'

Karen took a deep slow breath, and to her credit stayed calm in her response. 'Because of Jen. I can't help being protective, she's my sister.'

'Okay, I can understand that, but sorry, what's that got to do with me?'

'Tommy. This man, he sounds like a posh wally but he's frightening Jen and the kids. He kept phoning her, but after I blocked his number he started turning up on the doorstep. You promised Jen you'd sort it out, but he won't go away.'

Now I understood, and I told her to leave it with me, this time Charlie Quentin would keep his distance, I'd make sure of that. I apologised and meant it. Her shoulders dropped as she uncrossed her arms and sat back in the seat.

'Thanks,' she said and seemed to mean it too. 'It's the kids I'm worried about, him coming over shouting the house down, it scares them. And how do I explain that to their parents?' I must have looked quizzical, either that or she was terrified of silences, as she felt the need to add, 'I'm a registered childminder now. I was already looking after my little one Ella, and Chloe after school so I thought I'd do it properly. That's five I look after now. But I do it at Jen's house as it's got the space. You know their conservatory out the back? Tommy painted it up, nice and bright with lots of Disney characters, looks great.'

I nodded that polite nod you give when someone's talking about their passion but you don't give a shit. Karen gave a sniff, dabbed a tissue to her face, then, 'What are you doing here Mark?' I appreciated the calm, rational tone to her voice.

'I did some work for Sally recently, we were related. Did you know that?' I asked, then watched her shake her head. 'Distantly. It's complicated, you know, my uncle's wife's sister's cat's best friend's turn left at the traffic lights, that sort of thing. But she was a nice girl, I liked her. How did you know her?'

'Sophia,' explained Karen. 'I'm her daughter Sophia's child minder, and got to know Sally from there. Our girls are—'

'Hold on.' Something had chimed a bell inside my head. 'You're the child minder? You're the one that found her?'

Karen looked at me, her mouth gaped open seeming unable to speak, until, 'How did you know that?'

She had a point; how did I know that? Then it came to me, of course, it was in Brennan's folder, but how could I explain that away? No need to bother it turned out as her fear of awkward silences took over again.

'Yes, I did, and it was horrible, I can still see it when I close my eyes. And they questioned me, the police, they said she came home because the childminder told her to. They went through my phone, I had to prove where I'd been all day, it was horrible. Horrible.' And then she began to sob.

Well, this was awkward. Ten minutes ago I'd been her sworn enemy, now I assumed she wanted me to comfort her. I moved my hand in small circles across her shoulder blade, I don't know if that helped, but I really didn't want to begin getting intimate. I tried changing the subject, finding happier topics.

'So, both your little girls together. Do they get on?' was the best attempt I could muster.

Karen sniffed, nodded, dabbed her eyes and eventually spoke, thank God, I was running out of ideas.

'Yeah, they get along great, could be sisters… twins in fact, turns out they share the same birthday. They became best friends, so naturally we became friends. I guess Sally was my best friend truth be told,' and another dab of the tissue to her eyes, then as though she knew what I was going to say next, 'My mum's looking after the kids today.'

'She's given up the golf? Looks like a lovely day for it as well.'

'I know, she wasn't happy about it, anyway I've promised to get back by lunchtime so she can still get nine holes this afternoon.'

'Is she good with kids?'

'If none of them need hospital treatment by the time I get back, I'll be happy.'

'How's Sophia, what with what's happened?'

'Poor little love doesn't understand what's going on.' We paused, quietly letting the enormity of that statement hang.

'Sally told me she'd met someone, sounded excited.'

'I know, it's so sad,' said Karen.

I didn't recall seeing anyone looking like a boyfriend amongst the bereaved – Brazil was there of course, but he was no grieving boyfriend, he was just an arsehole with anger issues, same as every day.

'So, where's the boyfriend today then? I mean, if they were that keen on each other, talking of moving in and all that, didn't he want to say a few words?'

'He really did want to be here, but when I spoke to him, he said he didn't think it would be appropriate. It's complicated. He's married.

'Married?' I recalled Sally saying his ex was a nuisance but still being married? That sounds a bit more than a mere nuisance, that sounds like good old-fashioned trouble. I suddenly felt sympathy tinged with anger for Sally. Something wasn't right.

'Apparently, she's a proper nightmare, he's been wanting to leave her for ages, only stays with her for the sake of their boy. Sally said she's one of those that always make a scene, very jealous, says they're going kill themselves, you know the sort I mean?'

'Makes sense for him not to come I suppose,' I said, disappointed he wasn't here, I felt I was getting close, I desperately needed something to give Hamlet. 'Have you met him, the fella?'

'Course, I introduced them.' There was a hint of pride in her voice. 'I'd often see him and his boy up the park, and we'd get talking when the kids played. One time I was with Sally, bumped into him and I made the introductions, Cupid Stunt, that's me. His boy and our girls, they're best friends. His work takes him away a couple of days a week, Essex I think, so I've started looking after his boy too a couple of times a week, that way they're all together.'

'Nice. Got a photo?'

'Yeah.' Karen's tone suggested that she was enjoying the conversation, and without her hostile edge I was enjoying it too.

'Here they are, the Three Amigos.' She turned her phone towards me. I could see three ridiculously cute toddlers posing in their dress-up costumes: two Disney princesses and Batman.

'Cute. Any others?'

'Here you go, that's all of us at the Christmas party,' she said passing me the phone displaying the two mums either side of Santa Claus and the three children standing in front of them.

As I looked closely at the picture the boy's face looked back straight and direct down the lens, his long shaggy mop of blond hair brushed away from his face, Batman unmasked.

'That's Joe is it?'

'Joseph, yeah ... how'd you know his name?'

'You must have told me earlier,' I said, but my reply was distracted, I was too busy scouring the picture. The bushy Santa beard and wig obscured most of his face, but the eyes, the eyes were clear, I recognised them, but where from?

'Very nice.'

I handed the phone back to her wondering whether I'd ever track this boyfriend down: I'd been to her flat, been to her work, not a trace of him. This was the closest I'd got but it still wasn't enough. It dawned on me the only option left was to ask Karen directly, but not too directly, I couldn't be seen to know too much, not after my mistake telling her I knew she'd discovered Sally, otherwise Karen might suspect something. 'So that's him is it, her fella?' I asked. 'What's his name?'

'Bobby,' replied Karen. Bobby? Fucking Bobby? The only Bobby I knew was a pub landlord in Chatham, a fat old Irishman with the pisshead's customary red vein network spread across his cheeks like the London Underground out to Zone 6 and beyond, the only pulling he'd done for years was pints, not bright young women like Sally. It definitely wasn't him. I didn't know anyone else called Bobby, but I knew those eyes.

'Bobby? You're definitely sure his name's Bobby?' I asked.

'Yes,' said Karen, a slight edge to her voice, annoyance, 'Sally always called him Bobby, and he looks like a Bobby, so Bobby stuck, we all call him Bobby. Far less formal than Robert, don't you think Robert sounds a bit stuck-up?'

As I drove her home, I encouraged her to talk about their kids, it seemed like a safe topic and I let her words wash over me as white noise, I didn't give it any attention and simply grunted reaction noises every now and then, because my mind was otherwise occupied. When we finally pulled up outside Jen's house, Karen bid me a friendly goodbye, which surprised her more than it did me, and I drove away feeling happy because you see, Robert, now we're getting somewhere. The only trouble is I know loads of Roberts. And then I also know a lot of Robs. But I only know one Rob with eyes like Santa's.

-40-

ON MY WAY home I stopped at the big Tesco on the Bowaters Roundabout, found myself a quiet spot in the furthest corner from the store, and wondered what to do next. I watched the constant flow of traffic through the gaps in the conifers and listened to Pop Master on the radio as a distraction.

'In which year did Bryan Adams spend a record-breaking 16 weeks at No.1 with '(Everything I Do) I Do It for You'?'

'Nineteen ninety-one,' I said out loud, even though I doubted Ken Bruce could hear me.

'Ninety ninety-two?'

'*Ooh, one year out,'* Ken's catchphrase, then his soft Scottish tones confirmed, *'It was nineteen ninety-one.'*

See? Should have listened to me, Tina in Bradford, although the final round, name three Robert Palmer hits in ten seconds, good luck with that Tina, you're on your own there. The quiz moved on to the news, I lost interest and snapped the radio off. I still didn't know what to do with myself, and my procrastination wanted a coffee.

A SURPRISINGLY UPBEAT and happy young woman handed me a takeaway latte from the coffee concession. Her badge said she was Viorica. There was an unfamiliar green and red flag below her name, I asked her where home was – partly out of interest but mainly so she'd know I was looking at the badge and not staring at her tits.

'Belarus,' she replied, sounding like a sultry Bond femme fatale. 'You want a muffin?'

I declined and walked away regretting that I couldn't think of a quippy response. James Bond would have batted something straight back, but then could James Bond beat me at Pop Master? No, I didn't think so either. As I wandered slowly past the multitude of conveyor belts, the pole-mounted flashing lights above the tills caught my attention. I'd had a contract a few years back changing all of them over in stores across Kent, it was a nice tickle – good rates, fast in and out work, premium for working overnight, lovely.

'Mark! Mark!' I looked around to find who was calling me. 'I thought that was you,' said Mrs Wilkes. She was one of those women that always seem to be dressed for the gym, no matter what time of day, like even now when pushing a trolley laden with bags she was in her customary lycra and hoodie. 'Didn't recognise you in a suit, very smart.'

I smiled at the compliment, but she had realised too late the significance of my clothes. She raised a startled hand to her mouth, 'I'm so sorry. Was it Tommy's funeral today?'

'No. I'd actually just been to somebody else's funeral.'

'Oh, well that's okay then.' Rather a peculiar reply, but I sort of knew what she meant.

A few shoppers bustled between us, interrupting our silence, then she spoke again and this time the shoppers went round us making our conversation an island rather than a short cut.

'I'm glad I saw you, I've been meaning to call,' said Mrs Wilkes. 'The police have gone, and said we can move back in. When do you think you can come back and get going again?'

'Brilliant news. Start of next week suit you?'

Instead of looking pleased, she fiddled with her long-beaded necklace, clicking across each amber bead like a rosary. 'Please don't be cross with me,' she talked down towards her Nikes, 'but I don't want the kitchen anymore.' She took a deep breath before continuing. 'It just doesn't seem right. How am I expected to live, make dinner, carry on, knowing that someone was murdered there? It's just ... wrong.'

'But I thought you wanted me to come back? Didn't you say—'

'Yes, yes.' A tremble had crept into her voice. 'I want it all ripped out and done again new. I don't want a single trace of it to remain.'

'And Mr Wilkes? Is he okay about this?'

Mrs Wilkes pulled her phone from her handbag and called her husband, telling him she was with me and recounted our full conversation so far before handing the phone to me.

'My wife has decided she cannot set foot in that house again. I want your best price to rip out and install a brand-new kitchen, as well as giving the whole house a general tidy up, then we're putting it up for sale.'

How would I react if it had been in my house – would I be able to sleep at night, I wondered before having the presence of mind to let him know that what they were proposing was very expensive.

'I'm well aware of that thank you.' Mr Wilkes's attitude clearly hadn't improved at all I noted, whilst making a mental reminder to change my quote from very expensive to obscenely expensive.

'Look, I'm happy to grub it all out, but I still need to be paid for the work done to date.'

'I'm well aware of that too,' he said. 'I want you starting Monday, so I need your estimate pronto, understand? I've told the estate agent she can market the house from the start of next month, so you've got two weeks to do everything and get out, is that clear? I want rid of the bloody thing. There's been lots of distraught tearful women leaving flowers outside, it's very depressing.'

'If I get an invoice to you today, can you pay it?'

A frustrated sigh blew in my ear, he clearly wasn't happy about it, but to my sheer delight he said, 'Alright, send it over today and if I can I'll pay it on-line this afternoon, if not it'll be tomorrow. But don't take the piss.'

BACK IN THE van my coffee tasted sweeter with the thought that I might actually be winning: I'd be able to pay most of my debts without even touching Hamlet's money, and then if I can load something extra into Mr Wilkes's new estimate I might be able to clear the interest on Hamlet's debt and give him the whole lot back and walk away from this fool's errand.

-41-

WITH THE SUBTLETY of a Hellfire missile, Perry bounced through the kitchen door, announcing herself with a loud hello. I've never had anyone let themselves into my house unannounced like that, I thought it was a tv soap opera thing, I didn't know it happened in real life. Even Dad would tap on the glass first. I wasn't sure how I felt, part of me welcomed the intimacy, but a bigger part of me resented the intrusion.

'Hello to you too,' I said, once I'd caught my breath back after the surprise. 'What's that you've got?'

'This?' she looked at the envelopes clutched in her hand as though it was the first time she'd seen them, 'Post. Clinton gave them to me outside.'

'Clinton? Who the bloody hell's Clinton when he's at home?''

She looked at me wide eyed and open mouthed, 'Duh! The postman.'

Through the window I could see the postie a few doors down the street: dreadlocks bouncing rhythmically under the band of his large headphones as he walked, shorts in all weathers.

'I never knew his name was Clinton. He's been delivering here for years, he's never spoken to me in all that time, you've only been here a few days—'

'Yeah, he said you were a misery guts,' she replied playfully, but by now I could at least see it was me failing yet again to connect.

'Looks like a lot of bills for MP Electrical Limited,' she continued, flicking through the dozen or so envelopes in her hand, until she came across a small brown one. 'Oh, no, wait, looks like one from the taxman for a Mr Mark V. Poynter esquire'

Great, just what I need right now, a letter from Her Majesty's Revenue and Customs. I took it from her and dropped it on the table: the longer I leave it unopened the less I owe.

'So, Mark Vee?'

'Mark Five. It took them a while to create perfection,' I said and she smiled, held it for a beat and then:

'I didn't know you had a middle name. What's the V stand for? Vincent? Victor?'

'I don't want to talk about it.'

'Vladimir?' she said in a terrible vampire voice.

'Leave it.'

'Alright, calm down ... Veronica.'

An unwelcome warmth had bloomed around my cheeks.

'Oh, come on.' Perry gave me a playful nudge of the elbow, 'I promise I won't laugh, come on, tell me.'

I paused, drew in a deep breath, held it for one second two seconds three seconds, then, 'Vivian.'

'What?' she hooted with laughter, falling to her side on the sofa in hysterics.

'You said you wouldn't laugh!' I rose to my feet and crossed the room to face her, 'It's not funny.'

'But it is. Vivian.' she collapsed into giggles again. 'Come on, admit it, it is a bit funny. You certainly don't look like a Vivian.'

'Blame my Dad, he was a fan.' I was trying to stay calm, I didn't want to sound petulant.

'Of who? Vivien Leigh? I guess you're lucky he wasn't into Doris Day!' Cue yet more laughing.

'Viv Stanshall, actually.' I realised as soon as I added the *'actually'* I'd failed the petulant test.

'Of yes, of course,' she said, holding back her smile. I knew she didn't have a clue who I was talking about.

'Dad was a fan. Mark for Marc Bolan and Vivian for Viv Stanshall'

'I see.' she had regained her composure and dabbed her eyes with her cuff then, 'Hang on, Marc Bolan, he was Marc with a C. You're Mark with a K.'

'That was Mum's doing. She was happy to go along with his choices providing it was with a K, we're not Americans so spell it properly was what she said, so I'm told. Anyway, Bolan's real name was Mark with a K.'

'Well then, I learn something new every day,' she replied, before adding, 'Vivian.'

'Stop it. It's not funny. I don't like it. When they found out my middle name at school, they took the piss so much it'd choke a dialysis machine.' I was aware my tone had become sharper and slightly louder, she'd noticed it too, as the giggles stopped.

'Oh excuse me, boo fucking hoo, poor old Mr Doesn't-Like-His-Slightly-Posh-Silly-Name. My heart bleeds for you. How mean, the nasty boys teased you.' Her voice was harsh, her spine was as straight as a pole and her eyes were locked on to mine, never breaking contact.

'You want to try going to a school where the only person who looks like you is your own sister! Where you have to make your name so simple just to get anyone to talk to you. Where you've heard at least thirty horrible ways to describe you before you're seven, and ten thousand by the time you're seventeen! Where people actually stop and stare at you for eating a sandwich, oh I didn't know your kind ate English food, and the weird thing is they'd think there was nothing wrong in saying it. Forgive me if I can't feel your pain for your silly name, but believe it or not, some of us have had to carry a lot worse. So get over yourself, and man up Mark Vivian Poynter.'

An awkward silence filled every square inch of the room, neither of us knowing quite what to say or do, I'd messed up again and felt the shame burn red stripes under my eyes. She held the rest of the envelopes towards me, an olive branch in second class stamps. I took them from her and muttered I was sorry. With a tap along the short edge and then the long I lay them as a neat, smart pile on the table; a problem for another day.

'I'm on the graveyard shift tonight,' said Perry eventually and immediately it felt as though the black clouds had parted to make way for the sun. 'I don't start until midnight so thought I'd pop over, see if you fancied something to eat and also, how was the funeral, tell me.'

Sally's funeral, it seemed like ages ago. but it was only when Perry asked, I realised I hadn't even taken my tie off.

'Fine, nice, it was nice. You know, nice family, nice words.' I struggled to think of things to say, how do you critique a funeral?

'I was worried about you today,' she said, and picking up on my quizzical expression continued, 'About your dad. Sometimes funerals stir up emotions unexpectedly, you might walk in there right as rain for someone you barely knew but end up bawling your eyes out because without realising it the whole occasion has clicked all the buttons for someone you loved.'

'Ah I see. Thanks, but I'm fine. What have you been up to?'

I was desperate to change the subject. I appreciated her concern but those buttons… they're permanently flicked on and I can't find a way to get them off, I don't need a chorus of 'Abide With Me' to tell me my heart's broken.

'Well, actually, talking about your dad, I've been looking into mesothelioma.'

'Have you now?' I didn't like the way this conversation was going, I already had a touch of resentment simmering from the over familiar way she'd waltzed in and then given me a dressing down, and now this topic was drip-feeding petrol to it.

'I didn't realise that the Medway Towns was a national hotspot for it, second highest in the country.'

'It was the asbestos.' I knew all the facts, there was nothing she could tell me I didn't know already. 'The Dockyard used it in everything, all over the place, they probably even had it on their chips at lunchtime! Dad was a boiler maker, he'd seen more than his fair share of the stuff.'

'But there's lots of support groups,' said Perry trying to be helpful, but the fuel was drip drip dripping on my resentment. I couldn't afford to let it ignite an explosion but I knew what was coming next, and sure enough: 'And there's law firms winning compensation for the families.'

'No, no, no!' I immediately regretted my tone as she stared at me like I'd slapped her around the face. 'Sorry. Not interested. No.'

'But why?'

'It won't bring him back will it? Look, Dad was seventy-four, that's still pretty good by anyone's standards. Was he supposed to live to a hundred and fifty? How can I justify claiming the disease robbed me of crucial years with him?' She nodded as I spoke, she'd slipped into her caring professional mode again. 'The support groups are great, they do a fantastic job they really do, but I honestly don't think it's fair that I waste their time, not when there's families that need it much more than me.'

'Okay, I see where you're coming from, I was only trying to ... you know?' She looked at the floor as she spoke, keeping her eyes away from me 'And I thought maybe, you know, saying you had money problems, maybe...'

'No way. I refuse to use his suffering like a "Get out of jail free card" – it doesn't sit right, sorry.'

'Okay, okay, I understand, shall we change the subject?' she said. I nodded, she rose and approached me with outstretched arms which she then wrapped around me squeezing away any bad thoughts. My head cleared and all I wanted was to stay like this.

'Do you like Indian food? I cook a mean Balti, my mum's recipe, you've not had anything like it.'

It sounded great and I told her so whilst I loosened my tie. She suggested I have a shower, get changed and then come over when I'm ready. I liked the relaxed, easygoing attitude she had, although I still couldn't see me letting myself in unannounced, I'd be ringing the bell and waiting on the doorstep for the foreseeable.

She stood to leave and looked at me as though seeing me properly for the first time. 'Are you sure you're okay? You just look a bit… your eyes, they're a bit pink.'

'I'm fine, it's been a difficult few days, don't worry.'

'It's okay to be sad occasionally, you know.' She held me again and I felt as though I could melt. 'What's that they say: Sad is happy for deep people.'

'Who says that? Shakespeare? Churchill? The Dalai Lama?'

'Doctor Who. I like quotations, I collect them.'

'In that case you'd get on with a woman I met the other day.' I thought about the truth behind that comment then added, 'No you wouldn't. She was vile.'

'Go on then, do tell, I love a bit of bitchy gossip.'

'There's not much to tell, she's the manager at the old folks' home I went to with Disco, nasty woman, but her whole office was plastered with feminist slogans.'

'Nasty how? Did she call you Vivian? Sorry, joke.'

'Something like that,' I replied, realising too late that I'd taken the can marked 'Juicy Wiggly Worms', ripped the lid off and tossed it all over the floor. I never ever set out to cause offence unnecessarily, never talk about politics or religion that's what Dad always said, and I really wasn't in the mood for an argument, not tonight.

'She was just… nasty,' was the best I could muster. 'She just wanted to put everyone down. Men, I mean… female empowerment, beating the men in a men's world, that sort of thing.'

'Uh huh,' came Perry's response, very non-committal, she was holding back judgement, waiting to see where I was going with this. I knew there was no way those worms were going back in the tin now, they'd seen freedom and were wriggling for it with all their might. I rubbed the palm of my hand across my tired face, and probed an itch at the corner of my eye, deliberately putting off saying anything, hoping the subject would change by itself but she wasn't going to let it drop. 'Go on then,' she prompted; brilliant, looks like I'm having that argument after all.

And so, I told her about my visit to Kate Fuller's office, how she savaged the car dealership on speaker phone, how she'd rendered Charlie Quentin into a gibbering imbecile, and mostly how she spoke so disparagingly about her husband, like he was nothing more to her than an au-pair and errand boy.

I sat back against the sofa, my head turned and eyes locked on the dead black slab of the dormant tv, I'd already adopted a defensive posture against the argument that was about to roast me like a forest fire. Mentally, I braced myself, here it comes…

'God, she sounds like a right bitch.'

Well, I wasn't expecting that response it must be said, yay, go Perry. I clasped her face in my hands and kissed her on the forehead, and then promptly apologised for being swept away by the relief. I was beginning to ramble, I didn't know what I was saying, it was nothing more than a random reflexive mind dump, 'I am most definitely not a misogynist, I'm pro-women, very pro-women, I love women, all of them.' Perry took my hands in hers and told me shush. Gratefully I shushed.

'Calm down. Look I'm a feminist, and proud of it.' She spoke softly, but with purpose and confidence. 'Being a feminist doesn't mean I hate men, it means I hate ignorance and inequality, and if you do too, then you're a feminist as well because that's what it means, understand?'

I nodded, what she'd said made perfect sense to me.

'What she is, she's not a feminist, she's an obnoxious arsehole, and they come in all shapes, sizes, colours and genders. Believe me, I work around doctors, there's more than enough God complexes walking around there, I've seen every variety you can think of. Call it what you like: A Type, Alpha, Arsehole. It all starts with an "A" and all means someone who thinks everything in life is a battle that they have to win at all costs.' Perry was right I realised: Kate Fuller, Mr Wilkes, they're both the same, larging-it-off, thinking they're better than everyone else, in competition against a world who generally either doesn't realise or doesn't care.

'So, you collect quotations do you, got any other great words of wisdom?' I asked, feeling the time was right to lighten the mood and at last change the subject.

Perry looked to the ceiling pretending to be in deep thought, a finger on her chin adding to the comedic pose, 'The man who walks through airport doors sideways is always going to Bangkok.'

-42-

PERRY WAS RIGHT, her Balti was amazing. There's nothing to beat a good home cooked meal is there? The very fact it was her mum's recipe seemed comforting to her, and she chatted happily about her family and her childhood. I, on the other hand, did not. It's not that I didn't want to – although I wouldn't have wanted to – but it was because we were joined by Uncle Bern, who took it upon himself to entertain Perry with every embarrassing anecdote he could think of about me. He'd only popped in to remind me about Harpo, and to get him off my back I agreed we'd sort Harpo out in the morning, but hearing there was the possibility of a home cooked meal, he managed to scrounge himself a seat at the table. Not that Perry seemed to mind, for some reason she found him charming and funny.

I began clearing the empty plates away, leaving Uncle Bern and Perry laughing raucously at Bern's telling of my reluctant appearance as the donkey in the school Nativity play when the night outside screamed a single ear-splitting beep. Out the window I saw a single flash of amber lights, something had triggered the alarm on my van but no sooner had it started than it ended. Very odd.

Waiting by the window, I noticed movement around the van, someone was there. It was the same guy in the grey hoodie as before, the one I'd seen outside Sally's flat. I was certain of it, and this time I wasn't going to spook him, this time I wanted to see his face properly. I needed to be sure.

I opened the front door gently and sprinted towards the van as fast as a bellyful of curry and rice would allow. As I approached, I heard the rolling rumble of my van's side door being slid open, and the metallic clunking of things being tipped over.

I neared the van, the clunking continued, he hadn't noticed me yet, I trod as softly as I could and edged around the back of the van. The Clunker was hunched over, leaning in through the sliding doorway, busy rummaging through the contents of the van.

I raised both arms together ready to drop them on to his shoulders, I was one pace behind him, but he must have known as he spun round to face me. My raised hands dropped as planned only we were locked now, face to face. I looked straight into his eyes. He looked surprised but he must have realised my shock and surprise was greater because before I could react his arm swung up clutching a heavy drum of cable from inside the van. It struck me on the temple, a red flash went off in my head, I let go. I stumbled back on to the tarmac, more out of shock than pain, and as I sat there, I watched him run away. He didn't dare look back as he disappeared out of sight.

Uncle Bern and Perry helped me to my feet and hauled me out of the road. 'What was he after? Did he take anything?' asked Bern, looking toward the van for any sign of damage.

'No,' I said but I could hazard a good guess at what he was after. He must be working for Hamlet now too, lumbered with a debt too big to clear and forced to search for Sally's killer in the hope of shaking it off. He must have thought I had information, I must be ahead of the pack in that case, which was a perverse kind of victory I suppose.

'I think you'd better come here,' called Perry, from further up the road. Bern and I found her standing outside my lock-up garage holding my heavy-duty cruiser padlock; its shackle had been neatly severed by a mechanical cutter.

The garage stood open, looking as if a tornado had whipped through it at a thousand miles an hour scattering the contents everywhere. And then at the back, in the wreckage I saw three grimy transparent boxes, ripped open, tipped and tossed. Dad's things lay loose and torn amongst the ankle-deep debris. Mum's Staffordshire dogs like black and white pieces of eggshell, smashed to smithereens, the same as everything else I've come into contact with recently: my business, my reputation, my friends ... all broken and ruined.

Some reflex made me reach down to grab a stray piece of paper that had been lifted on the breeze, catching it before the evening wind whipped it away. I knew as I reached for it that it was an old photograph, from a time of white borders, bright primary colours and a flat dull finish.

In the picture my young dad grinned back, he'd have been about the age I am now, beside him sat Bern looking quite groovy in his dark glasses and Fred Perry, still sporting wavy black hair, both of them on deckchairs in front of a two-tone caravan, white over olive, cans of beer in hand. At their feet, a small laughing boy held a plastic yellow football. The camera was looking towards the sun and bright light blanched the top corner of the picture with white space, leaving her legs poking out below as the only trace of Auntie Val; my Mum was never great at taking photos.

'Let's see that,' said Bern, looking over my shoulder. 'Caravanning in Paignton, do you remember? Your dad borrowed it from one of his mates in the Dockyard and towed it down with that big old Granada he used to have. Took forever as your mum was scared it'd tip over if he went too fast. You learned to swim on that holiday too, remember?'

I did, I remember it vividly, it seemed to be sunny every day, the woodland camp site felt like a proper outdoor adventure to a little boy, I can picture Mum and Val both looking young and beautiful, and Bern promised me 50p if I could swim a width of the pool without armbands. And I did it. 50p was a lot of money in those days, especially when you were only five. It was probably the only time I ever got any money out of Bern. Happy times.

Perry broke me out of my nostalgia with a sob, I hadn't noticed how this had affected her, and I put my arms around her in comfort. Bern rubbed her shoulders, muttering, 'It's all okay darling, nothing to get upset about.' I was surprised how easily intimacy and reassurance came to him, and I recognised insecure pangs of envy and inferiority stinging me.

'We need to call the police,' she said, looking at us both, panic shining through her tears.

'No, the police won't be any good,' I said. 'Nothing's been taken, he's just made a mess, that's all.'

Perry protested but Bern made soothing noises, telling her I was right.

'Besides,' I began to say, then paused. How sure was I? Enough I reckoned. 'I know who it was who did this, they both looked at me expectantly. 'It was Adam.'

A silence passed.

'Who's Adam?' asked Perry.

'His brother,' said Bern. In my hand, Adam looked up at us both clutching his yellow ball, a time of innocence. Happy times.

BERN DIDN'T STAY much longer; he'd had his free dinner so he left. Actually, that's not fair. I think he realised he'd be better off out of the way given how I felt. He was very gracious in the way he thanked Perry, and I told him I'd see him in the morning.

'I like him, he's sweet,' said Perry, talking to my back. I'd been trying to make sense of what happened and had retreated into my thoughts, but not wanting to appear moody made myself busy washing up whilst Perry had seen Bern to the door. The water was too hot, every plunge into the scalding sink to seek out something to scrub clean turned my hands scarlet. It was painful, but not enough to care about. Perry approached from behind, wrapping her arms around my waist. I felt warmth against my shoulder blade as she rested her head on me. 'Are you thinking about your brother?'

Funnily enough I wasn't, in fact I'd been thinking about Mum. Adam was always her boy, no doubt about that. Maybe Mum dying is what set him off.

'I've never heard you talk about your mum before,' said Perry taking my hand, leading me to the sofa, 'What was she like?'

'Beautiful, like Helen Reddy.' As soon as I said it, I saw Perry's blank look, 'No-one remembers Helen Reddy anymore, the only reason I do is because Mum only ever had two cassettes in her car, one was by The Carpenters and the other was "The Best of Helen Reddy". In the picture on the front she had this sort of shaggy 70s pageboy hairstyle. Mum looked just like her.'

Perry fiddled with her smartphone while I spoke, and turned the screen to me, 'This her?'

'Yeah ... well, that's Helen Reddy. But Mum was the spit of her.'

'Very pretty.'

'Beautiful.'

'Do you remember the songs, were they any good?' She fiddled with her phone, and then all of a sudden music started to play through her Bluetooth enabled speakers, '...*I am woman, hear me roar, in numbers too big to ignore...*'

'I know this!' squealed Perry, turning the volume up, she now had to shout to be heard, 'Awesome song, we used to do this at karaoke when I was at college, I never knew who sang it though ... *I am invincible ...*'

I let her enjoy her sing-a-long and poured out the last splosh of red wine from the bottle, realising I'd had it all to myself – Perry wasn't drinking as she was starting work later and Bern was driving

– first time since I can't remember I'd done a bottle on my own, but I liked how it muffled my thoughts. Perhaps I wasn't thinking clearly, but at least I wasn't thinking painfully.

'Your mum had great taste,' Perry informed me when the song finished, making me smile, and we sat silently for a couple of seconds waiting for the next song to start, another one I recognised. Straight away, I was in the back of her Renault 5 coming home from the Pentagon Centre. Perry was happy to let it play in the background, and lowered the volume.

'We were very much a family of two halves, me and Dad, Adam and Mum,' I said, remembering how we were. 'Don't get me wrong, Mum and Dad were solid, they were very much in love right up to the end, 'til death do us part and all that, but for some reason that's how it was, Mum and Adam, me and Dad.'

Perry twisted the cap off a bottle of water with a hiss of escaped bubbles then gestured for me to continue.

'I never knew why, maybe because he was her first baby so she felt something special for him. To be honest I never really gave it much thought because, when she passed, I still had Dad. I was only a kid, just turned twelve but I was a young twelve if that makes sense.' She nodded that it did. 'And because of that, Dad was very protective over me. Adam was sixteen, maybe he felt there wasn't enough room for him, maybe he felt outside of the family now. I'm wondering if that's what set him off on the path he took.'

'And what path was that?' she asked, softly behind us Helen Reddy chanted about Delta Dawn.

'He wanted—' I didn't know what to say, or where to start. Was there one moment, a single incident that sparked it all off? If so, I couldn't see it. It was more like wallpaper – there every day to the point you stop noticing, wallpaper – quite sad, fucked up wallpaper, but wallpaper nonetheless. I'd stopped talking, I'd just petered out, as if I'd run out of power, Perry gently rubbed my back, trying to coax some life back in my dead batteries, but I didn't know how to go on, and gave up altogether.

'Okay, okay,' she said in soothing tones, 'How long since you saw him last?'

'Six years,' I said, six years and four months in fact, 'Didn't know if he was alive or dead, he just disappeared one day.'

'How? How can anyone just vanish in this day and age?'

'I don't know, if I ever see him again, I'll ask for a demonstration, shall I?' I snapped, and then immediately apologised, it wasn't her I was angry with.

She kindly accepted my apology, but wasn't going to let it go, 'There's CCTV cameras everywhere, phones can be tracked, and as for bank accounts…'

'I know. That's why I'd reconciled myself that he must be dead, it didn't make sense otherwise.'

'Well, you must be so glad then,' she said, squeezing me. 'Congratulations.' But I wasn't in the mood for celebrating. I know I should have felt relief, but I didn't. Instead my body shivered with icy cold anger, my skin was prickling and my nerves twitching. A normal person should be overjoyed their brother was back from the dead, but not me. I felt betrayed, humiliated, as if I was the victim of some cruel elaborate prank that the rest of the world was in on and now everyone's laughing and pointing fingers at me.

Perry spoke, I found her voice calming, 'We'll never know how until you ever get to speak to him, but well… you know… how?'

'Like I say, it was about six years ago.' I placed the empty wine glass on the table, leaned forwards and nudged it to the centre with my fingertips while I composed my version of events in my head, 'He'd got involved with stuff for Hamlet, working for him.'

'Him again?'

'We were all a little in awe of him back then if I'm honest.' I twiddled the circular base of the glass, rotating it half a turn, piecing together what to say next. 'We all thought hanging around with Hamlet gave us a bit of glamour, we never had to wait to get served at a bar, never had to queue outside a nightclub, doors were held open for us, we were like local celebrities. It was right before social media exploded, things weren't filmed or reported every second of the day on people's phones, so you could earn a bit of status being at the scene of the stories, especially after they'd got whipped up into legend by the gossips.'

Perry nodded, with a look that said she understood but didn't get it, that was fine, different upbringings, different aspirations.

'Trouble is, Hamlet doesn't give it away for free. If you want the perks then you have to pay for it. Some way or other. Adam seemed to love it. He'd had a few jobs, he'd worked for the Royal Mail, he'd done some gardening, he was working as an estate agent of all things when he disappeared, but I got the impression that turning pro, going full-time with Hamlet was what he'd always wanted, and we ended up arguing about it.'

'Why? Sounds to me like you were keen on it too.'

I reached for the wine glass but remembered I'd emptied it and the bottle too, so I twisted it another half turn on its stem; in the silent pause Helen Reddy serenaded me with some unfamiliar ballad.

'I don't know, maybe. But I was different. I'd get called in to do little jobs here and there, when he needed an electrical job done with no questions asked. And I was a lot younger, it was nice to get paid handsomely, have cash to flash around at the weekend. And I suppose it was quite nice feeling part of something secret and important.'

'Important?' she seemed surprised.

'Probably not the right word, but I can't think of a better way to describe it.'

'No, I don't think important is the right word at all. Significant, possibly, but definitely not important.' Perry didn't seem impressed, and with hindsight I couldn't argue with her.

'Anyway, Adam didn't have a trade or any skills, he was just used by Hamlet for fetching and carrying and a bit of driving. Strange now I think about it, he was so proud of himself, thought he was as cool as cowshit, but made me swear not to tell Dad. He knew Dad wouldn't approve. Dad always would say to us there's no quick way to getting rich, didn't that prove true this past couple of weeks for me.'

I noticed a space had opened up between Perry and me on the sofa, she had the look of someone that had wanted the truth only to wish it had remained a secret. But she could tell that, now I'd started, I needed to finish, that I'd bottled it up too long, and through just the gentle movement of her eyes urged me to carry on.

'His behaviour started changing, I began to suspect he'd started using drugs, more heavily than just weekend partying. We argued about it. By then I was already trying to distance myself and get out of that whole environment.'

Perry got up and headed towards the kitchen without saying a word or looking back at me. I slumped back on the sofa, and ran my hands through my hair, this was a challenge and it felt like I was losing. Perry returned with two bottles of water, handed one to me, and asked me why I wanted to get out.

'The more I saw, the less I liked it. The stardust, the glitter, it was all crap, it was a dirty ruthless business, I didn't fit in there, I knew I didn't belong.' I twisted the neck of the bottle and took a long sip, the bubbles felt dry as they popped in my mouth. 'We were at a party Hamlet was hosting in a room above one of his pubs. I needed the loo but it was occupied so I went downstairs, only to find that one was occupied too. Seeing as it was after hours and the pub was closed, I decided to go behind the bar to see if I could find a staff bathroom. I found it all right. But that was occupied as well, in this case by three blokes battering some poor sod to a pulp. I watched them slam his head against the edge of the toilet bowl three or four times, his eye was split, his front teeth gone, blood was sprayed up the white tiles, thick and the most vivid red I've ever seen. The guy looked like he'd checked out, they were just hurling him about like a toy, there was no resistance. The man nearest me leaned over and whispered *"Get yourself back upstairs, there's a good boy"* and pulled the door shut. Like an obedient little sheep, I did as I was told.'

Perry looked shocked, and a little disappointed but I was beyond caring, I was happy at last to finally offload this canker I'd been carrying about for years.

'That sounds awful,' she finally said.

I took another sip from the water to avoid saying anything further. After consideration I decided to leave the story there, I didn't know how she'd react if she heard the rest of it and I really didn't want to find out. But that wasn't the end of it. I went back upstairs and rejoined the party as though nothing had happened, didn't say a word to anybody, and tried to lose myself in the darkness and music. Twenty minutes or so later the same man opened the door, letting in a rectangle of light through the doorway, and caught Hamlet's eye on the opposite side of the room. I could see both of them from where I was. The man gave a solemn shake of the head, pursed lips. And I'll never forget what I saw next. Green and red and blue lights pulsed in time with the music across Hamlet's face as he slowly drew his extended finger across his throat. Across the room the man nodded as though saying "Message received", the darkness was sucked back into the hole as the door closed, and he was gone. I have no doubt what the message meant, and what the man was instructed to do. All my life I've liked to think I was a good person, that when the time came, I would stand up and do the right thing. But I turned and ran the first time I was told to, and I sat back and watched the order being given and didn't do a thing, never even told anyone, even now I can't bring myself to admit my complicity. It was at that point I knew I needed to get away, this wasn't the life for me.

'Adam and I had stopped talking, and he barely spoke to Dad too which broke his heart. A few months later I get a phone call from a pub landlord in Gillingham complaining about Adam. He said Adam's car was in their car park, been there for a couple of weeks and it was making deliveries difficult. I told him it wasn't my problem.'

'And what did he say?'

'He said he'd tried calling Adam a few times to move it but he wasn't getting any response, and then moaned that if he's on holiday he was an inconsiderate dick and his car was about to be towed if it wasn't moved pronto.'

The landlord hadn't been exaggerating, it looked like it hadn't been touched for a while, it was carpeted in sticky yellow dust dropped from the trees and the tyres sagged a little. I drove it home and left it outside my house where it sat untouched for a further four years, waiting like Greyfriars Bobby for its owner to come back, but no-one's seen or heard from him since.

When he didn't attend Dad's funeral, that's when I finally decided he was never coming back, and it was at that point I reconciled myself to being the last living person in my family, the end of the line. I sold the car at the same time as I got rid of Dad's stuff – apart from the sentimental bits now lying in pieces in my garage. I looked on it as making a clean break with the past, setting myself up as the sole survivor of the Poynter dynasty.

For years I've tried, with varying degrees of success, not to imagine Hamlet drawing his finger across his throat giving that same silent instruction about Adam, and now it appears he was alive all along. I'd reconciled myself to the thought he was with Mum and Dad, but now the wound had been ripped open and bled as raw as the day he disappeared. Where had he been, and why did he go?

-43-

JUST AFTER BREAKFAST time, Uncle Bern helped me tidy the mess in the garage, and then we headed over to Harpo's place. From the outside, it looks like what it is, an Airey House refaced in brickwork. Airey Houses were widespread in this area: cheap and quick to assemble prefabricated concrete panels making them the ideal Post-War solution to replenish the depleted social housing stock. They weren't particularly pretty to look at but semi-rural ones such as Harpo's, on the edge of the Medway boundary before you tip over the hill down to Maidstone, benefitted from having a lot of outside space.

Harpo had concreted over every available inch – front, back and sides – and then filled it with piles and piles of salvaged bits and pieces. Fabulous ornate terracotta chimney pots jostled for space beside a stack of tin baths, pallets of every kind of roof tile ran the length of the property, Victorian cast iron fire surrounds lived next door to 1960s glass blocks.

We parked the van on the front forecourt. I'd picked up some new infrared sensors designed not to be triggered by animals, so Fantastic Mr Fox wouldn't keep switching on Harpo's lights every time he took a short-cut across the yard. For what they cost, I couldn't be bothered getting into an argument with Harpo about it, I'd simply swap them over and get gone, shouldn't take an hour, and then we can drop back on to trying to earn a proper living.

Uncle Bern walked into the Airey House looking for Harpo. He doesn't live here, I should have mentioned that. Harpo has a very nice bungalow almost directly opposite on the other side of the road, obviously there's a good living to be made in junk. The Airey House is strictly business, downstairs front is his office and then downstairs back and all of upstairs is storage of everything that needs to be kept out of the weather: doors, handles, mirrors, plaster cornices, stained glass and so on, a Tardis treasure trove of old crap.

'Harpo … Harpo … Harpo,' Uncle Bern hollered at the top of his voice. Eventually he gave up, stood in the doorway and shouted for me this time. 'He's not here, does it look like he's at home?'

I looked across my shoulder over to the opposite side of the road towards Harpo's house, and I saw him waddling towards us clutching a half-chewed triangle of toast.

'Bloody hell Bern,' he said, between bites, every mouthful disappearing in to that nasty prickly infestation on his face, 'I could hear you all the way over there in my kitchen.'

'But could you hear us sitting on the toilet?' asked Bern.

'No,' said Harpo, looking a little confused.

'Because we could hear you.' Bern laughed loudly at his silly joke, and I have to admit I did too. Harpo stood still in the middle of the road, feet apart like a Wild West gunslinger and raising both hands held middle fingers aloft, flipping up the bird in stereo. That's when I saw him – behind Harpo, parked up on a grass verge five or six houses back, the silver Mondeo and yes, I could clearly see the man with the light bulb shaped head. He was watching me. I didn't want to spook him so I turned my full attention to Harpo by walking to meet him, placing an arm around his shoulder and then heading back towards Uncle Bern in the doorway. My neck itched, eager to turn around. I hoped this pantomime was working and Light Bulb Head would stay put for now.

Hamlet had sworn that there was no police surveillance on me, who is this guy?

I SWAPPED OVER the sensors, and Harpo seemed pleased. We shook hands on the forecourt and then I began to reload the van with steps and tools whilst Harpo headed home with Bern, promising him tea and toast. As he crossed the road, and as rehearsed, Harpo made a show of noticing the Mondeo, he gave Bern a nudge and pointed at it shouting, 'Alan! Alan!'

Light Bulb Head looked up, startled. But before he could react, Harpo and Bern were at the car.

'Alan, how are you?' continued Harpo. Bern had positioned himself right in front of the car, his knees virtually touching the radiator grille much to the driver's surprise, but much more of a surprise was the grinning Harpo's revolting beard at his window coming towards him like a minge with yellow teeth.

Grinning and gesturing to lower the window, Harpo kept the act going, 'Hello Alan, I thought that was you, didn't I Bern? I'm not actually open this morning, getting some work done, but anything you need, as I think they've just about finished. You've finished, haven't you Bern?'

'Yep, all done, we're finished.'

'See, they're finished. So, what can I do for you, Alan?'

The driver's head flicked between Harpo and Bern and back again; he was confused, and as long as he was confused, he was distracted, and that suited me. I ducked down low, I don't know why but that's what they do in the movies, and hurried along the opposite footpath before crossing the road. I pulled hard on the door, throwing it wide open and jumped in the passenger seat at which point the driver, Light Bulb Head shrieked like a little girl, 'Please don't hurt me, take the car, take the cameras, just don't hurt me. Please.'

With Bern and Harpo's help, we escorted him back to Harpo's office.

'Sit him on that bench over there,' said Bern.

'Bench? That's a genuine Victorian oak and velvet church kneeler in the Gothic style,' said Harpo, at his most pedantic. 'You break it you buy it.'

Light Bulb Head looked around bewildered but thankfully he'd stopped shrieking as it was beginning to get on my nerves. I leaned over him, and demanded he tell me who he is and why he'd been following me.

'My name's Graham. I'm a private investigator,' we were informed, not to mention intrigued.

'And why is a private investigator following me?'

'I was hired by a man called French, he wanted you followed.' Not a name I recognised, I was still none the wiser. 'You've been sleeping with his wife, he wanted photographs, for the divorce.'

'I don't know what you're talking about,' I said, only to feel a nudge at my elbow. Uncle Bern was holding Graham's digital camera. With his finger holding down a button, photos flicked past on the small screen in rapid succession, hundreds of them, all of me over the past week or so. I could feel my hands twitching again, the rage bubbling not far below the surface. I was surprised to find myself so angry at the thought of being spied upon.

Graham had clearly picked up on my mood, he looked as though he was about to burst into tears, with his lack of chin and round bald forehead it was like having a big baby in the room with us.

'Are you really a private eye?' asked Uncle Bern, 'I thought they were all meant to be like Raymond Chandler, you know, rough, tough guys. No offence like, but you're a bit of a wuss.'

Graham nodded in agreement, and stifled a sob. Bern and Harpo patted his shoulders to calm him down. Eventually he was in a fit state for Bern to coax the full story out of him.

'Thirteen years I'd been with BT, hated it every bloody day. Then when they offered voluntary redundancy, I leapt at it, and got a tidy little pay off.' Uncle Bern nodded appreciatively, Graham continued. 'After a few months I got bored at home, needed a job, wanted to do something different.'

'So, you became a private eye?' asked Bern, by now he'd settled down comfortably for a chat and a natter, 'How'd you get a job like that anyway?'

'I saw an advert. Correspondence course, do it online. So, I paid the fees, did the course, and set myself up as a private investigator. Got this job, jealous husband, figured how hard can it be?'

'But I don't know anyone called French, and I've certainly not been carrying on with any married women.' I said.

'You must have,' Graham had a bit more force in his voice than I expected given his less than robust performance so far. 'He was very clear in the brief. He said he'd employed you to decorate his living room and kitchen, and he's totally convinced you were boffing his missus when he was at work.'

'Decorating?'

'Yes. That's what you do, you're a decorator, Tommy Davies.'

'No, I'm not. I'm neither of those things.'

'Yes, you are, don't lie, it's even written on your van, Tommy Davies.'

'Tommy Davies is dead,' I told him and took the camera from Bern. After a few seconds of bleeping I held it in front of Graham, 'Look, you even took a photo at his bloody funeral.'

'Oh. Is that whose it was?' said Graham, sounding like he was beginning to catch up.

'Didn't you think to check?' asked Bern.

'You're right, maybe I should have, but look—' he took the camera from me, and flicked on several photos to show me sitting looking solemn in a pew, but Graham was pointing to the top corner of the screen at an elegant looking middle-aged lady in black two rows behind me. 'That's Yvonne French. I was convinced I'd caught you, so I didn't bother checking anything, I was more focussed on getting you two together, but you avoided her throughout.'

'That's because I don't bloody know her.'

'Oh yeah, that's right, you said,' the crestfallen Graham was now fully aware of his epic fail.

'How long have you been following me?' I asked snatching back the camera, I jabbed my finger at the button and let it flick through frame by frame.

As I looked through the photographs, Bern began chatting, 'You know, I think maybe you're not cut out for life as a private eye, son.' Graham looked up at him, held his gaze, and then nodded his sad agreement.

'Maybe it's just as well I didn't finish the course,' said Graham 'Otherwise I'd have to make the last payment, and pay the cost of the certificate. So, I suppose it's a blessing in a way, isn't it?' Bern and Harpo both agreed that it probably was.

'Bern, look at this.' I offered up the small screen, 'Is there any way of zooming in?' Graham showed me how to enlarge the image, and I showed it to Bern, a photo taken several days ago. I was crossing the road towards Sally's house, the van behind me, but what I was more interested in now was the man in the grey hoodie on the opposite side of the van that I wouldn't have seen. We zoomed in on his face, it was thinner, six years older, but it was definitely him.

'That's okay son, I did believe you, you know,' said Bern, 'Hello Adam, where've you been hiding all this time?'

I think Bern and I were both relieved at the thought he was still alive, even if we didn't know anything else, and we were grateful to Graham for giving us proof. We thanked Graham, and then left him to start the rest of his life, wishing him the very best of luck. Something told me he'd need it.

-44-

'YOU'VE STILL GOT the keys to Sally's flat? Call me when you're there,' commanded Hamlet and I duly obliged. Twenty minutes later I was standing outside, he answered his phone on the third ring.

'You there yet?' No pleasantries, quite rude, but I wasn't going to be the one to mention it, instead I confirmed I was. 'Had a call from the girl upstairs, says it sounded like someone was smashing up the place. What's it look like?'

'I'm outside on the pavement looking at the front. Looks fine, can't see in though, the curtains are drawn,' and as I said it, I tried to recall whether I pulled them closed last time I was here.

'Well don't just stand there like one o'clock half struck, get inside and have a look.'

I slipped the key in the door, but then the coward inside me took over and I went back to the van to find something lumpy, just in case. Clutching an off-cut of armoured cable I pushed open the front door, noticing it was in fine working order, no damage. The internal door leading into Sally's flat was also undamaged, and both the latch and deadlock held it tight. I pushed it open and jumped back, scared there might be someone behind it waiting for me, the door swung freely, opening to its full extent.

'What can you see? Anything?'

'The place has been trashed.'

I began describing everything as I found it: sofa cushions ripped open; shelves cleared, the contents swept across the floor; pictures pulled off the wall; drawers tipped out. The destruction flowed from room to room, even Sophia's bedroom had been turned over, her Princess toys scattered across the floor. On the other end of the phone, Hamlet didn't speak a word, but I could hear his fury. Moving to the kitchen, I tiptoed carefully over a carpet of broken crockery, I don't know why, was I trying not to tread awkwardly to avoid spraining an ankle, or was it out of respect for the family who used to call this home?

'Whoever it was, they've gone. Looks like they came in through the back,' I told Hamlet, staring down at a muddy paving slab lying in a circle of glass splinters, 'They put through the French window, came in that way.'

'What's it look like? Junkies? Thieves?'

As I surveyed the wreckage, I could see the television, a nice small hi-fi that looked new, a digital camera on the kitchen worktop – all portable, sellable stuff a thief would take.

'No, I don't think so.' I paused, wondering whether I should continue my train of thought. I did. 'I think they were one of your hunters, looking for information.'

'What?' Hamlet sounded like he was about to explode. I was grateful I was on the other side of town as I really wouldn't want to be around him now. 'If I find out who's done that, I will fucking murder them.'

I promised I'd make good the window and tidy the place up, he ranted a little longer then cut the call. I walked around taking photos to send to him, maybe tomorrow when he's calmed down a little. Then I called Uncle Bern, told him to pick up Disco, and to get themselves down here double pronto.

'FUCK ME, LOOKS like a bomb site,' said Disco, rasping a hand over his scratchy, greying muzzle. 'Where do we even start with this?'

I allocated jobs between us, and we got started. I separated what was to be kept against what was to be junked, and began carrying the detritus out to a neat pile that I'd formed by the front door.

'Is it bad?' said a voice behind me. I turned to be met by a woman in the doorway, late twenties I'd guess, jeans and T-shirt, long blonde hair tied back. I admitted it was.

'I didn't see anything, just heard almighty smashing and banging coming from downstairs,' she said.

'Did you call the police?'

'No, what's the point in that? They wouldn't have done anything. Anyway, you know who owns this place?' she jerked her thumb back at the property, I nodded that I knew. 'I called Mr Hamlet, he said he'd sort it out, and here you are.'

'Here I am indeed. And you didn't see anyone at all?' I asked, she shook her head, crossed her arms, looked defensive, but I could understand her not wanting to get involved. 'Did you know Sally?'

'Yeah, kind of, I knew her to say hello to, it was civil, you know what I mean?'

'I do. Do you know if she was being hassled by anyone, a boyfriend maybe?' The woman tightened her arms around herself and shook her head again. 'What about a big bloke, muscles, ginger hair, drives a Merc?'

Her eyes darted up past me towards the chimney pots on the houses opposite and she gnawed her lip, before giving a slight nod. Brazil. Steve. So, he had been here as well as phoning her.

'Know anything about him?' But again, the arms crossed as tightly as a straitjacket then she turned to leave. 'Look I know you've seen him. You told the police you'd seen his black Mercedes outside late at night.'

She'd had enough and this time she did start leaving, but as she left, she said over her shoulder, 'It wasn't black, I never said that,' and backheeled the door shut behind her.

IT HAD GONE seven by the time we'd got the place looking reasonable again. We loaded up all the broken and destroyed stuff. Bern offered to get rid of it all tomorrow, to which I made him promise me he wouldn't fly-tip it all down some country lane, that'd be all I need – my van with my name all over it spotted defiling some beauty spot. I could see Senia wetting his pants over that. Uncle Bern eventually agreed, and then offering Disco a pint at the nearby Palm Cottage they both disappeared for the night.

I drove to Hamlet. The club was putting its face on, ready to throw its doors open later that night: the same cleaning crew I'd seen last time were polishing and vacuuming. Brazil and Dunlop would be out minding the door later, but I passed them sat at a table eating something smelly from a polystyrene box.

'Evening gents,' I said in their direction. 'What's for tea?'

'Go fuck yourself, Poynter!'

'Nice. Enjoy.'

I knocked once before going through to the back office to find Hamlet within. I handed back the keys to Sally's flat then took out my phone and flipped through the photographs I'd taken, showing the mess it had been in. There were also a few 'after' shots too, showing it how I'd left it, tidied up and secure.

'Cheers, cheers,' he muttered, somewhat distracted. He pulled a huge bundle from his pocket, 'What do I owe you? Here,' he began throwing down notes before I'd even said a word. I hadn't expected to be paid and hadn't intended even raising it, but he'd offered and I needed the money more than him. I scooped it up without counting but I could see it was more than I would have asked for.

'Thanks.'

'You got a name for me yet. What have you found so far?' His tone was level and composed, but I had a sense that the fury wasn't far beneath. He picked up my phone again and began flicking the photos of Sally's flat back and forth again.

'Bastards. If I get my hands on them.' he came to the one of Sophia's bedroom and winced at the sight of her pretty little clothes ripped from drawers by hands unknown. 'She's just a little girl, some things are supposed to be out of bounds.'

He swiped back and forth through the pictures several times, I think just to pass the time whilst inside he plotted what he would do to the perpetrators should he ever find them, then suddenly he let fly a short sharp laugh.

'What's this?' He held up the photo of me as a kitten. Something chimed in the back of my head.

'Sally took that, she had an app for silly selfies, turns you into daft animals,' I said.

'Yeah, she'd done that to me too,' said Hamlet with a small chuckle in his voice, 'Turned me into a lion.' That figures, I thought. 'Bloody silly thing.'

'Great, okay, so you will remember it too then.' I noticed the excitement in my voice and tried to draw it back a bit. 'What did she use? Describe it.'

'Her phone,' he said, pausing, then: 'A new one. A red one.'

'Yes, exactly, that's right, but… gah, I need the police report to be sure.'

Hamlet opened a desk drawer and seconds later a copy of it landed in front of me, I flicked through the pages, yes, I was right, I turned the document around to him.

'Look at this. This is an inventory of Sally's belongings, and look at the photo and description, Samsung phone with cracked screen.'

Hamlet picked up the document and nodded sagely. 'And?'

'Where's the red phone?' I said, and his eyes lit up, now he understood, 'Senia can't have it or else it'd be mentioned. In fact, I'd be willing to bet, seeing as they've found this phone on her already, they don't even know about the new one.'

Hamlet threw open the desk drawers and began rummaging through them before slamming them closed with force, 'No, they searched here already.'

'Listen, this is what I'm thinking, they've had full access to her flat and car, so have we, and no-one's found it. But I heard they were very restricted here. Where did they actually search?'

'Just in here, the office, nowhere else.' Hamlet laughed, no doubt pleased with his lawyer's successful blocking of Senia's search.

'In that case, I think it might be somewhere in this building.'

Hamlet picked up his own phone and jabbed at the screen, listened and then a few seconds later cut the call, 'Straight to voicemail, the battery must be dead, follow me,' he said and we left the office.

In the main club area Hamlet clapped his hands together to attract attention, the three cleaners looked up.

'Speak English?'

One lady nodded her head looking very self-conscious as she did so.

'I am looking for a red phone. It is very important. Please stop everything and look for it. I will give you one hundred pounds if you find it and bring it to me.'

The lady spoke quickly and quietly to her colleagues, all three of them looked at Hamlet nodding. They put down their cleaning equipment, went into a huddle whispering in their own tongue then scattered in different directions.

Ten minutes later the English-speaking cleaner knocked on the office door brandishing Sally's smartphone in its red sparkly case. Her English wasn't strong enough to tell us where she'd found it so we followed her to the cloakroom just inside the entrance lobby and she pointed under the counter to an unplugged charging lead. I gathered it up, Hamlet thanked her and handed over the reward as promised.

'I like her,' he said. 'She was an accountant back home, now she scrubs toilets, but she's a bloody hard worker. I was thinking about maybe training her up to do the books here, only problem is she's still learning the language. I'll have to have a think about it. Anyway, here you go, you wanted it, what are you going to do with it now?'

It took about fifiteen minutes before the smallest sliver of charge appeared in the empty battery logo. The phone rebooted itself, I snatched it off the charging lead and waved it in front of Hamlet.

'Righty ho,' I said. 'What's her passcode?'

Hamlet looked at me blankly.

'Don't ask me, I haven't got a clue, how should I know?'

We tried a dozen or so different combinations picked at random, then the security measures locked us out, the tiny squirt of power ran out and the phone died again.

'Well,' said Hamlet returning to his seat behind the desk, his patience clearly as flat as the battery, 'You're Mr Electrics, you sort it out, I've got a club to run,' which I took as my signal that I was dismissed.

THE CLUB WAS waking up, the mood set by the low-level lighting, and chill-out dance music played. The cleaning crew had gone, replaced by the bar staff who were making preparations behind the jump for a busy night ahead. Brazil and Dunlop were ready too, earpieces plugged in and big padded black jackets to keep out the chill. They were loitering in the lobby, no point going outside until opening time, might as well stay in the warm for as long as possible.

I stood waiting for them to hold the door open for me, eventually, begrudgingly, they took the hint.

'Ta ta.'

I stood outside, the evening had moved into night and a chill descended. I waited a moment or two, then thumped on the doors, it swung open.

'One of you drives a black Merc don't you?' I said, 'I've just seen some skanky bloke pulling on the door handles, setting the alarm off, you may want to check it out.'

Brazil didn't need any encouragement; he was out of there like Usain Bolt's ginger twin. At last, I'd separated them. I followed him to his car, he was looking at it from all angles, seeking out the slightest imperfection.

'I'd like a word with you… Steve,' I said.

He looked up at me, then decided I wasn't worth it and began going back to the club.

'Don't walk out on me Steve. Either you hear what I have to say, or Hamlet will.'

That got his attention, he stopped and looked straight at me.

'What do you want Poynter?'

'I know, Steve. I know you had a thing for Sally.'

He shrugged and tried muttering something about how everyone did, she was a good-looking girl.

'No, Steve, it wasn't a nice thing was it, you took it further than that. I know about the photo you carry of her. I know you'd been turning up at her flat uninvited.'

'So what? You can't prove any of that, and she's not going to say anything is she?' That, I thought, was a particularly low blow, even for him.

'I've heard the answerphone messages,' I said, his face flickered, 'I've copied them over,' I lied, but he wouldn't know that. 'You know who she was to Hamlet don't you?' Brazil nodded. 'So what do I tell him?'

Brazil's expression looked blank, he raised his palms as if in query.

'He's piling the pressure on me, he keeps pushing me for information and updates, and by the look of things there's only me and the police so far that have heard the messages, and they don't know who you are. So, do I tell Hamlet, or do we keep this between ourselves?'

'Between ourselves,' he softly muttered.

'Okay,' I said. 'Give me your number, I might need you one day.'

-45-

SALLY'S PHONE HAD been put on to charge all night, and while I waited for my toast I tried as many random combinations to open it as I could before the security measures locked it. It was only four digits, that meant there could only be ten thousand possibilities, so if it disables itself for five minutes after seven failed attempts, then it should only take ... ten thousand divided by ... I gave up on the maths, but I knew how long it would take – too bloody long.

The burning smell reminded me why I shouldn't do long division in my head, and swearing profusely, I jabbed a fork into the toaster to remove my breakfast; it looked like a charcoal briquette, and tasted the same too. I threw it in the sink and began to sulk. A few minutes later a bleary-eyed Perry opened her front door complaining she'd been on nights and only just got to bed. She didn't seem too impressed by my emergency. 'I've run out of bread and milk and not had any breakfast.'

'Go on, help yourself. I'm going back to bed. Let yourself out when you're done,' she said, stopping halfway up the stairs to add, 'Don't make a mess.'

Perry only seemed to have healthy bread with seeds and bits in, but 'Any port...' thought I. I began looking for marmalade but, like my toast, the search proved fruitless. In the end it was a rather disappointing breakfast of healthy bread toast with a scraping of yellow stuff that had half the fat and none of the taste of butter and a cup of tea with red milk. I could see a trip to the cafe happening later in the morning.

Perry seemed to have gone straight back to sleep, so I washed up as quietly as I could and was ready to go. Then a thought occurred to me. I opened the understairs cupboard, my spare toolbox was still there containing Brennan's folder and the Peppa Pig bag of cash. I thought about adding Sally's phone to my secret stash, but at the last second changed my mind. I stuffed in it my pocket, and replaced the toolbox in its hiding place. I let myself out, and headed off to face another day.

A QUICK TRIP to the cafe later, and I was now properly fuelled for a day's labour. My phone rang, and I grabbed at my clothes, in my panic and surprise it felt like so many pockets and so many phones. I managed to find the right pocket and right phone just in time, a second more and it'd have cut to voicemail, 'Hello Jen, how are you?'

'Mark is that you?' she sounded scared.

'Jen. It's me, yes. What's the matter darling, is everything okay?'

No response, just a faint sniff.

'Jen? Are you okay?'

'It's Karen. I didn't know who else to call, Mark.'

'You've done the right thing. Tell me, what's wrong?'

'She's being hassled. She took the kids out to the playground. Said this man was following her. Said he's been watching them. She's worried he's going to do something to her. Or one of the kids.'

'Where is she Jen? I'll go and sort it out, leave it to me,' I said pulling into traffic. I was already on my way.

THE STRAND LEISURE park in lower Gillingham down beside the river, popular with everyone. The kids love it because of the huge playground, outdoor pool and miniature railway. And the doggers love it for its badly lit car parks hidden away from the main road. Fun for all the family.

I'd already promised Jen and Karen that I would stop Charlie Quentin bothering them, obviously he wasn't taking no for an answer. This time I would need to get the message across loud and clear, but I'd need back-up if I was too do it properly. I called Disco only to find he was out all day on a job for Boris The Plastic. Nothing else for it, I'd have to cash in my favour earlier than I'd ever expected. 'It's me,' I said, 'I need your help.'

THE BLACK MERCEDES rolled into the Strand car park and came to a halt next to me about ten minutes later. I'd explained to Brazil over the phone that a friend of mine, a young single woman, was getting harassed by a man who wouldn't leave her alone. Maybe he's a gentleman, or maybe it chimed a chord with his own recent behaviour, but Brazil agreed to help without question or complaint.

It had turned into quite a nice bright morning, so a lot of parents and carers had brought their kids down for a run-around in the fresh air.

'So, who is this bloke?' asked Brazil.

'He's just a posh wally,' I said scanning the view for Karen. 'He shouldn't be any problem, just flex your muscles and look butch.'

'Do you want me to hit him?'

'No,' I said, appalled at the idea. 'There's kids around. No, he just needs a short sharp shock, let him know he can't go around frightening ladies.' I'd spotted Karen. 'Come on, let's go.'

KAREN WAS SAT on a bench, a pile of coats, toys and snacks beside her as she watched the children clambering up a frame to reach the curly slide, only to whizz down it and then scramble back up again. They looked as though they were having a wonderful time and were oblivious to anything else, but concern lingered behind Karen's smiles of encouragement to the children.

She saw us approaching and raised a hand in greeting which I mirrored back to her.

'Hi Karen, all okay?' I asked.

She slowly shook her head and then looked off into the distance, tilting her head to the left, meaningfully. I followed her prompt and looked out across the vast playground, towards the outer perimeter. It was a busy jumble of colours and movement. My eyes swept back and forth slowly, methodically, and then I saw him leaning against the fence, his white shirt and denim jeans camouflaged neatly from this distance against the boats in the marina behind.

I gestured towards him for Brazil's benefit. He looked across, then said, 'I thought you said he was a posh wally. That's Cookie.'

Cookie. He'd been the one following Karen today, scaring her, watching her. Why?

Realising there was only one way to find out, we went across to meet him. The playground was full of families and movement, so he didn't see me until we passed through it and were almost upon him. We were still about thirty feet away from him when he saw us. His body tensed and he looked ready to run or to pounce, and I didn't know which would be worse. Still I approached.

His eyes were on me, he hadn't noticed Brazil who was trailing slightly behind. Cookie's lip began to curl into a snarl, his massive hands folded in to fists. Pounce. He was definitely going to pounce. I stopped, about eight feet from him, Brazil caught up and stood beside me, now Cookie saw him properly for the first time, confusion flickered across his face and the snarl shrivelled away. Why was I with Hamlet's man, was I there on Hamlet's behalf, was I under Hamlet's protection? I knew all of these questions were ticking over inside his tiny hateful mind. Cookie's stance loosened up, he had figured out neither running nor attacking were good ideas.

He spat a thick gob of white mucus on the ground in front of me.

'What're you doing here Poynter? Here to rob me again?'

'Cookie, look—' I stopped myself, why was I about to apologise to him – if he hadn't been a violent racist scumbag he'd have probably been paid by now. As it was, Hamlet stepped in and punished him; you reap what you sow.

Brazil had moved in front of me, he leaned in close to Cookie and demanded to know, 'Why are you scaring that lady over there?'

'I don't know what you're talking about.' Cookie flapped his hand in dissent, for some reason it made me think of a third division footballer's reaction to receiving a yellow card.

'Mr Hamlet's already warned you once. He won't do it twice, so, why are you scaring that lady over there?' Brazil's voice carried just the right amount of attitude, he'd obviously done this kind of thing before, I'm glad I brought him now as I couldn't imagine me and Disco coping with Cookie on our own.

Cookie sighed and scratched the back of his neck, 'I was trying to find out if she knew anything about the girl who was killed, Hamlet's girl.'

It made sense now, when Hamlet was telling Cookie '*You owe me*', it wasn't loose lipped secrets, it was for my benefit. Hamlet was letting me know Cookie was one of his hunters.

'She's the child minder, so I figured she or the daughter might know something, someone. When I tried talking to her outside her house this morning, she blanked me, I thought following her, letting her know I was there might change her mind.'

'Intimidation,' I said. 'You've resorted to intimidating helpless single women, you're pathetic.'

'Fuck you Poynter,' Cookie retaliated, people had turned to look at us, we didn't need Cookie making a scene but he hadn't finished. 'You think you're so fucking protected, Hamlet's little pet, everyone knows it's only because he feels guilty about your dipshit brother.'

What? What did he just say? Guilty about what? What did he know? Was Hamlet involved in Adam's disappearance all along, just like I'd always suspected?

'You wait Poynter. There'll come a time when he feels like he's done enough to make amends, he'll cut you loose, then you're on your own and we'll be coming for you.'

I was struggling: make amends, for what? Did he know why Adam disappeared, where he went? I tried to compose what I wanted to say, but Brazil got in and filled the silence.

'How'd you know she's the childminder?'

This abrupt diversion seemed to throw both Cookie and myself.

'How'd you know she was the childminder, who told you?'

'No-one told me, I found out,' said Cookie, he tapped the side of his head with his fingertip. 'I used my initiative.'

'You went to her flat,' I said, 'You did, didn't you?'

'Yeah, so what, initiative that's what that is. Want something done, do it yourself.'

'Well she doesn't know anything, we've already spoken with her, quite a lot. So, leave her alone, you're scaring the kids,' I said. My voice carried threat, but inside I hoped Brazil had my back if Cookie reacted badly to it.

Cookie looked around, spat on the ground near me again, and decided he'd be better off leaving than staying. 'I will get you one day Poynter, you'll see.'

'Goodbye,' said Brazil, getting between us; again, he delivered it well – whatever he does for Hamlet he's pretty good at it.

Without speaking to each other, we watched Cookie walk back to his car; he turned back to flick us a V-sign, and then he drove up the steep climb to rejoin the main road.

'Thanks Steve,' I said to Brazil, who shrugged his shoulders in response, and a thought occurred to me. 'You heard him, so can you let Hamlet know it was Cookie who went in Sally's flat yesterday, he'll know what I'm talking about.'

Brazil assured me he would. Good. That means I won't need to worry about Cookie for a long time to come.

Brazil left, and I made my way back to Karen. I let her know her tormentor had gone and wouldn't be coming back. She blew out a sharp breath, and thanked me, then looked back up at me.

'Sorry, you've just missed him,' she said. 'Bobby, he was here a minute ago.' Who the hell's Bobby? But then she reminded me, 'Sally's boyfriend, Bobby. He just picked up Joe to take him home for lunch. You might just catch him… oh, no, there he goes,' she said pointing off towards a small blue car pulling into the flow of traffic on the main road.

-46-

'WHAT THE BLOODY hell is all this? You'd better have a good explanation or I will be calling the police, for real this time!'

Perry stood before me with a face that only the seriously pissed off can get away with. In front of her on her kitchen table were the gruesome photos of Sally, Brennan's folder, and the Peppa Pig bag full of cash. 'Do not say work stuff!'

I had hoped that she wouldn't have opened the box. Was it too much to ask that secretly hiding a box in someone's house without their knowledge wouldn't pique their curiosity? But when I tried deflecting the anger and asking her what she thought she was doing going through my things, Perry pointed out the flaws in that tactic by skilfully eviscerating me when amongst other things she pointed out it had appeared in her house, 'As if by magic!'

'That, as you can probably tell from the rest of the folder, was Sally', I said gesturing towards the photos. The look on her face told me to stop being a smart arse. I leant against the kitchen counter top and sucked my bottom lip whilst I considered my response. The kitchen counter top was chipped along the roll and was delaminating at the edge, the sunlight traced knife marks across its surface.

'This kitchen's knackered. I know where a brand-new one is being ripped out, never been used, still got the wraps on most of it, I can get Disco in to fit here if you like, do it next week if you want.'

Her face hadn't changed, it still called me a smart arse.

'Won't cost you a thing, and I can have a word with your agent, a new kitchen must be worth three months rent free.'

That got a twitch, just briefly, the resolve was slipping. It had given me long enough to think things through and I'd come to the conclusion that I had to trust her and tell her everything, start to finish, so I did. Everything.

'AND SO, YOU think this Cookie moron knows something about Adam?'

I nodded to let her know that was my impression. Cookie would never have told me anything normally, but now it was even more unlikely he'd tell me anything once Hamlet had caught up with him for trashing Sally's flat.

'And are you any closer to finding who may have killed her?' She closed the folder and pushed it out across the table as she asked.

'No. I did have Brazil high on my list.' My list of one. 'But I'm confident now it wasn't him. It's the boyfriend I want to find, I think I know who he might be, but–' I didn't finish because a thought flashed across my mind, '*You were convinced Chapman was the cause of all your problems too, and look where that got you*', maybe it's better if I left things unsaid for now.

My phone rang, I moved to answer it, Perry used it as an excuse to head towards the fridge and began preparing lunch for us both as I made my greetings to the caller.

'I only phoned to say thanks for today,' said Karen, for it was she. I told her thanks weren't necessary. 'Okay, but it's a relief, the kids are in enough turmoil as it is without me getting all in a panic.'

There was a crashing noise in the background and a squeal.

'Stop that please Ella, say sorry to Sophia,' said Karen to the miscreants at her end. She apologised to me.

'I thought you said they were best friends,' I joked, but then something from our conversation after the funeral chimed with me.

'They are usually. Just a bit boisterous today'

'Karen, didn't you say they shared the same birthday?'

'That's right, fifteenth of October, Libra, the sign of communicators, which is about right, two proper little chatterboxes.'

I made a little bit more polite chit-chat, and then said goodbye a few minutes later. I reached for Sally's phone. Perry had been slicing up some tomatoes but stopped to watch me. The prompt for the passcode demanded feeding. One-five-one-zero I tapped, the screen flickered and – bingo – I was in.

PERRY AND I sat side by side, the phone before us on the table. I looked at her, she nodded as if to say, 'Let's do this', I re-entered the code, and the screen opened in vibrant colours, lots of app boxes arranged in a neat grid pattern.

I went straight to the photo album and the screen lit up with dozens of tiny images. I clicked open the most recent picture and it filled the screen. It was me, looking like a kitten thanks to that daft app she'd been playing with. Perry giggled. I scrolled backwards, saw Hamlet as a lion.

'That's him is it,' asked Perry, trying to see the man behind the mane. As we scrolled through, we found other photos that gave a clearer image of Hamlet, but one in particular was of special interest to me.

It was one of the more recent photos. A gang of partygoers. I recognised the location as Hamlet's club, eight friends squashed up close for a team photo, all draping their arms across each other making a wall of drunk celebration. In the middle was Hamlet grinning, his big arms outstretched around two buxom women I didn't recognise. Dunlop stood far left, one arm around a man I didn't know, his free arm raising a bottle of beer in salute. And to the right on the picture was Brazil and Sally and then someone I vaguely remembered.

All the people on the outer edges were looking towards the centre, towards Hamlet, always the life and soul of his own parties. I recognised it, and it explained why the photo in Brazil's car looked out of proportion, he'd cropped everyone else out of it to create his own fantasy sweetheart photo: an old romantic or crazy sicko? Maybe I should have taken this to Hamlet, but I'd made a promise. He'd upheld his end by helping me out with Cookie, so I needed to uphold mine.

I tried to rationalise it in my mind. He had a crush on her to the verges of stalker, but I knew he didn't hurt her. Firstly, as the upstairs neighbour was adamant the car she saw wasn't black, but also because he'd been at the club with Hamlet and Dunlop the whole time she was killed. It occurred to me that Nick Witham had said the telephone records were being rushed through, and I realised if anything came from that I'd have to reconsider, but for now, I'd keep my promise.

We flicked back through more of the photos, stopping at exactly what I was looking for. We examined the photo before us, capturing a moment on a sunny day out in the country as rolling hills rose up to meet the bright blue sky. Signs of a picnic, a tartan blanket was laid on the grass behind the open boot of a hatchback that looked loaded with the provisions for a fun day out; paper plates with remnants were pushed to one side to make room for them all to get in the photo, Sally, Sophia and a boy and a man squeezed up close for a selfie, sunglasses and broad smiles worn by all. They looked good together, her ready-made happy family.

'You recognise him?' asked Perry.

'That's Bobby,' I said. 'But everyone else knows him as Rob, Rob Beach.'

'So that's the boyfriend?' Perry squealed with delight. 'You've found him. Although, not wishing to piss on your chips, that's not a Mercedes, that looks like a shitty old Golf.'

She was right, you could clearly see the rear hindquarters of a dark Golf in the photo and it was an old one, a couple of generations ago model. We scrolled back through the photos in case there was anything else. And there he was, Rob Beach, in picture after picture, and their postures and actions left no doubt, these were people in a close relationship, more than just good friends. There were selfie photos of them snuggled up on the sofa, there were photos of them with their children, there were photos wearing silly hats and smiling at the seaside. They looked happy.

'Go to the messages, see if there's anything there,' Perry said. She seemed to be enjoying this whereas I was uncomfortable, as though intruding on Sally's confidences.

I tapped the envelope icon looking for messages between Sally and Rob Beach, and the screen filled with comic-strip style speech bubbles, the blue ones coming in from the right of the screen were from Sally and the grey ones from the left, Beach.

I scrolled upwards to reach the first message, about six months ago. I whizzed past the earliest ones, flirty chit-chat making me feel like a pervy voyeur and I didn't like Perry's rubbernecking on their intimacy. But it quickly turned more personal and functional the further we went, *'Today was so great. I wish we could be together all the time'* to which he'd replied, *'One day soon, you know me and Joe want that too'* but that prompted further intense messages like *'Leave her. You don't love her'* countered by *'I would if I could and I will once we can afford it'*, and they continued in this vein. *'I make you happy, she doesn't, that's all we need'* with the glib response *'Relax, it'll all come together when the time is right, just be brave a bit longer. Should get the £££ soon.'* The messages seemed to tie in with what she'd told me, about her hopes for being together in a ready-made family, although I didn't trust my own interpretation so I sought Perry's view.

'It's hard to tell as its written rather than spoken but, if I was a cynic, I might say it looked as though maybe he was less keen than her,' said Perry, echoing my own thoughts.

The messages took on a more serious tone as we got towards the most recent ones, *'I'm worried, I've never been this late before'* and *'I've bought a test kit'* and *'I've an appointment booked after work'*.

The messages in her final week alarmed me, *'You have to tell her about us, if you don't I will'* and the final message, from Rob Beach read *'Wait. Do not talk to my wife! It should be me. Don't do anything! Do not say anything to anyone. I will contact you.'* It shocked me that the last message was sent the night before she was killed.

'What do you think?' asked Perry, 'Could it be him? What do you know about him?'

I thought for a moment before replying, 'All I know about him is he's a lowlife scumbag. I'm sure he and Sally were having a relationship. But that's all I'm sure about. You've seen the text messages, they're hard to interpret. Was he offering to do the decent thing and stand by her, or was he fobbing her off? I can't tell, can you?'

She shook her head slowly, she understood my predicament: would I be handing Beach over to Hamlet unfairly and for no other reason than to save my own neck? She looked thoughtful and turned away from me, busying herself by filling a cup from the tap then using it to water a plant on the window sill. When she turned back, she seemed certain she'd found a solution.

'There's only one thing for it, you'll have to go to the police.'

'No, that would only make matters a whole heap worse. First, I'd have to explain where the phone came from, why I have it and why I hadn't given it in before. Then Hamlet would find out that anything the police do next is because of what's on the phone and he knows it's me that's got the phone, so I'd be a grass in his eyes and I really don't want that thanks. No, all that going to the police would serve is getting me even further into trouble.'

Perry nodded as though she'd expected me to say that all along. 'Okay then, let's come about this from a different direction,' said Perry. 'Tell me about Sally, what do you know about her?' But there wasn't really a lot to tell. I didn't know her very well, we were kind of related in a distant disjointed way, but never close, partly because of the age difference but also the very rarely seen Auntie Val was the missing link between the families. Sally was a nice kid, a loving mother, that was about all I could say.

'Do you think she had strategic importance?' asked Perry, to my confused face. 'I mean, she was close to Hamlet, practically his daughter-in-law, you said yourself there was history between him and Beach, could he have got with her as a cruel trick on Hamlet?'

'I don't know,' I said, the photos suggested one thing, the text messages suggested another. 'Do you want to hear how Hamlet sorted out Beach? Beach had started turning up in Hamlet's bars pushing his gear, which was a big no-no, it was like setting up a barbecue in McDonalds. Hamlet noticed and wasn't happy. So, one night he gets the DJ to cue up that silly Christmas song, *I Wish It Could Be Christmas Every Day*, by Roy Wood and Wizzard. Remember that bit at the end? When it fades out, with only the children's voices? Hamlet got the DJ to play that bit, just as they turned a spotlight on Beach at the same time. Oh, you should have seen it, it was like one of those old films where the dopey prison breaker freezes in a beam of light, that was Rob Beach, and then comes a child's voice repeating '...*when the Snowman brings the snow, the Snowman brings the snow*...' over and over again. And as it so happens, in a proper Hamlet coincidence, there only happened to be a couple of plainclothes officers from the Drugs Squad in that night, off duty having a beer, who knew? They were very interested in Mr Beach and took him in for possession with intent to supply. That was probably the last time I saw him. Until I bumped into him at Queen Mary's a few days ago.'

'Yes, Queen Mary's,' said Perry, she was excited about this. 'Let's think about that. There's Rob Beach: serial shagger, small-time dealer, fancies himself as a boutique supplier – is that the right word?'

'Boutique? Yep, that's what I was told.'

'Then, there's Charlie Quentin. Party animal. You suspect Beach was supplying Charlie Quentin with the drugs for his parties, am I right?'

'You are correct.'

'Charlie Quentin was desperate for cash to keep partying, and would effectively buy dirty cash from Tommy for a clean cheque?'

'That's right.'

'And Tommy had a lot of cash to shift. So if we've got this right, the relationship went Tommy to Charlie, Charlie to Beach and back again?' Perry said. I couldn't see where she was going with this, however the flash of brilliance behind her eyes suggested she knew exactly where.

'Think about what he says in his text messages to her,' said Perry. 'He talks about money, says he's expecting a large windfall any day soon. Where's that coming from?' I shrugged my shoulders, I didn't have the faintest clue. To be honest I hadn't given it a lot of thought, I'd assumed it was a delaying tactic to keep Sally from getting too serious or demanding. I'd never even considered there could be any substance behind it.

'Oh, you're useless, think!' said Perry, getting quite animated and excited, but any inspiration I'd had dropped faster than Gillingham's goal difference after Christmas. 'Let's assume it means what it says, he's hoping to come into some money.'

'Okay, let's do that.' I was getting the hump being the dumb sidekick and hoped it would be over quicker if I played along.

'Fact one,' said Perry holding up a thumb Fonz style, 'Beach supplies Charlie with dope. Fact two,' now extending her forefinger and thumb gun shape, 'Charlie buys it with cash acquired from Tommy. Fact three, this all happened at the old people's home. And fact four, Disco told you Tommy hadn't been discreet about his cash and people were noticing. Don't you see what that all adds up to?'

'No.'

'Seriously? Are you winding me up?'

'No.'

'Oh my God. Really? Charlie was getting his cash from Tommy, who had a ready supply of it. What if – and this is a big if – Rob Beach said in his text he was expecting a windfall of cash because he'd decided to cut out the middle man and go straight to Tommy?'

'But Tommy didn't do drugs.'

'Oh, for God's sake! Think! What if he went straight to Tommy because he wanted Tommy's money? What if he killed Tommy?'

Ah, now I understood. Could it be true?

'But what if…' I began, '…he was merely stringing Sally along, using her for easy jollies while the wife's at work? From what I've heard from Karen he's a good dad to that boy, but I've seen enough mates get tortured by ex-wives and girlfriends using their kids against them, Hamlet being a case in point. What if he didn't want her telling his wife because he feared losing the boy? What if he thought it came down to a straight choice between Sally or the boy, and Sally came second? What if he killed Sally?'

A moment of silence and reflection hung between us, broken by a noisy mewl from Mr Skinner announcing himself entering the room. Perry picked him up and rubbed her nose on the fur between his ears and he purred loudly.

'So,' I said. 'What if your what if and my what if were both correct?'

'Then in that case,' she replied. 'We're looking at a double murderer.'

I DON'T KNOW if you've ever had a similar conversation, but there really isn't anywhere you can go after that, so we just looked at the cat. The cat looked at us then jumped off Perry's lap and disappeared upstairs, so we looked at the stairs.

'Yeah, so like I say, I can get you a brand-new kitchen,' I said, trying to break free from the conversational quicksand. 'Never been used, still in the wrapping some of it, gloss white, very modern and smart.'

'How much?'

'Nothing. Not a bean. For me anyway but you might want to give Disco a drink for his time. Be warned, he drinks a lot.'

'Okay,' she laughed, and I felt the tension had been released from the room. She must have felt it too as she followed up with: 'We really have to tell the police now.'

'We can't. For a start it's all ifs and maybes, we don't have any evidence.'

'We've got more than the police currently have got against you. Don't you want to clear your name?'

'Of course I do,' I said, although I was more concerned about my standing with Hamlet than the police. 'Let me think about it over night, okay?'

She nodded, saying it sounded like a good idea, but for me there was nothing to think about, I simply wanted her to stop going on about it.

-47-

HEY. I NEED someone to talk to about this, someone who can listen and won't judge. I thought about talking maybe to Disco, but you know Disco when it comes to the gossip grapevine – he's Marvin Gaye, he's all over it. And I'm not talking to Uncle Bern – knowing him, he'd probably try charging me to listen, and knowing me, I'd probably end up paying.

And I'm certainly not talking to Hamlet, not yet anyway, not until I'm clear in my own mind what's going on. Tell him too early and it'd be carnage – there won't just be blood on the walls, it'll be dripping off the ceiling.

And Perry? I'd thought about it, but it'd mean sharing too much, more than I'm ready to right now, I think I've told her enough for now and things are good, I'd like to keep it that way.

So, it's you, Dad, just like it's always been you, Dad. I can't think of anyone I trust more. I miss you and wish you were here. I still talk to you every day. Although you already know that, don't you?

Sorry, I should have gone to see you and Mum when I was at Bluebell Hill Crem earlier, I simply didn't get the chance, it was all a bit odd. But the Garden of Remembrance's looking nice, the rose buds are beginning to appear, it'll be very pretty when they're fully in bloom.

Adam's back. But I don't know where he's been, or where he is, or why he went away. Have you got any idea? Did you ever hear from him? Any visits? I've been wondering whether he kept in touch with anyone, whether they let him know about you? Or it's something I'll need to do if and when I ever find him.

Anyway, I'm in a mess Dad, and I'm struggling to find a way out. You used to say there's always a price to pay for getting rich quick, didn't you, and you were right of course. I've been trying to make sense of it. I borrowed a load of money from Hamlet thinking it was safe and he'd claim it back from

Chapman, but I thought wrong. I borrowed money from Tommy as a quick fix to avoid getting my head kicked in. I've been thrown a lifeline of sorts from the Wilkes' because that'll cover all my trade debts, but as far as I can see I still need Hamlet's money – I need to pay back Tommy. Part of me says Jen wasn't even aware of it and what you don't know you don't miss: but I know. That's what's important. I know. And there's his little girl having to grow up without her dad, he'd have wanted her looked after, a good education, the deposit on a house, this money was meant for her future. I can't steal from her.

Tommy's money and Hamlet's money combined, that's just over three hundred and fifty thousand. I've got the Wilkes money coming, but even if I can squeeze a bit extra out of that, I'm still short of over two hundred grand. No matter what way I look at it, I can't do it. Chapman can't write me a cheque from beyond the grave, if you see him up there on a cloud somewhere give him a bloody hard kick up the arse from me, the twat.

The only way out I can see is give Rob Beach to Hamlet and hope he sticks to his promise to release me from his debt. Now, the Rob Beach I knew was an absolute arsehole, but even still it doesn't feel right offering him up like a blood sacrifice, he's got a little boy for God's sake.

I've still not learned to play that bloody banjo yet, Dad, but it did get a bit of a workout the other night, someone saying they were bit of a fan of yours back in the day. He was pretty good too. I didn't tell him though, least I have to do with him the better.

I've been trying to remember as much as I can about Rob Beach, but there's not a lot. He was just someone that was always there, everywhere we went. He was a small fry dealer, a good-looking lad, slept around a lot. That's about all I can remember, which is why I can't for the life of me work out why Sally was so totally smitten by him, but someone for everyone I suppose. Although there was certainly bad blood between Rob Beach and Hamlet. Surely he couldn't have strung her along as a cruel prank to get back at Hamlet could he?

I have to decide whether I throw him to the lions or not. I thought at first it simply came down to a matter of him or me, but now I don't think that's true. That little boy keeps coming back to haunt me.

I miss you Dad, more than I can ever put in words. I see you in my dreams most nights and it hurts to wake up. Something happens during the day and I'll think, 'Must tell Dad about that tonight,' and when I realise I can't the pain hits me again.

So, who am I to put another son in that position?

But then what kind of man steals a little girl's future?

That's my choice Dad: I ruin the boy's life or I ruin the girl's.

What would you do Dad?

-48-

'THEY'VE CLEANED IT up well, you can still smell the disinfectant, it's faint but it's there. Look, if you get down close you can still see a bit, come on, crouch down.'

I had absolutely no intention of crouching down in the hunt for brain matter and told Disco so in no uncertain terms. He was beginning to get on my wick. I'd asked him here to help me strip out and refit the Wilkes kitchen but you'd think he was a Jack the Ripper tourist. I'd already told him twice to put his phone camera away. However, despite my growing annoyance with Disco it was nice to be back on the tools, back in my comfort zone, getting on with routine, taking my mind away from my dilemma and my suspicions.

'Look, can you dismantle everything, and put all the units in the garage, Uncle Bern's coming this afternoon to take them away.'

'And the worktops?'

'Leave them, be careful, we're reusing them,' I said. Mr Wilkes had been true to his word and paid me, the money was in the bank and the relief was out of this world when I phoned all my creditors, people I'd known for years, and told them I could pay them at last – apart from Cookie. I figured if I was to be Hamlet's bitch I could at least benefit from his protection, so Cookie could go swivel for now, especially after what he'd done to Sally's flat and then to Karen.

Although, just because Mr Wilkes had paid me didn't mean I'd changed my opinion of him, he was still a nobhead, but I did feel obliged to play fair too. Well, within reason at least. I said we could reuse the bespoke granite worktops and the appliances that were still boxed and wrapped in the garage and that'd save him a large chunk of money. I could have saved him even more by only changing the doors and drawer fronts to the units, but I'd quoted for new carcasses and he accepted it which was handy because I'd promised the outgoing ones to Perry.

The Wilkes lived in a nice large detached house in a smart area; warm honey-coloured bricks, dark brown joinery, fake Tudor beams and a stand-alone double garage adjacent to the property. It was the sort of place I always fancied for myself one day back when I used to have ambitions for a wife, two children and a Labrador. A nicely done orangery extension doubled the size of the kitchen, creating a lovely bright family area that was larger than the entire footprint of my house. There were enough units coming out of here to refit both mine and Perry's small galley kitchens, and I felt I deserved a little perk after the week I'd had to be honest.

We were taking them whole, no need to collapse down to flat pack, and would work out how to arrange them in the best fit when we got them back home. Disco was making light work of unfixing them using a pump-action ratchet screwdriver. You don't see them very often these days, most of the younger guys probably wouldn't even know how to use one having been brought up on power tools and battery drills. It's an elegant tool from a bygone age, a polished wooden bulb of a handle and chrome retractable shaft that, with a click extends, to its full three feet in length, and with one long smooth movement Disco had the screw out.

Mrs Wilkes didn't want to be reminded of Tommy. *'Get something different, don't care what'* that's what she said. So, she's getting a Shaker style in a pale wood veneer with stainless steel bar handles; she should like it. Mr Wilkes did, because it was in the same price range as the previous white units.

With my account reactivated the Magnificent Maria was more than welcoming to me when I went in to place the order but I'd heard from Disco that her panel beater had been playing away with some strumpet at work, so I wondered if Maria was after some rebound, revenge romps. Not that I'd have been interested, as I'm with Perry now – like I say, the timing has never been right for me and Maria, it's just not to be. Anyway, ordering was easy enough, despite the distractions. I used the previous order as a shopping list for what was required. The granite counters would lay on top with no adjustment, and the appliances could just simply be popped into the openings and wired into the spurs already there, easy peasy lemony squeezy.

I'd welcomed the flurry of activity, the sorting out the payments, the placing the orders, arranging the labour; it took my mind away from my conversation with Perry, away from Rob Beach.

Whilst Disco swept up the kitchen area, I took the last unit to the garage ready for collection by Uncle Bern, who'd promised me he could get hold of a van big enough to shift everything in one trip. The one good thing Uncle Bern can do is scrounge, he has the brass balls to put people firmly on the spot to ask them for extreme favours and, I suspect, to get rid of him, they agree.

I found all my impounded tools in the garage, apart from the club hammer which I expect was still in Senia's trophy cabinet. From the smudges of fine black dust all over my hands I realised the police had fingerprinted them all. I plucked a towel hanging off Mr Wilkes' golf clubs and wiped my hands clean, then set about wiping my tools clean of the black muck with Mr Wilkes' golf towel.

In amongst my tools I found a radio, Tommy's radio, it wasn't that old but it was so splattered with paint splashes it looked like it had spent twenty years in a pigeon loft. I doubted Jen would have a use for it, so I decided to keep it out of sentimental reasons and gave it a rub down with the golf towel too.

I returned to the kitchen to find Disco gazing dreamily through the wall-to-wall bi-fold doors, hands down the track pants having a good scratch or at least a good rearrangement.

'Nice garden,' he said, seeing me in the reflection. 'Do you reckon Tommy was having a dabble with the lady of the house?'

'Probably.'

'Rampant little fiend, wasn't he?'

'He was,' I said, then Disco and I both burst into laughter, a bit of gallows humour. I felt relieved we'd dealt with the elephant that had been in the room since we arrived, and as we laughed, off it went with a trumpety trump, trump trump trump.

Thorpe's delivered the new kitchen units in dozens of flat cardboard sleeves. Their driver had been with them for years, he probably got his hi-vis waistcoat on his first day as any eye-catching neon had long since faded, rendering it threadbare and the grubbiest shade of smoker's cough yellow. Its wearer was an old boy with grey curly hair that always looked in need of a cut, a chubby, smiling face above a heavy round belly. Ancient blurred blue and green tattoos peeked through his hairy forearms. I'd never learnt his name, but Disco clearly knew him by the way they gossiped like old mother hens ferrying the deliveries into the kitchen before stacking them in a neat pile.

While Disco and the driver had a smoke on the driveway, I made a couple of calls.

'Just spoken to Uncle Bern,' I said. 'You won't be surprised to learn he's running late, so we may as well lock up and go for lunch. You can make a start on putting it all back together tomorrow.'

Twenty minutes or so later I pulled up outside the Golden Lamb. Disco looked confused and asked if I was coming in.

'No, not today,' I replied. 'Something I need to do. Actually, do us a favour, and put the word out about Tommy's van, see if anyone's interested in buying it?'

He said he would, I told him what I thought was a fair price and drove off promising to see him tomorrow.

-49-

I KNEW FULL well that by the time I'd got home Disco would be in his element regaling everyone at the Golden Lamb with his morning at the scene of the murder. It wouldn't surprise me if more than a little embellishment went on, I fully expected it to be described like a snuff movie in the Hammer House of Horror and I laughed at the thought, but my happy mood didn't last long.

'You've done what? Are you bloody insane?' Perry said, flapping her arms about for added effect. I was beginning to think it hadn't been a clever idea telling her.

'I needed to be sure before I hand him over to Hamlet. Sally was family to him, Hamlet won't be mucking about, it won't be tickles and trips to the seaside, the only fresh air he'll get from Hamlet will be a hundred feet of it when he drops him off the Medway motorway bridge.'

'You must be some sort of lunatic. Don't you see how risky this is? You could get hurt,' she said, but I was already well aware of that thank you very much. 'Tell me exactly what you've agreed.'

'Oh…kay,' I said, trying to buy time, aware she'd be looking out for half-truths and lies. 'I called Charlie Quentin, told him I wanted a deal like Tommy's, and he should come straight here. Half an hour later he was here, sitting in the same chair as you.'

Perry wriggled as though the chair had scabies.

'He was keen, wanting to know what I had. I put the Peppa Pig bag on the table, he looked inside and whistled, he actually whistled.'

'And what then? He agreed? Just like that?'

'Not quite. There was a lot of chin rubbing and head scratching going on, and then he pipes up with "That's a lot of dough", in a ridiculous Rich Boy Mockney accent.'

Perry giggled at my impersonation, spurring me to ramp up the exaggeration in my story, figuring that the more she enjoys it, the less trouble I'm in.

'So, I say to him, that's two hundred grand there, can you take it? And he's pacing up and down scratching his head, and then, finally he says to me, "I suppose so, I don't know." "What's the problem?" I say.'

Perry looked at me wide-eyed, prompting me to go on. I closed my eyes for a moment, but it was silly posturing to look thoughtful as I could very clearly picture him leaning against the window sill, his eyes darting outside every few seconds as though the chattering schoolgirls dawdling past were secret agents in an elaborate sting operation, his wooden beads hung down between the two open top buttons of his crumpled pink shirt and clicked with each turn of the head.

'"We've never done so much before," he says, "it was always little bits and pieces, the odd fowzan' or two," going all Mockney again on me. He said him and Tommy did twenty grand over four invoices in the same period a couple of times. But I could see that this much scared him.'

Perry shuffled in her seat, unhooking her leg from underneath her and swapping it with the other.

'So, I suggest, can we slice and dice it? Offering to drip feed it, ten grand a week, over five months. Know what he says?'

'Yes?'

'No. What he says is, great idea, but there's not enough time because the sale of the business goes through at the end of this month and then he's out.'

'What? Is he saying he'll be so loaded he won't need the cash?'

'Far from it. His family's selling the retirement home business, so yes, there'll be a lot of money coming to them but it's virtually impossible for any of them to get their grubby little paws on any of it. It all goes into a complicated offshore trust fund, and then they all get their monthly allowance and other than that the rest of it's untouchable. So, I knew I had to convince him and I told him, then this is your last chance, your final pay-off, get yourself a nice nest egg.

'So, he's thinking about it, he's pacing up and down, he's got his fingers steepled against his lips, and then suddenly he says, "Okay let's do it." And then he suggests that as there's three weeks before the sale goes through, we could break it down into three payments as he figured it'd be less noticeable that way.'

'Makes sense, I suppose,' said Perry, although her tone didn't support her words.

'Then he suggests making them irregular amounts, to make them less suspicious, put them through one big one, one medium, and then a small one to finish off.'

'So how are you going to justify such a big amount without setting off a big red warning flag?' said Perry, echoing my very own question to Charlie only a couple of hours earlier.

'He'd already worked it out. He says to me, there's all those works orders Tommy had that he hadn't been paid for, so he said he'd just reprint them with my name on instead of Tommy's. That covers more or less half the amount, then we'll work out how to pass the remaining balance through two more batches of bogus orders and invoices.'

'That sounds like an awful lot of money to account for. Especially as it had already been thrown out once before,' said Perry.

'But that's the clever bit, only a director can write a cheque, and only Quentin family members are directors. Last time it was my fault contacting Kate Fuller. But this time, we work around her rather than through her, and there's nothing she can do about it.'

'Except have you for fraud.'

'Ah no. You see, you're wrong, because, well… I don't know… the director signed it off, I suppose.'

'So she has the director done for fraud too.'

'True,' I said, pausing whilst my mind spun in panic trying to find a way out of this argument, and then inspiration, the spinning stopped, three bells in a row, jackpot!

'Look, best case, the cheques go through and Tommy's family end up with a clean set of books and nice bank balance, Jen might even be able to sell the business as a going concern. Worst case, Fuller finds out about it, stops the cheque, I get the cash back. But I'm confident there's no way the Quentin family would want to involve the police in anything, he's been a bit of a character in the past has Charlie and they've never involved the Law before, I can't imagine them doing it now.'

That seemed to reassure Perry's concerns.

'And hopefully the prospect of a hundred grand, possibly more, is enough to tease Beach out and get him sniffing around, see if he acts like I suspect he did with Tommy: bypassing Charlie entirely and just reverting to a dirty little thief sneaking up on the moneyman to steal the cash, only unlike Tommy, this moneyman will be ready for him.'

That didn't reassure Perry's concerns and brought us back full circle to where we started.

'Are you bloody insane?'

-50-

PERRY FOLLOWED ME back to the Wilkes' house to meet Uncle Bern, who unsurprisingly still hadn't turned up by the time we arrived, so as something to do I pointed Perry towards the garage.

I showed her the units that I'd put aside for her and she ran her hands across the smooth gloss surfaces and muttered appreciatively.

'And I spoke to your letting agent this afternoon.'

'Did you?' she sounded more defensive than surprised.

'Of course, I've known him for years, used to do all his landlord testing. Anyway, we agreed a new kitchen is worth three month's rent free. And he knows me, knows I won't rip him off, so he went back to the owner, even got the owner to agree to pay for new worktops and new flooring. Result.'

'Yeah, result,' she said, but I thought she'd be happier than that, certainly a little more grateful.

'Everything alright?'

'Yes. Thank you, thank you for doing all of this. But it seems a bit too much, too full on.'

'What? I'm fitting you a kitchen, not giving you a diamond ring? If you don't want it, fine, I'm sure I can sell it on.'

'No. Sorry. I'm grateful, I really am. I just—' she trailed off, she didn't know what she wanted to say and being neither clairvoyant nor patient, I left her to it and went to watch Uncle Bern arrive.

'Hola amigo,' his voice boomed across the street, shouting over what sounded like the first diesel engine to give itself asthma. The noise of it struggling to stay alive was pitiful. Somehow, he'd managed to borrow the crappiest, most beat-up box van in the Medway Towns: greying gaffer tape Xs patched over holes in the bodywork, one panel was red whereas the rest of it was the unpleasant shade of white milk turns when it goes sour, and in the dirt you could read the name of the previous owner where the labels had been peeled off but never cleaned. Good old Bern hadn't come up trumps yet again.

'How are you mate?' he said, pumping my hand up and down in a firm handshake, his eyes squinting at me through his thick glasses that only seemed to stay on by virtue of his scrunched-up nose, giving him the look of a constipated vole. 'Sorry I'm late, had a bitch of a day on a house clearance in Gravesend for Harpo, still, here now, shall we get cracking?'

He reversed the van up to the garage door with a crunch of gears and a farting exhaust. Keen to get it done, we hardly spoke, meaning it didn't take long to get the van loaded, and we were soon finished. I asked him to follow Perry back home, and then load the units in her house. I watched them drive away, then locked up the Wilkes house, got into Tommy's van and left.

BEFORE I KNEW it, I was drawing up at Queen Mary's. I slowed to a trundle and parked next to Old John's container.

'What are you doing back here?' he said, age hadn't mellowed him, the cranky old sod.

'Hello John,' I said, partly to be civil and partly for the sport of deliberately avoiding his questions knowing it would antagonise him. I began walking towards the building entrance.

'I said, what are you doing back here? I thought you were done.'

I ignored him and carried on walking towards the entrance doors, from behind I could hear him following me, he was certainly a lot heavier on his toes than the night he jumped me.

'And what are you doing in *his* van? Wheedled your way into that too have you?'

I stopped, I didn't like his tone or his insinuation but I knew the game he was playing, I'd needled him so he was trying to needle me. I turned to face him with the biggest smile I could muster.

'I'm trying to sell it. Interested? Very nice, full history, low mileage, still a bit of warranty left. Better than that old shitter you're still driving around in. Fancy trading up? I'll give you a fair price.'

'How much?' it always amazes me, no matter how antagonistic people are to you, the moment there's the chance of a deal they're your new best friend. I knew how much Jen wanted for it, so I added five hundred. Old John wrinkled his round face in disgust, resembling a balloon a week after the birthday.

'Talking of trading up, that's very pretty,' I said gesturing to the parking spot immediately outside the entrance where a highly polished red convertible Merc sparkled in the sunlight.

'Certainly is. It's Kate Fuller's, it's been getting repaired for the past week. Got it back today, just in time for the sunshine, meant to be nice at the weekend.'

'So, did they give her a courtesy car while it was off the road?' I said to Old John. Something didn't feel right, I was sure there was a different car in this spot both times I came before.

'No, she just used her husband's car for a few days, either that or he dropped her off and picked her up.'

'And what's that car?'

'A Volkswagen, I think.'

'An old one? Golf? Blue? Baby on board stickers?'

'That's the one, yes, why?' Old John wanted to know more but he didn't know why, he simply wanted to know. I wasn't in any mood to satisfy his nosiness.

'Her husband, what's his name?'

'Robert, why?'

'Rob? Rob Beach?'

'Don't know his surname, but yeah, they all call him Rob. What's all this about?'

'I don't know, John,' I said, speaking the truth, I couldn't see any relevance in it all other than it squared off another corner: I knew who Rob's 'nightmare' wife was.

To my surprise I began to feel a little sympathy for him. I could see why he'd fall for a bright, charismatic girl like Sally when faced with an obnoxious ball buster like Kate Fuller at home. I could imagine him, the Player, the Ladies' Man from the club scene, being made to feel grateful for every slice of bread, every teabag that she deigned to throw his way. I was starting to side with him, and then I remembered the suspicions that had led me there.

-51-

DISCO'S LADY FRIEND was manning the reception counter again, no need to be hostile, I'm a friend of a friend now. But what's her name? I dredged the grimiest recesses of my memory in the last few footsteps to the counter.

'Helen,' I said with a tinge of pride as I surprised myself by remembering it. She smiled, I think she took the sound of my self-congratulation as a cheery greeting. 'Remember me, I'm a friend of Disco's ... Dave ... David?'

'Yes, I remember,' she said, graciously putting me out of my discomfort.

'I'm looking for Charlie Quentin, is he about?'

'He was. Last I saw him he said he was popping outside to inspect the grounds, which is his code for going for a cigarette, he can't be far away.'

I thanked her, and retreated outside to see if I could find him. There was a smoker's bench just to the right of the entrance, close enough that it wasn't too far away, but far enough away to avoid the smell of smoke drifting back into the building. It was occupied by a tired faced, elderly lady staring into the middle distance. A smartly dressed woman sat beside her, her right hand kept massaging her left wrist as though she was desperate to look at her watch and call time on this obligatory visit. No sign of Charlie though.

I followed the footpath around the side of the building to an enclosed terrace garden that I bet is lovely in the summer, but peering through the wrought iron gate I saw that on this cold damp

Spring day it was empty. Empty, except for Charlie Quentin perched on the edge of a garden table, enough to rest against but not enough to get his bum wet. Circling him was Rob Beach, hands behind his head rubbing his closely clipped hair as he paced. I pushed myself up against the brick pier, sucked in my belly and held my breath as I peered around through the gate to find out what was happening.

'I don't know, fifty grand, that's a lot,' said Beach. Fifty? Clearly Charlie has finally understood financial prudence and is setting aside some of his cash windfall for a rainy day. 'You can definitely afford it?'

'Yes, for the what, fifteenth time. I'm good for it. And I want decent stuff, none of that cheap and nasty shite you sell the schoolkids.' Clang, the penny dropped: Charlie's not suddenly become the rainy-day saver, he's worried that any more than fifty thousand's worth of whatever he's into would be difficult to source – the more he asks for, the more it will be cut and watered down to meet the volume.

'Okay,' said Beach; from the way he'd stopped pacing and was now standing, arms crossed, feet apart, I could tell he'd reached a decision. My phone buzzed in my pocket, bollocks, luckily I'd had the foresight to switch to silent mode, but I was still concerned the vibration could be heard, carried through the quiet afternoon still air. Muscle memory knew exactly how to kill the call without needing to look at it. I drew in a slow long breath, grateful that the sound hadn't carried.

'I can get you fifty grand's worth, I need to make a few calls, but I think I can have it here day after tomorrow,' said Beach. Charlie thanked him and looked relaxed, until Beach added, 'Cash up front.'

'Oh shut up Rob, don't be ridiculous. I'm not giving you cash up front, what sort of mug do you think I am?'

'This is a substantial number Charlie, the biggest I've ever done, my people will want reassurance, and it's not like I can pay them on my credit card, get a few reward points. This is a cash business. They need to see the money.'

'Well how about I talk to them myself? They bring the gear, I bring the cash and we trade there and then?'

'You don't get it, Charlie, do you? The reason these people are where they are is precisely because they don't get their hands dirty at grass roots level, that's why they go through people like me.'

'So, what are we going to do then?' asked Charlie. I had a bad feeling from what I'd heard, it had sounded to me like Beach was prevaricating, all he wanted was the money, don't give it to him Charlie.

'I've got an idea, a compromise,' said Charlie, *No don't do it!* I screamed at him inside my head. 'How about half? Half upfront, half on exchange?'

'Yeah, that could work, let me make some calls,' said Beach, and I saw Charlie nod. Beach made a great show of extracting his phone from inside his jacket and I knew that was my cue to get out of there before I was spotted. Anyway, I'd seen and heard enough, my mind was made up, I knew Beach was my man. As the two of them performed handshakes and chest bumps I crept away quietly until I was around the corner, then I ran full pelt.

CHARLIE ROUNDED THE corner and found me settled on the arm of the bench looking nonchalantly at my phone. The two women still sat in silence watching the horizon, waiting for enough time to pass before they could politely say their goodbyes. Charlie called my name. I glanced up trying my best to look surprised to see him.

'Charlie, hi, I was told you were out inspecting the grounds so I was just texting you to find out where you were,' I said, slipping the phone back in my pocket.

'Yeah, I nipped out for a crafty ciggy, filthy habit I know but, well...'

'Sure.' I rose to my feet, and gestured for him to walk with me, away from the quiet ladies. 'So, tell me, our deal, are we on?'

'Yes, yes, of course we are.' As he spoke his phone pinged, he read the message and I read the big grin forming across his face. 'Yes, we are most definitely on, have no fear Mark, all systems go.'

He motioned for us to walk a little further, off the footpath to the edge of the grounds, the damp from the grass seeped into my trainers, brilliant, nothing I hate more than spending a day in cold soggy socks.

'I need at least fifty grand by tomorrow evening at the latest, can you do that?' he said.

'You know I can. But can you do all the paperwork your end?'

'Relax, writing an order and a cheque? I'll go in and do it now.'

'Hold on, hold on,' something had occurred to me for the first time. 'A cheque? Tomorrow? No. No way. I'm not handing any cash over until the cheque is in my account and cleared, do you think I'm daft? I'm not giving you all my cash for the cheque to be cancelled as soon as I drive away.'

Charlie's face whitened as I spoke, he was looking spooked and after a few open-mouthed moments he said 'But... we've got an agreement, a deal, you just need to trust me.'

'I don't need to do anything. I want cleared funds before I give you anything.'

'But I need it. Tomorrow.'

'Sorry, but...well. Too bad.'

Charlie looked as though he was going to be sick, and my toes were going numb, so I began to walk away, back to the firm footpath. I walked slowly expecting him to follow but he didn't. I increased my pace, moving in the direction of the van thinking *one day you'll be grateful to me Charlie as I might just have saved your life.*

'Wait,' Charlie's raised voice carried clearly across the distance. *No, no, no, do yourself a favour Charlie and let it lie,* I thought as he jogged towards me.

'I have an idea, I think I know how to do it; I will need to check something in the office but I'm sure it'll be okay, I'll call you later and you can bring the money tomorrow, I'll be here all day.'

'Go on then, if you can sort it, then you'll get the money' were my last words to Charlie, hoping he'd fail. Nonetheless, whether or not Charlie could magic up some kind of financial miracle, I left Queen Mary's knowing I had to act. I was confident Beach was my man, he hadn't changed from years ago and I'd seen it with my own eyes, I knew he was going to double cross Charlie. Maybe I was at fault? Maybe it was too much, too tempting? But from the way he spoke, the way he was insistent on money up front, I could tell there was no deal, and as for Charlie offering half, he was inviting himself to be robbed. Now I was convinced this was Tommy's downfall. Now I knew I had to act, and that's why I was in the beer, wines and spirits aisle.

I'd parked up at the Hempstead Valley, and entered the shopping mall hoping the person I needed was working today. After a dash up and down the aisles, to my great relief I found him on his knees unpacking a pallet of South African chardonnay.

He saw me approach and rose from his kneeling position, dusting his hands off on his maroon uniform before thrusting one out in front of him. I grabbed it in both hands and shook a greeting.

'Hi, you got a second? I need a word.'

'Sure, if you don't mind me finishing this?' he said, glancing at the boxes beside him.

'Do whatever you've got to do, mate. Don't let me get in the way.'

Spencer, for that was his name, thrust his huge paws into the nearest box and withdrew two bottles by the necks, which in a fluid movement he placed on the empty shelf in front of him. With his enormous shaved head and barrel chest he looked almost identical to Nick Witham, apart from his big bushy badger of a biker beard to Nick's clean-shaven dopey mug. To see them together you'd think they were brothers, which, given Nick's chosen occupation may have its advantages. I'd known Spencer nearly as long as I'd known Nick, way back when we were all at school together, and I liked him a lot, a very funny guy. I guess we always knew Nick and Spencer were an item even before we knew what that meant. Two big happy bears, still together all these years later, the most successful relationship out of any us and still going strong.

'Listen Spencer, I need you to tell Nick something important, but remember, you didn't hear it from me, okay?'

-52-

I WOKE QUITE early and checked my phone but there were no missed calls from Charlie, hopefully that meant he'd given up.

Uncle Bern arrived with Disco around nine, quite a late start by my standards but to hear them both whinge you'd think I'd woken them up at stupid o'clock for wetting the bed.

As Old John had said, the weather was improving in the run-up to the weekend and the Sun threatened to shine all day, so Disco began by setting up his working area on the decked patio area outside my kitchen. With Uncle Bern's help they had a couple of fence panels off, creating a clear open space across the back of mine and Perry's houses allowing us to work in both houses at the same time. Perry opened her kitchen door and cheerfully came out to greet us, offering teas and coffees all round.

Disco had looked at all of the units we'd grubbed out of the Wilkes' kitchen and had sketched out a layout for both our houses that used most of them, and he began walking around telling Uncle Bern which ones to move to my house and which were to stay at Perry's.

Whilst the pair of them began transporting the units between houses, Perry cooked them sausage sandwiches on my advice; 'If we don't keep them here once they finally arrive,' I'd said, 'they'll only disappear to the cafe and we won't see them for hours.'

As Uncle Bern, Disco and I sat outside on the dwarf wall enjoying our breakfast, Mr Skinner skipped over the lawn to see what was going on, and walked back and forth between the gardens deciding whether or not he approved of the missing fence panel.

'He's a handsome chap,' said Uncle Bern, stretching his hand towards Mr Skinner.

'Don't do that Bern, he'll rip your arm off, he doesn't like strangers, oh ferrfux...' I said as Mr Skinner rubbed his forehead against Uncle Bern's knuckles and purred loudly. Mr Skinner recoiled with wide open eyes as my hand approached him – even Uncle Bern, it seems, is preferable to me.

My phone buzzed and all concerns of winning the acceptance of an old stray left me when I saw it was Charlie's number on the display. I walked back inside the house for privacy. He sounded happy in his greeting.

'Mark, problem solved. Are you ready your end?'

'Charlie, what's going on?'

'I've fixed it – I needed to check but I was right, I do have the authority to make electronic payments. So, I can transfer the money directly into your bank account. If you can get the cash to me this morning, it can be clear funds in your account by the end of the day. Brilliant, eh?'

I told him he was indeed brilliant, as that's what he wanted to hear, no matter what I really thought, and told him I'd meet him at Queen Mary's in the next half hour. With a sense of uncertainty about what lay ahead I returned to the garden: 'Bern, put that cat down, we're going out.'

UNCLE BERN FOLLOWED me to Queen Mary's, and we parked up side by side close to Old John's container. Uncle Bern and Old John seemed to know one another, and Uncle Bern wandered off with him. Before I reached the entrance steps, Charlie had raced outside to greet me in a state of great excitement.

'Do you have it?' he said, and I nodded. 'Let's have it then.'

'No,' I said, 'Not until the money's in my account.' He looked a mix of confused with a dash of angry, but I didn't care. As I looked out over the car park, I couldn't see any sign of Uncle Bern or Old John, good, that's what I'd been hoping for.

'One of my associates has it,' I said, immediately knowing I sounded like a prick for saying associates. 'They're here, on site, and I've told them to hand it over as soon as I get the bank's message alert that the funds have arrived.'

Charlie looked out over the car park. Maybe because it was becoming a bright Spring day, it was busier than I'd seen it before. There weren't many empty spaces and people were coming and going constantly. Looking further out across the grounds plenty of people were strolling along the paths and sat on the many benches and seats enjoying the warm sunshine, there was no way to know whether any of them were with me. Charlie seemed to weigh his options and nodded agreement, muttering okay under his breath.

'Follow me,' he said, and he led me to his office, winning me filthy looks of suspicion and disgust from Kate Fuller as we passed her in the corridor. In his office he leant over his desk and gave his mouse a little wiggle, the screen of his laptop blinked back into life. I sat in a guest chair watching him tap away; he remained standing as he did so, and then after a minute or two he beckoned me over to look at his screen. The logo of a big bank was in the corner of the screen and as I read the text displayed I could see it was an instruction to make an electronic payment to my account for the sum of fifty thousand pounds, and adding a theatrical flourish he pressed the send button, the screen instantly changed to a confirmation screen: 'Satisfied?'

I FOUND UNCLE Bern in the resident's lounge watching a home improvement programme on the big communal television. Televisions in old people's homes are always huge, very bright and very loud. I couldn't talk over the sound, I could barely think, so I gestured for him to follow me to a quieter area, and after a rolling of his eyes, he made a big deal of following me to the empty dining area.

'I was watching that,' he said in all seriousness, sounding extremely put out by the inconvenience.

'I'm not paying you to watch telly. Look, I want you to stay here all day and keep an eye on Charlie Quentin for me from a discreet distance.'

'Who's Charlie Quentin?'

'You see that fella over there by the front reception on the phone?'

'What, the wally in the beads?'

'That's him. Just keep an eye on him.'

'What for?'

'Because I'm bloody asking you to, that's what for!'

'No, what am I watching out for, what do you think's going to happen?'

'Oh, I see, right, just make sure nothing happens. If anyone approaches him that looks a bit suspicious or nasty then you need to make an anonymous call to this number,' I said, handing him a piece of paper.

'Who am I looking for, anyone in particular?' I gave him a description of Rob Beach and he nodded, it looked as though it was going in, but I had to wonder.

My phone buzzed, a text alert, the transfer had arrived in my bank account, I had to keep up my end of the bargain. I felt the thick package inside my jacket, it was still there. I rose from my chair.

'Pay attention Bern, this starts now,' I said and went to hand over the cash to Charlie.

Uncle Bern made reassuring noises as he followed me out of the dining room, and plopped himself back in front of the television.

BACK AT HOME, all was going fine. By the time I returned Disco had removed the old units from Perry's house and stacked them in the back garden, he'd removed the wall tiles and ripped up the old vinyl floor. He'd also manhandled Perry's appliances – the cooker, washing machine and fridge freezer stood in a solemn semi circle, a Stonehenge of white goods in her living room.

The kitchen was now a dismal empty space with a faint echo. Bare unpainted patches of plaster once hidden behind cabinets were exposed for the first time in their history, you could tell it was decades because the plaster was grey, not pink like modern plaster done in the last twenty years or so.

Disco explained his grand vision to me, and pointed out that the cooker point and a couple of plug sockets needed to be moved, no big deal and so I gathered up the right tools and made a start.

'HE'S HERE, HE'S here, that bloke you were talking about, I've just seen him, walked right past me,' said Uncle Bern so quickly he was in danger of hyperventilating.

'Calm down. What's happening?'

'He was out the front fiddling with his phone. I guess he was sending a text message because a minute or two later your mate came out. He put an arm round your mate, and they walked off around the corner, do you want me to follow them?'

'No,' I said. 'Whatever you do, don't let them see you, just hang back.'

'Wait, they're coming back now,' said Uncle Bern, sounding like he was enjoying himself. 'Now they've stopped, they're talking, the other one he's patting his jacket, now they're shaking hands, all looks friendly, now your mate's gone inside and the other one's gone to his car, an old blue Golf just like you said.'

'Okay Bern, thanks,' I said. 'Tell you what, can you hang around for another couple of hours, just in case?'

There didn't seem much else to going on at Queen Mary's, the transaction had gone through and everyone seemed to be playing nicely with each other, so Disco and I motored on in the kitchens. It didn't sound like a violent confrontation, in fact it sounded quite amicable, but it didn't mean he wouldn't be coming back. Assessing the situation, I realised it was time to make a call. I waited for the connection to go through and a second later it was answered.

'I need to speak to him,' I said.

-53-

THE NEXT MORNING, I felt quite smug looking at what we'd achieved: the floor units were in as well as most of the wall units. Today we'd get the worktops on, fit a new sink and taps, install the appliances, reconnect the plumbing and electrics, and Uncle Bern could make a start on the wall tiling, which to everyone's amazement, is something he's actually pretty good at.

Uncle Bern dropped Disco off, the pair of them deep in conversation about a plumber we all knew who'd recently been sent down for fiddling his VAT.

'Uncle Bern, before you start here, can you quickly nip over to Queen Mary's, have a look around, make sure all's okay, and nothing happened overnight?' I said, and walked him out to the van, listening to him moan about Disco.

I came back, and then listened to Disco moan about Uncle Bern, eventually managing to fade him out by focussing on the music coming from Tommy's pigeon shit radio on the window sill. From what I could gather he only stopped moaning after Perry offered to make a run to the cafe for breakfast due to both kitchens being out of operation.

The three of us were sat drinking stewed tea from polystyrene cups and eating fried egg sandwiches when Uncle Bern phoned.

'He's not here. Your mate. He's not here, nobody's seen him this morning. His car's been here overnight, and I felt the bonnet like they do on telly, it was stone cold, no-one's seen him since last night.'

I cut the call and dialled Charlie's number, straight to voicemail, I hung up and redialled, voicemail, hung up, redial, voicemail. I had a very bad feeling about this, and punched in a different number, this one rang a couple of times before it was answered:

'Karen? Hello, hi it's Mark Poynter. Sorry for calling you out the blue like this, but I'm trying to get hold of Rob Beach. He's not with you on a play date is he? No? But he's left his boy there? Do you know where he is? No? Okay, no, no message, thanks.'

So, both Charlie and Beach had gone AWOL, the nauseous creeping of guilt rolled across my stomach, I punched in a third number, it was answered almost immediately.

'Spencer, it's Mark, that thing we were talking about, tell Nick it's happened.'

I put the phone down, my head was spinning and so were my guts, only in the opposite direction. Just when I thought the day couldn't get any worse, I heard the kitchen door creak open and the distinctive metallic tap-tap of a ring against the window pane.

'HI HONEY, I'M HOME' said Hamlet, sauntering in with the sort of confidence only someone in his position can pull off, the grit on the unfinished kitchen floor crackling under each footstep. Behind him lumbered Brazil and Dunlop, both looking around nosily to see what was going on.

'Doing a spot of DIY Marky Mark? It'll look very nice I'm sure,' said Hamlet, then turning his attention to Disco and Perry, 'You two, fuck off!'

'Hey, come on, no need to talk to them like that,' I said, this was my house and my friends, so the primeval part of me wanted to defend them, unfortunately I realised too late it wouldn't be the primeval part of me but the very easy to bruise fleshy outer bits of me that'll get the battering. But to my amazement Hamlet didn't react.

'Yes, you're quite right Mark, I apologise, that's no way to talk in front of a lady,' said Hamlet. 'So, will you please, pretty please, if you don't mind, it would be awfully kind if you please... fuck right off.'

Like the obedient dogs they were, Brazil and Dunlop moved forwards to shepherd Disco and Perry out. Disco's scowl was enough for them to keep their distance. He might be a shabby old mongrel but he's one mutt you don't want to poke. With a chivalry that was very evidently lacking from our new guests he helped Perry to her feet and guided her to the door. The surprise and anger were clear on her face, but Disco was whispering words to calm her down as he walked her out.

'It's okay,' I said to them. 'This won't take long, I'll come and find you when we're done.' Disco nodded and they were gone.

'You left me a message yesterday Mark, you wanted to talk to me, here I am, so talk.'

'Okay, but before I do, we had an agreement didn't we, I find you Sally's killer, you waive my debt, that was the agreement, wasn't it?'

He nodded his head whilst keeping his eyes fixed on me.

'No, say it, I want to hear you say it.'

'Yes, that's the agreement, you find him and we're quits. Does this mean you've got me a name?'

'Yes.. I think so.'

'And how certain are you? How do I know you're not simply setting up someone you've got a grudge against, someone who nicked your parking spot?'

'Ninety-five per cent,' I said. 'Short of actually seeing him do it, I think it's pretty conclusive.' And so, I told him about Beach, about Tommy's cash for cheque scam, about Charlie wanting fifty thousand's worth of dope, about Beach pressing Charlie for cash up front, about Sally's phone messages, about Beach's warning to stay away from his wife and I swear I saw Hamlet wince when last of all I told him about Sally being pregnant.

'Right you are Marky,' he said after a short reflective silence, 'I'm convinced. I'll take it from here.'

'And the debt?'

'Account rendered in full,' he said rising from the armchair. 'These two are my witnesses.'

Great, Brazil and Dunlop, watch them go skipping down the yellow brick road – talk about having men of straw as your only witnesses.

Hamlet and the scarecrows left the way they came in, they had the scent of blood and were on a manhunt. I collapsed onto the armchair. There was a muscle flickering in my jaw causing my teeth to chatter, and my mouth tasted bitter with bile.

I TURNED THE tap and filled a pint glass with water. I tipped my face to the ceiling to down it in one, I needed to get rid of the taste.

'Ahem.' Hamlet gave a fake cough to attract my attention, and I nearly soiled myself at the surprise. He was on his own. 'I've left them two in the car,' he said, 'there's something I want to talk to you about, in private. Not in here though, looks like a bloody building site.'

He wandered through to the living room and sat in my armchair, gesturing for me to sit beside him on the sofa. I meekly complied.

'I hear you and Cookie had a bit of a tête-a-tête recently. I hear Cookie was shouting his mouth off,' said Hamlet. I remained silent, neither confirming or denying. 'I heard he mentioned your brother.'

I tried not to react, but I don't think I succeeded.

'Is there anything you want to say to me?' asked Hamlet.

I tried to remain calm, I tried to remain tight-lipped, I tried to remain in control. But I knew what Hamlet was really saying, he was offering me a once in a lifetime opportunity: speak now or forever hold your peace.

'He's alive,' I said, 'I've seen him.'

Hamlet nodded, 'He's alive, yes, always has been.' He leaned forward and looked at me, or rather, he looked into me. 'You thought I'd killed him didn't you.'

'Not you personally.'

'Okay… I killed him, I had him killed … same thing really. But no, I didn't,' said Hamlet, there was a calm, smooth tone to his voice, as though he'd rehearsed these words. I sat back in the sofa, scraped my hands over my face, gripping my cheeks as I dragged them down then up, trying to shake out the fear and fatigue.

'I have been protecting him. For the past six years,' said Hamlet. I didn't speak, I didn't need to, my face asked all the questions. 'It was necessary. He's a good lad, but a bit too keen, got himself involved in something way over his head. So, he was given somewhere safe and sound to hide.'

'From Cookie?'

'Cookie? Cookie's just a loud-mouthed twat, forget about Cookie, he knows nothing. He's going to get what he's due for what he did to Sally's place. Desecration, that's what they call it.'

I nodded but I wasn't sure at what, whether it was Sally's flat or Cookie that was getting desecrated.

'Anyway Marky, the reason I'm here, I have a new offer for you.' Hamlet smiled as he spoke, with all the Monkhouse sincerity of a game show host, 'This is what I'm thinking…. you've given me Beach, thank you very much. So as agreed, you can take the cash I gave you, you're free to walk away with it and solve all your problems…'

What was going on? We had a deal, I'd given him what he wanted, this was unfair – but wait, he hadn't finished.

'So, option one, take the money and run. Or option two, you still owe me, but in return for you giving me Beach, I give you brother Adam.'

My head reeled, I gripped the sofa cushions convinced I would fall off otherwise, a yawning, lurching feeling crept up inside me and I feared I would vomit.

'So, what's it to be? Take the money, or I tell you where he's been and where you can find him?

-54-

I DON'T KNOW how long I'd been sitting there before Perry found me. She settled herself on the arm of the chair, put her arm around me, rested her head against me and with a light squeeze we sat in silence until, judging the moment, she spoke.

'Disco asked me to take him to the Bell, said he'd see you tomorrow.'

'The Bell? I've not been there for ages,' came my reply without thinking. I'd resorted to auto-pilot whilst the rest of me tried to make sense of what was happening. I gave a lazy shake of the head to her offers of something to eat or drink, but I was grateful for the gentle kiss to my temple before silence returned.

I was broken out of my trance by the ringing of my phone. 'Hello Bern, what's up?'

'Your mate, Charlie, they've found him.' His words felt like an icy finger running down my spine, my stomach slowly tumbled over.

'He's… dead? Is he?'

'No,' said Uncle Bern, 'but he's not in a good way. He took a proper clout to the nut, cracked his head right open, lost a lot of blood. They've taken him to Medway Hospital, intensive care probably, that's what the ambulance man said.'

'Who did it?'

'No idea. I told you, no-one's seen him since last night. Old John found him in his lock-up when he opened it up this morning, almost had a heart attack and dropped down dead himself when he saw him.'

In hindsight that's at least one highlight in this utter omnishambles, I'd have liked to have seen that.

'Whoever had done it had locked him in there and left him for dead. He's alive Mark, but only just. He's lucky Old John's an early starter as who knows what would have happened otherwise.'

I thanked Uncle Bern, and put down the phone. I wondered whether Perry could see the relief coming off me like steam, it felt so physical. The auto-pilot was switched off and I burst into tears: big wet blubbery tears.

PERRY COOED AND soothed, until I was ready to speak, to tell her why I felt so emotional. Her beautiful big brown eyes coaxed the words from me.

'I've got Jen's money back. Chloe will have the future Tommy wanted.'

Perry gently cupped my head in her hands, and wiped away my tears. 'You've done a wonderful thing, I can see you're emotional, but these are happy tears,' she said through a beautiful smile. I didn't tell her about Option Two, and tried to convince myself they were indeed happy tears.

ONCE I'D PULLED myself together, we found neither of us were in the mood for getting back to work. The spring sunshine was still there coaxing us outside. Proper beer garden weather. We decided Disco had the right idea, and felt we deserved a relaxing couple of hours under a clear blue sky and we too headed to the Bell.

Sitting alone waiting for Perry to come back from the bar my phone rang, Number withheld. Normally I avoid calls like this and against my better judgement I answered it with a tentative hello.

'Mark, it's Nick Witham, can't talk for long, got you a quick update. Rob Beach has been picked up in deepest darkest Essex, drug bust. Don't have many details other than he was waiting in a field for a light aircraft that never landed. Essex Police are keeping a tight lid on it, but apparently it was a big money undercover sting. Just thought you'd like to know.'

I thanked him, and as I cut the call Perry sat down and pushed a new drink across the table to me.

'You look very pleased with yourself,' she said, and as she raised a chilled glass of fizzy water to her lips I told her about the call I'd just received.

We clinked our glasses together in celebration and from inside we could hear Disco laughing uproariously with friends. It acted as the release trigger we needed, and we both started laughing as well.

-55-

HEY DAD, I think I've done it. I've dug myself out of the hole I was in. Just give me a minute, hear me out, I just need to say it out loud and make sense of it, make sure I've not missed anything, no holes.

So, the Wilkes money came in at the nick of time and I used that to pay off all the trade creditors. That left Tommy's money and Hamlet's money to pay back. Hamlet's waived his debt, that means I'm off the hook with him and can use his money to repay Tommy. I haven't got anything, but more importantly I don't owe anyone anything either, happy days.

Rob Beach killed Sally and Tommy, I worked that out and told both Hamlet and the police, but he got picked up by a different police force entirely, an anonymous tip-off apparently, so neither of them got him first so neither have got any reason to come back at me, especially as Nick said the tip-off came from a woman walking her dog suspicious of the men loitering about and worried they were perverts.

You know what Dad? I think I'm actually ahead for the first time, things are going right for me at last, and even the sun's come out, shining on the righteous. I like to think you put a word in for me, thanks.

Shame you're not here though, that's the one thing I can't change, and it's not fair. Well, it's not the only thing. Adam's alive, he's out there, and Hamlet knows where. He will tell me, in time, I just need to regain his trust. I'll find him, Dad.

Went to the Bell yesterday, first time in ages, last time I went there was with you. You were very ill then, not long before… well, you know. You were quite weak, you'd lost a lot of weight, too much. It was one of the hottest days of the year, do you remember? You insisted on sitting outside, I suppose looking back you knew just how ill you were and wanted to make the most of the sunshine for the last time but then all you did was complain that you were getting a headache.

Do you remember I thought there might be an old baseball cap in the back of the van? Your hair, it was so thin by then, but I couldn't find the cap so we had to make do with what I could find, remember? So, there you were sat in a pub garden licking an ice cream cone wearing a bright yellow construction hard hat. That was the last time I'd been there.

I told Perry about you in the hard hat, she laughed. Things are going good there, you'd like her. Who knows where it'll lead but without this millstone of debt around my neck, I think my head will be in a better place to give it, whatever 'it' is, room to grow.

Still not learned to play the banjo yet, in fact it's been hidden away since I saw it being played so well by, well it doesn't matter who by, but it made me jealous I suppose, so I packed it away. If I can't have it to feel closer to you, then no-one can. Silly isn't it?

'TALKING TO YOURSELF again are you?' came Perry's voice through the open door, promptly followed by herself. 'What's that you're holding?'

'This? Oh, it's my Dad's banjo, well it's the case obviously, the banjo's inside it.'

'Get it out then, let's have a look,' she said.

'Really?'

'Really. It's clearly very precious to you, so I'd like to see it. Please'.

Won over, I snapped open the buckles that held the hard-sided casing together and peeled back the lid. Her eyes widened, she reached to touch it and without thinking, by reflex, I recoiled. She looked up at me and in a gentle tone said, 'Relax, take it easy, I'm not going to break it,' and she reached in and removed it from its protective home. Its silver frets flashed in the daylight, the mother of pearl inlay created rainbow reflections on the ceiling.

She perched on the edge of the chair, gripped it close to her, formed a chord, no idea which one but when she strummed it rang as clear and as pure as you can imagine. Then to my amazement she began to play; it was a little clunky with some awkward chord changes, but there was a recognisable tune. She could play. She grinned, as she knew I was surprised and impressed in equal parts.

'I learnt to play the ukulele at college,' she said without me even saying a word. 'There was a course, a few of us did it for a laugh, I really got into it. Surprised myself there that I could still remember some of it.'

Well how about that then Dad? Told you you'd like her.

-56-

BY THE FOLLOWING morning, the remodelled kitchens in our side-by-side houses were well underway. Disco had finished the carpentry works, after all it was only swapping out old units for new ones, he'd galloped through it in double quick time. Uncle Bern was in my house making a start with the wall tiles, and would be ably assisted by Disco once he'd finished packing away his tools, providing the pair of them didn't get into another stupid argument – together they were like a pair of toddlers, and for that reason I was happy to be away from them. I was in Perry's house, moving some spurs in readiness to pop in the appliances. Perry meanwhile was in my house, upstairs in the bedroom, she needed to get some studying done and because I'd turned the electricity off in her house, I suggested she go to mine so she could use the wi-fi.

All was going well, through the open window I could hear Bern and Disco bickering next door but the radio diverted my attention away from them, and soon I was playing along with Pop Master and getting trounced by the woman contestant, but I was interrupted before the final question so I decided to call it a draw.

'I said, we're going down the caff for breakfast, do you want us to bring anything back for you?' said Uncle Bern leaning in through the window.

'Please. Get us a bacon roll, red sauce, cheers,' I said. 'And don't be long. We need to be out earning a living again, everything needs to be done by tonight.'

I watched Uncle Bern and Disco walk away together, united in their delight in getting one over on me and I didn't expect to see them again for at least an hour. I didn't mind, it gave me the chance to crack on without any interference, I'd almost finished the electrics and that'd only leave the wall tiling and flooring, and if all three of us jump on to that when they came back we'd have it sorted in no time.

Like all good plans, my interruption-free run was pretty soon interrupted by a ringing phone. I was of a mind to ignore it and let it run to voicemail but then I saw the name displayed.

'Hello Jen, darling,' I said into the phone. 'How are you? What can I do for you?'

'Hi Mark,' she sounded much better, she was alert and so much more like her old self, I hoped she was off the pills. 'Someone just called about the van, wanted to see it.'

'I'm at home today Jen, it's right outside, I'll be here all day, send them over.'

'Okay, I'll call them back now and tell them to go and see you, thanks,' she said and closed the call. I paused for a moment, and then decided no need to bother Perry if she's studying, I'll leave her in peace for now, and I got back to work.

I emerged from under the sink when the eleven o'clock news started on the radio, no sign of Bern or Disco, but I was quite pleased with the neat, tidy job I'd done of running in a new fused spur for the washing machine. I ached from being hunched down low so long. I put my hands behind my back and arched, belly forward shoulders back, trying to squeeze the ache out. As I leant back my peripheral vision caught a shape, a person, passing by the front window.

As I rolled my head around in circles, ear to shoulder, chin to chest listening to the crackles and crunches inside me, I wondered if that could be the person about the van. I slowly swept up the off-cuts of cable and conduit listening out for Perry, and sure enough, carried across the small width of garden I heard her call, 'Mark, can you please come here. Someone to see you.'

I responded that I was on my way, and a couple of seconds later I walked in through my own kitchen door, noticing that Uncle Bern deserved some credit as he'd actually done a very nice job with the tiles so far.

I entered the living room and found Perry. She was on her knees, eyes wide, clearly terrified by the enormous knife held to her throat. Gripping the knife in one hand, Perry's hair in the other stood Kate Fuller.

'Hello Mark,' she said beckoning me in.

'WHAT'S THIS ABOUT?'

'You know. Don't insult my intelligence. You know very well what this is about,' said Fuller, her eyes bulging with fury, her nose flushing even redder.

About Rob? But how did she know about me, I was convinced that I was in the clear, I knew Hamlet wouldn't talk and I was sure Nick Witham wouldn't have, how could she know I was responsible?

Perry wriggled in resistance, but Fuller tightened her grip on her hair, I could see her knuckles whiten and the roots of Perry's hair straining at the tension.

'Leave her alone,' I said. 'If it's about Rob, it's me you want.'

'What about Rob?' she said, 'What's he got to do with anything?'

'I had to tell the police, I had to, he's a killer.'

'What?' she laughed. 'What are you talking about? He's a useless streak of piss, doesn't have the balls he was born with.'

'He killed my friends.'

Fuller laughed again, 'He's a loser. A lazy, freeloading loser.'

'No. He's a murderer.'

'You're off your head. I've never heard so much rubbish in my life, stop talking crap, it won't work.'

'Your husband is a drug dealing murderer.'

'Shut up! He used to do a bit of weed, but he put that behind him years ago when he became Daddy Daycare.'

'Do you know where he is today?' I asked, and saw a flicker of uncertainty cross her face. 'He's been arrested by Essex Police in a drug bust worth tens of thousands.'

'Rubbish!'

'It's the truth. It was going to be the big pay-off he needed so he could leave you.'

'He'd never leave me, I'm his meal ticket. I'm the bread winner in our family.'

'He was only waiting for this big money deal and then he would have left you, taken the boy and gone.'

Fuller laughed, a nasty derisive laugh as though she knew something I didn't. 'Rob doesn't have any big deal planned, he's an idiot. He was waiting for my big deal.'

That surprised me, perhaps she did know something I didn't after all.

'Your big deal?'

'Eighteen months I've been working on this, kowtowing to cretins like Charlie Quentin and his family of inbreeds. Eighteen months, working hard, putting it together, driving it through. And then you come along. You will not fuck it up.'

'Right, now I have no idea what you're talking about. How about you tell me, it'd be nice to know before I knock you out. Just because you're a woman don't think I won't hurt you to protect my girlfriend.'

'Get back,' she jabbed the point of the knife straight at me. '"Just because you're a woman" – listen to yourself.' She laughed her snide laugh again.

Perry twisted, but Fuller tightened her grip and pushed the knife hard up under Perry's jaw, I held my breath in reaction, if she pressed any harder Perry would bleed.

'I've had to listen to pricks like you for years. I got a first at Cambridge, I worked my way up to this point, listening to patronising arseholes like you. It's not because I'm a woman. It's because I am better than you. I am better than your grubby friend, the painter. I am better than the Quentins. I am better than any of you!'

I'd surprised myself so far by staying reasonably calm, but Fuller appeared totally deranged. Her grey woollen suit strained at the seams, she was in danger of going full Hulk at any moment.

'I've worked so hard for this deal. The sale of Queen Mary's will go through at the end of the month, there's no question about that, I won't let you spoil that now. I'll be free of the Quentins, I get a place on the board of a FTSE100 company, a big bonus, six figure salary, it's so close and I will not fail. I do not fail.'

'How's it going to be? All happy families with your old man doing ten years on drug offences?'

'I've only your word for that. I don't believe you. This deal will go through and I will win, I always do.'

'No. Rob was going to leave you and start a new life somewhere else, away from you.'

'Liar.' Her face looked damp and sweaty, her eyes wide and unblinking. 'What would he want a barmaid for? I am better than a barmaid.'

'Barmaid? You know about Sally?'

'Of course I do. He can't keep any secrets from me, I own him. That was the deal. He gives me a baby before I'm forty, and I support him. I own his phone, I own his devices, I own him.'

'She was pregnant, they wanted to be a family,' I said.

'Lies! She wasn't pregnant. It could have been anybody's, she was a loose slag. Losers like him don't leave me, especially not for trash like that. He knows that now.'

She was sounding crazier by the minute. I was losing control of the situation. I tried to get on her side hoping it would pacify her: 'What do you mean by that?'

'He came to me, said he'd met the barmaid, but I already knew, I'd seen his phone and his messages, I didn't care, she wasn't his first bit on the side, probably wouldn't be his last, but he always comes back. I own him. But then he said he wanted to be with this one. He was wrong, he knew he was wrong.'

'How did he know he was wrong?' asked Perry engaging her caring professional voice, trying to get the rational part of Fuller to listen.

'Because he knew it would kill me. If he tried to leave me it would kill me, and Joseph.'

'Wait, you threatened to kill your own son to teach him a lesson?' somehow Perry still managed to retain her soothing tone of voice, but my head was reeling at the very suggestion Fuller was making.

'It would be his own fault, and he knew it. That's why he changed his mind and apologised to me. But she wouldn't take no for an answer and kept texting him, telling him to go with her. I'm not afraid of trash like her, I don't lose to her kind. So, I went to see her.'

It was dawning on me where this was headed and I was frightened for Perry, she shouldn't have been dragged into this. I looked at Perry pinned behind the blade, and prayed she wouldn't get hurt because of me and this horror show I'd created.

'I told her to leave Rob alone, but she was pathetic, said she loved him, that they wanted to be together, stupid bitch. I tried slapping some sense in to her. She went all melodramatic, started talking nonsense like something from a bad movie: "Do you know who I am? I'm protected. I can get you killed" and so on, absolute rubbish, carrying on like she was in the *Godfather* or something. She came at me with her claws, so I let her have it. I play to win. Always. I don't lose. I knew I was better than her.'

'That wasn't pretending,' I said, 'Didn't Rob mention it?'

She tilted her head as she looked at me, there was a sense of confusion floating across her fury-contorted face. Then it dawned on me, of course, it was obvious. I began laughing. Fuller stared at me, her teeth bared and gritted, she still looked demented, but for the first time she looked defensive with it.

'Of course, he didn't,' I said, laughing. 'He hasn't got the balls to leave you, but he's got the brains to get you killed. Suicide by Police, you know what that is? That's when someone deliberately provokes a lethal response from the police because they don't have the stamina to kill themselves.'

Fuller looked blankly at me and shrugged her shoulders. She didn't understand the point I was making. I only hoped it would be enough to make her realise she'd gone too far and to give up.

'Only instead of Suicide by Police, he's gone for Widowed by Gangster. Sally was protected, very much so – you'll know who her kiddie's granddad is if I say Hamlet, yes, you've heard of him haven't you. And right now, he's on a mission to get his hands on Rob to take his own form of justice as he thinks Rob killed Sally.'

She paused, thinking, then, 'So, let him have the silly bastard in that case, I don't care.'

'Well,' I said 'I'm no marriage guidance counsellor but I'm guessing he won't cover for you, especially if he knows you killed his unborn child. Hamlet will be coming for you very, very soon. Anyway, your Rob deserves everything he's got coming to him, he killed my friend Tommy.'

'Jesus you're stupid. No, he didn't. Why would Rob want to kill your grubby painter?'

'For the money?'

'I killed him. I've told you. Eighteen months I've spent, day and night, putting this deal together and I'm not having it ruined in the due diligence when the accountants discover you cowboys have been fiddling the books just to give Charlie Quentin some pocket money. I told him, the painter, to give the money back. He laughed at me. I told him I'd go to the police, he just laughed like it was all some big joke to him, and then he starting making filthy propositions. I put him straight there, and as he turned his back on me thinking himself the great comedian, I picked up a hammer that was lying on the side and swung at him. I didn't mean to kill him, but when I realised I had, I didn't care.'

Perry and I exchanged a look. We both knew I'd got it wrong again, only this time the repercussions would be a lot, lot worse.

'Okay, okay calm down. I agree, he could be quite filthy, quite inappropriate, disrespectful. I apologise on his behalf,' I said, trying to placate her and dampen her fury, hoping the sane part of her was listening. 'Tell me, why are you here? What do you want from us?'

'What do you think I want? I want the money back. You are not ruining my deal. Pay it back, I want the cheque, give it to me or I will kill her, then you.'

As I didn't have a cheque, I needed to find a way to buy some time.

'Okay, that's fine. I can do that. It's just over there, in my jacket hanging up over there, see it?' I said pointing towards the front door. 'Can I go over and get it, is that okay?'

She nodded, and we all slowly wheeled around keeping our eyes locked on each other until I ended up with my back to the front door and Perry and Fuller with their backs towards the kitchen. I was hoping somehow, if I could hide my hands inside the jackets by the door I might be able to send a distress text to Nick Witham or someone, Hamlet even.

Slowly, with my hands raised I stepped backwards, one slow deliberate footstep at a time still thinking inspiration would strike and I could find us a way out of this. As I maintained eye contact with Fuller I could see movement on the very outer edge of my field of vision slightly behind her in the doorway, but it took every ounce of concentration not to break eye contact with her, I couldn't see clearly what it was.

'Hey, you.'

Fuller turned and found Disco standing in the kitchen doorway, he held his ratchet screwdriver, his thumb flicked the switch and it shot out to its full three feet length and in one smooth Keith Moon motion he tossed it in the air end-over-end and snatching it by its pointy end swung it like a baseball bat. Its bulbous wooden handle struck Fuller on the side of the head.

'Ow! You fucker!' said Fuller, her hand shooting up to her face in reaction to the blow. Silly bollocks Disco had failed to put enough force behind his swing and merely annoyed her further. With her grip released, Perry dropped on her side and rolled away.

'Look what you've done,' said Fuller holding her hand out to Disco, 'I'm bleeding, that'll bruise. You dozy bastard, what'd you do that for?'

Fuller's questioning took Disco by surprise, genuinely bewildered, he began mumbling apologies.

'Hey! Bitch.'

Fuller turned to follow the voice and as she did Perry drove the narrow end of Dad's banjo case squarely into her face, her rosy red nose flattened across her face and she went down, her head hitting the floor knocking her clean unconscious. Perry, Disco and I all looked at each other before coming together in a group hug.

'You'll never guess whose outside – Pervy Ken. He's here to look at the van,' said the late-arriving Uncle Bern. 'What the bloody hell's been going on in here?'

-57-

HEY DAD, so, that was quite a few weeks wasn't it? Just taken a few days off to get over it all, went down to Brighton with Perry, met her folks.

But it all seemed to sort itself out in the end, the police came and took away Kate Fuller who admitted to killing Tommy and Sally, and also clobbering poor old Charlie. The uniform who attended our 999 call was Hamlet's pet copper Brennan. We had a few private minutes together, and next thing I'd heard was Hamlet's fancy lawyers had made the club available for a second search, 'in the spirit of collaboration', no knuckleheads blocking the way, access all areas, and lo and behold there was Sally's new red phone in the cloakroom where it had always been. I heard from Nick Witham that Senia was very interested in the texts and messages they found on it.

I also heard from Nick that Rob Beach had been bailed by Essex Police due to his co-operation in helping Senia build his case against his soon to be ex wife. Due to his restricted movements whilst on bail he's entrusted little Joseph to Karen's childminding service, and Sally's mum thought continuity would be good for Sophia so she's with Karen too, the Three Amigos ride again.

Charlie, thankfully, pulled through and was released from hospital within two days, but I did manage to spend five minutes with him in his private room shortly after he came to. Perry managed to sneak me in to see him and we got things straight. Sitting less than three feet apart, I emailed him to say there was a mistake and I'd been overpaid, he emailed back to say he'd misplaced the decimal point and instead of five hundred he'd typed fifty thousand. I emailed back some bad joke about having spent it on a yacht, but finished by confirming the money would be returned, and I did an online transaction bouncing it back to the Queen Mary account. As soon as he was discharged, he destroyed the paperwork and replaced it all to correspond with a small five-

hundred-pound order. All done before anyone noticed. I'm confident that when the accountants do their final due diligence for the sale of the business there won't be any cause for concern.

Charlie returned all of the cash to me, and I, in turn, returned it to Jen who was naturally delighted by this surprise windfall, and promised it would buy Tommy's daughter the best education possible. So that's nice, something positive will come from all of this.

Weather was nice in Brighton. It was good. Met her folks, all very nice, made me feel very welcome. Met her younger sisters and made some balloon animals and did a few tricks, now they think I'm the coolest boyfriend ever. They loved Fuzzy Duck. I mean, who doesn't?

You know what this taught me Dad? I didn't know Tommy at all. I would have said before all this he was one of my best friends, but it made me realise I was taking people for granted, just because they're there every day. I lived in the present. Maybe it was a defence mechanism, losing Mum, Adam, you. Enjoy them while you can but don't get too attached? Who knows? But, I've resolved to try and put a stop to it, and to try and open up to people – started last night in fact.

We went out for dinner, Perry and me, Disco and Helen from Queen Mary's, did you know Disco travelled the length of Asia north to south by motorcycle when he was twenty? No, nor did I. And she's actually very nice away from work when you get to know her too. I hope this can be the start of a new chapter for me.

Oh, and as for Mr Wilkes, his house sold within two days of going on the market, full asking price offer as well. So, they're buying a new place and he's asked me to do the kitchen and bathroom for him.

Things are looking up Dad, onwards and upwards.

And keep an eye on Adam, will you Dad? Keep him safe. Let him know I'll never give up looking.

MATTHEW ROSS

DEATH OF A PAINTER

ABOUT THE AUTHOR

Matthew Ross was born and raised in the Medway Towns, England. He still lives in Kent with his Kiwi wife, his children and a very old cat.

He was immersed in the building industry from a very early age helping out on his father's sites during school holidays before launching into his own career at 17. He's worked on projects ranging from the smallest domestic repair to £billion+ infrastructure, and probably everything in between.

A lifelong comedy nerd, he ticked off a bucket-list ambition and tried his hand at stand-up comedy. Whilst being an experience probably best forgotten (for both him and audiences alike) it ignited a love for writing, leading to various commissions including for material broadcast on BBC Radio 4 comedy shows.

Matthew moved into the longer format of novel writing after graduating from the Faber Academy in London in 2017.

'*Death Of A Painter*' is his first novel and the first in a planned series of stories featuring Mark Poynter and his associates.

Matthew enjoys reading all manner of books – especially crime and mystery; 80s music; and travelling and can't wait for the next trip to New Zealand to spend time with family and friends.

AUTHOR'S NOTES AND ACKNOWLEDGEMENTS

From the very outset, I should make clear that none of my characters are based on real people. Similarly, the Medway Towns in this story is my Medway Towns of memory, fantasy and fiction so I apologise for dropping dead bodies and a crowd of reprobates on it. I'd like to reassure anyone thinking of visiting that in real-life it's very lovely. I'm proud that it's my hometown, and to be a Man of Kent.

It has been a long journey to get to this point, and I am grateful for the help, guidance, collaboration and inspiration of so many people along the way.

I'd like to thank everyone at Red Dog Press for giving me this wonderful opportunity and having faith in me. Their encouragement, guidance and support has been there in abundance from the very beginning, and I realise I've been very lucky to be in their safe hands. It may well be the case that it was the amazing cover that made you pick this book up, and that is thanks entirely to Sean at Red Dog leading the design process with verve and passion. And I've truly been touched by the kind words of Chris McDonald and Heleen Kist welcoming me to the Red Dog kennel, it really feels like a happy home.

The building industry has been good to me providing a living for my family and I, as well as offering inspiration for (fictional) scallywags and mischief. I'd like to thank my many friends I've made for the good times and experiences we've had. So I'll give shout-outs to Stuart, Spencer, Tim, Carl, Smudge, Julian, Dominic and Richard – but everyone I've worked with has made their own impression on me, so thanks for that.

Then comes the writing. I will be forever grateful to Jo Caulfield and Kevin Anderson for taking a chance on me, a new, unknown writer: I learnt so much from you guys. And thank you David Tyler of Pozzitive for commissioning my material for the radio, it was such an opportunity and such fun. From working with you all I developed the confidence and self-belief to go for it and attempt writing a novel. That led me to the door of Faber Academy, and Richard Skinner – the best writing coach there is – thank you for the inspiration and words of wisdom. And thank you to my Faber Academy classmates for all the laughs, feedback and mutual support: Cassandra, Issy, Zia, Kerry, Chelise, Kim, Gabriel, Jonathan, Steve, Dani, Mary and Caroline.

I owe a big thank you to Francine Brody for the structural and editorial support – and for correcting my appalling punctuation.

Of course I must thank my family. Thank you to my wife Rebecca, who put up with me lost in my own little word for hours on end whilst I worked on this. Thank you to my two boys who inspired me that it's never too late to follow a dream.

Most of all, thank you to my father, the greatest man I've ever had the privilege to know. It breaks my heart that he's not here to see this but he always knew it would happen one day and held the faith in me even when I wavered. For his love and support I'm forever grateful.

And finally, thank you for taking the time and trouble to read this book, it's more appreciated than you may ever realise. If you enjoyed it please do leave a review, your feedback would be great.

I'd love to hear from you so please do feel free to get in touch with me. You can find me on Twitter @mattwross and contact me via Red Dog Press.

MATTHEW ROSS

DEATH OF A PAINTER